ANCIENT PRIDE

ANCIENT
PRIDE

By Michael Fridgen

ISBN: 979-8-9863148-2-2
eISBN: 979-8-9863148-4-6

FOR
DELANO OSWALD SMITH

Long before manger and cross
Generations of ancestors fated
Much love and then the loss
For Jonathan and the brave David.

When dead Patroclus shown
To Achilles with eyes dismayed
His love manifested in moan
Body and grief never decayed.

Hephaestion breathed his last
Alexander saw the approaching dire
Future gone with great love past
Their souls united in flames and pyre.

From Thebes, that most sacred land
They fought for home, kin, and scion
Affection in pairs formed the band
Perpetual rest of stone and lion.

Beauty beyond that of a mortal
Hadrian yearned for their infinity
The Nile, the devastating portal
Antinous was lost to divinity.

Nameless of the same soul
These men and passion unsighted
While aristeia not set in scroll
Their legacy is Anteros requited.

PROLOGUE

"No, I don't care what your ninth-grade English teacher told you," Professor Madison W. Freeman said. "Your English teachers were terribly uneducated. It's a problem. Aphrodite was not, and is not, the goddess of love."

She looked out over the lecture hall. One hundred and fifty college students sat in the elevated rows of seats with tiny tables attached to them. No one was looking back at her. She was used to it. She'd been teaching Greek mythology at the college level for thirty-nine years. Each year, the students cared less and less about the ancient people of the planet's past. She began to assume she spoke to no one. But she continued nonetheless.

"In fact," Dr. Freeman said, "much of what Aphrodite does in Greek myth could be considered antilove. She meddles with people's emotions and even causes great wars from her actions. So the Greeks never considered her the goddess of love—like your high school English teachers do. The ancient Greeks thought of Aphrodite as the goddess of sexual passion. And there is a big difference if you think about it."

She wondered if anyone was listening to her. Sure, maybe their interests had been piqued when she mentioned sex. But that was probably all they were thinking about anyway.

"Now," she continued, "many people believe that Aphrodite's son Eros is the god of love. You might know him by his Roman name: Cupid. But let me tell you that Cupid is only the god of unrequited love. That is, he is the god that can help when you love someone and they don't love you back. That's what he uses the arrows for, apparently."

She walked around her podium. She liked to walk while she lectured.

"But when you think about that, you'll realize that forcing someone into love can't really be love, right? If one person loves someone and the other doesn't love back, then to me, that's the end of the story. So Cupid has little to do with true love in my book."

She walked back behind the podium as sort of a grand finale to her lecture. The students continued to sit and stare blankly. Almost all were on their laptops. Professor Freeman had no way of knowing what they were doing on the devices.

"So who is the god of requited love? The god of true, deep, everlasting love? The god of that love that makes it unbearable to be separated from each other? Well, his name is Anteros. Now I know you've never heard of him. That's because historians don't want you to know where he came from. Historians have a narrative to push, and for more than a millennium, the story of Anteros didn't fit in their definition of what a god should be. So he was pushed aside, and Aphrodite was allowed to take his place."

Madison thought this would be a good place to stop the lecture. She could always feel when the students needed to get out of their seats or else they would explode. Also, it had been a long day, and she was tired.

"I'll see you next time," she said. "Have a good weekend."

The students quickly closed their laptops and stood. It was a mass exodus. Madison W. Freeman, professor of Greek mythology, looked at them and sighed. Thirty years ago, they all cared when she spoke about Anteros. They cared because he was interesting. But now?

She gathered her papers and started to leave. She didn't move as fast as she used to. By the time she climbed up the rows of seats to the back of the hall, it was completely empty. In silent stillness, she went to a heavy wooden door. She turned off the lights, thinking that nobody cared anymore. She was wrong.

CHAPTER 1

"Mom, she's weird," John Paul Saint Clara said.

"All nuns are weird," his mom replied. "It's part of their charm and their piousness."

"Well, she's weirder than any of the others—a lot weirder," John Paul replied. "All the kids think so. Why do you think they call her Sister Genitals?"

"I don't like it when you say that. You know I really don't. It's disgusting. Her name is Sister Gentillini. And I don't care what a bunch of sixteen-year-old public school brats think. I hope none of the Catholic-school kids call her that awful name. She's a holy woman."

John Paul didn't think either word—*holy* or *woman*—applied to Sister Genitals. He hadn't liked her since she yelled at him and his friends in front of a whole lot of people at a water park. He remembered being on a Catholic youth group field trip during which he had hung out with a group of public school girls. Gentillini didn't like that the girls were wearing bikinis. She said some awful things and called them a few names from the Bible that John Paul had never heard before.

"And while we're on the subject," his mom said, "I don't want to hear that you are hanging around with any public school kids. There are plenty of kids from your own Catholic school at the youth group—hang out with them."

They were in their family car, a top-of-the-line SUV decked out with every feature imaginable. John Paul knew it was a car they couldn't afford. John Paul and his mother entered the downtown area of Kaiserburg. Kaiserburg, population 18,463, was forty-four miles from the nearest big city and its sprawling suburbs. The downtown was basically one street, Main Street, lined with shops, bars, schools, and the Catholic-church campus.

His first name was John Paul. His last name was Saint Clara. His Christian name was Jerome. And his confirmation name was Benedict. He wanted to be known as just "J. P." But since his mother had heart palpitations anytime someone called him that, he resigned himself to the fact that he would always be John Paul. John Paul Jerome Benedict Saint Clara—as Catholic as all the popes put together.

"I especially don't like seeing you hanging around all those girls," she continued as she turned a corner and began driving down Main Street. "What is that kicking thing that the boys from your school do? You know, when they're outside kicking that thing?"

"Hacky sack," John Paul answered.

"Yeah, do that. It looks fun."

It wasn't fun. John Paul hated it and thought they looked ridiculous, kicking around a stupid little beanbag in a circle. Every once in a while, one of them would kick it by the heel from behind his back, and they would all cheer. John Paul guessed it was supposed to be somehow impressive.

"After I drop you off at church, I'm going to pick up Mary Clair from piano lessons. Then I'll pick up your dad at the KC Hall, and we'll come and get you when youth group is over. I think we'll go out for fish later. I know it's not Lent, but there is something about a Wednesday that makes me hungry for fish. I don't know why—perhaps I'm always reminded of Ash Wednesday when it's Wednesday."

He had one sister: Mary Clair Elizabeth Saint Clara—she hadn't been confirmed or chosen a confirmation name yet. Even though Catholics were not supposed to believe in birth control, he did not know any Catholic family with more than two or three kids. He sometimes thought about this and then tried not to think about this.

"Who's bringing the treat today?" Mom asked.

"That kid that sang the bad solo during Mass last Sunday," John Paul answered.

"Oh, his mom is an excellent cook—it should be good. She made some brownies for the last meeting of the Catholic Mothers Association. They were delicious, and I think they probably have a really clean kitchen. At least, she looks clean."

John Paul didn't hear anything his mom said about the bad singer and his mother's good hygiene. As soon as he thought about the treats, he thought about the break during which the youth group would eat the treats. Treat break had become his favorite time of the entire week. However, his excitement for break time had nothing to do with brownies or eating. As he thought about what he'd do during the break that Wednesday, his stomach filled with a nervous excitement that made him feel more alive than anything he'd ever done at church.

CHAPTER 2

"Oh, I just don't like that kid," said Sister Gentillini to another nun who was standing next to her in the church parking lot. The twin bell towers of Our Lady of Seven Dolors rose behind them. The nuns' convent sat next to the church, its ornate windows sparkling in the sun. On the third side of the parking lot, teenagers were being dropped off at Our Lady of Seven Dolors Catholic School for the parish youth group.

"Which kid?" the other nun asked.

"That one getting out of the car right there," Gentillini replied. "John Paul Saint Clara."

"That's not very charitable of you, Sister," said the other nun. "What's wrong with him?"

"I'm not exactly sure, but there is something wrong with him. First of all, he's always hanging out with these public school girls."

"That's not a big deal these days. Our Catholic students have to be able to get along with non-Catholics. They might as well start now. And maybe it's not such a bad thing that girls and boys are allowed to socialize with each other. It's better than when I was a kid, and all us girls were taught to live in fear of men."

Sister Gentillini was in her mid-thirties. She was quite young for a nun. She wore black pants and a white blouse, and her hair was concealed under a simple black veil. In contrast, the other nun was quite middle-aged, hair exposed, and she wore no sign whatsoever that she was a nun. Sister Gentillini was the only nun in the convent who wore a veil. She was proud of that and judged the other, older, nuns harshly. But in this pride, she still wanted more young nuns to join the order who felt like she did. She would never admit it, but inside, she was lonely.

"I told Father Ron," Sister Gentillini continued, "that it was a bad idea to let the public school kids join the same Catholic youth group as those in our parochial school. But you know how he is—everyone is welcome and all that. I especially told him that the public school girls should not be allowed to go to the water park with us. And do you know what happened?"

"What?" asked the older nun.

"Well, they looked like whores."

"Sister! I don't think that's really appropriate talk."

"Well, I can't help it if I think so. My mother never allowed me to run around like that—even at the swimming pool. I don't think God approves of such attire."

"Jesus probably went swimming with Mary Magdalene."

"Oh, Sister...really? I don't think our Lord went swimming with a prostitute."

"Why not? He let her wash his feet with her hair," said the older nun smugly.

"Go ahead and think what you want," said Sister Gentillini. "But we both know that girls who show it all to every man that comes their way will end up—well, all I'm saying is that John Paul Saint Clara doesn't make great choices with his friendships. But, listen, even more than that, I'm watching him. He always disappears during snack break."

"What is that about?" The older nun laughed. "You talk like you're running a kindergarten. Or a jail."

"All I'm saying is that he's never around for snack break."

"Where is he?"

"I don't know. But I'm going to find out."

"Maybe he's on a diet."

"Yes, maybe...a diet of the devil."

"Oh, Sister, really? I hope you're not serious."

"Go ahead and laugh, Sister, but I intend to find out what he's doing. Drugs probably."

"He has decent parents. Theresa and Bernard Saint Clara seem like good parents that have taught him well. I highly doubt he's taking drugs alone during snack break at Catholic youth group."

"We shall see..." said Gentillini.

"Sister," said the older nun, "I am going to pray for you."

Sister Gentillini shrugged her shoulders and looked up at the sky. She knew that most of the other nuns, all far older than she, thought she was old-fashioned and prudish. Not only did she not care what the others thought...she was proud of it.

The older nun was Sister Gabriel Luke. She left Sister Gentillini as soon as John Paul Saint Clara got out of his mother's car. She didn't want Sister Gentillini to continue speaking poorly about him, and she knew that Gentillini lacked the speech filter that others seemed to possess. She hoped that Gentillini was kidding, but she knew that the

Sister probably meant everything she said. As Gabriel Luke walked toward the convent, she said a prayer, softly, but aloud nonetheless.

"Dear Lord, please give Sister Gentillini a greater sense of awareness and charity to others. Please help her to not be so judgmental. Please help her to hold her tongue. If you aren't able to change her, then please arrange for her to be transferred to another convent because I'm losing my patience—a convent in a very strict town would suit her better. Kaiserburg is not the place for her."

CHAPTER 3

While Sister Gabriel Luke walked into the convent, another car was driving on Main Street in front of Our Lady of Seven Dolors. But this car did not pull into the church parking lot. Instead, it continued past the church and stopped near a community center just a few blocks away. Inside this car, Jayme Smith-Johnson and his mother found a parking spot next to the center that used to be the Kaiserburg Elementary School.

"Jayme," his mother said, "you have on two different socks!"

She laughed as she reached over, put her hands on the side of his head, and mock-slapped him on the cheeks.

"But I love you anyway," she said. "Even if you identify as a two-different-sock kind of person, then I support you."

"Mom," Jayme replied, "I didn't do it on purpose. I guess I just wasn't paying attention. It's not a statement or anything, so don't get excited."

"Well," she said, "just remember that I love you, no matter what. You can be anything you want—girl, boy, nonbinary—it's up to you."

"Yes, I know, Mom," he said.

Jayme looked down and saw that he was, indeed, wearing two different-colored socks inside his old sneakers. His joggers were clean but wrinkly. His T-shirt had just been pulled out of a large pile of shirts in his bedroom. The shirt depicted a movie poster from the original 1931 version of *Frankenstein*.

"It's just that," continued his mom, "I think we should have a serious talk. It's time. I think we should make an appointment for you to see a doctor to talk about getting you on some hormones."

"Can we talk about this later?" Jayme asked. "I don't want to be late."

"Why don't you talk about it with some of the others at the group today? Oh! Did I just say something wrong? Can I call anyone 'others' anymore? What should I have said?"

"I'm not sure, Mom. It's the queer youth group—so 'others' is probably fine."

"Well, I'm not sure. You should ask someone. Just ask what kind of hormones one of the transitioning kids is on."

Jayme was annoyed with the conversation. He didn't particularly enjoy the queer youth group and found many of the members as annoying as his mother. But it was easier to humor people than to confront them. He wondered if humoring his mom meant that he'd soon be on hormones? He had hoped that she would just drop it. But it seemed that lately, Jayme's gender had become a big deal to her.

"Just ask someone that takes female hormones how it's going for them," she said. "There are a lot of good doctors that we can go to in this state—and your dad and I are fighting hard to keep it that way. You've never been a typical boy—and I mean that as the biggest compliment. So why not embrace it and make a change?"

It was true that Jayme didn't feel like a typical boy. He also didn't feel like he necessarily needed to make a change.

However, Jayme was one of those people who was good at putting off decisions for another day. Like Scarlett O'Hara, a character from one of his favorite movies, he'd think about hormones tomorrow.

CHAPTER 4

"Ugh, I think I messed this one all up again," Sophia said to John Paul. They were sitting on the floor in the corner of a Catholic kindergarten classroom. Other groups of two teenagers were sitting randomly around the room.

"Look," Sophia said, "this one is all wonky. Why are yours so perfect?"

"Because it's not that hard to count to ten," John Paul replied with a small giggle.

"Shut up. It's not the counting that's the problem—it's getting the spacer knot in the right place."

Three plastic trays sat on the floor in front of each group. One tray held thousands of small, plastic blue beads. Another tray contained plastic blue crosses, each with a small white plastic depiction of the crucified Jesus attached to them. Blue plastic shields, slightly larger than the beads, lay in the last tray. Each shield depicted an image of Jesus on one side and his mother, Mary, on the other. Among all of this, a spool of white string had been placed between each group of two.

"The spacer knot is easy when you get the hang of it," John Paul said. "Just watch how I do it."

Sophia watched for a moment, then said, "I guess it's not that I can't do it right. It's more that I just really don't care."

They both started laughing. Sophia looked up and noticed that they had caught the attention of Sister Gentillini.

"Damn," Sophia said. "Sister Genitals is coming over. Oh well."

"Switch with me," John Paul said.

"Why? She already hates me," Sophia said.

"She hates me more," John Paul said as he exchanged rosary beads with Sophia.

They both sat silently and pretended to concentrate on their work as Sister Gentillini crossed the room. Out of the corner of her eye, Sophia noticed that while the nun was careful not to step on any of the trays scattered around the room, she managed to step on a few hands of the others in the Catholic youth group.

"Let me see," Gentillini said directly to Sophia. She held out her hand. Sophia shrugged and placed her rosary, the one actually made by John Paul, in the nun's hand.

"Looks good," Gentillini said after the briefest moment.

"How do you check them so fast?" Sophia said with a bit of amazement.

Gentillini didn't respond. She threw the completed rosary into a pile in the middle of the room.

"Let me see," Gentillini said to John Paul.

He gave her the rosary crafted by Sophia.

After the same insanely brief moment, she said, "This is terrible. The second Mystery only has nine beads; the third Mystery only has eight. Then the fourth and fifth Mysteries each have eleven. How do you expect the Blessed Virgin Mother to answer the prayers of illegal-alien children with incorrect Mysteries?"

Sophia watched, partly upset and partly entertained, at the interaction between the nun and John Paul. Gentillini took a step closer to him.

"I'm asking you," Gentillini said sternly. "This is not a rhetorical question, Mr. Saint Clara. These rosaries are being given to illegal-alien Mexicans in the United States. How do you expect the Blessed Virgin Mother to answer their incorrect prayers? Answer me."

"I guess," John Paul replied, "I was hoping that the actual number of beads wasn't that big of a deal to her."

"Well, it is," Gentillini replied.

Now Sophia was much more entertained than upset. She bit her bottom lip to avoid giggling.

Around her neck, in addition to a crucifix on a silver chain, Gentillini wore a white string with scissors attached to it. She took the scissors and cut the incorrect rosary in several strategic places. The beads fell and bounced all over the floor.

"Clean that up," Gentillini said to John Paul. "And make sure I check every one of your finished rosaries. And when Sister Gabriel Luke gets here, don't let her help you. You need to learn to get this right all on your own."

The nun left them. Sophia was amazed that Gentillini avoided slipping on any of the rosary beads rolling across the tile floor, even though she seemed to walk without looking down.

"I'm serious, John Paul," Sophia said to him softly. "I'm going to learn to walk like a nun."

"What?" he said with a small laugh.

"They walk like a cat. It's dignified and somehow sexy."

John Paul curled up, placing his arms around his knees. Sophia watched as he tried not to laugh out loud.

"I'm not even kidding," Sophia continued. "I'm going to drive the boys nuts at college next year. Just wait and see."

John Paul contained himself and sat up straighter. He began leaning over to pick up the beads that he could easily reach without standing up.

"Where are you going to college?" John Paul asked.

"Hopefully at Ohio Valley Catholic University," she replied. "Why do you think I'm even wasting my time at Catholic youth group? I need a letter from a nun or priest or someone like that. I wouldn't be here making Jesus necklaces if I didn't need to."

"I think they're Mary necklaces. And my mom says it's a sin to wear a rosary as a necklace."

"Whatever. My parents met at Ohio Valley Catholic, and they really want me to go there too."

"Do you want to go there?" John Paul asked.

"Sure, why not? It's as good a place as any. And I saw on a campus weekend visit that there is no difference to the party scene from a public college. You should join me in two years."

"Ugh. Don't even say it. My parents would be thrilled if I went to a Catholic university."

Sophia turned and looked directly at him. She wanted to say something but didn't. Instead, she began to help him retrieve the scattered blue-plastic beads.

"Listen," John Paul said to her quietly, "I'm going to leave during the snack break. Can you cover for me again?"

"Of course," Sophia said. "It's the least I can do since you switched rosaries with me. You faced the wrath of the Genitals—I owe you."

He laughed and said, "Thanks."

"Where do you go, anyway?" she asked.

John Paul didn't reply to her. He just shrugged his shoulders and looked down at the beads on the floor.

CHAPTER 5

"I hate doing this shit," Hunter said.

"Then don't," Jayme Smith-Johnson replied.

"I mean, what good is it?" Hunter asked. "Why should I film myself saying, 'It gets better' to a bunch of people that I don't know? I mean, what gets better?"

"Life, I guess," Jayme said.

"But all the kids watching this already know they have a shitty life, or they already know they have a great life," Hunter said. "I mean, the only ones that this will make a difference for are the kids that don't know. So if we tell them, 'It gets better,' aren't we telling them that they're not okay right now?"

The two boys were standing in a line around a classroom that had seen better days. Hunter smelled the musty air under the dim lights. He shuffled his feet slightly in the direction of the moving line, allowing the gap between him and the person in front of him to grow larger. At the front of the classroom, each student stood on a wooden crate and said, "It gets better" toward a teacher that was filming with a phone.

"I'm going to skip out," Hunter said. "I really don't want to be filmed. I'm only here because I'm your friend, and I was bored."

"This is for someone's senior project," Jayme said. "I don't know whose. But you'll need to do your own senior project in two years."

"Well, I can think of a better project than this piece of clichéd crap," Hunter said. "Besides, I've got you to help me—you know more about movies than anyone I know. I already planned that you'll create some kind of film for me. If you can't make something awesome to get me through to graduation, then no one can."

"Is that the only reason you come to Queer Community Outreach?" Jayme said. "To spend time with me so I feel bad saying no to you? I knew it."

They looked at each other and smirked. Jayme nudged Hunter to move forward as the line was way ahead of them.

"Well," Hunter replied, "I'm not here to get a date—that's for sure."

"Yeah, I know," Jayme said. "We all know—you're straight. You come out to us all the time."

"Good, but remember, if I was gay—you'd be the first guy I'd date. I mean, who else will watch horror movies with me? You'd be the perfect date if you didn't have a penis."

"I'm flattered," Jayme replied. "But I'm not willing to give mine up just to date you."

"Your parents don't think that. They'd love it if you'd hack that thing off."

"Don't remind me. Why am I the only gay guy that's losing his family because he's not liberal enough?"

Hunter laughed loudly and punched Jayme on the shoulder. Jayme punched him back.

"Hey!" said the teacher with the phone as she turned to look at them. "No inside jokes! It's rude—share with everyone, or keep the laughs to yourselves."

"Sorry, Miss Sommersmidt," Hunter said.

"It's just Sommersmidt," the teacher replied. "At school you can call me miss, but remember—there are no gender titles here."

"Oh yeah," said Hunter. "Sorry for that too, Sommersmidt."

The teacher went back to filming. Hunter glanced at a filthy clock over the door. He could barely make out that it was just after seven o'clock.

"Hey, Jayme," Hunter said, "isn't it time for you to get out of here?"

"Yeah," Jayme replied without looking at the clock. "I'm keeping my eye on it. I'll bail soon. They won't miss me as long as you stay in line."

"I'll stay in line, but you have to promise me something."

"What?" Jayme asked.

"Tonight, during your weird seven fifteen silent date," Hunter said, "you at least have to find out the guy's name."

"No way."

"Come on, Jayme, it's been long enough. How many weeks has it been?"

"This is the fifth," Jayme replied.

"So what? You just stand there and look at each other?"

"No, that's not what it's like. It's a bookstore—we both just happen to be shopping at the same time each week. That's it."

"That's stupid," Hunter said. "And it might also qualify as stalking. Ask him for his freaking name—take this to the next level. How else will you ever get into his pants?"

"Shut up," Jayme said as he shoved Hunter.

"Or at least find out where he goes to school. He must go to Seven Dollars."

Hunter knew that the correct name of the Catholic school was Seven Dolors. But like most of his friends, he thought it was quite funny to refer to is as Seven Dollars.

"He wears a school uniform like the Catholics do," Jayme said. "So probably Seven Dollars is right. But I just don't want to mess with it."

"Mess with what?" Hunter asked. "There's nothing to mess with. You just stare at each other through stacks of books."

"It's exciting enough the way it is," Jayme said. "Like I said, I don't want to mess with it. I like it."

"You're positive that you've never seen him anywhere else?" Hunter asked.

"Positive," Jayme said. "I don't even know if he lives in Kaiserburg. But I don't want to know. Are there other Catholic schools around? No, don't tell me—I don't want to know anything about him."

"Get his name...or this is the last time I'm covering for you," Hunter said. "I mean it."

"I'll think about it," Jayme replied.

Hunter watched as Jayme ducked behind a large kid on the other side of him. He slunk his way against the wall, away from the line of students, and left the room through the door under the clock. Hunter was excited for him and knew that he'd always cover for Jayme—even if he didn't find out his mystery guy's name.

CHAPTER 6

"Yep, that's right—Carlson's Used Books and Records on Main Street," said Bob Carlson into an old landline phone next to a cash register that was also old. He hung up the phone and looked for a pen and paper.

"Are they going to pick them up?" asked Fiona. "I'll just set them right on the back counter with their name on it."

"Thanks," Bob replied. "I'll write out a ticket for them. If they buy all those records, we'll be able to stay in the black for another month. Even if they buy just half of them, we'll be okay."

Fiona started moving several stacks of vinyl albums, in their cardboard sleeves, to a counter behind them. Bob watched as he sat back down on a stool that had seen better days; it rocked slightly as he sat, but he was used to it and wasn't bothered. Bob himself was older than the stool. He was in his mid-eighties.

As he watched Fiona carry the albums, he was grateful for the young woman who had become his best employee—probably the best employee he'd ever had. She was in her mid-twenties with streaky blond hair, made that way from years of bleaching it herself with peroxide. Along her right arm, she had a tattoo of the first sentence of *Alice in Wonderland*: "Alice was beginning to get very tired of sitting by her sister on the bank, and of having nothing to do." Bob knew she didn't have a sister and believed the phrase was much more philosophical than literal.

When she finished with the records, Fiona walked back to the cash register and sat next to Bob on her own stool. Her stool also rocked when she sat. She pointed to two copies of the same book that were sitting alone on a shelf under the cash register.

"What are those?" she asked. "Is there a name on those for the back counter?"

"Oh no," Bob replied. "I have a plan for those."

"Well, remember what I said? One small, unorganized pile leads to the complete mess you had in here before I started."

"I know," Bob said. "But I'll get rid of them tonight—I think...I hope."

Bob glanced around the store. Fiona had, indeed, organized his expansive merchandise better than it had ever been organized since he opened forty-four years earlier. The many tables of vinyl albums stood in neat rooms in the middle of the space. The entire perimeter was lined with bookshelves that were overflowing with books. It had taken Fiona—with Bob's reluctant assistance—over a year to organize all the used books into categories. But the many positive comments from customers convinced Bob that the work was worth it.

"Oh," said Bob, looking at his watch, "it's almost seven fifteen on a Wednesday. You know what that means?"

"Another exciting episode in the saga of the two most boring boys in the world?" Fiona asked.

"No!" Bob replied loudly with a laugh. "It's another episode in the wonderfully romantic 'will-they-won't-they' story of two shy young men. Two awkward young men that have more chemistry than Romeo and Juliet."

"You are a hopeless romantic. How have you stayed single all these years?"

"I've always been much more of an observer in life, and I don't mind."

"Well, those two drive me crazy—someone needs to make a move," Fiona said while softly caressing her tattoo. "How many weeks has it been that we've been watching them?"

"I think at least a month or so," Bob answered. "They are adorable. Remember the first time they were both in here, when it didn't seem like nothing at all? But then the one came back at the same time the next week, and when the other then came back at the same time—that was magic. I'm telling you, Fiona, it's better than TV."

"Yeah, well, they're going to lose half their audience if they just stand around awkwardly again, pretending to look at books that they obviously care nothing about. For God's sake, last week one of them was pretending to be entranced with the gardening shelves just because it gave him a better view of the other one over at automotive repair. There's no way either of them is gardening or fixing an old car."

Bob laughed and looked at the two books he'd placed under the register. Fiona leaned over to get a better look out of the storefront window. She ducked a bit to see through the backward painted letters that read "Carlson's Used Books and Records" from the other side.

"Well," Fiona said, "you're in luck. Here comes the one in the Catholic-school uniform."

"Tonight's episode has started." Bob laughed. "Next week, will you bring some popcorn?"

"Make your own." Fiona smirked. "I'm into books—not cooking. But I do enjoy looking through a nice recipe book just to see…"

Bob stopped paying attention to her when the shop's door opened and a young man stepped inside the store. The boy, in his neatly pressed school uniform, politely nodded a greeting at the two sitting behind the register. Bob and Fiona greeted him loudly, which made him blush as he rushed to a nearby bookshelf full of books about collecting antiques.

Bob swiveled on his stool to an old radio that was sitting next to them on a third stool. It was already playing a classical-music station, but Bob turned it up quite a bit.

"Is that supposed to be mood music?" Fiona said to him.

"Yep," Bob answered, "and also so that we can talk about them without them hearing."

"How sad are we?" Fiona said. "Too easily entertained."

"At my age," Bob replied, "you take what you can get. And there is nothing on any of those streaming services that is worth a piss. Even the history shows are about some nonsense like space aliens building the pyramids and all sorts of crap. I'll take a real—"

"Shut up," interrupted Fiona as the shop door opened again. "Here comes the more artsy one."

"I knew it," Bob said. "You are just as interested as me."

Bob and Fiona said hello to the other young man as he entered the store. He waved and said hello back as he immediately went to the first table of used records and started sorting through them.

"Oh Christ," Bob said, "he's got to do better than that. He's in the Lawrence Welk section. He should at least try to act casual with something hipper than that."

"Hipper?" Fiona laughed. "Is that the word that the kids are using these days?"

"Whatever." Bob smiled back. "But I do like that every week he wears a shirt paying homage to an old movie. This kid's got taste—seriously. Universal Studios' original *Frankenstein* is a masterpiece."

Bob watched the two guys intently while pretending to be extremely interested in the cash register. Fiona stood from her stool and began straightening a display of bookmarks sitting next to the register. Except for the sound of the classical radio station, which was now playing the overture to Mozart's *Marriage of Figaro*, none of the four in the store made a sound. Bob took a deep breath and relaxed. Bantering with Fiona and watching awkward young love made him feel alive.

Bob noticed that Fiona also enjoyed the evening—the bookmarks had been perfectly sorted for days, but she was still arranging them. He also kept his eye on his watch. He knew that the Catholic kid always stayed exactly twenty minutes, then left quickly. The artistic guy would saunter around for a few minutes and then also leave. If Bob were to intervene, he'd have to do it on time.

Fiona made a small smirk, drawing Bob's attention up from the register. For the first time in all these weeks, the two guys were looking at the same shelf of books. The artistic one was pretending to look for a specific book and had intently walked toward the Catholic guy.

"He's going to make a move," Fiona said quietly but expectantly.

"Oh," Bob replied to her, "I hope so. Come on, man; have some courage."

Bob looked at the time on his watch—only six minutes left. It was excruciating but wonderful to witness. Just then, the artistic one lunged to grab a book at the exact same time that the Catholic one started to stretch in a pretend yawn. Their arms collided. They each said, "Sorry," and took a step away from the other.

"Oh!" Both Bob and Fiona groaned simultaneously.

Bob said, "Okay—that's it. I can't take another week of this. We have to say something."

"Oh, finally," said Fiona, "we get to be in an episode. What should we do? We have to get them to actually bump into each other—that's how it's done in movies—like those on the Hallmark Channel at Christmas. You start talking to Frankenstein, and I'll take Catholic School. Then we just have to—"

"Nope," Bob interrupted, "that won't work."

"Of course it will." She laughed. "I've seen it many times."

"Well, it's not Christmas for another three months, and this is not a damn Hallmark movie. Listen, age is an advantage to me here. I know more about this kind of thing than you think. I know that there's a lot more going on around here than meets the eye. Even in this modern age of LGBTAQI-whatever, these two come from different worlds—and they both know it. Both these kids have been subjected to adults arguing over politics since they were born."

"What?" Fiona asked curiously. "Adults and politics? What are you talking about? You don't even know these guys."

"Oh," Bob answered, "yes, I do. When you get into your eighties, you know everyone you just met as if you'd known them for fifty years. I know exactly what these two are about. You see, everything they hear from every adult—in real life and on TV—is garbage talk from one side of politics or the other. It's a culture war, and you can't be in the middle. You don't think they've already picked up on the fact that one goes to Catholic school and the other doesn't? In a culture war, that's a big warning sign. Frankenstein is afraid that Catholic School might not even be gay—or if he is gay, that he might not know it. And Frankenstein is also quite unsure of himself. He's already been rejected by his peer group, or why else is he escaping to a used bookstore in the first place? His 'friends,' or whatever you call them, aren't into old movies like he is. He's not going to make a move because he's terrified of rejection. And the other one has been so repressed that just looking at a guy as he looks at you is enough excitement to fulfill his needs. Catholic School is not going to make a move because he's not going to take a chance on ruining these little weekly interactions—he needs them; they're all he has."

Bob looked back at Fiona and saw that she had been hanging on his every word. Her face showed an expression of wonder and admiration. Of love, even.

"Bob," Fiona said, "you are a marvel. I can't wait to be in my eighties and have that insight."

"You've got lots of time to get there—but we only have four minutes left to get to these two."

"There's always next week," Fiona said.

"That's another thing you learn when you're eighty—and sometimes you learn it the hard way—opportunities don't always come around again. There's not always next week."

CHAPTER 7

M rs. Theresa Saint Clara turned left with her SUV and pulled into a small parking lot in front of a building that looked like a warehouse. Next to the car, in large letters, a sign read: Knights of Columbus Hall, a Confraternity of Catholic Men. Her husband, Mr. Bernard Saint Clara, stood near the door of the building, talking to another confraternal man. She swung her car around the gravel lot and pulled up next to him. Mr. Saint Clara shook hands with the man he was talking to and got into the SUV.

"Hi, Theresa," he said to her as he climbed in and immediately adjusted the air vents so that they were blowing on him.

"Bernard, do you want fish tonight?" Theresa asked. "I feel like fish."

"Fine," he said as he looked around the empty back seat. "Where's Mary Clair? Didn't you pick her up?"

"The Trobecs wanted to take her to a movie," Theresa answered as she pulled back onto the street. "I didn't think you'd mind."

"What movie?" he asked.

"Something by Disney."

"Oh. Did you check to see if it was okay? I'm sure the Trobecs have good judgment. But, you know, Disney?"

"I checked the online version of *The Catholic Visitor.* They said it was fine—just a few minor things that I can talk about with her later tonight."

"If the *Visitor* said it was fine," he said, "then I guess it's okay. They are pretty good with these things over there."

"I think so," Theresa said.

Bernard reached up and rubbed a silver Saint Christopher's medal that was attached to the sun visor over his head. He used a finger to trace the engraved letters: *Saint Christopher, protect us as we drive.* Theresa loved that he often did this when he got into the car, even if it did make her self-conscious about her driving.

"Did you have a good time at the KC Hall?" Theresa asked.

"Of course," Bernard answered. "But Father Ron never showed up. He didn't leave any word with Jim, so nobody knows where he went."

"Oh, you know priests," she said. "Maybe he was called to the hospital or the funeral home?"

"Well, Jim is upset, of course. How long has Father been here?"

"I think at least seven or eight years."

"Time for him to move on," Bernard said. "He's too liberal. And he can take that nun—that Sister Gabriel Luke—with him."

"I've talked to her several times. She's not liberal, is she?"

"What? She's as liberal as Hillary Clinton. Apparently, she was talking about letting women become priests with the confirmation class. She got the girls in there all worked up. We all heard about it—good thing Sister Gentillini was there to set them all straight. Now there is a nun. It's nice to see a young nun with such a commitment to the church."

"You know, Bernard, the kids hate her," Theresa said. "They call her 'Sister Genitals.' "

"I know. And she doesn't deserve that. She gave probably the best lecture about the Blessed Mother that we've ever had at the Knights of Columbus. Really—we men were very impressed."

"John Paul thinks she's weird."

"Hmph." Bernard smirked. "I guess he probably would."

"What's that supposed to mean?"

"He's hanging around with the wrong crowd, Theresa. We've got to do something about that. Those public school girls are getting to him."

"I mentioned it to him on the way to Catholic youth group tonight. He wasn't very receptive."

"Well, he's going to be when I talk to him. I worry about him."

"I do too," Theresa said. "You don't think there is anything really wrong with him, do you?"

"Of course not," Bernard said.

"You know what I mean, don't you? You know what I mean when I worry about there being something wrong with him?"

"Yes, I know what you mean. I worry about it sometimes too. We just have to pray about it, and if we ever find out he's playing for the wrong team, then we need to do something about it. There's a lot at stake when we start talking about our son's eternal soul."

"I know, and I agree. I've even looked into it a little online. There are places that can help boys like him. I talked to one mom—anonymously online, of course—and she had great success with her son."

"But, Theresa, let's make sure he needs help before we give it to him. And if he does need to go somewhere, I won't hesitate to send him. He's been a little 'off' since he was born, and it would be nice to just fix this thing once and for all."

"I agree," she said. "It's nice to know that we have an option. Men get over this kind of thing all the time. I'll keep an eye on him."

They continued on their way as the streetlights began to glow. The sun was setting. They didn't speak at all for the rest of the trip.

CHAPTER 8

Ms. Abygail Smith-Johnson drove down Main Street toward a strip mall on the far side of town. She'd driven to the point where Main Street was about to turn into a county road. Two reusable water bottles sat in cup holders in her car. As she drove, she drank a smoothie from a Starbucks disposable plastic cup. The passenger seat was stacked with binders from the various community organizations to which she belonged. As she neared the strip mall, she placed the Starbucks cup between her seat and the door. She then started picking up the binders one by one and throwing them onto the back seat. Her husband, Sammy Smith-Johnson, was leaning against a mailbox at the edge of the mall. He got into the car quickly when she pulled up.

"You're late," Sammy Smith-Johnson said.

"I know, sorry," Abygail replied. "I dropped Jayme off at the Kaiserburg Community Center and stopped at the housing coalition to talk to Shantal. Well, you know how that went—they just can't shut up."

"Oh, who else was there?" Sammy asked.

"Just Shantal," Abygail answered.

Sammy shrugged his shoulders and reached toward the display screen on the dash of the car. He started pressing a few digital buttons.

"I need to switch the sync over to my phone," he said.

"Are you expecting a call?"

"Yeah, from Brandon Mussah."

"Oh really?" Abygail said. "Might this be a very important call?"

"Yes," Sammy replied, "it just might be. But it won't be if I'm late to tonight's meeting."

Abygail smiled and said, "I think we still have just enough time to get you to your meeting on time. Then I'll pick up Jayme, and maybe we will have something to celebrate tonight."

"Let's not count our chickens until they hatch," Sammy said. "But if it all goes to plan, Jayme may not have time for activities—not if we need to hit the campaign trail. He might be too busy."

"Stop referring to him as *he*. We just don't know yet."

"You just referred to him as *him*."

"I did?" she asked. "Well, I didn't mean to."

"Maybe we should stop pushing him? Maybe he's just a gay man?"

"No, Sammy, he's not," Abygail said. "A mother knows these things. I don't want him—them—to lose their one chance to fix things."

"I just think we might want to take it a bit slow," he said. "We just don't know how—"

He was interrupted as his phone rang throughout the car's speaker system. On the display screen, large red letters displayed the name "Brandon Mussah." Abygail and Sammy looked at each other. She bit her lower lip and took her hands off the steering wheel to show Sammy her crossed fingers. Sammy nodded his head and pressed a green button on the screen.

"Hey, Brandon, this is Sammy," he said. "I've got you on speaker in the car with Abygail."

"Oh hi, Abygail," said a voice over the speakers.

"Hi, Brandon," she replied. "Don't mind me. I'm just driving."

"Okay," Brandon said, "but I'm actually glad that I have you both together."

"What can we do for you?" Sammy asked.

Abygail glanced intently toward Sammy. He returned the glance.

"Well, Councilman Sam, we've talked about it a lot. And—well—I won't waste your time, and you need to know this before you get to the meeting tonight. So how does Representative Smith-Johnson sound? Congressman Smith-Johnson?"

Abygail and Sammy looked at each other with huge smiles. Abygail lifted her hands from the steering wheel once more to shake her fists with excitement. Sammy motioned to join her, then held up his hands, and brought them down in a calming manner. He took a large breath and exhaled slowly.

"Does that mean what I think it means?" Sammy asked.

"Yes," Brandon replied over the speakers, "we've decided to endorse you for the election. But as you know, it will still be a long road because we have some hurdles. We've just got to get through the primary, and then we'll be golden."

"I understand," Sammy said. "I sure appreciate the endorsement."

"We don't want to waste our money," Brandon continued, "so we're going to run a campaign in all the bigger towns in the district before the primary. As you know, this is a very liberal district, and our union wants to keep a big part of that. The primary election is the only thing that matters.

We need to show the Progressives that you are as progressive as them. These are the only people that count right now, Sammy. You can't win the election if you're not on the ballot, so we need to do what we can to make sure you win the primary. If you want our union money, then you'll need to start being as liberal as you possibly can—your family too. I'm not going to step around it—we're taking a big risk by endorsing a straight white man. But we believe you are the best candidate for us. So do what you can to liberalize your image—there are other factions already putting a woman forward. We need to beat them at the primary."

"Don't worry about us, Brandon," Abygail said. "I'm on board one hundred percent. And Jayme will be too. We'll all work on Sammy's image."

"Good," Brandon said. "We'll talk about the details more when you get here. But I have to go, or I'll be late myself. I'll see you soon."

"Brandon," Sammy said, "thanks again. You won't be sorry. Your money will be well spent."

"I better not be, Congressman," Brandon said. "Remember, your only thought right now should be about one word—*primary*."

The phone clicked off suddenly. Sammy and Abygail took a moment, looked at each other, checked that the call had completely disconnected, and then let out screams of excitement.

"It's finally starting!" Abygail yelled. "We're getting noticed!"

"It's more than that," Sammy said. "I'm finally getting more than a foot in the door."

"All that union money! I'm so tired of all this Kaiserburg crap and these people with their stupid problems calling the house all the time. Finally, our ticket to Washington—and dinner parties, Christmas at the White House, lunch with lobbyists—"

"But we have to calm down and get through the primary," Brandon said. "You heard what Brandon said. I'm a straight white man—that's a problem around here. Especially if the activists are running a woman in the primary."

"Yes, of course," Abygail said. "We will present a united Progressive front. You can't lose if we stick together with key talking points about climate change and affordable housing. All of us—the whole family—we'll be just as Progressive as those primary voters want. We'll get every climate activist, every union activist, and every LGBTQIA+ person to believe in your message. Jayme will help a lot to show how Progressive our family is."

"All of us, right," Sammy said. "You're right. All of us together will get those activists behind us in no time—even if I'm a straight white man."

Abygail sat silent in her joy for a few moments. She was already imagining herself as First Lady. She wondered if Sammy was also imagining far into the future.

Then out of nowhere, Sammy said, "You know what, Abygail? I might have been wrong before. Maybe we should go to a doctor and try to get Jayme on some hormones? It might be good for him—I mean, it might be good for Jayme to embrace who *they* really are. You know, they might like to talk about it and share their story with others. It also could be good for Jayme if I talked about it with people...about how proud I am of him—*them*—how proud I am of them. I can share the story of our family's acceptance and approval. We could do a lot of good."

"I agree," Abygail said.

CHAPTER 9

At Our Lady of Seven Dolors Catholic School, it was break time. Sister Gentillini started to make preparations, causing the students to relax and talk loudly as they moved around the room. It was a bit chaotic, and Sister Gentillini did not like chaos.

"Completed rosaries that have been checked by me in the bag!" Sister Gentillini yelled to the group of students scattering around the floor. "If they haven't been checked by me, then cut the strings and put the loose beads back."

"But I'm close to done on this one," said one of the students. "Can I just set it aside and finish it after the break?"

"No," Gentillini replied, "it's too easy for you to lose count and screw up. Unless it's complete—destroy it. And make sure all the loose beads get back in the right trays. I also don't want to see any plastic pieces lying on the floor. Did that kid go to get the snack or not?"

Before anyone could answer, a teenage boy entered the room with three large plastic containers. She took the containers from him and began to organize the snacks on a side table. At the same time, she glanced around the room, remembering that she wanted to keep an eye on John Paul Saint Clara. She chastised herself for not watching him closely. In a far corner, Gentillini saw Sophia cleaning up her trays—alone. Her eyebrows raised and her eyes widened.

"Did you see John Paul Saint Clara when you went to get the snacks?" she asked the boy standing next to her.

"Yeah," he answered. "I think he went out the back door in the kitchen."

"Why is he going out there?" she asked.

"I don't know," the boy answered, not realizing that her question was rhetorical.

Gentillini started to walk toward Sophia, then realized that she wouldn't get much of an answer from the girl. Instead, she quickly walked out of the kindergarten classroom and turned down the hall.

Since the sun had set, the hall was dark. Under her breath, she cursed the janitor for not turning the lights on. She'd almost reached the kitchen door when she heard someone calling her name from behind.

"Sister Gentillini," said Sophia, "can I ask you a question?"

Gentillini stopped and turned in the darkened hallway and noticed Sophia walking after her. She immediately suspected that this was some type of diversion tactic to get her attention away from John Paul. In Sister Gentillini's mind, Sophia and John Paul were thick as thieves.

"I'm looking for John Paul Saint Clara," Gentillini said.

"Oh," Sophia replied softly, "I think he went to the bathroom. I saw him leave, and I'm sure that's where he went."

"Hmmm," Gentillini said.

"But I have an important question for you," Sophia said quickly.

"Well, what is it?" Gentillini said. "I don't have a lot of time."

"Well," Sophia said, "I'm hoping to go to Ohio Valley Catholic next fall, and my parents wanted me to ask you about a class. They said that you are the best person to ask because you know the most about these things, and they trust you."

Gentillini knew this was a lie. She didn't remember ever meeting Sophia's parents. But at the same time, she believed that she really was the best person to ask about anything to do with Ohio Valley Catholic. Or anything Catholic at all.

"What is it?" Gentillini asked.

"So," Sophia said, "it's about the theology requirement for the first term. My dad wants me to take Catholic catechism, and my mom wants me to take world religions. What do you think?"

"Catholic catechism—of course. Your dad is right. Why in the world would anyone want to study other religions?"

"That's what I thought," Sophia said.

Gentillini turned to enter the kitchen. If Sophia really was trying to distract her, she should have thought of a longer and better question than that. As she went into the kitchen, she could tell that the girl was still following her, probably hoping to think of something better to say. Gentillini flicked on the kitchen lights and started walking toward the back door that led outside.

"Sister," Sophia said loudly, "I think I want to be a nun!"

Now Gentillini knew this was a ruse. She stopped and turned with a snap of her neck. This was too brazen of a ploy to let go. Sophia was visibly startled at how fast Gentillini had turned. Gentillini could not believe that anyone would stoop this low simply to cover for a classmate.

"Really?" Gentillini said. "*You* want to be a nun?"

"Ah, yes," Sophia said. "I've been getting a call—I mean, *the* call. Jesus has been calling me to be a nun."

"Really?" Gentillini said. "I got my calling from Mary."

"Well, yeah, of course I get calls from her too," Sophia said.

"What is it about being a nun that they are calling you to do?"

"Oh, you know, feed the poor and help the homeless. That sort of stuff."

"Do you really think you have what it takes to be the bride of Christ?" Gentillini asked.

Sophia didn't answer. Gentillini saw the wheels in the girl's head spinning as she tried to think of something to say.

"Sophia," Gentillini said, "where did John Paul go?"

"Who?"

"John Paul—you know, the boy you are always with."

"I don't know anything about him," Sophia said. "Honestly, I just wanted to talk to you."

"I thought you said that he went to the toilet," Gentillini said.

"He did," Sophia said, "but I'm sure he's out now. He's back in the classroom, honestly."

"You wouldn't know honesty if Saint Peter himself brought it to you on a silver tray," Gentillini said. "This is a terrible sin you have committed. Not only are you lying for the sin of another, but you are using the sanctity of the religious vows as a lie. You have made the Blessed Mother very unhappy. I hope you have a rosary in your bedroom because you are going to need it. And I better not see that you take the Holy Communion on Sunday unless you go to confession with Father."

Sophia didn't say anything. Gentillini tried hard to see, in Sophia's face, whether she was sorry. But, instead, the girl looked like she was a bit proud. This angered Gentillini to the point that she considered grabbing a large metal serving spoon that was lying on a nearby counter. She didn't think that she would actually hit the girl, but it might be nice to at least make that impression. She reached for the spoon. Just then, the outside door opened. Sister Gabriel Luke walked through and into the kitchen.

"Oh, hello," Gabriel Luke said, a bit startled to see people in the kitchen.

"Did you see the Saint Clara boy out there?" Gentillini asked.

"No," Gabriel Luke replied, "should I have? Is everything okay in here?"

"Yes, everything is fine," Gentillini said. "Isn't it, Sophia?"

"Yep," Sophia said, "everything is fine."

Sophia turned and walked quickly out of the kitchen. Gentillini noticed that her hand was still on the spoon. With a smoothness of gesture that only nuns can make, she retrieved her hand and placed it up the opposite shirtsleeve.

"Did you need that spoon for something?" Gabriel Luke asked.

Gentillini shrugged her shoulders, turned, and left the room, going back down the dark hallway. She imagined Gabriel Luke's suspicious face and delighted in it.

Sophia walked into the classroom while all the other students were eating some kind of cake. She was condemning herself for how stupid she had been. She couldn't believe that she wasn't able to think of anything better to say other than that she wanted to become a nun. It was probably the dumbest thing she had ever said. Still, hopefully, John Paul and she could have a nice, long laugh about it someday.

CHAPTER 10

"Hey there, guys," Bob yelled across the bookstore. "Why don't you come over here and talk to us for a bit?"

Both of the boys looked over at him. Frankenstein just looked a bit startled, but Catholic School looked like he'd just been discovered committing murder. Bob felt bad about Catholic School's stunned face but decided to press ahead.

"We don't bite," Bob continued. "We have a gift for you since you are frequent customers."

"Well, you're not really customers," Fiona said with a laugh. "You'd have to buy something to be one of those. But anyway, come over here."

"I really can't," said Catholic School. "I really need to go back somewhere."

"Now just wait a moment," said Bob. "You can be a little late—it's the least you can do since you visit here every Wednesday at the same time."

While Catholic School was talking, Bob noticed that Frankenstein looked at the other boy with a sense of wonder. Almost as if he was relieved to know that the guy he was crushing on could speak—that he was actually a real human and not a dream.

The boys walked over to the counter that held the cash register. Frankenstein walked much quicker than Catholic

School. Bob and Fiona stood from their stools, and Bob turned the classical radio station down.

"What's your name?" Bob asked Catholic School.

"John Paul," he answered.

"John Paul—well, it's nice to meet you. And you?" said Bob.

"Jayme," he answered. "Jayme with a *y*—in the middle and not at the end. I mean, it's J-A-Y-M-E. I don't know why, I just…"

Jayme's voice trailed off, as if he realized he was being awkward, and stopped speaking. A few long and silent moments followed. Bob let them pass. The feeling that something special had just occurred was overwhelming him. He noticed that not even Fiona dared to speak.

"I take it that you two don't know each other," Bob finally said when the time was right.

They both shook their heads. They didn't look at each other.

"I didn't think you went to the same school or anything," Fiona said.

"Sorry if I'm bothering you," John Paul said. "I'm sorry to waste your time and not spend any money here."

"Then why do you come here?" Bob asked.

Bob knew the answer to that question, but he wondered if John Paul did. Jayme looked at John Paul with expectation.

"I like books," John Paul said.

"Is that all?" Fiona said with a small chuckle.

"No," John Paul said as he shyly lowered his head and stared at the floor. "I guess it's not just for…"

"What about you?" Bob asked Jayme.

"I like old movies," Jayme replied. "I'm not sure why that's a reason to come here, though, since you don't sell old movies. I should have thought of…"

John Paul quickly looked up at him and smiled. Bob noticed them bonding over their awkwardness.

"Yeah," said Fiona, "I kind of got that you liked movies from the shirts you wear."

"But that's not all," Jayme said with sudden confidence. "I saw this guy in here a few weeks back, and I liked the way he looked—and I hoped he'd come back, and he did. Oh, I hope it's okay to say that I like the way he looks. I'm not shallow or body-shaming people that don't look that way—I'm just saying that I like the way you look."

Jayme turned and looked at John Paul as he said this. John Paul, still staring at the floor, nodded his head. Jayme smiled in relief. Then Bob watched as John Paul's face began to glow a brilliant shade of red.

"Well," said Bob, "now that you at least know each other's names, I have a gift and an assignment for you. There's no use just coming in here and doing absolutely nothing each week—it's a waste of time, frankly. And I don't have a lot of time. So here you go."

Bob reached under the register and retrieved the two copies of the same book that he'd placed there earlier. The books were the size of an average textbook, with a hard, glossy cover that reflected the store's overhead lights. He placed the books, side by side, on the counter.

The title, *Ancient Pride*, was printed in large gold letters on the front cover. Underneath, on the left side, there was a depiction of ancient Greece. On the right side, there was a depiction of ancient Rome. A brilliant rainbow stretched from the Parthenon to the Colosseum. Below the picture, in smaller letters, the complete title of the book and the author were displayed: *Ancient Pride: A Book for Gay Men About the Hidden Gay Men of the Past.* The book was written by Dr. Madison W. Freeman.

"Here you go," Bob said. "I want you to read the introduction and the first chapter. When you come here next Wednesday, we'll have a little book club. That way, you'll have a reason to visit us."

"Oh, I want to join!" said Fiona excitedly.

"I knew you would," Bob replied. "There are other copies around here someplace. If you can find one, you can join."

"Not a problem," Fiona said as she glanced at the boys and gave them a wink. "I can find any book anywhere."

"I can't, really," John Paul said timidly. "I really can't have this book. My parents would never allow it—I mean, they'd never allow any of this. And I really can't come back again. Sorry. I have to go."

Bob sighed with sadness. He had been afraid of this. Jayme looked like his heart had just been ripped out. Bob didn't know what to say. He stared at John Paul and wanted desperately to grab the boy and hold him for a few years until things got better. Bob was at a loss for words and actions.

"That's not a problem," said Fiona. "I can take care of the book for you."

She grabbed the book and stepped to the side of the counter. She seemed to move faster than what was humanly possible. Fiona reached under the counter and tore a large piece of brown parchment paper from a stiff roll. She placed the paper on the counter, put the book in the middle, and began to fold the paper into a cover. When completed, she took a few pieces of masking tape to secure her very neat work.

"What is your favorite subject?" she asked John Paul.

"Math," he replied.

Fiona grabbed a felt-tipped marker from a jar next to the cash register. She wrote *Advanced Algebra* on the cover and slid the book to John Paul. He hesitated, then took the book.

"Can I have one of those covers too?" Jayme asked. "My mom hates ancient stuff—even though history is my favorite subject. She never lets my dad and me watch any of it because of the patriarchy and all that. I don't know why I said that—it's too much information, probably. Anyway, she'll freak if she sees anything with Rome on it."

"Not a problem," Fiona said. "I can understand your mom; I sometimes have patriarchal problems myself."

Again, Fiona wrapped the book with extreme precision and speed. Bob, already greatly impressed with Fiona, was even more amazed at her many abilities. Fiona wrote *History* on this book and gave it to Jayme.

"Now you guys better get going," Bob said. "I don't want anyone that might be expecting you to worry. Or to be looking for you."

"Thank you," John Paul said as he turned to leave.

"Yeah, thank you," Jayme said. "Actually, I really owe you one—I've been trying to find out his name for weeks!"

When Jayme said this, John Paul looked back. He was even redder than before.

"No problem," Bob said. "We're here to help each other. See you next week."

"And don't forget," Fiona said, "introduction and first chapter. Hey! I kind of like organizing a book club. We should do this more often."

"You bet," said Jayme.

When the boys had left the store, Fiona let out a cheer. She and Bob instinctively slapped their hands together. They both laughed.

"That was the best episode I've seen in a long time," Fiona said. "You did good, Bob."

"Thank you, I thought so too," Bob said.

Bob felt quite good about himself. He and Fiona shared a moment of pride, then went back to work.

Outside, Jayme ran to catch up to John Paul. He didn't care about being late and knew that nobody else in the queer group at the community center would either.

"Hey," Jayme said. "It's nice to finally meet you, John Paul."

John Paul stopped and turned to face him. He was smiling. Jayme held out his hand, and John Paul took it. They shook their hands with the formality of two old Scrooges making a deal. Except one of the Scrooges was still bright red.

"John Paul—I like your name," Jayme said.

"I don't," John Paul replied. "I'd rather be called J. P., or something like that."

"No, *John Paul* has a good ring. It stands for something, like *Julius Caesar* or *Alfred Hitchcock*."

"I don't know who that is—the second guy, I mean. I know who Julius Caesar was."

"Alfred Hitchcock directed *Psycho* and a bunch of other really good movies. He always makes a cameo in his movies. I guess I know a lot of useless crap like that, mostly from movies."

"I like useless crap," John Paul said. "I don't know why I just said that. I really don't like useless crap all that much."

They both started to laugh. Jayme had never heard something so wonderful in all his short life as the sound of John Paul's laughter.

"I really have to go," John Paul said. "There's…people… nuns—I mean, I need to get back before they notice."

"Nuns? Right," Jayme said. "I hope I see you next week."

"Me too," John Paul replied. "Yeah, nuns. I have to go. I mean, I hope I get to see you next week."

Jayme turned and started walking toward the community center. For some reason, he couldn't stop the main musical theme from the film *Out of Africa* from playing in his head. The melody repeated in his dreams all night.

ANCIENT PRIDE

BY DR. MADISON W. FREEMAN

Introduction from the Author

Thank you for reading this book. It was a labor of love to write, and I feel it is probably the most important book I've written. I want to take an opportunity to explain what this book is about, and what it is not about.

This book is about men from ancient Greece and Rome, some mythological and some historical—but all of them real. These were men who were revered as heroes and respected as leaders. These were men who fought hard for their beliefs and were beloved by the gods. But these were also men who loved other men. Tragically, historians decided to tell the parts of their stories they liked and to hide (or eliminate) the parts they didn't like. This was a horrible injustice that I hope to undo in this book.

Many historians will tell you that we cannot know these men were gay because there is no definitive proof. These historians are my colleagues—I've worked with them my whole life, and they frustrate me. I can present to these historians the story of two men who lived together for years, ate together, worked together, and fought together, and one grieved when the other died. I can tell the experts all about the struggles and triumphs that these two men had together.

Yet when I suggest that these men were lovers, the historians will tell me I am wrong because there isn't any proof. In essence, they won't believe that Alexander the Great and Hephaestion were gay because we don't have a picture of them actually having gay sex. I state that this is absolutely ridiculous. Not only is this notion technically impossible, but it also portrays the incorrect assumption that gay relationships revolve around sex and nothing more.

We don't have a photograph of George Washington going at it with Martha in the backyard of Mount Vernon. There aren't any diary entries where Martha describes nights of torrid lovemaking with George under the cherry tree. There are no witnesses who saw George's wooden teeth caught on Martha's corset laces. George and Martha never had any children together—that is a verifiable fact. But everyone assumes that George and Martha Washington were in a heterosexual relationship. No historian has ever asked for proof to believe this. So why don't we afford the same liberty to Alexander and Hephaestion?

Yes, this is a book full of circumstantial evidence. That is the only evidence that we have. I'm not stating that circumstantial evidence is proof, but I am stating that circumstantial evidence is all we have in the case of George and Martha. What is the difference?

Now let's talk about what this book is not. This is not a book about gay rights or equality. There are no parades or flag waving in this book. You will not find that any of our heroes identify themselves with any sort of sexual labels.

These are modern aspects of society. We cannot apply our modern rules to those who lived three thousand years ago.

Please don't be disappointed when Emperor Hadrian does not give a rousing speech that legalizes gay marriage for the Roman Empire. Don't be disappointed when the Sacred Band of Thebes does not march on Athens and demand to be recognized by the news reporters of the time. And don't be disappointed when one of our heroes does what is expected of him and has a child with a woman. Survival was much more important these millennia ago. Being "yourself" was something that never crossed anyone's mind. This is a luxury of our modern age.

It's my hope that this book will both teach and inspire. I hope you will learn that being gay is not a new concept. I hope you will learn that gay people can do great things. I hope you will learn that love is intense and powerful. Mostly, I hope you will be inspired to share these stories so that others may be inspired. The ancient people knew that sharing stories was the best way to impart knowledge from one generation to the next.

Enjoy your reading,
Dr. Madison W. Freeman
Professor of Egyptian, Greek, and Roman studies

CHAPTER 11

"No," Jayme said to Hunter. "Stop being such a jerk." Hunter laughed loudly. It was a Friday—the Friday after the Wednesday when Jayme had learned John Paul's name, and Jayme and Hunter were walking home from school together. Hunter's dad lived a few doors down from the Smith-Johnsons.

"What?" Hunter said. "Are you serious? You actually did get his name?"

"Yes," Jayme replied. "I went up and asked him, and he told me."

Jayme knew this wasn't quite the way it had happened. He didn't tell Hunter about Bob, Fiona, or the book he received. But it was true that he'd talked to John Paul.

"Well, tell me. What is the dream guy's name?"

"John Paul," Jayme said with a small smile.

"John Paul, John Paul, ohhhhhhh, John Paul," said Hunter as he pretended to make out with the air.

"Stop it," Jayme said.

"How many times have you teased me about some girl?" Hunter asked.

"Too many to count," Jayme replied.

"I rest my case then," Hunter said. "But seriously, what else did you talk about?"

Jayme didn't say anything. Hunter stopped on the sidewalk and looked at Jayme. He rolled his eyes.

"Tell me you talked about something, not just his name," Hunter said. "His last name?"

"Okay," Jayme replied, "we didn't talk all that much. But he's very polite and clean."

"Polite and clean!" Hunter laughed. "What the hell does that mean?"

"It means he treats people with respect and smells good. That's all."

"Well, I guess good hygiene is important for you gay guys."

Hunter laughed again and started to continue walking. Jayme followed but at a slower pace than before. Hunter looked back, noticed Jayme's red face, and stopped for a second time.

"Look at you blush!" said Hunter excitedly. "Oh, man... you've got it bad!"

"I know. I know," Jayme said. "I'm screwed."

"Screwed in the good way?" Hunter asked with a smirk.

"No, really screwed in the bad way," Jayme answered. "I think he's really, really in the closet. He's not going to be able to handle being gay, and that scares me. I should just stop going to the bookstore before it goes anywhere. Why waste my time with some guy that probably will have panic attacks at the thought of being seen with me?"

Hunter started walking again. Jayme kept up with him this time. He wondered if he should say something else to explain his feelings about John Paul. But neither of them spoke for a few blocks.

"Listen, Jayme," Hunter eventually said. "Yeah, I get it that this guy, John Paul, goes to the Catholic school and all. But, man, look at you! You are exploding right now—I've known you for my entire life and never seen you like this. You got to give this guy the benefit of the doubt. Yeah, John Paul may have to work out a few things. But you've been there; you can help him."

"You've met my parents, right?" Hunter said. "I know nothing about being in the closet. When I told my parents I liked other guys, they threw me a party. A big old freaking rainbow party, remember?"

"Yes, of course I remember. I was there. It was awesome. The rainbow cake alone was worth your embarrassment."

"So how can I help anyone like John Paul?"

"You help him because you can. And maybe nobody else will. Yeah, he might freak out and run away. But you have to try."

"I guess," Jayme said.

"You guess?" Hunter asked.

"I know," Jayme said.

"Isn't that what Han Solo says in *The Empire Strikes Back*? You know, when Princess Leia tells him that she loves him?"

"That is not the same at all!" Jayme yelled. "You are so stupid."

Jayme shoved Hunter to the side. Hunter shoved back. They continued walking.

"Hey, Sophia," John Paul said into the phone, a landline, in his kitchen. "What happened when I was gone on Wednesday? It seemed weird when I got back to the youth group."

John Paul was home alone. It was Friday after school, and his parents were at a prayer meeting and dinner with some of the other Knights of Columbus. They would never trust him or his sister with their own cell phones. John Paul often called Sophia on Fridays when he was alone, before she went out for the night.

"Wednesday!" Sophia said loudly. "It was a disaster!"

"What?" John Paul asked. "What happened?"

"I made a total idiot out of myself; that's what happened. I had Sister Genitals stopped in the hallway because that stupid kid with the snacks saw you leaving the kitchen door."

"I knew he saw me!" John Paul said. "Oh, I knew I should have stopped and made some excuse to him. What happened?"

"I asked her something about a class at Ohio Valley Catholic," Sophia said. "But like an idiot. It was way too easy for her to answer. Took her less than a second. Genitals just went on, right into the kitchen. I followed her."

"Then what?" John Paul asked.

"It was awful. I couldn't think of anything else. So I told her I wanted to be a nun."

There was a long silence. John Paul didn't know if he should be shocked or if he should laugh.

"What?" he said loudly. "You did what?"

"Yeah, it was all I could think of. It was stupid. Of course, she saw right through me. I thought her head was going to explode. But it did get her off your track for a bit. She was going to hit me with a spoon, and then Sis—"

"Wait, what?" John Paul interrupted. "She was going to hit you with a spoon?"

"Yeah, she had her hand on one of those big metal spoons that the cafeteria cooks use to dish out crap. I was scared for a second. Then Sister Gabriel Luke came in from the outside. I was so happy to see her."

"I bet you were."

"Genitals calmed down when Gabriel Luke came in. I got out of there as fast as I could. I wanted to tell you when you came back, but you ran out of there as soon as youth group was over."

"Yeah," John Paul said. "It had been a long night, and nothing felt right when I got back. So I just wanted to get out of there. Sorry about that."

"Long night?" she asked. "You were gone for twenty-five minutes. What could be long about that? Anyway, you have to tell me what you've been up to. Now you owe me for sure."

John Paul grew nervous and didn't say anything. He'd been dreading this discussion since Wednesday night. He knew he put Sophia in quite a spot by asking her to cover for him. He realized that he owed her some kind of explanation. But he didn't know yet what to say.

"Come on, John Paul," Sophia said. "I know it's not smoking or anything like that; that's just not in you. So what is it? Are you going to that coffee shop with the pastries and sitting in there? Because if you are, you need to start bringing me with you. You can't eat croissants while I'm sitting with Genitals."

"No," John Paul said, "I'm not at the coffee shop. I just need a little time to myself. You know, just to hang out and think. That's all."

"It's not that creepy used bookstore, is it? Oh my God. Are you going in there looking for porn?"

"No!" John Paul said. "And it's not creepy in there. Plus, I don't think they have any porn—at least not that I've seen."

"So you *have* been going in there."

John Paul was, once again, at a complete loss for words. His mind raced so fast that he simply couldn't figure out how to speak. Sophia was also quiet for a few moments.

"John Paul, I gotta ask you something," Sophia eventually said. "Don't freak out on me. But let's say you were—hypothetically—going to look at a porn magazine…what would it be? Would you want to look at some sorority chicks washing a car? Or would you want to see a football locker's shower room after the big game?"

John Paul heard what she said. To him, it seemed that she was speaking in slow motion. He took a deep breath and sat down on a kitchen chair. Then he realized that he was fine. In fact, he was shocked that he wasn't panicking. In that moment, Sophia's question seemed as normal as could be. He looked around at his empty house.

"The football one," John Paul said. "I guess I'd choose the football locker room."

"Just to be clear," Sophia said, "I'm talking a regular *men's* football team. Like, all the naked people in the showers are guys, just to be clear."

"I know what you meant," John Paul said.

"John Paul," Sophia said, "so are you gay?"

"I don't know. Well…probably…I just don't always know what that means. But yes, I'm attracted to other guys. I just don't really like that word—or any word like it."

"I knew it!" Sophia said loudly. "I knew you played for that team!"

"How could you know?" John Paul asked.

"We hung around for an entire day at the water park. I was wearing hardly anything, and you never seemed to notice. And I looked good—a lot of the other guys noticed."

John Paul laughed. Sophia joined him. It felt good to laugh, even if he was a little scared.

"Okay," Sophia said. "So shut up for a second. Then what's the deal with the bookstore? Are you doing something creepy in there? Like in the back, like, you know, doing what people do sometimes?"

"No!" John Paul yelled. "Of course not! Stop it!"

"Then what?"

"There's a guy there. We just hang out. That's it."

"Who?" she asked. "Not some old creeper, right?"

"Oh, shut up," John Paul said as Sophia laughed. "He's our age, in high school. I mean, he must go to your school because I've never seen him before."

"What's his name? Do you know?"

"Yeah, I know his first name anyway. But I don't want to say—you know. He might not be okay with that."

"Oh, come on," Sophia said. "I would never say anything to anyone. You know that I'd feel terrible if something bad happened because I opened my big mouth. And it's just a first name, right?"

It was against John Paul's better judgment to answer her. But he did know that she would never do anything to intentionally cause harm to him. He felt that in his heart. In addition, part of him hoped that she did know him. John Paul wanted any information he could get about him.

"Okay," John Paul said. "It's Jayme, with a *y* in the middle and not at the end."

"I know him," Sophia said. "Yep, he's gay."

"What?" John Paul said in complete astonishment. "You really know him?"

"Of course," Sophia said. "Jayme Smith-Johnson. And he will definitely not mind that you told me his name. He's been out of the closet forever. I even went to the coming-out party that his parents threw for him. All the girls have a crush on him, so I don't blame you for hanging out at the bookstore, but he's fairly nerdy. You know, old movies, old music, history stuff—he's into that. But all us girls think that the way he looks during swimming class makes up for the nerdy stuff. He's got a great body. And he's very nice. We all talk about what a waste it is that he's gay. But anyway, I've been trying to hook up with his friend Hunter for over a year. He's just as dreamy but two years younger than me, and you know, I'll be eighteen next month and—"

"Okay," interrupted John Paul. "Now I'm terrified. Thanks."

"What? I'm trying to help. What are you scared of now?"

"A coming-out party?" John Paul said. "I can't compete with that."

"Listen, kid," Sophia said. "You don't have to compete with anything. You don't have to do anything. Hanging out and talking and stuff doesn't mean that you're having a relationship; it doesn't even mean that you're out of the closet. You can be friends with a gay guy, even if you're not one."

"But I am one," John Paul said.

"Proud of you, John Paul," Sophia said.

"And I don't think my parents would agree with you," he said. "I don't think they think anyone should be friends with a homosexual person."

"Okay," she said. "So let's talk about that. You might want to run away from all this, but I wouldn't think that's a good idea. You might have to make some tough decisions and put yourself first. Screw your parents."

They spoke on the phone for over an hour. John Paul experienced the full range of human emotion during that hour, from the high of freedom to the low of disappointment. Regardless, he slept really well that night.

ANCIENT PRIDE

AN EPIC LOVE

We'll start our analysis of history's hidden gay couples with the most profound example of same-sex attraction from the ancient world: the story of Achilles and Patroclus.

To the ancient Greeks, there was no more important myth than the stories associated with the Trojan War. These stories are the subjects of hundreds of poems, tragedies, and comedies. In fact, of all the surviving literature we have from ancient Greece, about 25 percent have something to do with the Trojan War. This is astounding when you think about the sheer number of different events that occur in a culture over one thousand years.

The blind poet Homer wrote down the famous epic poem *The Iliad,* but he didn't create it. Thousands of storytellers sitting around thousands of campfires honed these stories over the course of hundreds of years. None of these people had a problem that the central relationship in *The Iliad* is a love between two men. Yet some scholars today do everything they can to explain away the same-sex attraction between Achilles and Patroclus. Perhaps the reason is that Achilles embodies masculinity. He is the definition of what the word *man* has become. We can't fathom that this model of strength, bravery, and honor could also be gay.

I stated earlier that this story is a myth. That's correct. Because the people in the story interact with supernatural beings, it can't possibly have been true as it's written. But it's important to know that the people of the time—the ancient Greeks themselves—had no concept of myth. To them, this story was completely and utterly true. Not only that, but it was also central to their belief system and was the cornerstone of ancient Greek culture. Let's begin.

Long ago, a sea goddess named Thetis was forced by Zeus (the head god) to marry the human king Peleus of Pythia. Soon afterward, they had a son whom they called Achilles. Thetis, being immortal, was concerned that her precious child would someday die because he had a human father. So Thetis dipped the baby into the River Styx to give him immortality. (She held him by his ankle as she dipped—more about this later.)

Achilles grew in strength, speed, agility, and everything else that makes a fine soldier. As a young boy, he was already renowned for his fighting skills with swords and spears. He was also extremely good-looking, with perfect muscles and brilliant blond hair that glowed in the sun.

In the neighboring kingdom of Opus, King Menoetius also had a young son just a few years older than Achilles. This child, Patroclus, was similar to Achilles in his handsome appearance but quite different in demeanor. Patroclus was kind—very kind. His warm heart shone through his body. All the other inhabitants of the palace at Opus made remarks about the kindness of Patroclus.

However, one day when he was about twelve years old, Patroclus was playing some sort of a board game with another boy. The other boy was caught cheating. Patroclus, in a rare moment, lost his composure and pushed the other boy to the ground. The boy struck his head on a rock and died. King Menoetius was afraid that the act of killing—even if accidental—might change his son's famous demeanor. He wanted Patroclus to grow up far from the memories of this tragic incident. So Menoetius sent Patroclus to live the rest of his life in Pythia.

The moment that Achilles met Patroclus, everyone in their presence could tell that something special existed between these two. They were inseparable. It was apparent that they needed each other desperately. You see, each had faults, but together they were unstoppable. Patroclus balanced Achilles's aggressive manner while Achilles gave Patroclus much-needed resilience. A deep love developed between the two boys as they grew into men.

At the time, most armies were composed of men who were paid by a kingdom to fight. Achilles and Patroclus recruited the best men of Greece and formed a team of mercenaries. This small private army, the Myrmidons, became the most elite fighting squad of the era. Due to Achilles's extensive training program and Patroclus's skill with healing wounds, they were employed by various kingdoms and never lost a battle. Patroclus, Achilles, and their Myrmidons grew in fame.

Around this time, King Menelaus of Sparta returned home one night to find that his wife, Queen Helen, was missing. She was the most beautiful woman in the world (literally), and he wanted her back. Some of the people in the Spartan palace said that Helen had been kidnapped by a visiting prince from the city of Troy named Paris. Others said that Helen went willingly with Prince Paris back to Troy. Regardless, Menelaus was eager to retrieve her.

Menelaus's brother happened to be the most powerful king in Greece, King Agamemnon of Mycenae. Menelaus asked his brother to help him. Agamemnon was thrilled to accept.

You see, King Agamemnon desperately wanted to attack the wealthy and walled city of Troy. The powerful citadel of Troy sat atop a hill at the junction of the Aegean Sea and a narrow waterway that connected it to the Black Sea. Whoever controlled Troy controlled all shipping between the West (mainly Greece and Egypt) with the East (mainly Persia and beyond). Agamemnon probably didn't care all that much for Helen. But he did want the city of Troy. Soon one thousand Greek ships sailed for Troy—the Myrmidons were on one of them.

Troy was ruled by King Priam and his son, the mighty Prince Hector. They probably weren't all that thrilled when Prince Paris, Hector's gorgeous younger brother, showed up with the queen of Sparta—even if she was the most beautiful woman in the world. However, as many parents have learned the hard way over the last few millennia, there's not much you can do when your kid falls in love. (Except perhaps start a war that leads to the annihilation of your entire culture.)

The war lasted for ten long years. Each side had their victories and their defeats. But the Greeks were never able to penetrate Troy's enormous walls, and the Trojans were never able to eradicate the thousands of Greeks camping on their beach.

During all this time, Achilles and Patroclus had grown into mature men who were inseparable. They ate together, slept together, sang together, and dressed each other's wounds incurred in battles. They were perfect complements to each other, and it was evident that these two men, together, made one perfect person.

All of this came to a climax in *The Iliad* when King Agamemnon wanted a slave girl who belonged to Achilles. Achilles refused to give the girl to him; however, Agamemnon took her anyway. This resulted in Achilles making a firm vow that he, Patroclus, and the Myrmidons would no longer fight for the Greeks.

Without the Myrmidons, the Greek forces were beginning to rack up more losses than wins. Agamemnon's friend, King Odysseus of Ithaca, begged Patroclus to persuade Achilles to rejoin the fight, as too many Greeks were dying. Patroclus, always wanting to save Greek lives, agreed and thought of a plan.

Patroclus thought that if he dressed in Achilles's armor, he could rally the Myrmidons and the other Greeks to fight with renewed strength. This way, the Myrmidons could rejoin the war without Achilles having to break his vow. When Patroclus approached Achilles with the plan, Achilles reluctantly agreed.

Patroclus dressed in Achilles's armor. Of course, he'd been watching Achilles's every move for many years, so it wasn't difficult for Patroclus to imitate him. Patroclus jumped on Achilles's chariot, pulled by two magnificent horses that were gifts from Zeus, and rode toward the Trojan walls. The plan worked. The Myrmidons and thousands of Greek soldiers grabbed their weapons and ran to the battle. However, Patroclus got caught up in the excitement of it all. Before he turned the chariot around, Trojan Prince Hector saw him, thought he was Achilles, and killed him.

When Achilles learned that Patroclus had died under these circumstances, he collapsed onto the sand. He wailed in pain and screamed that he "loved Patroclus more than all others and loved as dearly as [his] own life."

His mother, the sea goddess, rose out of the Aegean to comfort him. But when she touched him, she trembled, as she saw her son's soul burn with the wrath of grief. Achilles could no longer be human because he was missing half of his humanity. Essentially, he turned into a machine. He ordered that Patroclus's body be put in his bed. Achilles refused to eat, drink, wash himself, or sleep. All night, he lay awake next to the dead body of Patroclus. He did this for weeks.

But what would Achilles do with all that time he had during the day? Well, he slaughtered Trojans—by the thousands. He was a killing machine. Both armies watched in awe as Achilles, fueled with rage, obliterated Trojans. He committed all sorts of crimes against the standards of warfare as he mercilessly took vengeance on behalf of Patroclus. And each night he lay next to the dead body of his love. He stared at the ceiling of his tent. The only thing he wanted was to have Patroclus back with him. Since that couldn't happen, the Trojans needed to pay.

Nothing could prepare the Trojans for what occurred next though. Achilles finally had the opportunity to fight with Hector, the man who had killed his love. Achilles easily killed the Trojan prince. Rules of warfare dictated that since Hector was the son of the king, Achilles should allow the Trojans to claim his body. Hector should be given the respect he deserved by having a proper ceremony and cremation. But instead, Achilles strapped Hector's corpse to the back of his chariot and dragged him around in the dirt. At least he'd found something new to do during the daytime. Day after day, Achilles drove around the walls of Troy with Hector's dead body trailing in the dust.

While it was probably fun to watch at first, the gods eventually got tired of sitting up on Mount Olympus, looking at the spectacle of Achilles versus the Trojans. They eventually decided to intervene and sent Hermes, the messenger god, to speak with the one person whom Achilles might listen to: King Priam himself. It might seem an odd choice, since Achilles and Priam were bitter enemies, but sometimes the gods were wise.

Priam smuggled himself into Achilles's tent and threw himself at his feet. The king wailed for the loss of his son, Hector. For the first time, Achilles saw that grief was a product of intense love that really had nowhere to go. His heart started to mend. Achilles decided to fix a meal that he and Priam ate together. They spoke of the love they had for Patroclus and Hector. It truly took grief to conquer grief.

Achilles agreed to let Priam take Hector's body. Patroclus's body was also given a proper ceremony and cremation. Then Achilles could feel that his time was also at an end. He had learned how to be human...how to feel.

Achilles dressed in the finest new armor that his mother had brought for him and rode toward Troy. Prince Paris, standing on one of the city's towers, saw him approach. An excellent archer, Paris strung his bow with an arrow and let it fly. The arrow swiftly flew through the air and pierced Achilles in the very spot that his mother had held him when she dipped him into the River Styx—his ankle. Since the magical water had not been able to cover this place on Achilles's body, he was vulnerable. He died.

The war came to a quick end when Odysseus thought of the brilliant idea of constructing a giant horse out of wood. One morning, the Trojans woke to find that the entire Greek army had left on their ships. All that remained on the beach was the giant horse, which the Trojans thought was a really nice gift. So they brought it inside the city's walls. That night, as the Trojans slept soundly, Odysseus and a few other Greeks who were hidden inside the horse sneaked out and opened the massive gates of Troy. The rest of the Greek army had sailed back and was waiting outside. They streamed into the city and killed everyone—completely erasing Troy from existence. (Or so they thought...stay tuned. Achilles and Patroclus weren't the only same-sex couple in Troy at that time.)

Achilles left strict instructions before he died. The Myrmidons carried out these instructions with valiant loyalty. The body of Achilles was given a proper ceremony and cremated. But instead of the normal procedure of putting his ashes in an unused urn, Achilles had directed that his ashes be put into the same urn that held the ashes of Patroclus. The Myrmidons mixed the ashes and buried the urn under a small hill near the sea. The hill was marked, and for centuries, people made pilgrimages to the shore to pay homage to the tumulus of Achilles. You can still visit it today.

I cannot stress enough how important this myth was to the ancient Greeks and the Romans who came after them. Many of the Greek playwrights, poets, and historians wrote of Achilles and Patroclus. Some of these works are quite explicit about their relationship and show the two heroes as lovers.

The fame of Achilles and Patroclus as lovers carried on over the centuries. There are many works of art that depict Achilles in agony over the dead body of Patroclus. My favorite painting is by the eighteenth-century Scottish painter Gavin Hamilton. It's titled *Achilles Lamenting the Death of Patroclus*. This painting is the best depiction of love that I have ever seen. Mighty Achilles has collapsed with a tormented face.

He reaches for the body of kind Patroclus with one hand and uses the other hand to keep everyone else away. I am deeply moved whenever I see this painting.

Many of my colleagues in our modern era refuse to even entertain the idea that Achilles and Patroclus were a gay couple. They say it's because Homer doesn't specifically talk about the two men having sexual intercourse. Homer mentions that they do everything else together over the course of their lives, but he does not mention sex. However, Homer doesn't state that Odysseus and Penelope had sex, but historians all agree that this was a heterosexual couple. Why?

I believe that Achilles's all-consuming grief is evidence in favor of them being gay. Achilles's grief is extensive, to say the least. The man refused to eat, and he slept with Patroclus's dead body for days. I don't know that anyone would do that for a really good friend, especially in the ancient times when death rituals were imperative.

However, the most important evidence lies with the fact that the ashes of Achilles and Patroclus were mixed in the same urn for all eternity. This is the only example—from all antiquity—of two people being buried like this. These two were in love. End of story.

CHAPTER 12

After finally learning Jayme's name and coming out to Sophia on the phone, John Paul was flying high with excitement. Then he read chapter one of *Ancient Pride*, and his whole mood came crashing down. Worse, he didn't know the reason, and he couldn't explain why the chapter depressed his spirit.

The next Wednesday, he had every intention of boycotting the bookstore all together. He thought about throwing *Ancient Pride* into the trash at a gas station and never thinking about it again. However, there was a problem: Sophia knew Jayme. There was no escape, as John Paul was certain Sophia would never allow it.

John Paul arrived at the bookstore earlier than usual, around 7:00 p.m. His goals were to thank Bob, return the book to Fiona, and give them a note to give to Jayme. His aim was to avoid Jayme altogether. The note explained that he needed to go back to his old life, and he hoped to be left alone. But when John Paul arrived at the store, Jayme was already there.

"Hey!" Jayme said as John Paul entered.

Upon seeing him, John Paul was instantly regretful that he'd come. Jayme crossed the store quickly and made a motion as if to give John Paul a hug. But John Paul quickly stuck out his arm and shook hands with Jayme before he had a chance to get closer. When Jayme backed away, he had a quizzical look on his face. John Paul felt bad about that.

"Good," said Bob, "you're early. Let's go in the back. We'll have more privacy there, and Fiona has it all set up for us."

"Ah, Bob?" John Paul began. "I don't think this is going to work out. Thanks for the book, but you can have it back. I really should get back."

"Oh," Bob responded, "you can't go now. Come on—give it a chance. You don't look too good, John Paul. Why don't you sit down a bit? I promise that if you're still not okay by the end of this, then you never have to see me again. How about trying it for five minutes?"

John Paul glanced briefly at Jayme. He looked hurt and confused. Now John Paul felt even worse. He also looked at Bob and saw the disappointment in his face. John Paul decided that it wasn't right to leave in this way. So he followed Bob into the back room of the store.

Fiona greeted them when they arrived. She had set a mug of cappuccino and a pastry by each of four seats around a round table. In the middle of the table, she'd placed a bronze-colored statute, about fourteen inches tall, of an ancient warrior holding a shield. They all sat down.

"So, Fiona," Bob said, "John Paul here is a little anxious tonight. So we're just going to talk and eat a bit. Sound good? Like maybe about five minutes?"

"Sure," Fiona replied. "Let me know if you need anything, John Paul. The bathroom is just through that door right there."

John Paul didn't think it was possible to feel even worse at this moment. But when Fiona mentioned the bathroom, he couldn't help but get a little nauseous. He thought that he might have to get to the toilet sooner rather than later. He also thought that he must look worse than he thought he did.

"Well," said Bob, "tell us, Jayme, what did you think of the first chapter of *Ancient Pride*?"

"Frankly," Jayme said, "it made me really angry. Has anyone else seen a 2004 movie called *Troy*? It stars Brad Pitt as Achilles? It was a huge blockbuster?"

All of them shook their heads to indicate that they had not. Jayme gave an audible sigh.

"Okay, well," he said, "in that movie Patroclus is portrayed as Achilles's cousin. That's it—a lousy cousin that is much younger than Brad Pitt. Patroclus is in about two scenes total. The story is similar, with Patroclus dressing like Achilles and ending up getting killed. But I always wondered why Achilles goes so batshit crazy when his cousin, who he's barely talked to, who has been on screen about two minutes, gets killed by Hector. I never understood that part because I didn't know the whole story. Yeah, I knew that the movie was based on a famous Greek story, but I'd never researched it or anything. I'm angry that in 2004, they didn't think it was okay for Achilles and Patroclus to be in a gay relationship. If they'd have shown that, I would have understood the movie."

"That's exactly why—" Bob started to say.

"Oh." Jayme interrupted Bob in a raised tone. "And one more thing before I forget. I was researching online and found a clip where the director of *Troy* was being interviewed. The reporter asked him about the change from gay couple to cousins. The director responded that he didn't think the people of 2004 were ready for a same-sex relationship. However, I then discovered that in the ancient times, the most famous playwright of the era, Aeschylus, wrote a play called *The Myrmidons*. This play was entirely about Achilles's relationship with Patroclus, and apparently, Aeschylus hides nothing—they are full-blown lovers. So how, Mr. Director of *Troy*, are 2004 audiences less evolved than those that saw the play three thousand years ago? Okay, sorry to interrupt you, Bob. Now I'm done."

"If you're going to say something that articulate," Bob said, "feel free to interrupt me anytime."

"Hear! Hear!" Fiona said as she pounded her fist on the table. "I'm proud to know you, Jayme."

John Paul listened to the words of Jayme's speech, but he hadn't really heard them. Instead, he was focused on the multitude of feelings within himself. He was mad that he didn't have the insight of Jayme and upset that he didn't feel free to leave. He was annoyed at Fiona for suggesting that he might have to be sick in the toilet. He was mad that Bob had given him the book in the first place. And he was angry with himself that he had told Sophia. Mostly, he felt defeated that he couldn't control any of this. All these emotions blended together, deep within him, and melted into a pot of frustration.

Bob, Fiona, and Jayme continued to talk for the next twenty minutes. John Paul heard bits and pieces, but none of it made sense. *Achilles. Patroclus. Homer.* They kept saying names that just flew past John Paul. Then Bob turned the conversation to give him a chance to speak.

"Do you want to say anything, John Paul?" Bob asked. "You look a little better—not a lot better, but you have to start somewhere I guess. You don't have to talk about the book. How are you doing?"

John Paul didn't want to say anything. He just wanted to leave the book on the table, next to his untouched pastry, and leave. Then words started coming out of his mouth. He was saying things that he'd been thinking for a few days. The words just came. He knew it was the frustration talking, and he was powerless to stop it.

"None of you understand," John Paul said. "You can talk about Achilles and Patroclus—and yes, it makes me mad—but none of you can understand how terrible it was for me to read this stuff. I was happy last week. Now I'm miserable. And I don't know how to say that."

"Sometimes," Fiona said, "no, oftentimes, ignorance is bliss. You learned a harsh truth about history and how it pushes people down. It's okay to feel bad about that."

"No, that's not it," John Paul said. "I know all that. At least, I can get my head around that because it makes sense to me. Historians are people, and sometimes people are afraid of things they don't understand. I live with people that hate gay people, so believe me—I'm not shocked that people don't want these two guys to be gay. I'm not mad about the hiding of the relationship."

"Then what's the frustration?" Bob asked.

"I don't know," John Paul said. "I'm just frustrated."

"I think you do know," Bob said. "You'll feel better if you say it."

"Okay, fine," John Paul said. "I'm frustrated that these two—Achilles and Patroclus—found each other and had this great thing. I'm jealous as hell! And these two guys lived thousands of years ago. I want that. I want someone to love me like that, and I'm terrified that I'm never going to have it. I want someone to go—what did you say, Jayme, batshit crazy?"

"Yes, that's what I said," Jayme replied.

"I want someone to go batshit crazy because I died!" John Paul shouted. "I don't care about coming-out parties. Yes,

Jayme, I know Sophia, and she told me all about yours with the rainbow cake. I don't care about historical injustice and rainbow cakes and equal treatment. Hell, I don't even care about gay marriage. I'm so depressed thinking about what I will never have. It would be better if I had never read it. I just want someone to love me best of all, like how Achilles loved Patroclus. I'm jealous of them—jealous as hell! And they're myth. I'm jealous of people that aren't even real."

Fiona sat with tears running down her face. Jayme looked shocked. Bob sat with a serene look on his face.

"Do you feel better?" Bob asked.

"Yes, thank you!" John Paul replied loudly. "Sorry."

"I know your frustration, John Paul," said Bob. "I've often felt it myself. But I've never heard someone explain it so well until tonight. I've had the frustration of never finding a life partner. But to admit that I'm jealous of those that have it is really difficult. Jealousy is a hard thing to admit. I'm proud of you."

"Yeah," said Jayme, "and I think it's even worse when you consider that the guys you are jealous of lived so long ago. Things are supposed to get better with time, but they haven't for people like you, John Paul. I'm sorry—really, I'm sorry. Things are way better for me, and I have to remember that not all people like us live like I do. There are still a lot of homophobic parents out there."

"I'm sorry too," John Paul said. "I feel so much better. I also feel really embarrassed."

John Paul started to eat his pastry and drink a few sips of the cappuccino. He was also thinking about Bob. Knowing that Bob never found a life partner was hard to hear. It made him want to appreciate what little he had.

They spent the next few minutes eating and talking about how good it felt to say what was on one's mind. Then they realized that they needed to get back to their lives.

"Before you leave," Fiona said, "can I take a photo? Only if you want to. I'd like to remember this moment if it's okay with you guys."

"Of course, fine with me," Jayme said.

John Paul didn't know how to respond. Taking a photo was a big step for him because it would be permanent—and he couldn't control who would see it. On the other hand, he really wanted to have a photo of Jayme.

"Whatever," John Paul replied. "I might as well. I'm already going to hell for saying that I'm jealous as hell, so whatever."

"Okay, you two, scooch your chairs closer and smile."

"It's 'scoot' your chairs closer," said Bob.

"Yes, Bob," Fiona said. "Thank you."

The boys laughed. Jayme put his arm around John Paul. John Paul's heart nearly came right out of his chest. Fiona took the photo.

Jayme and John Paul left the store side by side. Jayme walked with him toward the Catholic school and convent, but just for a few steps. Then he put his hand on John Paul's shoulder and turned him to face him.

"Hey," said Jayme. "I really like you. I just wanted you to know that I really like you. I don't think I have any idea of what you're going through because it's so different from my experience. But I want to help, if I can, because I really like you. Sophia told me all about you; it was freaking amazing to hear. That's all…that's all I wanted to say."

John Paul didn't respond. Jayme stood and looked into his eyes.

"Except this," Jayme said quickly. "Do you think we can do something together sometime? I don't care, whatever it is, but just the two of us. How about it?"

"I would really like that," John Paul said. "I'm not sure how to make that happen, but just hearing you ask me that makes me very happy."

"Cool," Jayme said, "let's talk next week. Maybe Fiona can help us figure out a way. She's probably good at that. So… next Wednesday. Chapter two, right?"

"Chapter two," John Paul said as he turned and walked away.

CHAPTER 13

Theresa Saint Clara looked carefully around the library of Our Lady of Seven Dolors Catholic School. She wanted to make sure it was empty. She needed to make a phone call using the school's phone, and she didn't want to take any chances of being overheard. It was night; the school was empty. She had sneaked over after a meeting of Catholic mothers down the hall.

A large statue of Our Lady of Seven Dolors stood in the corner. Theresa stopped in front of it and said a quick prayer. The statue depicted Mary, the Blessed Mother. Mary looked sad and had carved tears coming down her face. The Seven Dolors were seven times that Mary was sorrowful, like during the crucifixion and burial of Jesus. Theresa was always very annoyed when she'd hear someone refer to the church and school as "Our Lady of the Seven *Dollars*." She had written several television and radio stations over that issue. She detested people from the public school who used the phrase as a joke.

Theresa went behind the librarian's desk and found the phone. As a volunteer in the library, she knew where everything was. She was also on the school's Committee for Quality Literature and had spent hours in the library looking through books and deciding whether they should be shelved or trashed. Most of the trashed books came from community donations. One time, she discovered a book that was even too terrible for the trash; she promptly took that book home and burned it.

She dialed a phone number that she'd written on a small piece of paper in her purse. It rang several times. She was almost ready to hang up.

"Hello, this is the Freedom Center for Boys," said an older-sounding male voice.

"Hello," Theresa replied, "I…ah…just have a few questions."

"Of course, I'm here with answers. Are you a parent looking for help?"

"I'm not sure," she said. "But I talked to another mother online, and she gave me your number."

"That's okay. We get lots of calls like this. My name is Joseph, but you don't have to tell me yours. We understand that you might want to stay anonymous."

"Thank you," said Theresa. "I really don't know if it's right for me to call, but I was just looking for some background information about your program."

"Of course," said Joseph. "I assume you have a son that you're worried about?"

"Yes."

"And, does he have a father that lives at home?"

"Of course," said Theresa. "We are a good Catholic family."

"That's great," Joseph said. "That actually helps a lot. Well, we are a residential program for boys that need a little extra help navigating this modern world of ours. Everything is done anonymously."

"I guess, my main question is: Is your facility clean and safe? Is it bright?"

"Oh. You really want to know if this is a jail, right?" Joseph said with a laugh.

"I guess," Theresa replied. "I'm sorry if that offends you."

"Not at all. It's a normal question. No, this is not a jail. We have dorm rooms with lots of windows and no bars on them. The boys are free to leave whenever they want; all we ask is that they check in and out with our front desk. We like to keep things very secure, mostly to protect the boys from people on the outside that often want to get to them."

"I can understand that."

"The boys complete a two-month course of work and education. We teach them how to use work to clear their minds, and we give them the tools to train their bodies. I've invented a therapy system that uses the name of Jesus to reprogram young minds. That's basically it. You can visit and call anytime."

"How much does it cost?"

"Our center is run on donations from dioceses all across the country."

"And you have success with this?" Theresa asked.

"We've had hundreds of graduates. We have a high success rate—nearly one hundred percent."

Theresa didn't like to hear that it was *nearly* 100 percent. She was desperate for a guaranteed fix. Her son's soul depended on it, as did her family's reputation.

"There is one more thing that I'm concerned about," Theresa said. "How do I know that…well…I'm not comfortable sending him to a place where he can meet other boys that are like him. Isn't that just a recipe for disaster? How do I know he's not going to come back worse?"

"That's a great question and one that most parents ask. This is what sets Freedom Center for Boys apart from the rest. See, the other places are typically camplike settings. They have the boys together, and all sorts of problems happen. I don't mind saying that these places are disasters. We don't allow our boys to meet each other. I believe this is our key to success. Our boys stay in dorms and have scheduled times to use the bathrooms and showers. Rest assured, he'll never see another boy like him—until he's not like them, and then he's fine to have male friends again."

"I like the sound of that. But he'll get to talk his problems out, right? It's not solitary confinement or anything like that?"

"Of course not," Joseph said. "He'll have contact with our staff when he's working and when he's learning. We'll also lead his Catholic spiritual direction."

Theresa was silent for a few moments. She liked some things that Joseph had told her, but she disliked others. Her biggest fear was that he would make the situation worse and drive John Paul to choose an alternate lifestyle.

"I'm not sure that I can make a decision right now," Theresa said. "I have to say that I was overjoyed when the mom I met online talked about a center that was just a few hours' drive from where we live. And she said many good things about you. Do I just call again if I need more information?"

"Yes, you can do that," said Joseph. "But you should know that we have a long waiting list. However, we do have an opening coming up in a few weeks, and I'd be willing to put your son up to the top. You sound like you are good Catholic people, and we'd like to reward that."

"Thank you very much," Theresa said earnestly.

"Just so that I know, if you call again, what is your son's first name?"

Theresa whispered into the phone, as softly as possible, "John Paul."

"Well, now I know we can fit him in," Joseph said. "Any boy with a name like that deserves to live a long and normal life in the path of Christ. Just keep in touch and call anytime. And God bless you and all mothers."

Theresa didn't say anything. She hung up the phone.

Abygail and Sammy Smith-Johnson were also in a library—the Kaiserburg Public Library. They sat with Brandon Mussah, the chair of their political party's campaign-finance committee. He had stacks of papers in front of him.

"Yeah," Brandon said, completing a thought, "so that's why it's important to get some articles in the papers. You're already well-known here locally, but we need to get you into the suburban and city papers. We'll work on the big-city papers next."

"Does anyone read the paper anymore?" Abygail asked.

She immediately regretted asking this question. She didn't want to do or say anything that would upset Brandon and the powerful, and wealthy, union that stood behind him.

"Primary voters do," Brandon said. "They might be the only ones that do. But they are also the only ones that count right now."

"So how are we standing at this moment?" Sammy asked.

"The numbers look good here locally—real good," Brandon answered. "But I won't beat around the bush. We don't look so good in the first-ring suburbs and the inner city. Unfortunately, that's where all the primary voters live. So we need to work on that. Your opposition in the primary is polling better right now."

"What should we do?" Sammy asked. "Door knocking in that area?"

"Of course," Brandon said. "We need a good ground game; it's the only way to get liberal voters. And let me tell you, these are the really liberal voters. I want to do a flyer and take them door-to-door. A flyer that really talks about your Progressive ideas."

"Sounds great," said Sammy.

"And I think we need a back-page story about your trans kid—Jayme, right? Didn't I meet him a few times at the call center?"

"Yes," Abygail answered.

"Maybe it would be good if the message came from you directly, Sammy. Just write a few paragraphs about your support for your trans kid. Talk about hormones and that kind of stuff. Oh, it's great if you say you were apprehensive about it at first, but you love them so much that you were willing to learn. And now you are behind them. By the way, while we're on the topic, I think I saw Jayme walking down Main Street with a *Frankenstein* shirt. Could that be right?"

Both Abygail and Sammy started laughing while Abygail said, "Yes, that would be them. They like old movies and all that sort of monster stuff."

Without laughing, Brandon said, "Well, that needs to not happen. A *Frankenstein* shirt is exactly the wrong thing for a trans person to be seen in. Do what you can to soften the image…maybe more pinks. Old movies are fine as long as they're not *Gone with the Wind* or anything controversial. I'm sorry if you think I'm going too far by telling you what your kid can wear, but this is politics. We need your vote in Congress, and we're willing to help you get there. But if you want union money, you need to be able to win. And to win, your trans kid can't be a Frankenstein."

CHAPTER 14

Sister Gentillini did not like Carlson's Used Books and Records. She thought there were way too many books about God knew what. She was terrified of them. However, Carlson's also had a large bin of used Bibles for under one dollar. While she didn't appreciate how they were just thrown in there, they made great cheap gifts—that is, when she could find a Catholic one. She diligently checked each Bible for the seven books in the Old Testament that Protestant Bibles were missing. When she found a good Catholic Bible with all completed books, she then checked for a proper translation.

About one in every thirty Bibles she checked met her approval. That day, she'd found two that made the cut. Now she felt an intense urge to wash her hands after touching all those heathen Protestant Bibles.

Gentillini took her two Bibles and walked toward the counter, where a woman with tattoos was standing near a cash register. Gentillini despised tattoos. To herself, she quoted a verse from the book of Leviticus that instructed all believers to not tattoo any marks upon their skin. This woman at the counter was obviously not a believer—at least not a believer in anything that Gentillini believed in.

Then she stopped suddenly. She'd noticed a pile of books stacked up on a table. She checked to make sure that nobody was watching her. The tattoo woman was busy messing with her phone and a printer. Gentillini hesitantly reached out her hand and softly touched the cover of one of the books: *Pride and Prejudice* by Jane Austen.

"Oh, how I loved this book," Gentillini said softly, not realizing she had actually spoken the words.

She stood there, motionless, and thought about the characters in the book. She remembered the romance. She remembered how, when she was younger, she yearned to be swept off her feet in a tornado of romance. She recalled how much she used to desire the touch of someone hard and muscular in the night, someone who would wrap his strong arms around her to keep her warm and tell her everything would be okay.

She picked up the book and stroked the spine. She thought about all the dreams she'd had as a young girl. Nuns weren't allowed to have memories, but in this rare instant, Gentillini wasn't a nun. She thought about reading books during summers by the lake and in front of warm fireplaces decorated for Christmas.

She looked up suddenly when she heard a cough. It was the tattooed woman. Gentillini found herself back in the bookstore, as a nun, stroking a copy of an old book. She threw the book, quite hard, onto a pile of books where it didn't belong.

"Immoral crap," she said and walked up to the counter.

"I'm sorry," the tattooed woman said, "did you say something?"

Gentillini didn't reply. She just set her Bibles nicely on the counter. The woman smiled and went to the cash register.

Gentillini looked down. Right next to her, on the counter, sat a printer that the tattooed woman was using. The printer was in the process of printing a picture on glossy photo paper. Line by line, the photo jerked incrementally out of the device.

"That's two dollars and thirteen cents," the woman said.

Moving again with her catlike nun reflexes, Gentillini procured a coin purse from under her sleeve. She counted out the change. The photo kept moving forward.

"Would you like a bag?" the woman asked.

"Of course," Gentillini replied.

While the woman was getting a paper bag and placing the Bibles into it, Gentillini glanced once again at the slow-moving printer. Now the photo was about 75 percent complete. Since it had printed top-side first, Gentillini clearly saw that it was a photo of John Paul Saint Clara. He was with another boy, one she didn't recognize.

Her first thought was that the Saint Clara kid was hanging out with another public school student, one who wasn't Catholic. She wondered if she should tell his mother about it. Then she noticed that the boy she didn't know had his arm around John Paul. They looked friendly. Too friendly. Way too friendly.

"Here you go," the woman said as she handed the bag to Gentillini. "Come again."

Gentillini took the bag and stole one last and long glance at the photo. The boys were sitting at a table. There were three books on the table. One had a brown-paper cover that read, "History"; the other had the same paper cover, but it read something about algebra. However, Gentillini's full attention was focused on the third book. She could see the title of this book clearly: *Ancient Pride*. The book had a rainbow on its cover.

"Is there anything else?" the woman asked.

Gentillini just shook her head and stared into the woman's eyes with the intention of looking into her soul. Then, without saying another word, Gentillini moved swiftly out of the bookstore. As she was walking out of the door, she committed the cover of the book *Ancient Pride* to memory. She wanted to look it up online as soon as she got back to the convent.

ANCIENT PRIDE

AN EMPEROR AND HIS HEARTBREAKING LOVE

Our first example, Achilles and Patroclus, was a myth. Now we will move on to something that is fact. This chapter is verifiable in the historic record through written accounts, eyewitnesses, and countless sculptures of the couple.

Emperor Caesar Traianus Hadrianus Augustus, simply known as Hadrian, was not just any ordinary emperor of Rome. He was one of the most famous and was a member of a group of emperors that the Romans called "the Five Good Emperors."

Hadrian came into power after the emperor Trajan, who was obsessed with conquest and growing the Roman Empire. Contrastingly, Hadrian adopted a policy of securing the Roman borders to maintain the current size of the empire. He was much more concerned with the people of his empire learning how to get along with each other than he was with conquering new people to get along with.

Even during his life, it was commonly known that Hadrian was sexually attracted to other men. Although he was married to a woman, as was expected of him, there is no evidence that they ever had sexual relations. Hadrian had no children. However, there was quite a long list of men whom Hadrian had been seen kissing during his lifetime.

A young man named Antinous came to Rome during Hadrian's reign. Many historians believe that Antinous was Greek but born in modern-day Turkey. We don't know why he came to Rome. Some think he was a slave, and others think he came to study. We also don't know how Hadrian and Antinous met. All we do know is that it was love at first sight.

Antinous was an extremely good-looking man. Today we would say he was "eye candy." How do we know this is true and not just an exaggeration? Well, due to circumstances that we'll speak about later, there are many surviving sculptures of Antinous. These sculptures were crafted with Antinous serving as a live model for them. So we pretty much know exactly what Antinous—and Hadrian, for that matter—looked like.

Antinous not only had a good-looking face, but he also had an extraordinarily beautiful body. As we can see from the sculptures, he had an unusual balance of muscle that was neither too much nor too little. His proportions and symmetry were beyond perfection. At the same time, he appeared to be the boy next door and also a mighty warrior.

Hadrian took one look at this perfection and wanted to meet the young man. From there, their relationship grew. We know from the writings of the time that Antinous was more than eye candy. He was able to speak with Hadrian at his exalted level. They spoke about politics, building projects, and the future of the empire.

One of the most memorable aspects of Hadrian and Antinous's time together is their extensive desire to travel. Over the course of several years, they traveled to visit many parts of the vast Roman Empire that had never seen a living emperor. During this time, Hadrian built his famous wall in the northern part of Britain to define the Roman boundary. This wall, Hadrian's Wall, can still be visited today.

Unfortunately, tragedy struck when they visited Egypt. Hadrian went to the land of pyramids to approve funds to renovate a massive underground burial chamber called the Serapeum. While touring the extensive tunnels and tombs, Hadrian became ill. We don't know exactly what kind of illness Hadrian had acquired. All we know is that he was confined to his bed on a barge floating in the Nile River.

The sickness went on for days, and all were afraid that the beloved Hadrian might not live. Antinous was worried beyond belief about his love.

Now we must take a moment to understand some of the religious thoughts of the ancient Romans. They were quite different from our own. Because these were people who were accustomed to visiting many temples and giving offerings to many gods, they believed they could get the gods' attention in sometimes drastic ways. Antinous was no exception.

Antinous, the beloved companion of Hadrian, felt that he could make a bargain with the gods. He would give his own life—and his beautiful body—in exchange for Hadrian to become well again. And this is just what he did. Antinous jumped into the Nile and drowned.

That night, Hadrian woke. He felt fine. Then he was told of Antinous's death. His grief was immense. But unlike Achilles, he went on with new strength. For in Hadrian's mind, Antinous had made the ultimate sacrifice for love. Hadrian would not let Antinous die in vain.

Immediately, Hadrian instructed the Egyptians to build a great city at the place in the Nile where Antinous died. That city, Antinoöpolis, stood for centuries. In the center, there was an elaborate temple to the god Antinous.

That's right—in an unprecedented move, Hadrian proclaimed that Antinous had become an immortal god. He felt that his act of true love had made him the equal of Apollo, Mercury, Mars, and the other gods. Soon Hadrian ordered that all Roman cities must build temples to the god Antinous and erect statues in his image. And they did. The people of the empire were so inspired by Antinous and his act of love that they readily obliged. People worshipped at the altar of Antinous for generations. It did not matter that he was gay; all that mattered was that he loved and was loved.

Hadrian went on to live out his life as emperor. He died at his villa in Rome, the same place where he'd had Antinous's body buried.

Today, because there are so many temples to Antinous scattered across such a vast empire, we have more surviving statues of Antinous than any other ancient Roman. It is impossible to find a museum in Italy that doesn't have at least one carving of the young god. In fact, the Vatican itself contains several statues.

If you ever visit the Vatican, look for a room called the Sala Rotonda. Inside this round room, you will find a colossal statue of the god Antinous. But don't stop there. Stand right in front of the statue and turn around. You will see that Antinous is looking across the Sala Rotonda, directly into the face of another statue—the statue of Hadrian. Yes, for centuries now, in the seat of the Holy Catholic Church, in the pope's own museum, Antinous and Hadrian stare into each other's eyes for all eternity.

CHAPTER 15

Jayme walked down the street quickly. It was Wednesday, and he was excited to get to the bookstore. His phone vibrated in his pocket. He took it out and noticed it was Sophia.

"Hey," Jayme answered.

"Hi," said Sophia. "I can't talk long because—well, you know—I'm also on break from the Catholic youth group."

"No worries," Jayme said. "What do you want? Is John Paul with you?"

"He just left here," she said. "He'll be there soon. But listen. He seems nervous again."

Jayme briefly frowned when he heard that John Paul was nervous. Then he remembered how new John Paul was to all of this. Jayme wanted to give him the time and space that he needed, but he was also sixteen and infatuated.

"Jayme," Sophia said, "I've been thinking about this, and…I don't want you or John Paul to get hurt."

"I don't want that either," Jayme said.

"So what I mean is…if you don't think you have the patience for John Paul, then you should get out of it now before you get in too deep. Do you know what I mean? He could really get hurt. So could you."

"I understand where he is coming from, and I think—"

"I'm not sure that you do. His family is deeply Catholic. He's been told every day since birth that it's not okay to like other boys. He also believes that everything he's been told by the Church is true. This isn't going to change overnight. It might take longer than you want to wait. If you don't think you can have the patience, then you need to get out before you lead him along too far and break his heart. Really, Jayme, I don't think you know how conservative his parents are."

"Well," Jayme said, "someone has to wait for people like him. Or they'd all end up alone."

"Yeah, I get that. But waiting a bit is one thing. Thinking that you need to be his savior is another. Get it?"

"I get it. But the truth is, I'm not concerned about him. Everyone wants to be free."

A few moments of silence followed. Jayme slowed his walk.

"Everyone wants to be free," Sophia eventually said, "but not everyone *can* be free. There are a lot of other things to consider. Family, for one."

Jayme began to wonder if he should be more concerned about rushing to get to know John Paul better. Maybe it wasn't the right thing to do. Maybe he was letting his physical attraction to John Paul get in the way of his thoughts. But he'd push those thoughts aside and think about them tomorrow.

"Just don't treat him like he's your special project," Sophia said. "Got it?"

"I'm not my parents," Jayme said. "I don't need a project."

"Good. Just be happy, I guess—as long as nobody gets hurt."

"I see John Paul coming around the corner now," Jayme said.

"I have to go," Sophia said. "Genitals is coming toward me."

"What?" Jayme said. "You have genitals coming to you?"

"Ask John Paul. Bye, Jayme."

Jayme ended the call and walked quickly toward John Paul. They shook hands when they met on the sidewalk, directly in front of the bookstore.

CHAPTER 16

John Paul was less nervous as he shook hands with Jayme outside the bookstore. He really wanted to hug Jayme instead, but since they were on the street, and Our Lady of Seven Dolors was right down the block, he didn't feel comfortable. Even though he was less nervous, it did not mean he was completely free from anxiety.

They walked into the bookstore. John Paul heard Fiona call for them from the back room. Again, the round table was set with cappuccinos and pastries. The same statue of a Greek warrior was in the middle of the table. Bob was already sitting on one of the chairs. Next to him, there stood a cane with a four-pronged base. John Paul hadn't seen Bob with a cane before.

"Ignore the cane," Bob said before the boys had a chance to ask. "There's nothing to see there."

"Nothing to see?" Fiona said. "Bob, you need to stand in your truth. You must learn to let others help you. How will we know if you need help if you don't ask?"

"I don't need another lecture from you," Bob said.

"Apparently you do," Fiona answered. "You see, boys, last Monday Bob here fell in the store. He tripped on a stack of old Bibles that had been put in the wrong place—right on the floor. He twisted his ankle. But here's the worst part. He was too noble to call for help, so he just crawled up on his stool and pretended that everything was fine. Eventually his friend Gabby, who just happened to stop by the store unexpectedly, saw he was in pain and took him to urgent care."

"Are you finished giving out my complete health history?" Bob asked.

"Yes, I am," Fiona said. "See, now there are two more people you can call that already know you might need help. We all need people in our lives, Bob, even you. You said last week that you wanted a life partner. Well, who's to say that has to be one person that you're in love with? Maybe for you, we can be your life partners. Ever think about that?"

"Let's just all sit down and shut up," Bob said.

The boys sat. John Paul thought that the banter between Fiona and Bob was a little humorous, but he didn't show it because the situation was fairly serious. He hoped that Bob listened to what she said about asking for help. And Fiona's words made John Paul feel less alone because they probably made Bob feel less alone.

"Okay," Bob said, "chapter two. This was about the Emperor Hadrian and his number-one boy toy, Antinous. Did both of you get a chance to look up pictures of Antinous and his sculptures?"

"I sure did," Jayme answered. "If he really looked like his sculptures, then I can see why Hadrian never wanted to be very far from him! The man was smoking hot."

"He really was," Fiona said. "I don't think you'd even have to be attracted to men to be attracted to a body like that."

They all laughed.

"Did you get a chance to see any of the art?" Jayme asked John Paul.

"I did," John Paul said. "I'm not allowed to really use the internet—well, it would have raised some red flags probably with my parents. But the chapter talked about a specific statute in the Vatican Museum. Fortunately, a Catholic high school library has lots of books about the Vatican and the art. So yeah, I was able to see a few of the sculptures of Antinous. And I saw them right in our Catholic-school library."

"He's hot, right?" Jayme asked John Paul.

John Paul wasn't ready to answer that question. He'd recently gotten better at thinking of himself as gay. But he wasn't ready to think of himself as a gay man who was able to entertain any thoughts of sex. He knew he wanted to, and he knew Antinous was hot, but knowing in your brain and actually saying it out loud were two different things. Instead, John Paul just smiled and nodded at Jayme.

"And to think," Jayme continued, "the ancient people idolized him. When Hadrian proclaimed that he was a god, the people didn't care that he had been the emperor's lover. They saw the ultimate act of love that Antinous performed and worshipped him anyway. Even in temples and all that stuff. It's amazing, really."

"I guess I have a kind of problem with that," John Paul said.

He noticed that the others around the table looked at him with a bit of surprise. He worried that he might have made some kind of mistake against book club etiquette.

"Maybe I said that wrong," John Paul quickly added. "Sorry."

"Don't be sorry," Fiona said. "Go ahead. I think we're just happy that you have something to say."

"Hear! Hear!" said Bob. "Let's hear it."

"Well, the ancient people didn't really worship Antinous. They had many so-called 'gods,' and they did what they did at their temples and everything. But they couldn't have worshipped Antinous the same way that we worship our God."

"Why not?" Bob asked. "They felt the same way about all their gods that the Christians feel about their one God."

"I don't see how that is possible," said John Paul. "To worship a gay god the same way we worship Jesus? I just don't see it."

"Well, perhaps Jesus was gay," Fiona said.

John Paul was instantly filled with a sense of sin and guilt. He felt that he should not be part of this discussion. He started to panic that he was, once again, alone with his thoughts.

"No, sorry, wait," Fiona said. "I'm sorry if I said that too quickly. But wait. What am I apologizing for? This is how I feel. Your Jesus lived at a time when it was imperative that everyone marry and have kids. He was Jewish—Jewish people are still obsessed with marriage. Yet your Jesus never married, never had kids, and lived with a group of other men the whole time."

"And then there is Lazarus," Bob said.

"Lazarus?" John Paul asked. "What does he have to do with any of this?"

"Lazarus lived with his sisters Mary and Martha," Bob said. "These were three unmarried siblings living together. Doesn't this seem highly unlikely according to the social norms of the time? There are people that think that Mary and Martha were probably a lesbian couple, and Lazarus was a gay friend. Besides, John Paul, Jesus only cries one time during the entirety of the Gospels—and it's the moment he finds out that Lazarus has died. The Bible simply says, 'And Jesus wept.' "

John Paul was both confused and annoyed. He didn't like being preached to by nonbelievers. And he really didn't like it that they made a bit of sense. And he really, really didn't like it that Bob could quote from scripture. He looked at Jayme and saw that he was just sitting back and smiling.

"There's just no way they loved Antinous the same way that we love Jesus," John Paul said. "I can't believe that."

Then a new voice came from the doorway. "That's because you're thinking of Jesus as a man and not as a god."

They all turned and saw an older woman walking through the door. John Paul immediately recognized her as Sister Gabriel Luke. He was instantly terrified that she saw him there.

"Hi, Gabby," Bob said. "I hoped you'd stop by."

Gabriel Luke went immediately behind John Paul's chair and hugged him tightly from behind.

"I love you, I love you, I love you, John Paul Saint Clara!" Gabriel Luke said excitedly. "And God loves you."

Fiona got up and retrieved a chair for Gabby. But before she sat, she also hugged Jayme from behind and told him that she loved him.

"This is my friend, Gabby," Bob said. "But I think John Paul knows her as Sister Gabriel Luke."

"You're a nun?" Jayme asked.

"We don't all dress like we're in *The Sound of Music*," Gabby said as she laughed. "Right, John Paul?"

John Paul just smiled. He wondered if everyone now knew he was gay. He worried about that for a second, then realized it was the first time he'd referred to himself using the word *gay*. He was briefly happy about that.

"Now I was listening for a bit before I came into the room," Gabby said. "I didn't want to startle you and was waiting until you left. See, Bob told me about all of you and your book club, but I didn't know if you were ready to know that I know. Anyway, I wanted to check on Bob, and I walked back here and heard you all talking. Here is your whole problem, John Paul: You are thinking of Jesus as a man and not as a god."

"He was both, right?" John Paul said.

"Yes, and the whole concept of the Trinity makes many people very confused," Gabby said. "See, we tend to think of God as a god, and we think of Jesus as a man. Nobody knows what the heck the Holy Spirit is—that's why people just think of it as a shapeless ghost. But anyway, when you just heard Bob and Fiona talking, you started picturing Jesus as a gay man. That's wrong, because he was also a god—the same God as his father. And if straight people are made in God's image, then so are gay people. And that makes God, and Jesus, at least, in part, gay. Understand?"

"But you keep saying that Jesus was *a* god, instead of Jesus was *the* god," John Paul said. "The ancient Greeks could not have understood how much we love our one God when they had so many."

"Wrong again," Gabby said. "Don't you think that our God was part of all those Greek myths? Of course he was! When the ancient Greeks wrote about love and courage, our God was there. When they wrote about evil people reaping what they sowed, our God was there. Our God was everywhere in the ancient times. Maybe he just had other ways of showing it."

"Can I ask a question?" Jayme said. "I admit that I've never been to a church. All I know about religion comes from the movie *Ben-Hur*. But I know that I was born gay. Nobody will change my mind about that. That means I have to believe that God—whatever god—made me gay. If *Ben-Hur* teaches me that God is all about love and kindness, then I must believe that God is perfectly fine with me loving other guys. Right?"

"Right," said Gabby. "And well said. John Paul, you would be an idiot not to go on a date with this guy. I hope you listened well to what he just said. He just saved you about three years and ten thousand dollars of therapy."

Fiona let out a loud laugh. She nodded her head in agreement. John Paul blushed.

"While we're on the subject," said Jayme, "and before we have to go, I really want to go out with you, John Paul. How about Friday night?"

John Paul felt a stir of excitement from deep within him. In that moment, he didn't care about Antinous, Jesus, or Ben-Hur; he just wanted badly to go on a date with Jayme.

"I want to," John Paul said, "but I don't think I'll ever be able to."

"Nonsense," Gabby said. "I need to bake unleavened bread to use as Communion for the upcoming holy day. I was complaining to your mom that it was so much work for me all alone, and she volunteered you to help me. I told her we'd do it on Friday night. Now, John Paul, I don't want to be a liar, so you have to come early and help me bake bread. Then you can come over here and meet Jayme."

John Paul wasn't entirely satisfied with this arrangement. He didn't like that Sister Gabriel Luke wasn't being entirely honest with his mother. He was also still scared. But he really wanted to see Jayme—just Jayme and nobody else.

"Okay," John Paul said, "but we can't really do too much in public. Is that okay?"

"That is great," Jayme said. "Just leave everything to me. Remember, I'm a movie buff. I know how a great first date is supposed to go."

CHAPTER 17

J ayme lay on his bed, propped up by a few pillows with *Jurassic Park* pillow covers. He'd had them since childhood and wasn't ready to part with them yet. His parents used to not care; it wasn't until lately that they had started paying attention to the things he had in his room. Come to think of it, it wasn't until lately that they had started to pay attention to him at all. He found it disconcerting.

He'd nailed a large poster for the film *Casablanca* above his bed. On it, Humphrey Bogart and Ingrid Bergman were forever crying and kissing in front of a World War II–era plane while a sinister Nazi looked at them. Jayme loved the drama of it. The rest of his room was a disaster, with clothes and childhood toys strewn about. He always intended to organize but never got around to it.

He was talking to Hunter on his phone. At the same time, he was looking through a copy of *National Geographic* that had a photo of a golden Egyptian death mask on the front.

"I think I really only ever talked to her, like, three times before," Jayme said, "but since she found out about John Paul and me, she's been calling a lot."

"She's always been nice to me," Hunter said. "For one of the more popular girls, she seems to be nice to everyone."

"Sophia's one of those people that can sort of mix with more than one group," Jayme said. "I wish I was more like that."

"Maybe it's because nobody likes you," Hunter said. He paused and then laughed loudly.

"Funny," Jayme said, "but shut up."

"So what are you doing for your big date on Friday? Please don't tell me you're taking him to one of your film festivals. He'll die of boredom before you ever get to first base. Hey, what is first base for gay guys?"

"I'm not sure," Jayme said. "Shirtless kissing?"

"From what I've heard about gay guys," Hunter said, "isn't it always a home run?"

"That is a stereotype."

"It's a good one."

"Anyway, we can't really go anywhere. So I'm planning something really nice at the bookstore."

"The bookstore? You're taking your dream guy to Carlson's Used Books and Records, a place you've been together tons of times before, on a special date? Good luck with that."

"It's not the place that matters," Jayme said. "It's what happens inside the place."

"Are you sure this is going to be okay?" Hunter asked. "I mean, I don't mean to rain on your parade or anything. But are you sure this is going to work? You've been out of the closet forever. Can you be with a guy like John Paul?"

"I've thought a lot about it," Jayme said, "and yes, I can. It used to worry me. But listen. I figured some things out after our last meeting. Appreciating other people and their differences goes beyond race, gender, body size, and all that other stuff. I think that appreciating other people also means appreciating their backgrounds because they can't help where they were born or who their parents were. Sure, it was shocking when I heard John Paul say that he believes in a one true God. My parents have never hung around anyone that would be like that. The closest thing I ever had to a god was Santa Claus—and my parents stopped that when I was, like, five."

"Oh, too patriarchal?" Hunter asked.

"Who knows? Too patriarchal, too white, too able-bodied, used elves and reindeer as slaves—it was probably all of those together. But maybe it's not so bad to have something to believe in."

"Like a magical man that can heal the sick and walk on water?" Hunter asked.

"Well, maybe I'm not ready for all of that. But there are pieces of it that I can handle."

Jayme heard a knock at his door. "What?" he yelled.

"It's me," his mom replied. "Can I come in?"

"Yeah, just talking to Hunter."

Abygail entered the room, carrying a large paper grocery bag stuffed full of something. She left the door open, looked around, and shook her head at the mess. She sat on the bed.

"Okay, man," Jayme said, "I gotta go."

"Have fun on Friday," Hunter said. "See ya."

Jayme ended the call and threw his phone on a pillow next to him. He looked at his mom with a small smile.

"What's all that stuff?" Jayme asked, pointing at the grocery bag.

"I went to the thrift store and got you some new clothes," Abygail said.

Jayme was annoyed. He was discerning about the kind of clothes he wore, and he didn't like other people's suggestions, especially his mother's.

"You know I like to be with you when you shop for my clothes," Jayme said.

"I know," she replied, "but I happened to be in that area and saw some things you'll like. Look at this."

She rummaged through the bag and pulled out a T-shirt. She held it up for him to see. It was light green and displayed a picture of Princess Leia from *Star Wars* swinging on a rope. Under the picture, it read "Girl Power" in large pink letters. Jayme was appalled. He'd never wear that shirt. He wanted to tell his mom that in the only scene where Princess Leia swung on a rope, it was because Luke Skywalker was carrying her, as he was saving her life.

"Here, look at these," Abygail said as she rummaged again through the bag.

She held up a pair of pants that were halfway between shorts and full-length pants. Jayme didn't quite know what they were. They were black and looked like they were made of a stretchy fabric.

"You like black, right?" Abygail said.

Jayme didn't say anything. He just sat back and smiled a little.

"I also got you something else," Abygail said. "Please just listen. Your dad and I are really concerned about you, and we want to do everything we can to make sure you have a happy life. So I went to see a doctor. Their name is Dr. Ramirez-Ogle. They use *they/them* pronouns. We talked a lot about you. They think it's important that you start on hormones as soon as possible. You're already well into puberty, so hopefully it's not too late."

"Mom," Jayme said, "I just don't think that I want to. At least not right now."

"But see, Jayme," Abygail said, "that's the problem. You don't really know what you want to do, and when you do, it could be too late. Dr. Ramirez-Ogle was great at explaining why you don't know what you want. We talked about how you have always liked artistic stuff and about how you liked to play with dolls when you were younger. We talked about how you're attracted to men. They are convinced that you are trans, even if you don't quite know it yet. One of the symptoms of your condition is that you will deny the condition. Understand?"

Jayme didn't say anything. He was used to his parents going ahead with any idea they had, but this was different. This was his body. And of all the things he was worried about, he was most worried that his penis would get smaller and that his voice would begin to sound too high.

"There's no harm in trying these hormones—the doctor told me. You can try for a month and see what you think. They think you'll notice a difference quickly and want to stay on them. They gave me a bunch of free samples. Do you want to keep them in your bathroom? Or do you want me to bring you one? You're supposed to take two every day, one in the morning and one at night."

"I'll take care of it," Jayme said. "Put them in my bathroom, on the counter, and I'll take them."

"That's great," Abygail said. "Good choice. And remember, you can talk to me about anything. So when you're ready to talk about bras and stuff like that, I'll be here."

Now it appeared that there was something for Jayme to worry about that was worse than a shrinking penis. At least nobody could see what was in his pants. But he really didn't want to start growing boobs. His mom left, leaving the grocery bag on the bed. He buried his face into his T. rex pillow.

CHAPTER 18

On Friday night, John Paul left Sister Gabriel Luke as she put the unleavened bread in the ovens. She wished him the best of luck, and he walked from the Catholic campus to the bookstore. He was anxious, excited, and full of energy. He never realized before just how good the feeling of anticipation could feel. He'd waited for this moment for two days, and now it was here.

When he entered the store, he saw that there were several other people shopping. He'd never seen another customer besides Jayme in there. But he figured that it was Friday night, and that probably made a difference. He waved at Fiona while she was helping someone with some records, and he walked up to the front counter, where Bob sat on his stool. He still had his cane next to him.

"Hi, John Paul," Bob said. "I hope you are ready. Jayme's been here ever since school got out. He's got the whole storage room all decked out for you. And don't worry. Nobody will bother you; Fiona and I will see to that."

"Thanks, Bob," John Paul said. "Thanks for everything."

"Just relax, and have a great time," Bob said. "My mother used to tell me not to do anything she wouldn't do. But I hope you do more than I would, especially since I can't do much these days!"

Bob laughed loudly. John Paul smiled and walked through the back room where they met for the book club. In the rear of that room, there was another door that led to a storeroom. The door was closed; John Paul knocked on the door.

"Come in," he heard Jayme say.

John Paul opened the door to a room of wonder. He didn't know what was normally stored in this room because everything had been cleared out. A small square table sat in the middle of the room. It had been perfectly set with plates and silverware. A candelabra containing four candles, all burning warmly, sat in the middle of the table. Another small table, off to the side, held food and utensils. The entire room smelled like garlic and bread.

Jayme must have brought some type of star projector because the ceiling was sprinkled with sparkling lights. John Paul closed the door, and the stars got brighter as his eyes adjusted. He could hear something. Very soft voices talking. He turned around and saw that above the door, a movie was being projected onto a blank wall. It was the original *Ben-Hur*. The soundtrack to the film was playing softly.

"I thought I'd show *Ben-Hur*," said Jayme, coming up to John Paul from opposite the entrance door. "I thought it'd be nice to have something playing that was—wait, have you seen it? I sometimes forget that not everyone likes old movies."

"Yeah, I've seen it," John Paul said. "I actually like it a lot."

Jayme hugged him. John Paul hugged back and hoped he smelled good. He'd taken two showers at home and had worn clean clothes and some of his dad's cologne, but he'd been kneading bread for the last two hours. Then he stood back to look at Jayme. His curly shoulder-length hair had been blown dry so that it was more full than John Paul had seen it before. A few strands of his bangs fell across his forehead and over his eyes. He was wearing brown dress pants and a blue button-down shirt. The top three buttons were unbuttoned. Even though his collar was crinkled on one side, John Paul thought he was the handsomest person in the entire world, even better-looking than Antinous.

"Can I help you fix your collar?" John Paul asked.

Without waiting for Jayme to answer, John Paul walked up to him and straightened the collar. Then he smoothed Jayme's shirt fabric over his shoulders.

"There, perfect," John Paul said.

"You look great," Jayme said. "I've never seen you out of your school uniform before. You look really good."

John Paul blushed. He wore black pants and a red shirt that was buttoned all the way up. He wore a red-and-black tie.

Jayme started taking plates and putting pasta on them. John Paul saw that it was from a local restaurant that was one of his favorites.

"I asked Sophia," Jayme said. "She said you'd like this food. Have a seat."

John Paul sat. Jayme brought two plates over and sat across from him. It must have occurred to Jayme that the candelabra was a bad centerpiece because he quickly moved it to the side table so that he could see John Paul. He laughed. They started eating.

"You know," Jayme said, sort of breaking the ice, "Charlton Heston is pretty good as Ben-Hur. But I don't think he's all that great-looking. I mean, he's no—"

"Messala?" John Paul said.

"Yes! I was going to say that. Messala is so freaking hot in this movie."

"For sure. He's the reason I got my mom to buy the DVD. She, of course, loves all the times that Jesus is in it."

"You know, the actor that plays Messala—Stephen Boyd—he was gay in real life. He was even out to a lot of other actors. Well, at least the ones he could trust."

"I didn't know that."

"You still buy DVDs?" Jayme asked.

"Yeah," John Paul said, embarrassed. "My parents don't trust streaming."

"Well, I'm surprised my parents haven't blocked *Ben-Hur* from my account. They'd freak if they saw how white, straight, and religious it was. Even if, in my opinion, Ben-Hur and Messala had to be in love with each other. Why else would Ben-Hur hurt so much when Messala betrays him?"

"But it must be nice having parents that support you, right?" John Paul asked.

A few moments of silence followed. John Paul could tell that Jayme was thinking of something to say.

"I guess," Jayme said. "It has helped a lot because I'm gay. But—well, I don't want to get into it."

"Please," said John Paul. "I want to know what your life is like."

"Okay, well, sometimes it sucks. Like especially right now. My dad is running for Congress—for the House of Representatives. It's what him and Mom have wanted since before I was born. They are both obsessed with it, really. Right now, everything is about the primary because he has to win that, or his dream is over. Nobody gets a second chance at the local level. You lose once, and you're poison—or so I've been told every week for the past ten years. But if you win, well, you live to campaign another day."

"Sounds like a lot of stress."

"That's not even the worst part. So they've come up with this stupid idea that they'll get a lot more of the superliberal vote if they have a trans kid. And since I'm an only child, I guess I'm the only option."

John Paul was taken aback by this information. He wasn't quite sure what to think of it.

"Wait, what did you say?" John Paul asked.

"They are pushing me to be trans. They say it's because they love me and want what's best for me, but I know it's about the election."

"You're serious?"

"Yep. They even got me hormones and everything."

"Jayme...I'm...well, I don't know what to say. I thought I was the only one here with parent problems. But are you really taking pills? Do you want to?"

"Oh God, no!" Jayme said loudly. "I really don't. I mean, I think that people should have the right to be trans, and it would be great if all those people had parents like mine. But I don't feel that I'm female, and I never have. I'm just a guy that likes guys. Anyway, the pills are in my bathroom. I just flush one at a time when I'm supposed to be taking them."

"Oh good," John Paul said with relief. "I'm not sure that I..."

He didn't finish his sentence. Jayme looked up quizzically.

"You're not sure what?" Jayme asked.

"Well, I don't want to hurt your feelings. But I'm not into being with someone that might want to...you know."

"You know what?"

"You know. Cut off his penis."

"Ahhhh," said Jayme. "So now I know what you're into."

Jayme laughed. John Paul blushed a bright shade of red.

"Does this mean you can admit out loud that you're gay?" Jayme asked. "You know that being a guy that likes it when other guys have a penis is probably the definition of being gay."

"Yes, Jayme, I'm gay. There, I said it."

"How do you feel?"

"Really, really great."

"Good," said Jayme.

"Wait a second though," said John Paul. "So I can't fit in with my family because I'm gay, but you can't fit in with your family because you're not gay enough?"

After a few moments of silence, Jayme laughed as loudly as John Paul had ever heard him before. John Paul joined in the laughter.

"I never thought of it like that," said Jayme. "But you're right!"

They laughed and ate more. The movie continued to play above them.

"Will you ever tell your parents that you're gay?" Jayme asked.

"Oh man," John Paul answered. "They'd never accept it. I'd be out on the streets or in one of those camps where they change you. Will you tell your parents that you don't want to be a woman?"

"Hmm," Jayme said, "that's complicated. At least not right now with the election. My mom doesn't do well when she doesn't get what she wants. I'm sort of afraid of her at times... I have some actual scars to prove it. Oh shit. Can you just forget I said that? I really don't want you to think I'm some sort of victim. I hate that shit."

John Paul's heart sank. In all his years of being secretly gay, and a sinner in his parents' eyes, he'd never been physically hurt—just emotionally, spiritually, and mentally. But sitting in front of him now was a guy with supposedly understanding parents, and he'd been physically hurt. John Paul wondered what kind of a world this was. Was there a place for either of them?

"John Paul," Jayme said, "you look like you just went a million miles away. I'm sorry if I shocked you. Really, I didn't want to talk about that, so forget it."

"I can't really forget it," John Paul said, "but I won't talk about it unless you want to. I was just thinking about how similar our problems are, even though our families are so different."

"Oh!" Jayme jumped up. "I have dessert, and I don't want it to melt. So let's eat it now."

He brought over two small containers of gelato from the side table and placed them where the candelabra had been. But before sitting down, he grabbed his chair and placed it right next to John Paul's. Then he sat.

John Paul's heart was beating out of his chest. Jayme leaned over.

"Can I kiss you?" Jayme asked.

"Yes," John Paul replied.

They each leaned over and kissed. It was just a light peck, lips to lips. They pulled back and smiled. Then they leaned back in and kissed again—slightly harder and longer that time. They pulled back.

"You okay?" Jayme asked.

"More than okay," John Paul answered.

They kissed some more. *Ben-Hur* kept playing above them, and the gelato melted.

ANCIENT PRIDE

THE ARMY OF LOVE

Now we turn to what might be the most interesting example of gay men in the ancient world. This chapter tells of a rare group indeed. The story of the Sacred Band of Thebes appeared in the writings of the ancient historian Plutarch. But ancient historians, just like the modern ones, tend to bend the truth to fit their narrative. Consequently, many historians of the Middle Ages believed this group did not exist at all—until archaeologists in the late 1800s made a discovery that proved that the entire story was real. This is truly an example of myth becoming reality.

About four hundred years after *The Iliad* had been written, Greece experienced its great classical age. This was the time of the philosophers and playwrights. This is when Socrates, Plato, Aeschylus, Sophocles, and others were working. However, Greece was still a collection of city-states, each with its own government. Sometimes they worked together, and often they fought. Just like today, humans found it difficult to get along.

Thebes was a beautiful city-state north of academically powerful Athens and east of the mighty military state of

Sparta. At the time, each city-state had its own army. But these armies were not like ours today. Instead, they were large units of mercenaries paid to fight for a specific city. The army of Thebes was not composed entirely of men from Thebes who were willing to die for their city. It was actually composed of men from many places who joined the Theban army because it paid the best at the time. If Sparta raised its wages, then these men would just as easily put on an "I Love Sparta" T-shirt and bid farewell to Thebes.

It all started when a small group of Spartan mercenaries rode into Thebes and staged a military coup, replacing the Theban government with Spartan dignitaries. The Thebans who had been in power were exiled from their city. Of course, they weren't happy about this. Neither were the citizens of Thebes, who would prefer to run their own affairs without paying taxes to Sparta.

A man named Gorgidas had an idea of how the military could function differently. He disliked the mercenary system because it took all the loyalty out of fighting. In addition, Gorgidas has been a student of the philosopher Plato. He remembered Plato's words from a famous document called the *Symposium*:

> *If there were only some way of contriving that*
> *a state or an army should be made up of lovers*
> *and their beloved, emulating one another when*
> *fighting at each other's side. They would overcome*
> *the world. For what lover would choose to be seen*
> *by his beloved abandoning his post or throwing*
> *away his arms? He would be ready to die a*
> *thousand deaths rather than endure this. Or, who*
> *would desert his beloved or fail him in the hour of*
> *danger?*

We must take a step back and remember that homosexuality was considered quite normal for the Greeks at this time. Gorgidas, taking Plato's words literally, would not have found it difficult to find male couples living and loving together in Thebes.

It was important to Gorgidas that all the members of his new group be citizens of Thebes. He wanted loyalty, first and foremost. So he scoured the city-state and found 150 couples, no doubt choosing the buffest and most skilled men he could find. The historian Plutarch tells us that at this moment, the Sacred Band of Thebes was formed.

The Sacred Band moved outside the city to train together. We don't know exactly what the training entailed, but we do know that it was extensive and effective. The three hundred men lived and trained together, day and night, for months. Everyone in Greece was astonished one night when the Sacred Band marched into Thebes and easily took back their city from the Spartan authorities. But they didn't stop there.

Encouraged by their success and the fame they received, the Sacred Band decided to get some payback from Sparta. Many thought this was complete madness, but those people didn't know that when gay men set their hearts on something, nothing can stand in their way.

The Theban army of mercenaries, after having witnessed the success of the Sacred Band, joined them as they marched toward Sparta. Soon other mercenaries wanted to be a part of this excitement. Sparta didn't stand a chance. The Sacred Band of Thebes took the fabled city and placed Theban politicians in charge. The Greeks were astonished that Sparta had fallen.

The more they succeeded, the more they attracted additional armies to follow them. However, the core Sacred Band always remained with 150 couples. Plutarch tells us that the Sacred Band fought as a single unit, with each man within arm's reach of his lover. Two men fighting as one became four men fighting as one, then eight men fighting as one, until all were so coordinated with each other that couples on one side of the formation knew exactly what was occurring to couples on the other. They were a fighting machine.

Battle after battle was won by the Sacred Band. Thebes became the unifying city-state in all of Greece. Athens fell to them. Corinth fell to them. For the first time in history, Greece was one united country.

Who could stop the Sacred Band of Thebes? Well, as it turns out, only a gay couple could defeat a couple of gays.

For centuries, Greeks traveled to the Oracle of Delphi for religious guidance. The Oracle of Delphi was a woman who lived in a cave at a place called Delphi. She was called the "Pythia," a religious title for a woman who could speak directly to the god Apollo. People would arrive with offerings. Poor people brought animals to sacrifice, and rich people brought gold and silver. Then they would ask the Pythia a question. She'd go back into the cave, talk it over with Apollo, and give the traveler their answer.

However, since the time of intellectual enlightenment in Athens, there were people who were skeptical of the Pythia. What if she was taking all the money and just listening to some old guys in the cave who told her what to say? What if Apollo wasn't in there at all? It had begun to be a little too coincidental that Apollo always seemed to agree with whatever side had the most money.

Then a group of men attacked the Oracle of Delphi. We don't know where they came from or how they were organized. But they controlled the whole area and exiled the Pythia, along with her entourage. Of course, the Pythia and her priests weren't too happy about this, especially since the outlaws started spending all of the gold they found in the cave system.

The Pythia appealed to the rest of Greece for help. This was, after all, the most important religious site in the entire country. But to her dismay, the cities of Greece weren't all that interested in helping her. The belief that she could speak directly to Apollo must have degraded to the point where most citizens were uninterested.

So the Pythia appealed to the north, to Macedon. King Philip II of Macedon had long been looking for a reason to attack Greece. His son had just come of age, and Philip saw that the young man showed much promise in military leadership. The son's name was Alexander—yes, *that* Alexander, the great one.

Philip and the Macedon army rode down into Greece and easily liberated the Pythia, placing her back in her cave. (But they kept much of the treasure for themselves.) Then Philip decided that since they were already down there, why shouldn't they try to take the whole country? So the entire Macedon army advanced toward Thebes.

The Sacred Band, with the Theban army behind them, moved to the north. The two massive armies met at a place called Chaeronea.

Philip had put his son, Alexander, and his son's lover, a man named Hephaestion, in charge of dealing with the Sacred Band of Thebes. It was a wise move on Philip's behalf. (We'll learn a lot more about Alexander and Hephaestion in a future chapter.) Alexander studied their previous battles and noticed that the Sacred Band was not functioning as a unit as part of the Theban army. Instead, the Thebans used the Sacred Band as sort of a really big weapon. Because the Sacred Band was so tightly knit together, the army wielded them as a single man would wield a large sword. So Alexander thought that all they had to do was remove the weapon and throw it away. Alexander became great and ruled the world for a reason: He studied hard and was never wrong.

Alexander and Hephaestion sent one thousand soldiers to surround the Sacred Band and cut them off from the Theban army. Then they sent two thousand more soldiers to surround those soldiers. The goal was to move the Sacred Band as far away as possible.

Soon the distance between the Sacred Band and the Theban army became large enough for Philip's Macedon forces to attack. Which they did. The Thebans were destroyed.

This was war—not a tea party. Alexander kept the Sacred Band surrounded by his growing forces until he gave the order to annihilate them. None survived.

Then something surprising happened. While the rest of the dead Theban army was left to rot in the fields—as was customary for the time—Plutarch tells us that Alexander ordered the Sacred Band of Thebes to be treated with respect and dignity. A large burial site was excavated. The bodies of the Sacred Band were placed in straight rows, many linking arms with their lovers. They were covered with dirt. Alexander then had a giant lion, carved from marble, placed in front of the mass grave. That is the last that Plutarch tells us.

The years went on—thousands of them—until the lion had disappeared and Plutarch's story became just that: a story. Then, in the early 1800s, a British man was riding on a horse around Chaeronea. The horse stumbled on a piece of marble. It turned out to be the broken head of a lion. The man got together some people from a nearby village, and they dug up the rest of the lion. It had broken into many pieces. They stored the lion in a barn and left it there.

In 1881, an archaeologist named Panayotis Stamatakis, who knew about Plutarch's writing and the discovery of the lion's head, began to dig around the site. He and his team quickly found the mass burial site, exactly as Plutarch had described it. There, right before him, rows of skeletons lay buried in the dirt, many of them still with their arm bones linked together. The Band of Thebes was no myth and no historical distortion by Plutarch. No other ancient burial site has ever been discovered with this many men lying this neatly. No other ancient burial site has ever been discovered with soldiers linking arms in pairs.

I can't help but wonder what would have happened if the Sacred Band of Thebes had been composed of twins. Wouldn't this army of twins be well-known all around the world today? Wouldn't we have a Hollywood movie about these sets of twins that fought to the death? Do the gay men of the Sacred Band of Thebes deserve less?

There are two lessons to learn from the Sacred Band of Thebes. The first is that anything is possible if dedicated people come together, work hard, and care about each other. The second is that it's not a great idea to mess with the Gay Men's Chorus.

Regardless, Panayotis Stamatakis and his friends reassembled the lion in the early 1900s. It stands there today, the Lion of Chaeronea, as a marker of the Sacred Band of Thebes.

CHAPTER 19

The next Wednesday, Fiona was straightening the bookmarks again when the door to the bookstore opened. A woman walked through with a cardboard tray holding four cups and a white paper sack. Fiona looked up.

"Hi, Becks," Fiona said. "You didn't have to bring that over here; I was just about to come and get it."

"You get the same thing every Wednesday," Becks said, "so I thought I'd save you a trip. How's Bob?"

"He's in the back," Fiona said. "He says he's fine, but I think this fall sort of scared him more than he thought it would. He seems to be extra careful about everything he does, and he doesn't want anyone to see that he's moving slower. He's stubborn sometimes—well, more than sometimes."

"Well," Becks said, "he needs to get over that. It's no secret that older people move slower. Anyway, I gotta get back to the coffee shop. This order is on me."

"Hey, that's nice. Grab a book on your way out."

Becks set the drinks and paper bag on the counter. She turned to a table and picked up a book that was on top.

"*Pride and Prejudice*?" Becks said. "Any good?"

"Literally not my cup of tea," Fiona said. "Not yours either, I'm afraid."

Fiona walked to a bookcase near the door. She looked around one of the middle shelves, selected a book, and threw it at Becks. Becks caught it and looked at the title.

"*Pride, Prejudice, and Zombies.*" She laughed. "By Seth Grahame-Smith."

"Yep," Fiona said, "it's right up your alley."

"Thanks," Becks said as she left the store.

Fiona chuckled a bit, then went back to the counter. The door opened again. Jayme and John Paul walked through together. They were laughing. Fiona was overjoyed to see them walking together.

"Now you two are arriving together?" Fiona said. "That's a change from a few weeks ago."

"A lot has changed," John Paul said.

"What's so funny?" Fiona asked.

"Nothing, really," Jayme said. "We just started laughing, I guess, when we saw each other."

Once again, they both started giggling. Fiona rolled her eyes. She thought of her first giggle with someone she was infatuated with.

"Oh," she said, "I remember those days. Well, Bob is in the back."

Fiona took the snacks, and the boys followed her to the back room. The table had been set as usual, with the Greek statue in the middle. They greeted Bob, who had his cane next to him, and sat down.

For once, they started by eating the pastries and drinking cappuccino. They talked about school, the weather, and the general happenings around town. Also, for once, nobody was keeping an eye on the time. Fiona made a mental note of this. Something had changed, she thought, and for the better.

When they started to discuss the chapter in *Ancient Pride* about the Sacred Band of Thebes, both boys revealed that they were captivated by the story. Bob was just as enthralled, especially with the discovery of the mass burial site. He offered more information about the site that he'd learned online. Everyone seemed impressed that he'd used the internet. Then Fiona decided to speak up.

"Okay, boys," Fiona said, "I get how exciting this all is, and, Bob, I'm considering you one of the young boys on this one. But here is where I'm coming from. Yeah, it's all great that gay couples could do this amazing service for their community. However, it involved a lot of killing. Were they really celebrated for being who they were—loving couples? Or were they just being celebrated for what men were doing all the time—killing other men?"

"Sometimes it's nice to be considered one of the boys," Bob said. "You just put those words in my mouth, and they're perfect for the Sacred Band of Thebes. See, both of your assumptions are correct. For once, these guys were the envy of the established world. Sure, it was because they were good at killing. But at least they weren't being ignored anymore."

"And where were the women?" Fiona asked. "Sitting at home. And I don't see any lesbians in this story either."

"That's because this isn't a book about them," said Bob. "Sure, the Sacred Band was a group of killers, but we can't all be as nice and caring as the Amazons."

"Oh," Fiona said, "he's playing the big card now, I guess! You're right, and I'll eat my words."

"The Amazons are featured in *The Iliad* itself!" Bob said.

"Like Wonder Woman?" Jayme said.

"Exactly," Bob said, "that's where the Wonder Woman backstory came from. The Amazons were a culture of women that didn't need men. They show up in many Greek myths, including those surrounding the Trojan War. These women were ruthless warriors—every bit as 'killers' as the Sacred Band. They are very important. It takes Achilles himself to kill the Amazon queen in many versions. So if the Sacred Band of Thebes killed many people, so did the Amazons."

"Okay," said Fiona, "your point is well taken. But the Amazons are myth, and it's been proven that the Sacred Band was real. Doesn't that mean—"

"So far," interrupted Bob. "The Amazons haven't been proven to be real so far. Perhaps there is proof lying right now under some pile of rocks on an island in the Aegean Sea. That could be your new goal, Fiona. Go and find them."

Fiona, looking in Bob's eyes when he said this, saw that he was only half kidding. He actually thought that there was a discovery to be made. More than that, he believed that Fiona might be the one to do it. Fiona got the sense that it wasn't so much he believed she could find the Amazons; it was that he believed she could do something great—whatever she wanted to do. She felt good.

During this entire time, which had gone on way past their normal twenty minutes, Jayme and John Paul didn't say much. It was evident that they'd both read the chapter, but they were much more interested in each other than they were the Sacred Band of Thebes. Fiona cut them a lot of slack. She could tell that Bob was doing the same.

After Fiona and Bob had finished bantering, Bob said, "Okay, now each of you have to say one thing you learned from the chapter. Then you really need to go. You're both very late."

"Umm," said Jayme, "I learned a lot. But to be honest, the biggest thing I got was that I'm frustrated there isn't a really good movie about this whole thing. I've got it all planned out—how it could be filmed, I mean. Lots of blood. And then you'd have the juxtaposition of Alexander and his boyfriend hunting down this band of gay guys."

"That's amazing," Fiona said. "I think that movie could do really well. You'd have to show the Pythia of Apollo in her cave with all her minions around. And then the look on the Spartans' faces when they've been beaten by gay guys. I'd go see it."

"What about you, John Paul?" Bob asked.

"I'd see it, for sure," John Paul said.

"No," Bob said. "What did you learn from the chapter?"

"That the life I have isn't enough," John Paul said. "I want more. Of course, I don't want to go killing anyone. And I don't think I'm one of those that will ever be in a parade or anything like that."

"Then what is the 'more' that you want?" Jayme asked.

"I want to be free to go to Chaeronea," John Paul said. "I want to go there with a man that I love. I want to stand in front of that lion and feel pride. That's the *more* that I want."

"Once again, John Paul," Fiona said, "you really let the story tell you about something you're missing in your life."

"Is that bad?" John Paul asked.

"No," Fiona said, "not at all."

Jayme asked, "Is it bad that I don't do that? I don't really think that I think like that."

Fiona took a moment to answer. She drank a long sip from her cup and broke off a piece of pastry.

"It's not *bad* at all, Jayme," Fiona said. "I think you believe your life is so much better than John Paul's simply because your parents are supportive of gay people. But that doesn't mean that you're not missing something. It's okay to think about what you really want. And, John Paul, it's okay for you to picture things like they'd be in a movie—to have fun with the stories."

She took another drink. She hoped she wasn't being too preachy. Fiona wondered if she was turning into her annoying, know-it-all aunt.

"Anyway, I'll shut up," Fiona said. "You guys can figure it out."

John Paul held the bookstore door open for Jayme as they left together. For the first time, he wasn't afraid to be seen outside with Jayme. He wondered if perhaps the true story of the Sacred Band of Thebes had given him the strength and confidence that he envied in Jayme.

They turned and walked together down Main Street, toward the bell towers of Our Lady of Seven Dolors. John Paul intentionally walked slowly. He'd always loved walking downtown at night with the streetlights glowing romantically. In the dark, even the drab and dated core of Kaiserburg turned into a beautiful, charming place to walk.

"Can I ask you something personal?" John Paul said.

"I'd love it if you'd ask me something personal," Jayme replied.

John Paul took a deep breath. He hesitated, but the ambience of the evening gave him courage.

"Do you believe in Jesus?" John Paul asked.

"Well, John Paul," Jayme said, "I'm not going to lie to you, even if I know it's not what you want to hear. No, I don't believe in Jesus being a god, or having any magical powers, or anything like that. Maybe he was a real person, I guess. Sorry."

"No, it's okay," John Paul said. "I just wanted to ask, and I'm not really sure why. It's just that—well—I don't know anyone that isn't Catholic. I've only been allowed to hang out with people who believe in Jesus. There is so much that is new for me right now, and I'm not always sure what other people are thinking."

"Yeah, I get that," Jayme said. "Now I have a personal question. Do you think that you have to believe in Jesus to be a good person?"

"I think I did but not anymore. I mean, look at Bob and Fiona. They are so nice and have done such a great thing for me—I mean, us. How can I believe that they aren't good people?"

"There are good people all over this whole large planet that have never even heard of Jesus. I can't believe that they are all bad people, or going to hell, or whatever."

"I can't believe that either," John Paul said. "I hope I don't believe that."

They were getting close to the Catholic campus. John Paul turned and led him along the side of the church, toward the courtyard.

"I learned a lot from you last week," John Paul said, "when you talked about feeling that if God had made you gay, then he must be okay with that. I realized in that moment that you know more about faith than I do. I've been thinking a lot about it. Everything I know is from what other people tell me. Then you come along, not even believing in Jesus, and you teach me something I never realized before. And it makes so much sense to me. I *know* that I was born this way. I *know* that God made me this way because I did not choose it. So he must be okay with it. If not, then he made a mistake, and I don't think that's possible."

"From what I know about it," Jayme said, "no loving God would ever create love, create people, and then create some people that aren't allowed to love. It doesn't make any sense."

Inside John Paul's mind, his brain cells were firing with new synapses. The words that Jayme had just spoken created the most profound statement John Paul had ever heard.

"You're amazing," John Paul said. "I think you just solved a huge problem I've been having."

"*You're* amazing," Jayme replied. "If we were in the Sacred Band of Thebes, I would be happy to be fighting while tied to you."

They entered the courtyard. John Paul pointed toward the door where he would enter the school. They said their goodbyes. Then as John Paul walked to the school, he was filled with a courage that he just could not resist. He stopped and turned.

"Hey, you!" John Paul said in a raised voice that echoed in the courtyard. "I'm from the Sacred Band of Thebes, and you are about to be attacked!"

"What?" Jayme said as he turned to face John Paul.

John Paul ran toward him. He grabbed Jayme and pulled him forcefully into a tight embrace. He felt Jayme, just as forcefully, returning the embrace. They started kissing. Then, right there in front of the statue of Our Lady of Seven Dolors, John Paul knew what it felt like to be alive.

CHAPTER 20

That same Wednesday night, Sister Gentillini and the rest of the Catholic youth group were assembling food rations for the poor people of Guatemala. They were standing around tables in the school library, dishing rice and dried beans out of large sacks and into small ziplock bags. Nobody, not even Gentillini, knew how the ziplock bags turned into food rations. But the missionary nuns of Guatemala asked for these shipments monthly.

Gentillini didn't particularly like her missionary sisters. She felt that since they'd been in Guatemala for over fifty years and things were actually worse, the sisters should probably come back to the United States, where they would be of more use.

To her dismay, at some point during the organization of the ziplock bags, she lost track of John Paul Saint Clara. She would impose a penance on herself later for committing such a lapse. She began to look for him all over the school, even though it meant abandoning a bunch of teenagers working with rice and beans.

Gentillini knew that the public school girl, Sophia, was covering for John Paul. She kept an eye on her as well, but nothing out of the ordinary seemed to be happening as far as the girl was concerned. But someone new was following

Gentillini's every move: Sister Gabriel Luke. Gentillini developed a sixth sense that Gabriel Luke also knew something about the Saint Clara boy. Something was going on that Gabriel Luke knew about. Gentillini wanted to know it too.

Gentillini decided to do a sweep of the hall and kitchen to look for John Paul. With her nun ability to see out of the back of her head, she felt Gabriel Luke behind her. She turned.

"Sister," Gentillini said to Gabriel Luke in the hall outside the library, "do you need something?"

"Oh no," Gabriel Luke replied, "I was just checking on you to see that you're okay. I saw you leave the library."

"Why should I not be okay?" Gentillini asked.

"No reason," Gabriel Luke replied. "I was just concerned that you were ill."

"I hope you have enough rosary beads to say a penance for that lie," Gentillini said. "I'd say one hundred Hail Marys if I were you."

"I have nothing to be penitent for," Gabriel Luke said. "And I can take care of my own Hail Marys, thank you very much. What makes you think I'm lying? I thought you were ill."

"Then please, leave me alone," Gentillini said.

"Sister, please leave *these kids* alone," Gabriel Luke said. "You are not the Savior, nor are you their parent. You're not the police. You're not even their guidance counselor—I am! I have a master's degree in counseling, and you, Sister, with all due respect, you have a degree in liturgical planning. Listen, I know you are looking for John Paul. He's fine. Stop being paranoid. He likes to have some time alone. You'd know that if you bothered to get to know him instead of trying to hunt him down all the time. He's outside, reading, like he always does during the break. And yes, sometimes he goes a little over time. But I've seen him. He's fine. I will swear before God and the Holy Mother that John Paul Saint Clara is outside of the school, reading."

"And where exactly is he doing this reading outside?" Gentillini asked. "And what is he reading exactly?"

"I told you," Gabriel Luke said. "He wants to be alone. And what he reads is his business. Have some trust and just let him be. This is not a suggestion, Sister; it's an instruction from a professional! And now I will leave because I, unlike some people, have trust that you will make the right decision."

Gabriel Luke turned angrily and walked back into the library. Gentillini was furious. She did not appreciate being spoken to like that by one of her fellow sisters. How dare Gabriel Luke accuse and speak down to her? The reason why Gentillini demanded decorum from the students was because she cared about their futures. She cared about whether they were going to heaven or hell. In her opinion, she was the only nun who truly cared where these kids would end up.

She wasn't just furious; she was also frustrated. Gentillini knew that Gabriel Luke was on the good side of their Mother Superior. Gabriel Luke and the Mother Superior had been close friends since they were young nuns. Gentillini knew that Gabriel Luke called the Mother House at least weekly to chat with Mother Superior. So there was no use for Gentillini to report Gabriel Luke's verbal assault. However, none of this would deter Gentillini from finding the truth and protecting John Paul from himself. She might not be *the* Savior, but she could be *a* savior.

She walked down the hall and turned into the darkened kitchen. She didn't bother turning on the lights. She walked through the rows of dim counters to the back door that led outside and opened it.

Three buildings occupied the space of the campus of Our Lady of Seven Dolors: the church, the school, and the convent. The backs of all three faced a small courtyard that the nuns had turned into a spiritual garden. The garden was not lit. But the lights from the nearby streets gave a dim glow to the area, except for the place where the two bell towers of the church created large shadows.

The center of the garden contained a raised area made from large, flat stones. On top of these stones, a life-size statue of the Blessed Mother stood. It had been cast all in white. She wore a crown on her head and stood on a serpent. Gentillini took a moment to bow to the statue. She was about to walk through the garden, toward the street, when she noticed two darkened figures entering the courtyard opposite her. With her catlike movement, she darted behind the stack of stones that held up the statue. She crouched there, silent and motionless.

The figures walked closer. The night was still. Her senses were heightened. Then she saw that one of them was John Paul Saint Clara and the other was the boy from the photo whom she'd seen earlier in the bookstore. Now she knew that Gabriel Luke was lying. John Paul was not alone, and he was definitely not reading. And she realized that John Paul was up to something that was leading him straight to the gates of hell.

The boys came closer; they were speaking in low voices. She strained to hear.

"This is where I go," John Paul said. "Through that door."

"I'll see you Friday night, right?" the other one said.

"Yeah, but this time I'm doing all the planning," John Paul replied. "See ya."

They hugged each other. Gentillini cringed when she saw this. Then John Paul turned and walked toward the kitchen door. But suddenly, John Paul stopped and turned back to the other boy.

"Hey, you!" John Paul said in a raised voice that echoed in the courtyard. "I'm from the Sacred Band of Thebes, and you are about to be attacked!"

"What?" the other boy said as he turned to face John Paul.

John Paul ran to the other boy and leaped toward him. He grabbed him around the waist and pulled him into an embrace. The other boy grabbed back, and they started kissing—really kissing. They were locked.

Strangely, Gentillini did not cringe at this. Her mind flew, almost as if her life were flashing before her eyes. She instantly remembered a boy she knew in high school. She sat next to him in several classes through the years. She remembered wanting to touch him—desperately wanting just to touch his arm. And his hair. But she never said anything to him. Then she thought about a boy she knew in college. They were in the choir together. They ate lunch together in the cafeteria every day. They laughed and talked a lot. She wanted him to kiss her. But she never said anything for the three years that this continued. One day, he started dating another girl. Gentillini read the scriptures at their wedding.

Now, as she crouched and watched these two boys kiss, she was filled with frustration and rage. Of all the emotions that humans are capable of conjuring, jealousy must be the strongest. She had done everything right. She never showed even the slightest breach of decorum. She never came close to breaking the smallest of sexual sins. And how was she rewarded? With nothing but loneliness. Yet here were these two boys, committing the most disgraceful and abhorrent sin—but they were in each other's arms, the very opposite of loneliness.

"If I need to follow the rules," Gentillini said to herself, "then everyone needs to follow the rules."

CHAPTER 21

"This whole thing seems odd to me," Bernard Saint Clara said.

He walked with his wife across the grass of a city park. The grass was wet, and Bernard hated that his dress shoes were getting full of loose grass and dirt. There wasn't anyone else around, and the place seemed unsuitable to him.

"I've been asked to visit with Father at the church before, and I've even met with the sisters in the convent reception room. But why a picnic table in a deserted park? Doesn't seem right to me. Are you telling me there was no private space in the school where we could have met?"

"Bernard, please," Theresa said. "Sister Gentillini said that it's very important, something to do with John Paul, and she didn't want to start any gossip by having us show up at the convent. We need to do this for our son."

"You didn't tell me it had something to do with John Paul!" Bernard said with a raised voice. "Why didn't you tell me? Did you know about this? Is he in trouble?"

"I didn't tell you because I didn't want you to raise your voice," Theresa said. "Remember, she might be just a nun in our little convent, but she is still a holy woman and part of a religious order. She is just as concerned about John Paul as we are—maybe even more than us because she can be impartial."

By this time, they'd walked through a group of trees and saw Sister Gentillini, sitting at a picnic table. The table was old, wooden, and badly in need of paint. It was also bare. Gentillini had brought nothing with her. Bernard didn't want to even sit on the splintered bench, but he figured he had no choice when Theresa gladly sat down across from the nun.

"Hello, Sister," Theresa said.

"Sister," Bernard said.

"Thank you for coming," Gentillini said. "I apologize for the secrecy, but I didn't think we should speak on the phone, and I'm afraid the convent isn't a great place to meet. There are those there that might not like what I have to say, and gossip is a tool of Satan."

"Is John Paul in trouble?" Bernard asked. "I think he's a pretty good boy, but if he's done something, then let's get it out on the table."

"Yes, Mr. Saint Clara," Gentillini said. "I'm afraid that John Paul is in a lot of trouble. Very serious moral and spiritual trouble. But no, he's not in trouble at school, and nobody else knows."

"I know what it is," Theresa said.

"What?" Bernard said with shock.

Bernard really had no suspicion of why they'd been summoned to this meeting. He was beyond surprised that his wife could know something about his son that he did not. Of course, Theresa and he had worried together about John Paul playing for the other team, but surely, Theresa would never involve a nun in that.

"What's going on here?" Bernard said. "Don't beat around the bush. Just get to it."

"Just stay calm, Mr. Saint Clara," Gentillini said. "We will get through this. Remember, with the Lord, all things are possible. So I've been watching John Paul for some time. He's been leaving the school during Catholic youth group. I wasn't sure to where, and he has a few friends covering for him. But I discovered that he's been hanging around Carlson's Used Books and Records—you know, that bookstore just down the street from the church?"

"Yes, I know the bookstore," said Bernard. "He certainly does not have permission from either of us to be in there, especially when he's supposed to be doing service with you."

"I know that," Gentillini said, "and it gets worse. It appears that he has met a boy there, a boy from the public school. At first, I gave them all the benefit of the doubt. However, last night, I saw them, with my own eyes, kissing each other in the church courtyard. Right in front of the statue of Our Lady."

Silence. Bernard felt a darkness drop from his head all the way down his back. So this was all about John Paul playing for the other team—a team that Bernard despised.

"How can this be?" Bernard said. "You are certain of this? Right in public?"

"With my own two eyes," Gentillini said.

"And you said you knew?" Bernard asked as he turned to look at Theresa. "You knew he was with another boy? Theresa, how could you?"

"No, of course I didn't know he was with a boy," Theresa said. "I've had a suspicion that he was like this, that he had this affliction. You've had that suspicion too, Bernard. But Sister has just confirmed it, and now we must do something..."

Theresa started sobbing. She put her head on the table. Bernard scooted away from her on the splintered bench. He was disgusted and embarrassed by all of this.

"All right," Gentillini said, "stop that crying. It does nobody any good. Now that we know about it, we need to decide what to do about it. We must remember that this is not the act of John Paul. He is a soul created in God's image. We must remember that this is entirely the act of Satan. Only Satan could do such a terrible thing. Satan in the guise of a boy in a bookstore."

"It would be better if I had just been told that he had cancer," said Bernard. "Or that he was killed in a car accident. That would be so much easier."

"Stop that talk!" Gentillini yelled. "Think of what you are saying! It is not your right to take a life or even wish for one to be taken, even under these circumstances. John Paul, even with this affliction, is still a creation of the Lord. And the Lord will prevail over Satan. Remember, the Lord has said that if your arm is your sin, then cut it off! It's better to live without an arm than to risk not going to heaven. Don't you see? We must not throw out the whole boy. We must just cut out the part that is corrupt. We must eradicate the affliction."

"I know how," said Theresa in a soft voice. "I've already been working on it. I found a Catholic place that takes care of these things. The Freedom Center for Boys. I've talked with Joseph there. He can cure this. I'll call him again and arrange for John Paul to go there."

"I know of a place in Texas that does this sort of thing," Gentillini said.

"But that's so far," Theresa said. "Freedom Center for Boys is only a few hours away."

"I've never heard of it," Gentillini said. "Are you sure it's reputable?"

"I talked to a mother who had her son there," Theresa said. "He was cured of the affliction. Let me call back and talk to Joseph; he seemed like a wonderful, God-fearing man."

"No," said Gentillini. "You are too close. Satan will use a mother's love against the son every time. I will contact this center and make sure it is indeed Catholic. We don't want to make matters worse by sending him to some Protestant faux religion."

"Thank you, Sister," Theresa said. "I would appreciate that. I can't do it; I'm too tired of it all."

Bernard followed the conversation. He wondered how his life had come to this. How had he, Bernard Saint Clara—who had done everything right—come to talk about fixing his sinning son in a deserted park? And then the worst fear of all came over his body: the fear that the other men of the Knights of Columbus might find out about this. He was terrified of this possibility.

"Who else knows of this?" Bernard asked.

"I have suspicions that one girl knows," Gentillini said. "Sophia. We'll have to find a reason why John Paul is absent for a bit. Perhaps he went to spend time with some cousins or something? And also, Sister Gabriel Luke might know."

"What?" Bernard said. "A sister of your order might know about this? Will she tell others?"

"She might," Gentillini said. "She doesn't seem upset by it."

"You mean, she approves?" Bernard asked with disgust.

"The convent walls are holy," Gentillini said, "and they present a greater satisfaction to Satan when he breaches them. I will take care of both Sophia and Gabriel Luke. Rest assured—there will be no gossip on this account."

Bernard, purposefully ignoring his wife, reached across the table and grabbed both of Gentillini's hands. He held them firmly. He needed to put all of his faith into competent action and not crying hysterics.

"Sister, thank you," he said directly into her eyes. "You are our only hope. We will pray for you and for our son."

"I will contact this Joseph and let you know when we will transfer John Paul to his care. In the meantime, you must search your house for a book. It will be wrapped in a brown-paper cover that says either 'History' or 'Algebra.' Tear the cover off, and you will find a piece of garbage called *Ancient Pride*. We'll need that book when we take John Paul."

ANCIENT PRIDE

AN OLD TESTAMENT OF LOVE

This chapter presents, undoubtedly, the most controversial couple in the book. Nobody worships Antinous anymore, and very few, if any, consider Zeus the ultimate power in the universe. But David and Jonathan are a couple featured in the holy texts of both the Christian and Jewish faiths—religions that billions of people practice today. I have included their story in this book because Judea was a Mediterranean area that had many ties to Greece and Rome over its long history.

The story of David and Jonathan also presents a unique dichotomy because of its source material. This dichotomy has people divided into two distinct groups.

The first group of people are those who believe the Bible is the undisputed, literal word of God—their one God, known as Yahweh to the ancient followers. These people believe that it's incorrect to interpret the Bible; instead, they must believe in it entirely. But a problem presents itself in the two books of Samuel, part of the Old Testament. The Bible clearly states that David loved Jonathan more than any woman and that they kiss each other. The issue is that the words of the Bible do not match the narrative that the people in this group want to believe. So they feel it's okay to interpret this particular story to mean that David and Jonathan were just really, really good friends.

The second group of people are those who believe the Bible is a collection of myths, composed by regular humans, and translated thousands of times into hundreds of languages. They believe that the book is an allegory that must be read with many interpretations. However, the story of David and Jonathan *does* match their narrative. So this group feels that the story must be an example of a gay relationship.

Do you see the dichotomy? Those who believe the book don't believe the story. And those who believe the story don't believe the book.

Since I have no knowledge of the reader's personal beliefs, I will present the story and let you, the reader, decide. And even though we live in a world that forces people to choose between black and white, under my philosophy, you are free to think of this story as something between, if you like. Let's begin with the story of David and Jonathan, found in the two books of Samuel.

Long ago, the people of Judea were at war with the Philistines. Judea was part of an area south of modern-day Israel, and the Philistines lived between them and the Mediterranean Sea. The Judeans were ruled by King Saul. As the war continued to rage, the king became ill with melancholy. Basically, he became depressed. He wanted to find a distraction from his worries.

Nearby, King Saul's representative found a teenage shepherd boy who was quite a fine harp player. He could sing, tell stories, and even make up his own verses. The boy was named David, son of Jesse. David went to live in the court of King Saul and entertained him with his talent. During this era, having a person like David in your court was sort of like having a subscription to Netflix.

Saul's biggest problem was a particular Philistine man named Goliath. This was a giant of a man, literally. Goliath was huge, with bulging muscles and the strength of many ordinary men. He'd been terrorizing Judean villages for some time. Everyone wanted him stopped.

One day, Saul sent David to bring water to his soldiers on the front line of the war. While David was there, Goliath showed up. David, proving that one single young person can impact the course of history if they want it badly enough, took his slingshot. He grabbed a rock and sent it flying into Goliath. Goliath fell dead. David then chopped off his head and gave it to Saul. This brought David instant fame among all in Judea.

Now David was no dummy. He knew that fame was fleeting and that if he wanted to grab real power, he'd need to solidify his position within the royal family. Saul gave David permission to marry one of his daughters; however, he required David to prove his worth by killing one hundred Philistine men. Apparently, Goliath had not been enough. And to further prove that he had actually killed the Philistine men, David needed to bring Saul one hundred uncircumcised penises. David, being the overachiever that he was, came back to Saul with two hundred uncircumcised penises. I imagine the young David approached the throne and said something like, "Here is your bag of dicks, Your Highness." (To be fair to Saul, this request was not that unusual. In the ancient world, it was common for a soldier to provide proof of the number of enemy men he slaughtered by keeping their penises. In fact, the Egyptians at one time paid their warriors according to how many penises they collected in a given battle.)

So David was allowed to marry one of Saul's daughters and join the royal family. But as it turns out, David wasn't interested in the daughter. He was interested in Saul's son Jonathan. The Bible states in the first book of Samuel, "And it came to pass, when he had made an end of speaking unto Saul, that the soul of Jonathan was knit with the soul of David, and Jonathan loved him as his own soul (1 Samuel 18:1). And Johnathan had David reaffirm his vow out of love for him, because he loved him as he loved himself (1 Samuel 20:17)."

However, as it so often does, jealously reared its ugly head. The people of Judea could not stop talking about how wonderful David had become. Not only had he single-handedly killed Goliath but he had also killed two hundred Philistines to prove his loyalty to Saul. Many started to think that maybe David should be king. Of course, this angered Saul and sent him into a fury. He went to David and shouted terrible things at him. He even said that David's relationship with his son Jonathan was a disgrace. If the two men had really just been good friends, then why did Saul make the effort to demean their relationship?

Saul decided to have David killed. He went so far as to hire a few assassins. However, Jonathan found out about this plan. He quickly warned David, and the two of them fled into the countryside, where they lived in a cave.

After some time had passed, it appeared that Judea was once again under attack. Jonathan still felt loyalty to his people, and even to his father. So he decided to join the battle, even though David desired to stay away from it. David somehow knew that Jonathan was going to his death.

The Bible states that when Jonathan was ready to leave, David got up from the south side of the stone and bowed down before Jonathan three times, with his face to the ground. Then they kissed each other and wept together, but David wept the most. Jonathan said to David, "The Lord is witness between you and me, and between your descendants and my descendants forever (1 Samuel 20:41–42)."

Indeed, Jonathan was killed in battle, along with his father, King Saul. When David was informed of Jonathan's death, the Bible states that David said, "I am distressed for you, you have been very pleasant to me. Your love to me was more wonderful than the love of women (2 Samuel 1:26)."

Since David was the only one left standing from the royal family, he became mighty King David, arguably the most famous of all Hebrew kings. In fact, David is so revered that his bloodline was chosen to eventually produce the Messiah. Remember, Jesus was born in Bethlehem, the city of David, because Mary's husband, Joseph, had to return there since he was of the lineage of David. Yes, this does mean that David had children. He had multiple wives, at the same time, and fathered a child out of wedlock with the concubine Bathsheba.

Now we are left with the ultimate question: Were David and Jonathan gay? Unfortunately, there is no answer. Another question: Did David and Jonathan have a sexual attraction to each other? Well, you can look at the evidence and make a decision. Here is what we do know: David and Jonathan had an extraordinary relationship that was based on love. That relationship bothered Jonathan's father. When Jonathan died, David was sad. King David, despite having written about his love for another man, was revered enough that his bloodline produced Jesus Christ.

CHAPTER 22

It was the next Friday, two days after they'd kissed at the church. Jayme woke and turned over in his bed. He should have been excited and full of anticipation for his date with John Paul that night. Instead, he was sick. His head pounded with each labored beat of his heart. His bedroom was spinning. He needed to get to the bathroom. Fortunately, the door to his bathroom was right next to his bed.

He barely made it to the toilet; he vomited until all that was left were dry heaves. His stomach was queasy, and the muscles around his stomach were now sore. He crawled back into bed and used his cell phone to call his mom. She didn't answer. Jayme hoped she was still home. Then he heard her coming up the stairs.

"What's wrong?" Abygail asked as she entered his room.

"I don't feel good," Jayme said.

"Are you nauseous?" she asked. "Headache?"

"Yes," Jayme said. "How do you know?"

"Dr. Ramirez-Ogle said you'd get this way during the first couple of days."

"The first couple of days of what?" Jayme asked.

His head was spinning so much now that he closed his eyes and burrowed into his pillow.

"Of taking your hormones," she answered. "Remember? You'll feel a bit off for the first few days, but it will pass. The doctor said it would be like that. You just have to get through these first couple of days, and you'll feel so much better."

Jayme considered what she'd just said. He knew that he hadn't taken any of his hormones, as he'd been flushing them down the toilet. So he couldn't be sick from the medication. He didn't want to tell his mom that he hadn't taken the pills; he knew she'd be extremely upset. But at the same time, he had to tell her because there must be something else wrong with him. The only way for him to get help was to be honest.

"Mom," Jayme said softly, "I have to tell you something. I haven't taken any of the hormones. I don't want to. So I don't know why I'm sick now."

"I figured," Abygail said. "That's why I crushed a bunch of them and put them in your food for the last three days."

Jayme was frozen with shock. His brain strained to process this information. Jayme's mind was suddenly flooded with images of being younger, of his mom standing over him with a yardstick. Was she violating his body again?

He tried to decide how he should react. Was it okay for a mother to poison her son with medication he didn't want to take? Maybe. Maybe not. He couldn't decide what to do.

"Honey," Abygail said, "in a few days, you'll feel fine. And then you'll be happier than you've ever been because you'll feel more like your true self. Your outside will start to match your inside. You just don't know what's good for you because that's part of the problem. So I have to know what's good for you. I have to act to protect you from yourself."

"But I don't want to feel this way," Jayme said. "Can I talk to Dad?"

"Dad is very much in favor of this. Who do you think smashed up the pills?"

Jayme did not like how her tone had suddenly changed. He'd witnessed this before. He grew scared. Again, he thought of his younger self, lying on that same bed. He remembered his bedroom door and what they'd done to it.

"Listen, Jayme," she said harshly, "you are not going to screw this up for us. This is the life we want, and you will—*will*—help us get there. Your dad will be in Congress, and you will thank us when you get invited to the White House. Don't you want to live in Washington? Do you want to live in this dump Kaiserburg forever?"

Jayme lay on the bed, still not moving much. He just wanted someone to help him feel better. He had an urge to call Hunter. He slowly reached for his phone.

"I'll take that," Abygail said as she took the phone from Jayme's bed. "You don't need to call anyone right now. And don't worry; I'll turn off your internet so that you can get better without distraction."

Jayme gathered the strength to look up. His mom began to leave the room, then she turned. She walked over to his closet and the pile of clothes lying next to it.

"And these need to go!" Abygail shouted loudly.

She began grabbing hangers of clothes and throwing them on the hardwood floor. The hangers clacked against the floor and made Jayme cringe. He thought of the sound of the yardstick. He stuffed his face farther into his pillow.

"I don't want to see any of this stuff! I'll come back later with some trash bags, and we'll get rid of it together. You've got your new stuff to wear—your new stuff from the thrift store."

She walked toward the door.

"Oh and, of course, I'll bring your food at mealtime. Rest up because we need to join your dad onstage next week at a union fundraiser. It will be our family's unveiling. You need to be there, looking bright. I'll be back with your breakfast."

She left and closed the door. Jayme heard the sound of a large metal latch being slid on the other side of the door. He hadn't heard that terrible sound since he was a little boy. It made him shiver. He passed out in the bed.

CHAPTER 23

John Paul and his sister were always picked up in front of the Catholic school by their mother. She didn't want them riding the regular school bus, which was shared with students from the public school system. John Paul stood along the curb with many other students in their school uniforms, who were waiting for their family's SUVs to retrieve them. John Paul kept an eye out for his sister, and before long, she came across the lawn.

"Mom's coming to get you," Mary Clair said, coming up to him, "but I'm going home with Anna. See ya."

John Paul shrugged his shoulders at her, and she walked away. He didn't much care what she was doing because it was Friday. In a few short hours, he'd be baking bread with Sister Gabriel Luke and then rushing over to the bookstore to prepare for his evening with Jayme.

Even though he wanted to plan everything himself, he didn't have the freedom from his parents to do so. Instead, he enlisted the help of Gabriel Luke. She and Bob sometimes went onto the roof of the bookstore to look at stars. She suggested that John Paul take Jayme up there with a picnic dinner. While Gabriel Luke was making the bread dough, John Paul would assemble the picnic in the convent's kitchen.

Standing next to the curb, waiting for his mom, he was excited to get home, take a shower or two, and ask to go to the convent early to help Sister Gabriel Luke with the bread. But then he heard his name being called.

"Hey, John Paul," a girl about his age said as she walked up to him, "I have a message for you."

He recognized the girl as a friend of Sophia. He didn't know her name. She walked up to him in her Catholic-school uniform, holding her cell phone up. Again, he wished his parents would let him have one. Most of the other students, even in the Catholic school, had them.

"Hi," John Paul said. "A message for me? From who?"

"From Sophia," the girl said. "She knows you don't have a phone. Here it is: 'J wasn't in school today, and he didn't answer my call, probably sick.' That's it. Does it make sense to you? I hope so because I don't know anything else. And I don't know who J is."

The girl laughed. John Paul was saddened by the message, but he pretended to chuckle anyway.

"Yeah, it's fine," John Paul said. "Have a good weekend."

"You too," the girl said as she ran toward a school bus.

John Paul didn't have any real way of contacting Jayme. He hoped he was all right. There were many reasons that he might have missed school; he might not be sick at all. John Paul thought that the only thing he could do was continue with his plans. At the very least, he thought, Jayme would call Bob at the bookstore if something was really wrong. And Bob would tell Gabriel Luke.

John Paul hoped that Jayme wasn't ill. Some of the concern was that he never wanted to see Jayme uncomfortable. But most of the concern was because John Paul really wanted to see, and feel, Jayme next to him. John Paul realized it was selfish of him, but he couldn't help it. He couldn't stop thinking about the kiss in the church courtyard, and he wanted more.

At last, Theresa Saint Clara pulled up in their car. He got in.

"Your sister's going with Anna," Theresa said as he put on his seat belt.

"I know," John Paul said. "She told me."

He immediately sensed that something wasn't right. His heart began to beat just a bit faster. His mother's face looked pasty and whiter than normal. And she hadn't looked at him while he got in the car. Even when she was speaking about his sister, she kept her eyes straight ahead. He didn't say anything.

They pulled out of the parking lot and started down the street. They passed the bookstore. Then they took a left at the next intersection. This was not the way home.

"Where are we going?" John Paul asked.

"We have to make a stop," Theresa said robotically, still looking forward. "We will meet your father."

Now John Paul began to feel funny in his stomach. His instincts were telling him that something was definitely wrong. First was the news that Jayme might miss their date and now this. His mind was racing.

"Did I do something wrong?" he asked.

"We'll talk about it when we get there," Theresa answered.

As they drove, his heart beat faster. All he could think of was that they knew. They somehow knew. They knew he was gay. He wanted to jump out of the car.

They took a few more turns and then came to a stop along the edge of a city park. Theresa told him to leave his backpack in the car and to follow her. John Paul obeyed. He followed her around and through a bunch of tall pine trees. He saw his father standing next to an old picnic table.

Then he saw Sister Gentillini standing next to him. Her arms were folded up in her sleeves. A large cooking pot sat in the middle of the wood table. He'd seen this kind of pot before when the cooks served soup at school. But what was it doing here? However, there was a second item on the table, and it made his heart completely stop. It was a book. A torn brown-paper cover revealed that the book was titled *Ancient Pride*. Scraps of brown paper lay around it, including one scrap on which Fiona had written, "Advanced Algebra."

He turned and started to run, but his mother caught his arm. She yanked hard, with more strength than he'd imagined she'd have. She threw him to the ground. Now his father walked up to him, grabbed both his shoulders, and hoisted him to his feet.

"Sit!" Bernard yelled, pointing to the picnic table's bench.

John Paul immediately went to the bench and sat. He started to cry. The three adults stood around him and stared down. Nobody said anything for a long time. He just kept crying.

"Sister Gentillini," Bernard said, "why don't you tell John Paul what you saw last Wednesday?"

"I saw this boy," she began, "this boy, John Paul Saint Clara, kissing another boy in the courtyard of the Catholic church. In front of the statue of Our Lady."

"And I found this book in your bedroom," Theresa said.

John Paul sat frozen. He didn't know what to do. Should he deny it? How much did they know? What would happen to him now? He was in shock.

"Do you have anything to say?" Bernard asked.

John Paul just shook his head and looked at the ground. He stopped crying. He wanted, more than anything in the world, just to not be at that place at that time.

"We have found a place for you to go," Bernard said. "It's a place where they fix boys like you."

"You will find Christ there," Gentillini said.

John Paul looked up quickly. He was alarmed.

"I want to go home," John Paul said. "To my bed. Please. I promise I won't ever do anything like this again. You can watch me all the time if you want. I don't want to go away somewhere."

"It's too late for that," Theresa said.

"No," John Paul begged, "please, just let me take care of this on my own. I can do it; I promise. You can watch me. I know I can do it."

"You can't," Gentillini said. "Satan has ahold of you, and you need help. Trust us, John Paul. You can find Christ again, and you will be whole...and normal...in his image."

"A very nice man named Joseph is going to help you," Theresa said. "It's just for a few days. It's called the Freedom Center for Boys. It's in a nice house—not some kind of camp in the woods or anything scary. Trust us. This is for your best. And it's only a few hours away, so you'll be home quickly once you're better."

"And you don't have a choice," Bernard said harshly. "We need to stop talking like he has a choice. I'm his father. He's going, and it's final."

"What about school and my fr—"

"I am your father, and you are going! If I say there is no school and there are no friends, then that is the way it is."

His father wasn't making any sense. John Paul knew that this was a terrible sign. He'd never known his father to lose his composure. What would he be capable of if John Paul resisted?

"Sister Gentillini has kindly offered to take you," Bernard said. "You will go with her in the convent's car. You don't need to bring anything; everything you need will be there."

"But first," Gentillini said, "you must make an act of penance. Satan will not allow us to arrive safely unless you banish him with an act of true repentance. This book, *Ancient Pride*, is the most disgusting collection of words I've ever encountered. The author was surely guided by an evil hand. The smut she wrote about David and Jonathan is enough to make me fall on my knees and beg Christ to be forgiven that I had seen such words."

Gentillini took the book and dropped it, hard, into the pot. She bent down and reached into a bag lying on the ground. She retrieved a small bottle of lighter fluid, unscrewed the cap, and squirted a steady stream of the liquid into the pot. Then she bent down again and took a small box of matches from the bag. She gave the matches to John Paul.

"You must burn this book," Gentillini said, "as a sign that you want to be forgiven and that you want to change. You must admit that you have sinned a great sin in the eyes of the Lord."

John Paul looked at the box of matches. He thought about Achilles and Patroclus. He thought about the Sacred Band of Thebes. He thought of Antinous and Hadrian, of David and Jonathan. He thought of Jayme. He thought again of Jayme.

"Oh for heaven's sake," Gentillini said, frustrated.

She grabbed the matches from him, tore the box open, and forcefully took a match. She stroked it against the rough table. The match lit instantly. She snatched John Paul's right hand. While holding the match in her right hand, she used her left hand to smash his hand against hers. With their hands together, she dropped the match into the pot. It instantly went up in flames.

CHAPTER 24

Sister Gabriel Luke opened the flour bin in the convent's kitchen. She began scooping out cups of it into a large plastic bowl. Above the counter where she was working, a two-foot-tall statue of the Virgin Mary sat on a shelf fixed to the concrete-block wall. The statue was painted in full, bright colors. Gabriel Luke always liked this statue. It was more cheerful to look at than the other more sorrowful statues of Our Lady of Seven Dolors spread around the church campus.

She didn't need any yeast. Bread for Catholic Communion was supposed to be the same as the bread that Jesus offered during the Passover meal. Since the Hebrews of the first Passover didn't have time to wait for yeast to rise, all bread made in remembrance of that event was unleavened.

Gabriel Luke looked at a clock that was fixed to a wall directly across from the Virgin Mary. She noticed that John Paul was late. She kept working.

Earlier that afternoon, she'd seen Sister Gentillini leaving in the convent's car. Gabriel Luke didn't know where she was going and hoped that she wasn't going to be back for dinner. The nuns ate their dinner late, after evening prayers. Gentillini often dominated that conversation by speaking about whatever modern atrocity she'd witnessed that day. Gabriel Luke hoped for a nice, quiet conversation without her. But then she realized that she wasn't being very charitable to Gentillini, so she said a quick prayer.

Time went on. Gabriel Luke was now covered with flour as she finished kneading an enormous mound of dough on the counter. She checked the clock and realized that John Paul was almost an hour late. This was not in his character, nor in his mother's. The Saint Clara family was always on time. She went to a large stainless steel sink and washed her hands and arms.

A telephone connected to an old landline sat on a small table in the corner of the kitchen. A directory of all the homes in the parish of Our Lady of Seven Dolors was curled up next to the phone. The directory was old and stained. But the Saint Claras were an old family and would be listed. She located the correct number and dialed it. There wasn't any answer. She knew that John Paul did not have a cell phone, but the parents surely did. But she didn't know any other numbers and gave up.

She was about to walk back to the dough when she decided to give Bob a call. Perhaps John Paul went directly to the bookstore for some reason. She knew his number by heart.

"Carlson's Used Books and Records," Bob's familiar voice said when he answered the call. "How can I help you?"

"Hi, Bob," she said. "It's Gabs. Is John Paul over there?"

"No, not that I've seen," Bob replied. "Just a minute."

Gabriel Luke could hear Bob yell something at Fiona. She heard Fiona yell back.

"Nope," Bob said. "Fiona hasn't seen him either."

"Hmm," Gabs said. "He's never late. He had a whole plan for tonight, and he's not here. Is Jayme there?"

"No," Bob said, "but I wouldn't expect him until about now, so he's not all that late. Why? Do you think something is wrong?"

"No, of course not. I just...well, something just feels off. Like there's something not right with the universe."

She thought for a few moments in silence.

"Bob," Gabs said, "do you think we made a mistake in all of this? I mean with getting those two guys together?"

"Well," Bob said, "there wasn't much *we* to it. It was mostly me."

"Yes, I was trying to be nice. Do you think you made a mistake? Pushing these guys together?"

"I didn't have to do much pushing. Neither did Fiona. We just helped a little."

"Or," said Gabs, "a lot?"

"Are you concerned about something, Gabs? What do you think is going on?"

"I guess I'm concerned about John Paul's parents. They are extremely conservative Catholics, Old Catholics, the kind of Catholics that liked things better when Masses were in Latin and women had to cover their heads to attend them. Maybe this is all too much for John Paul."

"Maybe that's exactly why we *had* to do something, Gabs. That poor kid was jumping out of his skin when he saw Jayme. In my view, it was torturing him to let him go on like that— abuse, really. Aren't we here to help those we can? That boy was suffering, and so was Jayme; I could tell. I wouldn't let a boy and girl suffer that way if I thought their parents would disapprove of their relationship, so why should it be different for two boys?"

Gabs thought for a moment, and said, "That's a pretty good point. Well, we can't change anything now. Wait a second…"

Another nun, an older nun who walked extremely slowly, came into the kitchen with a note for Gabriel Luke. The nun bowed a little when she handed the note to her. Gabriel Luke took this bow as a sign that the older nun was in the middle of a vow of silence. She bowed back, and the older nun slowly left the room. Gabs read the note.

"Okay," Gabs said, "I just got a message that was left for me from John Paul's mom. It turns out that he went to spend the weekend with his cousin and won't be making bread with me tonight."

"Do you know what *deus ex machina* means?" Bob asked.

"Yes, Bob," Gabs said. "Even as a nun, I can still read pagan Greek drama. *Deus ex machina* is a term from Greek theater. It is used to explain when something happens at just the right moment of the story to move the story forward, even if it's too coincidental to be real."

"Don't you think," Bob said, "it's a bit deus ex machina that you got that note just at the perfect time while talking to me?"

"One person's deus ex machina is another person's sign from God," Gabs said. "And God always knows the right moment. Something isn't right. I don't buy this cousin thing about John Paul. Listen, I'm going to finish baking this bread because, well, what else am I going to do? But if you or Fiona hear anything about either of those boys, you need to call me right away."

"There's a million reasons not to worry, Gabs," Bob said. "We're talking about teenagers. They probably already had a big fight and have sworn not to see each other ever again.

I don't think we need to worry about anything. But yes, I will let you know if we hear anything."

"Thank you, Bob. Have a good night," Gabs said.

She hung up the phone.

"A million reasons to worry?" Gabs said aloud to the Virgin Mary on the wall. "How about one more? Gentillini never drives the car—she never has anywhere to go."

CHAPTER 25

Hunter was bored. He was lying on his bed, tired of gaming and without any ambition to do anything else. It was Friday night, and he had absolutely nothing to do. He hadn't been on a long run for a few days. He wondered where his running sweats with reflective stripes were. If he could find them, he'd go for a nice long run. But in order to find them, he'd have to get off the bed.

His phone rang.

"Saved by the bell," he said out loud.

He looked at the phone and saw that it was Jayme's new friend Sophia. Hunter didn't know how her number had even been programmed into his phone. He considered that Jayme might have put it in there, hoping to connect the two of them.

"Hey," Hunter said when he answered.

"Hi, Hunter," Sophia said. "It's Sophia—you know, Jayme's friend."

"Oh yeah," he replied coolly. "What's up?"

"Have you talked to Jayme today?" she asked. "He wasn't in school."

"Yeah," Hunter said, "he sent me a text and said that he's sick. He just wants to sleep for a few days."

"Oh, okay," Sophia said. "I tried to call him two times, and he didn't answer. He should have sent me a text too. Rude."

"Yeah, well," Hunter said, "I called a bunch of times and left messages. I didn't get the text until tonight. He must be really sick; it's not like him. I'll see how he's doing tomorrow."

"I guess I was concerned because…well, it's Friday, and he's got a date with John Paul. You know that I know John Paul, right? You know who John Paul is, right?"

"Yeah, I know all about it. It's all Jayme ever talks about anymore."

"Well, I can't get ahold of John Paul either. He doesn't have his own phone because his parents are weird, but nobody answers at his house. It's weird because I had a friend deliver a message that Jayme wasn't in school today. I was really expecting John Paul to call me right away, but he never did."

"Are you sure John Paul got the message?" Hunter asked.

"Yeah," Sophia replied, "my friend read it to him right outside of school. Anyway, that's what she told me."

Hunter suspected that Sophia liked him. He didn't quite know why, because they hung around with completely different sets of people. But he knew that he wasn't unattractive, and he could tell when a girl was looking at him.

"Hey, Sophia, do you want to go get something to eat?" Hunter asked.

"Ah, I can't," she said. "I'm going to hang out with some friends."

"Ditch them," Hunter said. "We can talk about Jayme and John Paul. It will be like community service."

Hunter recognized that was an odd thing to say; it didn't make any sense. But he'd said it.

"Okay," she said. "I'll see what I can do and call you back."

She ended the call. Hunter sighed when he realized that he'd now have to get off his bed.

Down the street from Hunter, Jayme attempted once again to open his bedroom door. Not only was the door firmly secured, but pushing on it also made him feel sicker than he already was. While the dizziness and nausea had stopped, Jayme's body ached, and he was exhausted. His anxiety level wasn't helping either.

He went back to bed and pulled the blankets up around him. He tried to be as still as possible to calm his body. His thoughts went back to his childhood. Jayme remembered being trapped in the same room, but instead of his body aching from medication, it was sore from being beaten with a yardstick.

The hard truth that he was trying to reconcile in his mind was the fact that he loved his parents. He'd known from a very young age—as long as he could remember—that he was different from most other boys. His parents always supported him. They fought for him. They celebrated the fact that their son was gay. They also encouraged his passion for old movies and music. If he set aside his mother's erratic temper and his father's complicity, he'd have had a perfect childhood.

He wondered if it would have been better to have grown up like John Paul in a religious house. Sure, he would have been abused emotionally instead of physically, but at least he'd have a heaven to believe in. And most of all, he'd have received a lot more sympathy from those around him.

It had been difficult for Jayme to hear about how wonderful his parents were all the time. He was constantly reminded—by teachers, friends, and family—how lucky he was to have such supportive and Progressive parents.

It was easy to condemn the religious parents because their abuse was so apparent. Jayme was frustrated that others couldn't see what he saw in the supposed "parents of the year" who cared for him.

He began to realize that he wasn't only attracted to John Paul for the way he looked. Jayme was also looking for someone to show him how to believe in something that brought comfort in the night. He wasn't, and would never be, ready for the entire Jesus-loving fanatical package. But he could benefit from some of the peace that it represented.

Peace could only come, though, if he wasn't living in his house. He resolved that he must get better, he must find a way to leave the house, and he must see where his relationship with John Paul may lead. He fell asleep thinking about all these things.

CHAPTER 26

Neither John Paul nor Sister Gentillini said anything during their car trip to the Freedom Center for Boys. John Paul sat in the front passenger seat of the convent's sedan. He was extremely nervous, and Gentillini's driving wasn't helping the matter. She seemed anxious, taking curves faster than she should. He wondered if she really knew how to drive correctly. John Paul was getting carsick but didn't dare complain or ask for her to pull over. He did not feel safe around Sister Gentillini and wanted to just get wherever they were going. But when he thought about it more, he didn't want to go there either. He was confused, sad, and worried.

They drove out of Kaiserburg on the main highway and continued through a rural area for over two hours. Gentillini wasn't using any type of navigation technology. John Paul assumed she had studied the route. She must have been fully prepared. He wondered why she cared so much and if she was getting some perverse joy out of his turmoil.

John Paul, with his analytical mind, had always loved maps. He also had a great sense of direction. Consequently, he knew exactly where they were. He paid careful attention to each turn and each passing town. His parents told him he would only be away for a few days, probably just the weekend.

He hoped he could believe them. But if not, he felt better knowing where he was on the map.

Then a strange question entered his mind: Did he want this to work? On one hand, life would be easier if he weren't gay. His parents would be so much happier—and infinitely prouder. He could become a doctor, like he'd always wanted. He could marry a nice Catholic woman and have nice Catholic kids. He could be a trustee of the parish and a member of the Knights of Columbus. And best of all, he could go to heaven.

But on the other hand, there was Jayme. Gay people could get married now. They could find a way to have kids. And John Paul could still be a doctor. But there would be no parents, no church to turn to for support, and no heaven. But he'd learned from *Ancient Pride* that he'd been lied to about history. Maybe he'd been lied to about heaven. Perhaps he wouldn't need parents and the church if he had the Sacred Band of Thebes behind him.

Suddenly, he realized something. When he imagined a life with a woman, he was seeing it in tones of sepia—like an old black-and-white movie. But when he imagined life with Jayme, he was seeing it in full Technicolor. He wondered why this phenomenon occurred in his mind. It must be some sort of sign. He hoped so.

Eventually, the roads became smaller as they turned through a rural area. Sister Gentillini began to drive quite slowly until she saw a gravel road with a broken-down mailbox next to it. She turned left onto the gravel road. The sun had now completely set. John Paul should be sitting with Jayme on the roof of the bookstore. Instead, the convent car bounced around a bunch of ruts for about a quarter of a mile.

They came to an odd two-story house. The front looked like an old farmhouse from decades ago. John Paul saw that the exterior had areas of old, weathered siding and other areas of unfinished plywood sheets. He was expecting the Freedom Center for Boys to look more institutional and, well, larger.

The gravel road became the driveway of the home. There wasn't a garage. There was a large outdoor light on top of an electrical pole just beside the house. John Paul couldn't see much, but what he couldn't see probably wasn't much either.

Gentillini pulled the car right up to the front of the house. When it stopped, she switched off the ignition and opened her door. John Paul opened his and stepped out.

He had nothing except the clothes he was wearing— his school uniform. He had no phone, no toothbrush. No books, underwear, pajamas, or anything that might bring him comfort.

Three rickety wood steps, badly in need of paint, led up to the front door. But as they were walking toward them, the door opened, and a man stepped out. He was tall and skinny, about the same age as John Paul's grandfather, and he had gray facial hair that was trimmed short. He wore jeans and a plaid-flannel shirt. He didn't look too unkind. In fact, John Paul thought he wasn't bad looking at all.

"Welcome," the man said. "You must be Sister Gentillini."

"I am," Gentillini said, "and you must be Joseph."

"Yes," Joseph said, "and this here must be our very special boy, John Paul. Jesus loves you, John Paul."

As he was saying this, Joseph walked quickly up to John Paul and wrapped his arms around him in a tight embrace. John Paul felt awkward during the hug; he would have preferred a handshake.

"Remember, John Paul," Joseph said, "Jesus loves you and wants you to join him in heaven. Together, we will make that happen. Sister, I'm sorry to be so rushed and send you on your way, but you have quite a journey home to make. I'm sure you understand."

"Of course," Gentillini said.

She turned and walked back to the car. John Paul thought that she would at least want to see the inside of the place. Didn't she have any paperwork that she had to do in order to drop him off? She didn't say anything to John Paul. No words of wisdom, no encouragement, no calming prayer—the only person within one hundred miles whom John Paul actually knew just got in a car and left.

"Come on in," Joseph said. "It's dark out here."

Joseph grabbed John Paul's arm, just a little too tightly, and brought him up the stairs and through the front door. It was indeed just a regular house. A living room sat off to their right, and John Paul could see down a hall and into an open kitchen. A staircase ran up the wall to their left.

The house was in a state of renovation. Half of the walls were exposed without Sheetrock or drywall, and half were complete. There was a stack of large white pipes in the living room, next to an old couch. Several electric tools sat on the floor around the couch. The kitchen looked like it was in the same state.

However, it was what John Paul didn't see, or hear, that alarmed him. The house was completely silent. It was after dark, but not nearly late enough for the other boys to be in bed. In fact, there was no sign that there were other boys at all. There was no garage, yet there were no other vehicles sitting in the yard. And now that John Paul thought about it, there hadn't even been a physical sign outside that read, "Freedom Center for Boys."

"Are we here alone?" John Paul asked.

Joseph didn't say anything. He grabbed John Paul's shirt-sleeve and led him up the stairs. John Paul didn't have much choice but to follow up the unfinished steps.

"You'll find everything you need in your room," Joseph said. "I've put a sandwich in there for you since you missed dinner. Just wait until tomorrow; we will have some good meals here."

He led John Paul through the first door at the top of the stairs. John Paul didn't have a chance to see what other rooms looked like on that floor.

Joseph flicked on the light to John Paul's room. John Paul's mood went from anxious to beyond depressed. A large piece of wood paneling had been nailed over the room's only window. There was a single bed along one of the bare off-white walls. An orange jumpsuit, like the kind that inmates wear, was spread out on the bed. On a small nightstand next to the bed, there was a plate with a sandwich on it. The wood floor was unfinished, and a light bulb without a fixture hung from the ceiling.

"You're real lucky," Joseph said. "I just finished the plumbing in here today, so you have your own toilet and sink. I know they're not much, but it beats having to share. And it's much better than having to go downstairs all the time."

John Paul saw a very old toilet sitting in the corner of the room—without any sort of wall or partition around it. A sink, stained with many brown rings, sat next to it on a wobbly pedestal base. However, all the PVC piping connecting the fixtures was new and sparkling white.

"Go ahead and eat, John Paul," Joseph said. "You'll sleep naked and wear the jumpsuit during the day. So go ahead and strip off your clothes. I'll take them with me."

John Paul panicked. He definitely did not want to do this. He stood very still.

"Oh, no problem," Joseph said. "This isn't a prison. Just throw your school clothes on the floor, and I'll get them tomorrow. I'll see you bright and early in your jumpsuit. Good night."

"Wait," John Paul said. "How will I know when to wake up? And what if I get thirsty?"

"Oh," Joseph said with a laugh, "you'll know when to wake up! Don't worry about that! We get an early start around here, and you won't be able to sleep through it. There's a cup on the sink for you to use if you get thirsty. Now sleep well. We have a lot of work to do tomorrow."

Joseph left and closed the door. John Paul heard the sound of a lock turning, but he checked the door anyway. It was locked. He slumped to the floor and clasped his hands together. He started to pray. But for the first time in his life, he didn't pray to Jesus, Mary, God, or even any one of the thousands of Catholic saints. Instead, he said aloud, "Whoever is out there—I need help."

He cried himself to sleep on the floor.

CHAPTER 27

Sister Gentillini pulled into the convent's garage just after seven o'clock in the morning. She was angry that she'd missed morning prayers because it meant the other nine nuns of the convent would know she hadn't come home. But she also knew that none of them would ask where she'd been; they were taught to live in trust. Although Gentillini didn't know if this unwritten standard would be followed by Sister Gabriel Luke.

She would have been back in plenty of time—she should have arrived hours ago—but she felt so tired at one point during the drive that she had to pull over and park in a small-town Catholic-church parking lot. She wasn't accustomed to driving. She fell fast asleep and didn't wake up until the sun was already up.

There was no door on the convent's garage. It was more like a carport built entirely out of large stones. The convent was almost one hundred years old, and in those days, the Catholics built out of brick and stone.

The nuns always used the rear door to the convent, which was the most convenient to get to the church and school. Only visitors to the convent used the front door facing the street. Because the rear door led past the dining room, Gentillini decided to go around to the front in order to avoid any nun who was still eating breakfast. She walked on the asphalt driveway back around the building. When she got to the front door, she noticed that some sort of brochure had been shoved into the side of the door. She made an audible grumble as she took the brochure, folded it, and put it in her pocket. Gentillini hated all kinds of litter and unwanted items put in her space. She hated all unwarranted intrusions into her life.

She opened the door and walked into the convent's small reception room. A nun was sitting in there, reading a prayer book. They nodded at each other. Gentillini walked through a small hallway. Contrary to popular belief, convents did have mirrors, and the nuns were free to look into them. She looked at herself in a mirror that was halfway down the hall. As she was the one nun out of the ten in the convent who still wore a black veil, she wanted to make sure it was on straight, as if she'd just gotten dressed. She was glad she checked because her veil had been a complete mess. She fixed it.

She turned onto a small landing that led to a staircase. There, she saw Sister Gabriel Luke coming down the stairs. Gentillini frowned. There was no way to avoid her.

"Oh, Sister," Gabriel Luke said, "I was looking for you. Were you here last night?"

Gentillini was offended at Gabriel Luke's lack of propriety, trust, and respect. She looked at her silently.

"I apologize, Sister," Gabriel Luke said. "I'm sorry to breach your confidence. It's just that I wanted to use the car last night, and I heard that you had it. I was worried that something was wrong since you were out all night. And I don't remember that you've ever driven so late at night before. I don't remember if you've ever driven at all."

"Everything is quite normal," Gentillini replied. "Thank you for your concern."

Gentillini started to walk up the stairs. She turned her body sideways to scoot past Gabriel Luke.

"It's just that," Gabriel Luke said, "I wanted the car to check on a student, John Paul Saint Clara. You see, he didn't show up to help me bake bread like we had arranged, and I was concerned. I was going to drive over to his house. It's not like him to even be late, let alone not show up at all."

Gentillini stopped on the second to the top stair. What was Gabriel Luke playing at? Did she suspect something? Why was she asking specifically about John Paul?

"I wonder that you didn't just call the Saint Claras on the phone," Gentillini said.

"Oh I did, but there wasn't any answer. It was unlike John Paul."

"Well, I'm sure his parents know where he is."

"Yes, of course," Gabriel Luke said. "They did eventually send a message. It turns out that he went to visit his cousin."

"So everything is fine then?" Gentillini asked.

"Yes," Gabriel Luke replied. "Have a good day."

Gentillini didn't respond. She just walked directly to her cell and closed the door behind her. The other nuns referred to their bedrooms as simply "rooms," but Gentillini liked to use the term *cell* since that is how the nuns of old thought. Her cell contained a comfortable single bed, a dresser, a private bathroom with shower, a small desk with chair, and a statue of Our Lady of Seven Dolors sitting on a shelf that was hanging on the wall.

She continued to wonder about Gabriel Luke when she started to undress. She wanted to get into fresh clothing. As she took off her long, dark skirt, she felt the brochure from the front door in her pocket. She took it and threw it in the trash can next to her dresser. She began to take off her veil.

Then a photo on the brochure caught her eye. It was a picture of the same boy who was in the photograph with John Paul Saint Clara. She bent over and retrieved the brochure. She took a closer look at it.

Yes, she was convinced it was the same boy who'd had his arm around John Paul. And it was the same boy whom John Paul was kissing in the church courtyard. She read the brochure. The boy was Jayme Smith-Johnson, child of Sammy and Abygail. Sammy was campaigning for Congress. He was advertised as a Progressive liberal in favor of abortion and public schools. Gentillini discovered that the boy, Jayme, was actually a transgender teenager in the middle of transition. Sammy and Abygail Smith-Johnson were very much in favor of the transition and wrote how proud they were of their child.

Perhaps the Saint Clara boy was more innocent than she initially thought. Perhaps he'd been corrupted. Yes, he still had free will to choose, but maybe the right choice had been harder to see than Gentillini thought. She couldn't tolerate the Smith-Johnson family. They were the very worst kind of people and were destroying a culture of decency. They obviously had no fear of the Lord. Wasn't it enough that they had to corrupt their own child? Why did they have to go after a nice Catholic boy like John Paul?

Gentillini shook her head, took the brochure, and walked over to her desk. She sat down and got some paper out of a drawer. She grabbed a pen. She began to write in her customary beautiful penmanship. Nobody had ever accused Sister Gentillini of illegible writing.

Dear Mr. and Mrs. Johnson,

*Please refrain from distributing your campaign
filth to the good people of Kaiserburg. It is not
welcome. I know for a fact that your son has
corrupted other boys he has recruited into his
perverse lifestyle. What you do in your own home
is your business, but it becomes my business when
you advertise it in a brochure and place it on my
door. And it's my business when I personally know
a good, God-fearing boy that your son perverted.
It's shameful.*

*We, the good people of Kaiserburg, will not
tolerate any recruitment among our young people.
Keep your trans-whatever away from our children.
I will say a prayer for you because you need it.*

*Sincerely,
A concerned citizen*

Sister Gentillini had written many political letters before,
mostly about the issues of abortion and school choice. She
was well aware that all candidates must file their correct
residential address with the state's office of elections. This
was a piece of public knowledge that she'd easily obtain.

She said aloud, "We'll see how they like coming home to
find a paper stuck in their door."

ANCIENT PRIDE

THE GREATEST LOVE

Throughout history, there have been many great military leaders. From world wars to the American Civil War, from the Crusades to the Napoleonic Wars, armies have been led by dynamic and successful commanders. The Romans alone gave us at least a dozen such leaders. But none of them reigned as high as Alexander the Great. Nobody conquered as much in as little time while earning the admiration of so many.

This chapter is absolutely real. Alexander the Great was so famous that his life was documented by eyewitnesses and historians. We have many accounts of what he did, why he did it, and whom he did it with. We have statues of his likeness from places all around the Mediterranean.

Alexander was born in 356 BC to the King of Macedon, an area to the north of Greece. When he was thirteen years old, he was sent to study with the philosopher Aristotle. While at Aristotle's school, ancient historians tell us, Alexander had sexual relationships with a few other boys. We even know the names of some of these boys. (It should be noted that at age thirteen, Alexander was considered to be old enough for sexual activity.) Then one day, he met another boy around the same age as himself. This boy was named Hephaestion. They were together every day after that.

In their early years, they studied the Greek language, philosophy, drama, and mathematics. They also trained in the arts of warfare and statesmanship. As they turned into young men, Hephaestion became indispensable as Alexander's chief aide. Hephaestion chose who could see the young prince of Macedon, briefed Alexander every day on world events, and even screened his mail.

At this time, they also started a relationship. Ancient historian Claudius Aelianus wrote that "Hephaestion was the object of Alexander's love." It was no secret that Alexander disliked sexual intercourse with women; many writers wrote of this knowledge. However, he did marry (more than once) and had at least two children. We can assume this was more out of an obligation to the throne than out of love. According to the historian Arrian, Alexander arranged for his first wife's sister and Hephaestion to get married. He did this so "that Hephaestion's children should be joined in affinity with his own."

While they were establishing themselves as competent military leaders, and before Alexander's father died, the two men found themselves at the Battle of Chaeronea. As we learned in an earlier chapter of this book, this is where Alexander was given the task of defeating the Sacred Band of Thebes, the Theban army made of 150 gay couples. After studying past battles at which the Sacred Band was victorious, Alexander and Hephaestion devised a successful plan to eliminate the elite army forever.

I wonder how they felt after defeating the Sacred Band. On one hand, the famous band was considered unbeatable.

Alexander and Hephaestion must have felt great satisfaction in their victory. However, their victory came at the expense of killing not only three hundred amazing warriors but also killing 150 couples who lived in the same love as Alexander and Hephaestion. We know that, unlike other defeated soldiers, the Sacred Band of Thebes was given an honorable burial, and their bodies were treated with great reverence. Alexander, his father Philip, and Hephaestion were seen paying homage to the dead members of the Sacred Band by several eyewitnesses. It was recorded that King Philip II wept profusely at the grave site and declared, "Perish any man who suspects that these men did or endured anything shameful." Philip and Alexander ordered that a giant stone lion be carved and placed at the grave site. The lion still stands there today.

Alexander became King of Macedon when his father died. He then eventually became king of…well, everything. Hephaestion was always at his side. After he conquered and united Greece, he traveled to Egypt. There, he defeated the Egyptians, removed their pharaoh, and took control of the country. He ordered that the Egyptians build a city for him, called Alexandria, on the Mediterranean coast. Hephaestion helped to create the first street plan for the city.

Alexander loved Egyptian culture and wanted to be considered the Egyptian pharaoh. He and Hephaestion journeyed to the Egyptian city of Siwa and visited a well-known group of prophet-priests. They rode up to the temple at Siwa with all their armies. The two men made sure that the priests saw the massive gathering of soldiers, each holding a sword. Alexander asked the priests if they could consult the gods and tell him anything that would justify his claim to the Egyptian throne.

The priests looked at all the soldiers and weapons and said something like, "Oh yeah…it seems you are Egyptian. We've just heard from Amun-Ra, our main god, that you aren't the son of Philip II of Macedon. In fact, your mother had sex with Amun-Ra himself, and he is your true father. You are a god." Alexander and Hephaestion must have been thrilled.

From Egypt, Alexander conquered throughout the rest of Northern Africa and the Middle East. Somewhere in Persia, he captured the Persian royal family. The historian Arrian wrote that one day Alexander and Hephaestion went to visit the captured queen of Persia.

Now while Alexander received all the fame, Hephaestion was supposedly taller and better looking. The queen thought that Hephaestion was Alexander, and she bowed deeply before him. When the mistake was revealed, the queen was horrified at making this mistake. (In the ancient world, queens were executed for far less.) But instead, Alexander laughed and said that "her error was of no account, for Hephaestion, too, was an Alexander."

Many writers of the era wrote about Alexander's obsession with *The Iliad*, the epic poem about the Trojan War. He believed that he was the new Achilles and often called Hephaestion by the name Patroclus. We are told that Alexander slept with a copy of *The Iliad* under his pillow. While in the Middle East, Alexander and Hephaestion traveled to the site of Troy on what is now the coast of Turkey. They were shown a place where the local people believed that Achilles and Patroclus had been buried in the same urn. Alexander laid a wreath there in honor of Achilles, and Hephaestion did the same for Patroclus.

Perhaps my favorite written account of the relationship of Hephaestion and Alexander is from the ancient Greek philosopher Diogenes. He wrote that Alexander loved only Hephaestion, and they were together, intimately, until the day they died. He wrote, "Alexander was only defeated once, and that was by Hephaestion's thighs."

Unfortunately, Hephaestion acquired a fever when he was just thirty-two years old. Alexander sent for a doctor named Glaucias. We don't know exactly what kind of fever he had, but most likely it was something like typhoid fever. Hephaestion, under Glaucias's care, improved. So Glaucias went to the theater. Hephaestion ate a boiled chicken with wine, felt sick again, and died.

The events surrounding Hephaestion's death are told to us by the historians Plutarch and Arrian. Apparently, Alexander flung himself over Hephaestion's body and stayed like that for three days. He didn't sleep, eat, or drink—he didn't even get up to use the facilities. He spent his time either wailing loudly or staring at nothing with the silence of grief. (Sound familiar? If not, please reread the chapter about Achilles and Patroclus.)

Alexander ordered that Glaucias be executed. He ordered that the temple of Asclepius, the Greek god of medicine, be burned to the ground. In the city of Babylon, he built the largest funeral pyre anyone had ever seen. He ordered that the Egyptians build a massive shrine to Hephaestion in the city of Alexandria. Last, he organized the greatest funeral games that had ever been held by bringing three thousand Greek men to Babylon to compete in athletics, music, and literature.

Historians tell us that the funeral pyre itself cost ten thousand talents. In today's money, that would be about

$200,000,000! The pyre was sixty meters high and was built out of wood and solid gold. Giant red banners hung on its sides, and there was a space inside for a choir to sing a lament. (Hopefully the choir was able to leave before the pyre was burned, but in the ancient world, it would not surprise me if they weren't.)

Arrian wrote, "Hephaestion's death had been no small calamity, and I believe Alexander would have rather been the first to go than live to suffer that pain, like Achilles, who surely would rather have died before Patroclus than to have lived to avenge his death."

A few short months after Hephaestion's death, Alexander caught a fever and died. The greatest military leader the world had ever known died from a simple illness. I believe his spirit was so weakened with the grief of Hephaestion that he had no fight left in him.

That is the end of our story. But now I have an assignment for you. Go back and reread this entire chapter. However, this time, whenever you see that name, "Hephaestion," replace it with "Diana." You will soon discover that there can be no doubt about the relationship between Alexander and Hephaestion. If Hephaestion had been a woman, their love story would give us the greatest power couple in all of history. Hollywood would have made sweeping dramas about their passionate love. There would be statues of them embracing in every museum in Europe. But because Hephaestion and Alexander were of the same gender, we have none of that.

We know that Alexander's body, because he was the pharaoh of Egypt, was taken to Alexandria. He was mummified and entombed in an alabaster sarcophagus visited by thousands of people over hundreds of years. It is well documented that Cleopatra often prayed at Alexander's tomb, and she once brought along her lover Julius Caesar. Alas, the tomb was lost to history and has never been discovered.

We don't know where Hephaestion's ashes were laid to rest. It's my hope that, one day, an adventurous archaeologist will discover the tomb of Alexander somewhere beneath the modern city of Alexandria. I hope that when the sarcophagus is found, Alexander's mummified body will be holding an urn...an urn full of the ashes of love.

CHAPTER 28

Jayme woke up, turned his head slightly, and saw light coming through his bedroom window. He assumed it was Saturday morning. He took a deep breath and realized that he felt better than he had the day before. His head wasn't spinning anymore, and his stomach wasn't queasy. But he was very, *very* hungry.

When he turned over in bed, his copy of *Ancient Pride* slid off the covers and landed on the floor. He had read the chapter about Alexander the Great during the night, hoping it would help him relax. However, when the book fell, it landed in such a way that a chunk of pages in the middle was folded back. Jayme groaned and ignored it, leaving the book lying there. He did not feel much like Alexander the Great this morning.

He recalled that he'd been in and out of consciousness throughout the night and previous day. He remembered seeing his mom enter the room with a bowl every now and then. He remembered seeing her throw clothes into black trash bags. He remembered her telling him to eat to feel better.

He propped himself up in his bed. There were two bowls of something, with spoons, on his nightstand. There were also two bottles of Gatorade. He smelled the bowls. They were full of chocolate pudding. He was extremely thirsty, but when he examined the Gatorade bottles, he discovered that the seals had been broken on each of them.

He slowly sat up. Aside from the hunger and the thirst, he was doing okay. He got up and went into his bathroom. He put his mouth on the sink's faucet and drank directly from the tap. Then he went back to bed.

Jayme didn't know what he wanted or what he should do. But he did know that he did not want to take any more hormones. Just looking at the chocolate pudding and Gatorade made him gag.

He wanted to talk to Hunter. Once again, he got out of bed. He went to his laptop that was sitting on a desk. There wasn't any internet service available. He checked the settings. Someone must have changed the Wi-Fi passcode. He checked his gaming unit hooked up to a nearby TV. Same problem: no internet.

He looked out of his window. His room was on the second floor, on a side of the house facing a neighbor. The neighbors were an older couple who were friendly with his parents. Perhaps they might help if he could yell at them. But what then? His parents would be furious, and there was no proof that he'd been mistreated. Then Jayme saw something that completely removed the neighbors from the equation.

In their front lawn, right next to the sidewalk, they had driven a political sign into the ground. The sign had a large blue star with red lettering. It read: "We all do better when we all do better—vote Sammy Smith-Johnson for Congress."

Jayme's heart sank when he now remembered that his mom told him that his dad had crushed the pills for his food. He had nowhere to turn. He went back to his bed.

He began to think that compliance might be his only hope. They'd have to take him out of the house sometime so that he could help them campaign. Maybe he could let them think that he was cooperating until he could run away and stay with Hunter.

Again, he got out of bed. He grabbed the bowls of pudding and the Gatorade. Taking them to the bathroom, he scraped the pudding in the toilet and flushed it. Then he poured the juice down the drain. He wondered how long he could go without eating. He made sure to rinse one of the Gatorade bottles well and filled it from the faucet. It didn't taste great, but it was unmedicated water.

As he watched the last of the Gatorade swish its way around his sink and down the drain, he thought about all the people in the world who actually were trans. It was such a shame to discard medication that was lifesaving to those who really needed it. This thought made him hate his parents even more. There were people who could actually use their help—people who would love to have parents so supportive of their transition. His parents could have been a gift to someone in need. But here they were, using that gift as a way to abuse.

Then he heard the latch slide on the outside of his door. He left the bowls and bottles in the bathroom and went back to his bed. Abygail walked into the room with another bowl and another Gatorade.

"Good morning, honey," she said. "How do you feel?"

"Better," Jayme answered.

"Did you eat?" she asked.

"Yes," he said, "and I drank the Gatorade."

She didn't reply as she set the new bowl and bottle on the nightstand. She looked around the room and went into the bathroom. She collected the empty bowls and threw the bottles in the bathroom trash.

Jayme wanted to do what he could to show her that he was compliant. He took a spoon and ate a tiny amount of the pudding—just enough to make it believable. He made sure that she saw.

"I saw one of dad's signs in the neighbor's yard," Jayme said.

"Oh yes!" Abygail said excitedly. "It's amazing to see them popping up all over town. It's really happening, Jayme, finally. We've got door knockers from the union going door-to-door with a new pamphlet. It looks great—your picture is on it! Our numbers are already looking better."

"What picture of me?" Jayme asked.

"Oh, people love it," Abygail said. "You're wearing a black T-shirt that says: 'I failed my gender assignment.' People think it's hysterical."

"I don't have a shirt like that. How is there a picture?"

"The campaign put one together. It looks so real! It's amazing how much stuff you can get done when you have real money coming in."

Jayme started to feel sick again. Maybe it was the hormones reappearing, or maybe it was the thought of his entire school thinking he was something that he wasn't. Then, for the first time since he woke, he thought about John Paul. Was John Paul upset that he didn't show up for their date? What would John Paul think if he saw the campaign pamphlet?

"You should get some more sleep, Jayme," Abygail said. "You don't look completely well. Oh, on Monday I'm going to Dr. Ramirez-Ogle to get something for you."

"What?" he asked.

"I'm not stupid, Jayme," Abygail said. "I know you didn't eat or drink anything I brought you. And I know you probably won't—no matter how hungry you get. I've arranged to pick up some injections for you. I told the doctor that you weren't tolerating the pills at all. You just don't know what is good for you, and we have to help you. Just wait until you feel so much better from the injections. Mark my words: By next week at this time, you are going to run up to us and thank us."

With that, she turned and left. He heard the latch slide. He sat up in bed. His eyes were wide with panic.

CHAPTER 29

John Paul woke fast and bolted out of bed. Somewhere in the house, a dog was barking so loudly that the wall was vibrating. He was terrified of whatever animal was making that sound. He was still wearing his school uniform.

The dog stopped barking. He heard the sound of someone climbing the steps, then he heard a key in the lock on his door. The door opened, and Joseph walked into the room. He looked the same but was wearing a different color of plaid flannel. For the first time, John Paul noticed that Joseph wore a ring of keys that was attached to his belt with a chain.

"I told you that you wouldn't have trouble waking up," Joseph said with a laugh. "That was Max. He barks like that exactly an hour before sunrise—does it every day. I don't know why, but I take it as a sign to get the day started. Well, you better change into that jumpsuit and get downstairs for breakfast. Can you do it yourself, or do I have to watch to make sure?"

"No," John Paul said, "I'll do it. But do I ever shower or anything?"

"We'll shower each day when we're done with our work," Joseph said.

"Shower together?" John Paul asked with a disgusted expression.

"Of course not!" Joseph shouted. "Let's get this right out in the open. I am not, or have I ever been, homosexual. Now get dressed and get downstairs."

Joseph turned and slammed the door shut. This time, John Paul did not hear the lock. He wondered if he could just try to run downstairs and out of the door. But he was afraid of Max, who he imagined was a rather large animal. He took off his clothes, kept his underwear on, and put on the orange jumpsuit. It was scratchy, and he immediately hated it. There wasn't a mirror in his room, and he was glad about that. He put on the black dress shoes from his school uniform; he hoped he was allowed to wear them.

He opened the door and stepped out into the hallway. There were other doors, just like his, each of them closed. He counted six. He couldn't imagine that the house had been built this way, but from the look of the crude wood-work and exposed framing, he assumed that it was a work in progress. He cautiously walked down the stairs. Joseph was in the kitchen, next to a large dining table that was also crudely made from bare lumber.

The largest German shepherd John Paul had ever seen sat on a cushion in the corner, near the table. This must be Max. John Paul walked softly past him and took a seat on an unfinished bench at the table. The dog looked up at him. John Paul looked back with a bit of fear. Then Max got up, walked over, and placed his head in John Paul's lap.

"Max!" Joseph shouted. "Get away from there. Leave the boy alone."

Max didn't move. He didn't show any sign that he'd even heard the man.

"That's Max for ya," Joseph said. "He's all bark and absolutely nothing else. I'm afraid you'll have to eat with him
lying on you like that."

Joseph walked over to the table and began placing food
on it. He brought a plate of pancakes, a dish of scrambled
eggs, a carton of orange juice, and a frying pan full of bacon.

"We'll eat a big breakfast and a large dinner," Joseph
said. "We don't stop for lunch because it's a waste of time,
and nobody needs to eat that much."

"I'm here alone, right?" John Paul got the courage to ask.

"Yep," Joseph said.

Joseph stood next to the table and looked at John Paul.
He sighed.

"I guess we should get the unpleasant stuff over before
breakfast," Joseph said. "It's the right thing to do."

John Paul did not like the sound of that. He instinctively
put his hands on Max's head, almost as if he was asking the
dog for help.

"Yes," Joseph said, "you're the first one here. I mean,
you're the only one here right now. You're going to help me
get the rest of the place ready for more boys. See, you aren't
here by accident. You were sent to me by Jesus. We've got a
lot of plumbing to do, I guess. And I'm going to help you
get over your problem—well, me and the Lord are going to
help you. See, I had a problem sort of like yours but not the
same. I cured myself with the help of Jesus, and I'll teach
you how to do the same. Then you can help me when other
boys come for help. We're going to build all this together and
run it together. We will have the best and most successful
Catholic men's treatment center in the country."

He seemed to have it all planned out. John Paul wondered if he'd get to have an opinion about all of this. Probably not. He wanted badly to run out of the door.

"So here is the unpleasant part," Joseph said. "I've got to make sure that you stay here because I'm acting as your parent now. So I made a thing out of a dog GPS tracker."

Joseph went to a counter and retrieved something made of metal. It looked like it had been fashioned out of a single handcuff with an additional metal chunk welded on. Joseph walked to John Paul and kneeled on the floor next to him. Since Max would not move, Joseph scooted over to the over side. He placed the object around John Paul's ankle.

"I know it's rough," Joseph said. "I tried hard to smooth it out with a torch. I think your ankle will toughen up, and it won't be a problem. Just remember that it will set off a whole bunch of alarms if you cross out of the yard. And it shows your location on my phone. We're miles from anyone, so I'll get to you before you get to anyone else. But hopefully, you won't try anything like that. I won't like it, and neither will Jesus."

Joseph got up. John Paul leaned over and felt the device. He'd take a better, and more analytical, look at it later.

"Do my parents know that I'm wearing this?" John Paul asked. "Do they know what it looks like in here?"

"Nope," Joseph answered. "They don't know much. Sorry to tell you that. They didn't even care enough to send you to an established conversion place. That's good for me, but I feel bad for you. Honestly, I do. And that nun that brought you—I talked to her on the phone, and she's not living in this century. I'm sorry to say that you don't have the right people looking out for you. They believed everything I told them on the phone. And I told them that they shouldn't contact you for months because any contact will just set back your progress."

"Months?" John Paul said. His heart fell low.

"Oh, don't be like that. It won't be all bad. We're going to have some fun here too. I'm a good person, doing the Lord's work. Look, I said that you don't have the right people looking out for you. That's going to change because now you have me. Those people—your parents and that nun—got you into this mess in the first place, and I'll get you out. I can tell already; we are going to be together for a long time. God sent you to me to help build this dream, a dream he gave me one night. We're going to save a lot of boys and then men. When we build all that I have in mind, we're going to be unstoppable. Then people will look at me with respect and admiration."

Max nuzzled his head farther into John Paul's lap. John Paul was too scared now to think about anything other than his fear.

CHAPTER 30

Hunter was spending Sunday night at his dad's house, which was four houses away from the Smith-Johnson home. His dad had gone to his girlfriend's place, so Hunter was fairly certain he'd have the house to himself for the whole night. He loved nights like this. He could do whatever he wanted and stay up as late as he wanted. He didn't care if he got much sleep before school on Monday morning. He was used to it.

He was lying on the couch when his phone rang. He checked and saw that it was Sophia. He hadn't talked to her since they'd met on Friday night. Hunter thought they had a good time together, eating at a fast-food restaurant and staying to talk for two hours. But he knew that she was two years older than he and was going to college soon, so their relationship, or whatever it was, would be short-lived.

"Hi," Hunter said as he answered the phone. "How are you?"

"I'm okay," Sophia said. "How are you?"

"I'm well. I had a good time on Friday."

"So did I," Sophia said, "but I called to ask you if you've talked to Jayme."

"We texted yesterday and today. Not a lot, but a few times. He's still too sick to do anything."

"Yes, but did you actually talk to him—like, hear his voice?"

"No," Hunter said, "just over text. But I did go over to his house today."

"Oh," Sophia said, "but you didn't see him?"

"No. His mom came to the door and told me that Jayme was too sick. I just told her to tell him to call me when he was better, and I left."

"Okay," Sophia said, "but I'm now really worried. I did something kind of bad. Well, not really, but I've been texting him, and his responses were not normal. And there weren't as many as there should be. So anyway, I sent a text that said, 'Hey Jayme—John Paul is upset that you missed your date. You should text him.' "

"Yeah," Hunter said. "I guess I see where you're going with this. It was a test or something?"

"Yes, and he failed. He sent this text back: 'Okay, sent John Paul a text, and everything is fine.' Hunter, do you see the problem? I know with absolute certainty that Jayme is not the person that responded. Jayme knows that John Paul does not have a phone. So whoever I've been texting with, it's not Jayme."

Hunter sat up on the couch. He was starting to understand why she was concerned.

"What?" Hunter said. "This is crazy. This is some sort of crappy-TV-movie crazy."

"I know!" Sophia said loudly. "But there is no way he sent me that text. I don't know his family much. Is there something weird going on? They always seem like such great parents for him. But I think his dad is in an election or something. Maybe that's causing some problems? Do you know what's going on?"

"So," Hunter began, "yeah, there is a little family drama over there. I don't want to get too much into it without talking to Jayme. When he was a kid...well, you've got me worried. I mean, it was tough for him when he was a kid."

Hunter didn't feel comfortable telling her about Jayme's past. He knew that Jayme did not have a great childhood, as his mom was sometimes unstable and almost dangerous. He also knew about his parents' insistence that Jayme was trans and that they were forcing it on him. Hunter knew about the latch on Jayme's bedroom door; he'd seen it many times. That latch was now the most frightening thing in his mind.

"I probably haven't been texting with him either then," Hunter said. "Who has his phone? His mom?"

"I don't know," Sophia said. "But there's more. I can't get ahold of John Paul, and he wasn't at Mass this morning. His whole family was there, but he wasn't. I went up and asked his mom where he was, and she told me that he's visiting his cousin and won't be back for maybe two months. I asked about school, and the dad looked weird and told me that John Paul was going to be homeschooled by the cousin."

"Who visits their cousin for two months to be homeschooled?"

"I know. It's weird and completely out of character for their family. I mean, Catholic school is really important to them. But do you remember what we talked about on Friday?"

"That his parents might have sent him someplace to be cured of his gayness?"

"Hunter, I know how it sounds," Sophia said. "But I can't stop thinking it. He's gone for two months during the school year? I don't buy it. If he were on drugs and was going to rehab, then maybe. But John Paul has never done anything like that. And now Jayme can't be contacted. What?"

"But there's no way these two things are connected? Right?"

"Well, I've been thinking about that," Sophia said. "What if someone saw them at the bookstore? What if John Paul's parents saw them? They'd send John Paul away in a flash and probably make it hard on Jayme. But you have a better chance of talking to Jayme than I do of talking to John Paul. Aren't you in his neighborhood?"

"Yeah," Hunter said, "but what am I supposed to do about it? I already knocked on his door and talked to his mom."

"Go look into his window or something."

"Sophia, it's on the second floor."

"Get a ladder."

Hunter started laughing, then stopped quickly when he realized that she was silent.

"I'm not kidding," Sophia said. "I think something bad is going on. Listen, I wouldn't ask you to do anything like this if I could think of any other reason for these two to be out of contact."

"Okay," Hunter said, "I'm not making any promises, but I'll see if I can figure something out."

"Okay. Just let me know. And thank you. Oh, I really need to find a way to calm down."

"Just take a few deep breaths," Hunter said. "Jayme is the brother I never had. I love the guy. I won't let him down."

They said goodbye and ended the call. Hunter sat on the couch and tried to think of some way to contact Jayme directly. He got up, went to his bedroom down the hall, and logged onto his gaming system. None of Jayme's avatars were online. He thought this was strange because Jayme liked to at least check in with his games once a day or so.

He thought about writing a note, wrapping it to a rock, and throwing it at the window. However, that would only work if the window were open, which it probably wasn't. Maybe he could throw some small rocks to get Jayme's attention. But what if someone else was in the room? It might make the situation worse.

Then he remembered that his dad had a long painter's ladder in the garage—the kind that folded up on itself and was easy to carry. Hunter had used it last summer when he and Jayme had gotten a Frisbee stuck high up in a tree. The second floor couldn't be that high, could it? All he needed to do was look through the window.

"Damn you, Sophia," Hunter said. "Why did you have to say *ladder*?"

He put on his sturdy sneakers and a black jacket. He went from the house into the garage. The ladder was folded into three pieces and was leaning against a wall. He didn't open the garage door; instead, he took the ladder out through a back door. It was lightweight and easy to carry.

He decided to walk across the three backyards between their houses. All these neighbors had fences, and he could walk right along them undetected. He was glad that it was very dark. Either there was no moon, or there were clouds covering it.

Hunter came to Jayme's house. He knew the exact window because he'd been in that room many times. He was glad to see that it was the only window, on that side of the house, that had a light on. He wondered if he'd go to jail if he were caught doing this. But other kids in school had done things that were way worse—and for reasons not nearly as good as checking on a friend.

He stood under the window and pressed in the metal gears that made the ladder unfold. He lifted the ladder and leaned it against the house, right under Jayme's window. He checked to make sure that the ladder was on even ground. It wasn't completely stable but stable enough he guessed. He started to climb, taking it slow and easy.

He progressed even slower as he got to the top. He stretched his neck and clung tightly to the ladder. He could peer just over the windowsill. Because the light was on, it was easy to see inside the room.

The first thing he noticed was that the room was not a complete mess. This was unusual. There weren't piles of clothing thrown about. The door to the bathroom was open, with the bathroom light on. Then he saw Jayme lying on his bed. He was under his covers, and his head was face down in a dinosaur pillow. He looked really sick.

Hunter felt bad and instantly started to climb down. Then he stopped. He'd come this far. He should really talk to Jayme. Anyway, he figured that this whole thing would make a great story for them to laugh about someday. He climbed back up to the top and knocked on the window—softly at first, then just slightly louder.

Jayme stirred in bed, turned his head, and then jumped right up. Hunter was afraid that he might have scared him. Jayme leaped onto the floor and ran to the window. He didn't seem as sick anymore. He opened the window.

"Hunter!" Jayme said loudly. "What are you doing here?"

"I came to check on you," Hunter said. "I just—well, it was Sophia's idea. We wanted to make sure you're okay."

"Are you on a ladder?" Jayme asked.

"No, I'm freaking Superman," Hunter said. "Of course I'm on a ladder. And I don't like it. So are you okay?"

"No, I'm not. I need to get out of here. Let me grab some stuff."

"What's going on?" Hunter said. "Are you here alone?"

"Yes," Jayme said as he searched his room. "My parents are gone."

Hunter watched as Jayme found a backpack in his closet. He went into the bathroom, grabbed a few items, and came back into the bedroom.

"I'm going to borrow some of your clothes," Jayme said. "Okay, I'm ready. Help me get on the ladder."

"What?" Hunter asked. "Why can't you just come out of the front door if you're home alone?"

"Because I'm locked in here," Jayme said.

The latch. Hunter hated that latch. Sophia was right. Something had been very wrong. Hunter felt terribly sad for his friend. How could any parents do something like this?

Jayme put his backpack on his back and started to climb through the window. Hunter guided his foot to the top rung of the ladder.

"Wait!" Jayme said. He went back into the room, grabbed something, and came back to the ladder.

"Here," Jayme said, "carry this. Or just drop it on the ground. It will be okay."

He passed Hunter a book. Hunter had never known Jayme to be much of a reader of books. He looked at the book and saw that it was titled *Ancient Pride.* Hunter shrugged his shoulders and let the book fall to the ground. It hit the ladder a few times as it fell.

CHAPTER 31

There were two things that were good at the Freedom Center for Boys: the food and Max the dog. Everything else was terrible.

It was Sunday night, and the sun had set. But that didn't matter much to John Paul. With a boarded-up window in his room, it was always dark. He thought about smuggling a crowbar back to his room to get the plywood off the window. But then why would it matter? He was never in the room during the day anyway.

Saturday and Sunday had both begun with a big breakfast. There was no denying that Joseph was an excellent cook. The kitchen cupboards and side pantry were completely full of supplies. John Paul was glad that at least he wouldn't have to worry about starving. However, the sheer amount of stock that Joseph stored meant that they could exist for a long time without any other human interaction. This terrified him—Joseph did not seem mentally stable to him.

Joseph was constantly telling John Paul about all his plans for the Freedom Center. None of them were based in reality. After the initial house was finished, Joseph wanted to build two dormitories in the backyard, one for the homosexual men and one for men who had some other sins to cure. John

Paul soon discovered that there was a long list of conditions due to sin that Joseph could cure, including cancer.

All of this, according to Joseph, was coming directly from Jesus. Nightly, Joseph had dreams in which the destiny of the Freedom Center for Boys was revealed. He talked nonstop about this future during their meals. John Paul was to play an integral part in all of this; he had been sent to become Joseph's partner in this dream. When Joseph eventually died, John Paul was to take over. Joseph was quite sure of this. John Paul was definitely not.

If Jesus had really ordained all of this, John Paul thought, *then why do I have to wear an ankle monitor and orange jumpsuit? Wouldn't Jesus have supplied a young man who wouldn't run away?* And even if John Paul was, somehow, the chosen one, did the ankle monitor have a technology greater than the power of God? If John Paul was this crucial to the mission and he ran away, wouldn't Jesus just tell Joseph where he was?

They worked all day Saturday and Sunday on the plumbing in the other upstairs rooms. None of it was interesting to John Paul, and he grew tired of the tedious work. He'd already carried enough PVC pipe up the stairs to make him wish that indoor plumbing had never been invented. And then there were the fixtures—the awful used toilets and sinks that Joseph had received as a donation from God knows where.

For some reason, Joseph was obsessed with the appearance of the PVC pipes. He meticulously measured and remeasured each pipe. All the PVC had to be scrubbed clean after installation. He freaked if he saw even the smallest dab of putty or glue. But then, after all this meticulous work, Joseph didn't care if the toilet they installed was disgustingly dirty. This made no sense to John Paul at all.

It also made no sense to him that they'd worked all day on Sunday. Joseph was extremely Catholic; he talked about it all the time. Yet there was no mention of attending Mass or receiving the Eucharist, the Holy Communion that Catholics were required to receive every Sunday. John Paul didn't ask about it. He didn't ask about anything and volunteered nothing. He'd probably said ten whole sentences since he'd arrived on Friday, and seven of them were to Max.

Max had taken an instant liking to John Paul. He was constantly placing his head in John Paul's lap during meals. And while they were working, Max sat next to John Paul—at least until Joseph got annoyed and ordered the dog to go to his bed, which Max always obeyed. John Paul did not mind attention from Max at all. At least someone loved him, even if it was a dog. His parents had abandoned him. Jayme probably hated him for disappearing. He wondered what Jayme was doing at that minute.

He closed his eyes and tried to relax as much as anyone in his situation could relax. He thought about the first time he'd ever seen Jayme. It was mostly due to an accident.

John Paul was at Catholic youth group on a customary Wednesday night. The group was making crucifixes out of burned matches to give to poor people somewhere. John Paul loved making these crosses because he thought they were beautiful. The burned ends of the matches created dark contrasting lines when glued together to a cardboard base. The ends would never burn evenly, and that gave the cross a natural, random look.

He sat next to Sophia; she also liked making these. They were in charge of using a candle to light each match, let it burn for a moment, and then extinguish it in a dishpan full of water. At one point, Sister Gentillini got on their case because the dishpan water had become too dirty with soot. She told John Paul to dump the water outside.

John Paul took the dishpan and went out the side entrance of the school. He dumped the water and turned to go back inside; however, the side door had locked behind him. So he started to walk around the building. That's when he looked down the street and saw the coffee shop.

He didn't know why he wanted to leave the church campus so badly. All he knew was that he was filled with a tremendous desire for freedom—and to do something that was wrong. He enjoyed the feeling that these emotions created in his stomach. It was unpleasant and somehow desirable at the same time.

John Paul set down the dishpan and walked down Main Street. He wished he was wearing anything other than his Catholic-school uniform. When he got to the coffee shop, he looked through the window and saw that it was packed with people. He lost his nerve and turned back toward the church. That's when he passed by the used bookstore and didn't see anyone around.

He decided to go inside, if only for just a second. He'd become completely exhilarated by the thought of being somewhere he wasn't supposed to be. John Paul opened the door and went in. He didn't look around. He went straight to the closest bookcase and started looking at the book spines.

He heard a cough near him. When he turned to look, he saw Jayme, standing next to a crate of old records. John Paul stared at him—he couldn't look away. There was something about how Jayme's clothes fit that John Paul really liked. In that moment, John Paul didn't even feel guilty about looking at another guy.

Suddenly, Jayme glanced up, and their eyes met. John Paul immediately ignored him and turned back to the bookshelf. He looked at more book spines but didn't read any of the titles. He was busy attempting to persuade his brain to take another look, even though the brain thought this was a bad idea. But he couldn't resist, so he turned his head again. This time, Jayme was already staring at him. Jayme smiled. John Paul smiled back. And that was all there was to it.

Later, he'd learn that Jayme was in the bookstore looking for a recording of the soundtrack to an old Elizabeth Taylor movie titled *Cleopatra*. But as John Paul now lay on his bed at the Freedom Center for Boys, all he wanted to think about was that first time that he saw Jayme. That is, until another persistent thought that he had the past two days entered his mind.

"Does this ankle monitor work?" he said to himself. He bent over and started examining it until he fell asleep.

CHAPTER 32

Abygail Smith-Johnson woke up Monday morning, showered, dressed, and made sure her hair looked just right. Sammy had already been up for over an hour and was working downstairs in his home office. The night before, they had been in a long meeting with the campaign managers and didn't get home until after midnight. Now they were up early. There would be no rest until at least after the primary and hopefully no rest until after the general election.

While she should have been exhausted, Abygail wasn't. She loved every minute of the campaign. She especially loved getting a daily itinerary of where Sammy and she needed to be, when they had to arrive, and what they were expected to do. She felt like a movie star. This would be another busy day. After she received her schedule from Sammy, she'd need to find time to pick up Jayme's injectable hormones from the pharmacy. She was sure the campaign would understand an unscheduled stop.

She left her bedroom and went to check on Jayme. When she came to his door, she slid the large metal latch to the side and opened the door.

Jayme wasn't on his bed. She checked the bathroom. Then she began to worry. The worry turned into complete panic when she noticed the open window. Abygail ran to the window and looked out. She didn't know how, but Jayme had left the house through this window.

"Sammy!" Abygail yelled at the top of her lungs. "Sammy!"

She waited in the bedroom, breathing in hard, labored breaths. Sammy, already dressed in a full suit, came running in.

"What?" he yelled back.

"Jayme is gone!" Abygail said. "Look!"

"You sure?" Sammy asked in a normal voice.

"There's not too many places for him to be, dear," she said sarcastically. "The bathroom is empty."

"Shit," Sammy said.

"I know." Her mood turned from panic to anger. Then it turned from anger to rage.

"He's going to tell people what we've been doing," Sammy said. "He's going to say we're forcing hormones on him. He's going to talk about it all, Abygail—"

She held up her hand to silence him. Her mind was running a million miles a minute. Like politicians had done for centuries, she needed to control the narrative before it controlled them.

"This can't be the end," Abygail said. "We have to think of something. If we can get to him, it still might be okay. His friends have been texting me. It must be one of them."

"Why are his friends texting you?"

"Try to catch up, dear. What do you think? I have Jayme's phone. They've been texting him, and I've been answering. It's either Hunter or Sophia. Probably Sophia—she's Catholic, you know. They hate us."

"Nope," Sammy said. "He's with Hunter. I guarantee it. Hunter's dad lives just down the street. Come on."

Sammy led her through the hall and down the stairs. They went to the front door. When they opened the large decorative door, a paper fell onto the threshold.

"What's this?" Abygail said as she picked up the paper. She read it aloud.

After she had finished, Sammy said, "That's nothing. We've got a whole box of letters just like that at the campaign office."

"Yeah," Abygail said, "I've seen them. But this one was in my door. What's wrong with people?"

She was about to crumple the letter and then continue to Hunter's house. However, she suddenly stopped. She read the letter again carefully. She stepped back and closed the door. Perhaps this was their salvation, a way to control the narrative.

"What?" Sammy asked.

"It says here that they will say a prayer for us because we need it," Abygail said. "Does that sound like a threat to you?"

"No, it's nothing."

"But they're talking about Jayme, and then they threaten us. Do you think whoever wrote this letter kidnapped our Jayme?"

"Abygail," Sammy said. "You're being ridiculous. He ran away and is with Hunter."

"You believe that," Abygail said, "and I might believe that. But the media doesn't have to believe that. They don't even have to know that."

"What are you saying?"

"I'm saying that we stay ahead of this thing. That's how the real politicians do it. We don't let Jayme tell them anything about hormones. Our trans child has been taken from us by conservative freaks. If Jayme says something, it will already be too late. The media will love this; they won't want him to ruin it."

"Abygail, this will never work. For one, we've got a camera on the doorbell. The police and the media will want to see it."

"Okay," she said. "It doesn't really matter, but sure, let's look at it."

"Doesn't matter?" Sammy said.

Sammy shrugged his shoulders and motioned for her to follow him. He entered his office and sat down at his desk. He pulled up the camera footage on his computer. Abygail hunched over him to look. Whatever she saw on the video, she would make it fit what she wanted the media to see.

There it was. At 2:46 in the morning, someone walked down the street, up the Smith-Johnsons' sidewalk, and up their porch steps, and placed the letter in the doorjamb. It was dark, but the camera had a night-vision feature.

"It's a woman, right?" Abygail said.

"I think, yes," Sammy said. "But I can't tell who. Can you?"

"No, but look at the skirt. What kind of woman wears a skirt that long in the middle of the night? Weird."

"Is there something on her head?" Sammy asked.

"I think it's just long, dark hair," Abygail said. "These religious freaks don't cut their hair. I think it says something about it in the Bible."

Sammy played with the controls of the video for a bit. He wasn't able to find a frame with a clear-enough image to identify the woman. Abygail was actually glad about that.

"It's better if she can't be identified," said Abygail. "Harder to prove that she's not right wing. And if she can't be identified by sight, then she can't be located. They can't interview someone that they can't find. She looks right wing—she looks almost Amish or something. Are you with me now?"

"I don't know," Sammy said as he sat back, away from the computer. "I don't feel good about this. We should at least find Jayme first."

"And let him ruin everything?" Abygail said. "I know him, Sammy. He's not on board with us. He hates the hormones. He'll ruin us."

"But there's no proof that he's been kidnapped. Once the media smells it, they will run with it, and there's no turning back."

"There is proof—there is the letter. And how do you think the Clintons got so much power? By letting others control the narrative? No! They grabbed it for themselves. They had nothing to do with Whitewater, remember? And my God, Monica Lewinsky! Bill basically sexually assaulted her, and he came off looking like a goddamn saint! If you want to be in Congress, you'll listen to me."

Sammy didn't say anything. She could see the wheels in his head starting to turn.

"Look at all these politicians, all the terrible things they've done," Abygail said. "They've done much worse than anything we could even think of. What you really do makes no difference. It's how you tell the media to react that matters."

"Okay, okay," Sammy said. "With a big risk comes a big reward."

"I'll call the police and report that Jayme's missing," Abygail said. "You call Brandon and tell him. We need to have a press conference as soon as possible—before Jayme has a chance to show up somewhere."

ANCIENT PRIDE

A REFUGEE COUPLE

For this chapter, we will turn back to the myths we learned in the first chapter: the myths of the Trojan War, as told in *The Iliad*. Not only was the Trojan War important to the Greek people but the later Romans were also enamored with it. In this chapter, you will see how a couple of gay Trojans lost everything, journeyed to a new land, and helped to create the greatest empire the world has ever known.

You might remember that the great city of Troy was ruled by King Priam and his sons, Prince Hector and Prince Paris. But there was another prince of Troy who would play an important role to the ancient people, especially to those of Rome: Prince Aeneas.

Aeneas was the son of King Priam's brother. His mother was Aphrodite, the goddess of sexual passion. Like Achilles, he has a mortal father and an immortal mother; consequently, he was mortal. During *The Iliad*, Aeneas fought in several of the many battles. During one battle, the god Poseidon appeared and stated that Aeneas could not die. Instead, Aeneas was destined to lead the refugees of Troy away to a new land, where they would become a great people again.

And according to the ancient Romans, that is exactly what happened. After the Greeks had stealthily left their wooden horse and attacked the city, Aeneas, as the highest-ranking survivor of the Trojan royal family, decided to escape. (His mother, Aphrodite, helped to convince him.) He gathered his son, his father, and his wife. However, his wife was killed as they were about to escape. Aeneas then fled to the nearby mountains, where he was united with all the others who had survived. These refugees from Troy—the last of the Trojans—decided to follow Aeneas and start a new life somewhere else. Among these refugees were two inseparable men: Nisus and Euryalus.

Most of what we know about Nisus and Euryalus comes from the poet Virgil. During the time of the Roman Empire, Virgil wrote about Aeneas's journey from Troy to Italy in an epic poem called *The Aeneid*. Like *The Iliad*, *The Aeneid* is based upon stories passed down from campfire to campfire over the course of hundreds of years.

Virgil does not attempt to conceal Nisus and Euryalus's relationship in any way. They were described as "pious lovers" and were never separated throughout the entire epic. Nisus was said to be an expert at weaponry, especially arrows and javelins. Euryalus was described as the most beautiful man of all the men to leave Troy. Euryalus was especially close to his mother, who had also escaped from Troy.

The Trojan refugees found some ships (it's a long story) and sailed around the Mediterranean, having adventures at various islands (it's a really long story). They encountered quizzical humans, magical creatures, and the wrath of a few gods. Aeneas was especially hated by Zeus's wife, the goddess Hera. We will learn more about that hatred in a later chapter. (Note: The myth of Aeneas is a Roman myth written in Latin. Consequently, Zeus is known as Jupiter, and Hera is known as Juno.)

We first encounter Nisus and Euryalus after the death of Aeneas's father. As was customary, the Trojans held a series of athletic games in remembrance of the deceased man. These games were an important part of the funeral experience for the Greeks. After the body had been cremated on a funeral pyre, several days of competitions were conducted. The more important the dead person was, the more spectacular the games would be.

The Trojans began their games with a footrace. They sacrificed a lamb to the gods, and the runners took off. Nisus and Euryalus were both in this race. However, as they neared the finish line, Nisus slipped on the blood of the sacrificial lamb. He fell to the ground. Now there are two versions of what occurred next. Myths, just like our news today, are told and retold according to whatever view the narrator wants to impart. It's not unusual at all to have several versions of the same myth.

In one version, after Nisus slipped, Euryalus stopped to help him, allowing someone else to win the race. In another version, after Nisus slipped, he tripped all the other runners so that Euryalus would win the race. One version was altruistic, and the other was…well, cheating. Regardless, the story illustrates that these were two men who looked out for each other.

So the Trojans jumped from place to place, from peril to peril, always looking for the perfect spot to start a new city. Aeneas often gained information about where this city should be from various entities on their journey. At one point, he traveled to the underworld to speak with his father.

Eventually, the Trojans arrived on the shore of Italy at the mouth of the Tiber River, just downstream from what would become Rome. Aeneas was sure this was the place to start his future great city.

However, there were already other people living there. But this was not a problem because the king of these people liked Aeneas and the Trojans. So he gave his daughter, the princess Lavinia, to Aeneas. But this *was* a problem because the king had already promised Lavinia to a local man, Turnus, leader of a tribe of warriors called the Rutuli.

The Trojans and the Rutuli began a war, right there at the mouth of the Tiber River. At one point, Aeneas decided that he would row upriver to see if he could gather support and men from other tribes who might also dislike the Rutuli. He left his son Julus in charge.

However, soon after Aeneas left, the Rutuli attacked and completely surrounded the Trojan encampment. This was a big deal in ancient warfare. If your camp was surrounded, it meant no food, no water, and no sanitation, and it pretty much guaranteed death. So Nisus and Euryalus, our couple of the hour, decided to go after Aeneas. They hoped to bring him back with lots of new soldiers who could attack the Rutuli from outside the surrounded camp.

One night, they sneaked out of the Trojan camp. They crept silently through several rows of Rutuli who were camped in circles around the Trojans. The Rutuli were fast asleep and did not wake. Nisus and Euryalus were amazed at how easy it had been to get past the Rutuli. Then the couple noticed empty wine casks…many, many empty wine casks. The Rutuli had drank themselves into a stupor and were completely passed out—all of them.

In the bloodiest scene of the entire *Aeneid*, Nisus and Euryalus took advantage of the situation and started to stab the Rutuli with their swords. They stabbed and stabbed for hours, hacking apart hundreds of Rutuli soldiers. This scene, although bloody, is a reminder that it's not a great idea to drink yourself to sleep when you're in the middle of something important.

Eventually, Nisus and Euryalus realized that they were pushing their luck. One of the Rutuli was sure to wake up and shout at some point. They decided to try to steal some horses from the Rutuli and make their way up the river. However, in the process of locating horses, they were discovered. Nisus ran quickly into the woods, with Euryalus close behind. But when Nisus felt he was safe and stopped, Euryalus was nowhere to be seen. Nisus immediately ran back to look for him.

Suddenly, a horrific scream filled the air. It was Euryalus. Nisus crept around some trees and saw that a group of Rutuli had strapped Euryalus to a tree. They assumed that this man had been responsible for the carnage around the Trojan camp. The Rutuli took torches and burned Euryalus's beautiful face. Then they burned other parts of him. His painful screams filled the air and penetrated Nisus's soul.

Nisus, an expert with spears, leaped out of the bushes. He grabbed two spears that the Rutuli had stuck in the ground and threw them simultaneously. Each spear found its target, and two Rutuli instantly fell dead. Another Rutuli took his dagger, walked up to Euryalus bound to the tree, and slit his throat. Blood gushed out, fueling Nisus's rage. He grabbed another spear and easily impaled the Rutuli who had just killed Euryalus. Then another Rutuli grabbed a spear and killed Nisus. The two men who had never been separated in life were now joined in death.

When the rest of the Trojans back in their camp woke the next morning, they initially rejoiced because they saw all the dead Rutuli from the night before. Julus, son of Aeneas, was ecstatic when he heard that Nisus and Euryalus were seen sneaking out of the camp. He assumed they had done the killing and were now on their way to find Aeneas. He proclaimed a day of rejoicing in honor of the great couple. But then a horrific shout erupted inside the Trojan camp.

Julus climbed up a ladder to look. Two Rutuli marched around the Trojan camp; each carried a large pole. On top of the poles were the heads of Nisus and Euryalus. Horrified, Julus grabbed his bow and shot both of the Rutuli. Then he instructed that his men scour the countryside until the complete bodies of Nisus and Euryalus were found.

Nisus and Euryalus were reunited with their heads and with each other. They received all the proper funeral rites and were revered by the Trojans for their bravery and commitment to each other. Because of Nisus and Euryalus, the Rutuli were severely weakened.

Eventually, Aeneas returned and completed the war by killing Turnus. He married Lavinia, and the Trojans began to live next to the Tiber River. Aeneas's son Julus had children, and his name lived on as their surname: Julius.

Generations later, because of the help of two gay men, one of Julus's descendants would become the mighty Gaius Julius Caesar. The Trojan people became the magnificent Romans. These proud people never forgot the story of their origin and held a yearly celebration called the Games of Troy. During this festival, lavish athletic contests, chariot races, and gladiatorial fights took place to honor the two men who had defeated the Rutuli and established the Roman homeland. These games, dedicated to Nisus and Euryalus, took place annually for centuries.

The next time you are at Olive Garden, you can sound really smart if you explain to the table that Italian food is really Trojan food. If they doubt you, just tell them all the story of Nisus and Euryalus.

CHAPTER 33

Jayme put *Ancient Pride* down. He had slept all right in Hunter's bedroom after having eaten everything Hunter could manage to locate in his dad's kitchen. He woke early, mostly out of nervousness, and didn't want to wake Hunter, who was also sleeping in the bed. Jayme had been reading about Nisus and Euryalus. He was thinking about whether they were sympathetic heroes or not. They killed a lot and might have been cheaters. But they saved their people.

He had no idea what was going to happen that day. He knew he couldn't go to school. And of course, he couldn't go home. Maybe he'd need to be gone just long enough to scare his parents. Maybe he could go home later in the week, and they'd pretend that nothing happened. If they'd accept that he was just a gay guy and not trans, perhaps they could all get back to where things were before the campaign.

However, his main objective for the day was to locate John Paul. He couldn't really rest until he knew where John Paul was. Hunter told him that Sophia had lost contact and hadn't seen him in church on Sunday. Jayme was concerned. He thought he'd start at the bookstore and ask Bob. Of course, he'd have to be careful about who saw him. He thought he could trust Bob and probably Fiona. But he didn't want to get anyone else in trouble either.

Hunter turned over. His eyes opened, and he sat up. He wore sleep shorts and a tank top. Jayme put his book down and looked at him.

"You know," Jayme said, "you look great in pajamas. You're going to make some girl very happy someday."

"You should be very glad that I'm as secure with my sexuality as I am," Hunter said. "Otherwise, you'd be sleeping on the floor, brother."

"The thought of touching you makes me gag." Jayme laughed. "But, Hunter, really, thank you for everything. I don't know how to repay this."

"If they arrest me," Hunter said, "get me a good lawyer."

Jayme felt terrible at this statement. He didn't want anyone else to get caught up in the mess his parents caused. But he didn't know how else to proceed.

"You can stay here as long as you want," Hunter said. "As long as my dad doesn't find out, anyway. So you're gonna have to stay in my bedroom and be quiet. I can bring you food."

"I can't stay here all day," Jayme said. "I need to find out what's happening to John Paul."

"How are you going to do that?" Hunter said. "Just give his parents a call?"

"I'm going to see if Bob knows anything at the bookstore," Jayme said. "Can you ask Sophia if she's heard anything? I still don't have a phone."

"Listen, Jayme, I've thought about this since last night. I'm willing to help you, but I don't want Sophia involved. She's almost eighteen and can get into a lot more trouble than we can. I don't want her to know that you ran away. If she doesn't report that she knows where a runaway minor is, she could go to jail. I'm going to tell her that I saw you last night at your house, that I talked to you, and you are really sick. I'll tell her not to call or text."

"That's fine," Jayme said. "It makes sense—and it's the right thing to do. But does she have any idea about where John Paul could be?"

"Yes," Hunter said. "I'm getting to that. We had a long talk on Friday night, and I learned a lot about Catholics. Sophia's sort of Catholic-light, but John Paul is a full-on, Pope-kissing Catholic. His family is, I mean. But Sophia thinks they might have found out he's gay and sent him somewhere to be cured. She thinks there's no way he went to visit a cousin for two months, and nothing else makes sense."

"It also doesn't make sense that they sent him to a change camp," Jayme said. "Those places aren't even real. They're just in made-for-gays movies."

"No, they're real. Sophia had a hard time even admitting it to herself. But she can't shake the thought. She did some research online, and yes, Jayme, those places are real. And they're not illegal. Now, listen, she told me that there's a good nun and a bad nun. The—"

"What the hell?" Jayme interrupted. "Now there are good and bad nuns involved? This *is* a movie."

"The bad nun has a name that sounds like 'genitals.' Stop interrupting me because I'm serious!" Hunter said when Jayme attempted to speak. "Her name sounds like 'genitals,' and I can't remember the exact name. But she would be the most likely to have helped John Paul's parents find a place for him where they would change him."

"Well, they can try, I guess," Jayme said. "But I don't believe it's actually possible to change someone's insides like that. But what about the good nun?"

"I remember," Hunter said. "Sister Gabriel Luke."

"Wait—I know her. She was at the bookstore. She's a good friend of Bob's. He calls her Gabs."

"You know her?" Hunter said. "You sure?"

"Absolutely," Jayme said. "I met a nun at the bookstore named Gabriel Luke. She had no problem that John Paul was gay and, in fact, was really happy about it."

"Okay, that's good," Hunter said. "A good start, anyway. Maybe you should try to talk to her?"

"Are you really going to school?" Jayme asked. "And let me do this all on my own?"

"Yes, of course!" Hunter said. "I love you, man, but I also have to be smart. I need an alibi for when your parents call the police and report that you ran away."

"No need to worry about that," Jayme said. "They'll be terrified that I'll accuse them of abuse. They aren't calling anyone."

CHAPTER 34

Monday started early for John Paul, with Max barking up a storm before daybreak. He used the toilet, put on the orange jumpsuit, and waited for Joseph to unlock his door. It was only the third morning since his arrival, and it already seemed routine. This scared John Paul. John Paul liked numbers and symmetry. He was analytical and was drawn to patterns. He could easily be comforted by routine. But could he ever be comfortable here?

He heard Max right outside his door. He wished that Max was able to unlock the door. But then Joseph came up the stairs, and the day began with another breakfast. Joseph cooked while John Paul sat on a chair and played with Max.

"Today, after breakfast," Joseph said, "we won't start working on the plumbing. On Mondays and Fridays, you'll have your therapy session in the mornings. Then we'll work in the afternoon. I'm still trying to figure out how we'll do it when more boys are sent here. I can't be in two places at once. Well, I suppose Christ will let me know one of these nights."

Finally, the part that John Paul dreaded the most would begin. He was about one-quarter afraid of any physical pain involved and three-quarters afraid that the therapy would mess up his mind for the rest of his life. And there was also the ever-present fear that it might actually work. Despite everything, deep inside, he realized that change would be a bad thing for him.

Thinking of Jayme at night, while in bed, allowed John Paul to relax. Aside from playing with Max, it was the only retreat from reality that John Paul had. He replayed in his mind what it felt like, physically and emotionally, to kiss Jayme. He could remember exactly what Jayme's back felt like when he moved his hands over the outside of his shirt while kissing. He remembered how alive he felt. What if Joseph was about to take that away?

John Paul recalled how his daydreams of Jayme were in color, while imaginations of having a heterosexual life were in sepia. He wasn't ready for Joseph to take the colors away.

They ate in silence. Then John Paul cleaned all the dishes to Joseph's standard. Again, there was the odd dichotomy in Joseph. He insisted on spotless dishes and pans, yet they were placed into rotting cabinets that were caked with old grease and dirt.

John Paul hadn't been allowed to see all of the house yet. He'd never seen Joseph's room on the first floor, nor the basement. He was scared of the unseen basement and had a feeling that was where the therapy would occur. He was right.

Joseph opened a locked door on the first floor that revealed a staircase descending straight down. He turned on the lights. John Paul was relieved to see that the basement was well lit. As he walked down the unfinished wood stairs, he saw several work lights hanging from the unfinished ceiling. They had been connected with extension cords in a crude way, with long spans of cord draping over exposed beams.

A large, and odd, contraption sat in the middle of the room. It looked like a treadmill without the tread. The platform where a person should walk had been removed. A wooden chair sat there instead. There were all sorts of cables lying on the floor around it. John Paul also noticed a blood pressure cuff on the unfinished cement floor.

Max attempted to come down the steps, but Joseph forced him back up and closed the door. John Paul heard Max whining and felt bad for him. Joseph then yelled for Max to go to his bed. The silence that followed led John Paul to believe that the dog obeyed.

Now at the bottom of the steps, John Paul saw that the treadmill was facing the only television he'd seen in the house. It was an older television but in good shape. He wondered how it got a signal. He'd often wondered how Joseph accessed the internet—especially how the ankle monitor sent a signal. John Paul hadn't seen any sort of router or modem anywhere. He even toyed with the idea that Joseph was lying and there wasn't any signal at all.

"Okay," Joseph said, "so this is all my own invention— well, mine and Jesus's. We might try to make it look a little prettier, but it works. That's all that matters. I'm very proud of this whole thing. Won't it be great when we have a whole row of these with men using them? So you just sit right there on that chair."

John Paul sat down apprehensively. Joseph started by placing the blood pressure cuff around John Paul's left calf, on top of the jumper's orange fabric. Then Joseph unzipped the top of the jumper. John Paul hated that intrusion into his personal space and body. He wondered if he should just start running up the stairs and risk whatever punishment Joseph would impart.

Joseph bent down, grabbed some wires, and began taping them to John Paul's bare chest with regular masking tape. Some of them didn't stick well, and Joseph became frustrated. He used more tape.

"This tape works better on me," Joseph said. "I guess I have more hair on my chest for tape to stick to. We'll have to work on that—maybe use black electrical tape? That's not very expensive. Okay, now you have to reach forward and put your hands on those metal plates."

John Paul grabbed the metal bar in front of him, just like someone on a treadmill would. He didn't mind the position he was sitting in, but he hated the feeling of Joseph touching him with the tape. He felt violated and wronged.

"Okay, the heartbeat monitor from the treadmill won't work without the motor running. We haven't figured that out yet, but we'll get there. So the motor is a little loud."

Joseph turned on the treadmill's display. He turned on the machine to a slow walk. John Paul looked down and saw the rotating axles of the treadmill. But with the entire platform removed, they rotated nothing.

Joseph bent down and picked up a small, plastic display that was connected to the blood pressure cuff. John Paul noticed that there was nothing special about it; anyone could have purchased it from any sort of pharmacy. Joseph also retrieved some sort of device from the floor that was connected to the taped wires on John Paul's chest.

"We have to get some sort of table in here," Joseph said. "Usually, I just hold this stuff on my lap when I'm in the chair. I guess I didn't think of that. Okay, I'll just stand behind you because then I can see your pulse on the treadmill and watch these other things. Okay, this is good. Oh shoot, I forgot the TV. None of this will be any good without that."

Joseph set the devices back onto the floor and walked over to the television. John Paul saw that there was a DVD player sitting on the floor in front of it. Joseph fumbled with it for a few minutes. There was a cardboard box of DVDs, not in cases, that he searched through for some time.

"Oh!" Joseph said. "Where is my brain? We forgot to pray. That's the most important part. Let's bow our heads."

John Paul lowered his head but kept his eyes open. It felt odd to pray with his hands stretched forward instead of folded together in the customary Catholic manner.

"Lord," Joseph began, "John Paul has come before you to be cured of his homosexuality. He knows he has sinned this grievous sin, for the good Sister told me she saw him kissing another boy in the courtyard of Our Lady of Seven Dolors. He begs your forgiveness for violating our most precious Mother in that way. He comes to you now, humble, for your divine cure. Help him to overcome his thoughts about men. We ask this through Jesus Christ, our Lord. Amen."

John Paul, being as studious as he was, knew that "Amen" was a way of saying, "I believe." He did not say "Amen" at the end of the prayer. He worried that Joseph would notice, but the man seemed much too interested in himself and his contraption than to worry about what John Paul was doing.

Joseph turned on the television. He used the buttons on the DVD player to navigate. He didn't have a remote control. The television started playing a gay pornographic movie. John Paul had never seen one of these movies before. In fact, the only naked man he'd ever seen was himself. Of course, he'd looked at handsome men in advertisements and in regular television shows. He loved it when his mom bought him new underwear, and he could look at the guy on the box. But he had never seen a pornographic magazine or anything like what he was seeing now.

John Paul knew he was gay—he had no doubt about that. He knew that he loved to look at Jayme. He loved the feel of Jayme. But what he saw on the screen in front of him was disgusting. Three overly muscular men—full of tattoos, sweaty—were having sex. At least, that's what John Paul thought they were doing. Nothing about it appealed to him. Even their private parts were nothing John Paul wanted to look at.

Joseph went back to his devices, standing at John Paul's side.

"Okay," Joseph said, "well, I can see that you are very excited now. Yes, everything is elevated."

John Paul wondered how this could be true when he didn't like what he was seeing. Also, he never felt the blood pressure cuff inflate. This whole thing was completely ridiculous. He relaxed and didn't worry anymore about pain. To John Paul, Joseph was quite incompetent as a therapist.

"Here's what you have to do," Joseph said, "you just, in your mind, think of the name *Jesus*. Just repeat his name over and over in your mind, but keep watching the TV. Use the name of Jesus to stop believing that the images are exciting to you. Feel that his name has more power than the images on the screen."

John Paul didn't know how long he sat like that, and he certainly wasn't repeating the name of Jesus in his head. He felt that it had been probably about thirty minutes. At one point toward the end of the therapy session, the scene that he was watching on the television came to its conclusion. John Paul was aghast at that conclusion and thought it was extremely unsanitary. He wondered if he was truly gay, after all? Maybe he was just a little gay? He certainly never wanted to do anything like what he'd just seen.

But another scene started playing. This time, it was just two guys. Only one was overly muscular. The other looked normal, with healthy skin, nice hair, and good teeth. John Paul found him attractive. He liked the look of his body. John Paul could understand how this guy could be someone he'd want to touch. But with Joseph standing next to him, he didn't find that he got too excited. This scene played for a bit, then Joseph walked over and switched it off.

"All right," Joseph said, "well, we have good news. You were very excited for most of the session, but right at the end, I saw a bit of progress. I think you must have found that the name of Jesus was working. Did you feel it?"

John Paul didn't know what to say since the whole thing had been so absurd. He wanted to tell Joseph to at least hook up the blood pressure cuff next time, then decided that Joseph was less dangerous in his overconfidence.

"Ummm," John Paul said. "I guess I felt that it was easier to ignore the guys on TV at the end. Yeah, I think that concentrating on the name and all made it easier."

"That's right," Joseph said. "The more we practice, the easier it gets. If you keep repeating the name, you will get to a point where the thought of men having sex is disgusting. You can take that tape off you now."

John Paul easily peeled the masking tape from his smooth skin. He wished he had access to the internet so that he could research how heart-monitoring patches actually worked. He was sure there had to be more to it than using masking tape to attach exposed wires to someone.

As John Paul climbed up the steps toward the kitchen, he couldn't help but think about that guy from the last scene. He hoped that during Friday's session, Joseph would start the DVD right in the same place.

CHAPTER 35

Sister Gabriel Luke looked out the window of the convent's reception room. Two older nuns, who were retired, sat behind her, watching television. She knew that Sister Gentillini was still upstairs. Gabriel Luke was waiting for Gentillini to leave so that she could investigate her suspicion.

Gabriel Luke had already watched the sisters who were teachers at the school leave for the day. She was the school's guidance counselor and didn't need to be in her office until later. Sister Gentillini worked in the parish office as the liturgist; she was responsible for planning each Mass, with the approval of Father, of course.

The retired sisters who were watching the news were discussing some of the stories from that morning's program. Gabriel Luke didn't pay attention to them. She didn't want to waste time discussing things that some people in a newsroom thought were important for her to discuss. There were actual, real events happening right in front of them that were important—events that could impact real people.

Where was John Paul Saint Clara? This was the most important thought running through Gabriel Luke's mind. And what did Gentillini have to do with it? Gabriel Luke was a guidance counselor. Of course, she'd heard of the horrible practice of reparative therapy—the pseudoscience technique of making gay people straight. And yes, the thought that John Paul was wrapped up in it had crossed her mind. But could his parents have actually done something like that? Could Gentillini?

Finally, she heard the familiar sound of a sister coming down the stairs. She moved silently, as all nuns were able to, around to the other side of the room. There, she could see Sister Gentillini as she descended the stairs and went into the kitchen. Gabriel Luke stood there for a bit; the retired nuns didn't pay any attention. She heard the back door open and close.

But Gabriel Luke was surprised when she saw, through the window, Gentillini walking across the street in front of the house. She should have just walked across the courtyard to the parish office. Where was she going?

Gabriel Luke didn't want to take too much time watching Gentillini. She had a task. She crossed the reception room and walked up the stairs. At the top, she stood in the long hallway that contained the nuns' bedrooms. Each door was identical. She passed her own door. Then she stood at Gentillini's door. She put her hand on the doorknob.

There were no locks on the doors. A lock would not be considered appropriate, according to the rules that the nuns lived by. Trust in each other was as important as air to them. Yet Gabriel Luke was about to violate that trust grievously. She paused to think about it.

Yes, going into another sister's room without asking was a terrible offense. Looking through her things made it exponentially worse. However, wasn't she helping Gentillini in the long run? If Gentillini really had done this terrible thing—sent John Paul to some sort of concentration camp for young boys—then entering her room to correct the matter was the trustful thing to do, right? Gabriel Luke convinced herself of this and turned the doorknob. She walked into the room.

At first, it looked identical to her own. Same furniture, same statue. But Gentillini's room was austere, like the nuns of old. There was little color, and nothing was out of place.

Gabriel Luke's own room had many more books, and her bedspread was much more colorful.

Gabriel Luke went right over to the desk, the only place where she saw papers, and sat down. She started reading everything she could find. She opened drawers carefully, attempting to leave things exactly as they were.

There were a lot of notes about liturgical things—things that Gentillini wanted to change inside the church. There were also pages of prayers that Gentillini had written herself in her beautiful penmanship. Gabriel Luke admired the penmanship and some of the prayers. Some of the other prayers, however, Gabriel Luke found old-fashioned and almost disturbing.

In the top middle drawer, she found a small notebook. It had a hard cover and contained lined pages. In it, Gentillini had written phone numbers for people in the parish, along with a few addresses. It also contained a few lists of things to bring to various places. It was basically a notebook of mundane life—something Gentillini probably used to jot things down when she was on the phone.

And then there it was—a page right in the middle of the notebook. In Gentillini's beautiful penmanship: Freedom Center for Boys, Joseph. Underneath, she'd written a set of driving directions. Without pausing, Gabriel Luke took a blank piece of scrap paper from one of the other drawers and copied the page, exactly as it was written. She double-checked to make sure she had it correct. She folded the paper and placed it in her pocket.

Gabriel Luke looked to make sure everything was normal when she left the room—well, normal for Gentillini. She closed the door and went to her own bedroom. She should be in her office at school, but she was too depressed and confused to go there. She sat on her bed.

What should she do with this information? Call the Saint Claras? John Paul was their child, not hers. He was a minor, and they had full authority over him. Even if she felt it was abuse, others might not. Should she confront Gentillini? She'd never admit to anything and would probably make matters worse. Could Bob and Fiona help? Maybe they could drive to this place and check it out. Should she call her friend, the Mother Superior? Maybe. But the fact that Gabriel Luke had violated the sacred trust would probably be a worse offense than Gentillini bringing a boy to a conversion camp.

She wasn't proud of herself. And she wasn't proud that she was a nun. She didn't like either of those feelings. She was frustrated and had no answers.

"Gabriel Luke, Sister?" She heard a voice calling from downstairs. "Are you up there?"

She got off her bed, opened her door, and walked to the top of the stairs. One of the retired nuns stood at the bottom.

"Oh, Sister," the retired nun said, "I thought I saw you go up there. We have to pray. A child has been kidnapped right here in Kaiserburg. The parents are on TV. Will you pray with us?"

CHAPTER 36

Gentillini, like most modern nuns, had a cell phone. But unlike most modern nuns, she refused to use a phone that could access the internet. Instead, she used an old flip phone that was specifically made for elderly people.

She woke up that Monday morning feeling unwell. She'd slowly been feeling bad since dropping off John Paul Friday night at the Freedom Center for Boys. Something wasn't right. When she woke up this morning, the feeling that she had done something wrong was growing. It was unlike her to feel this way—most unlike her—and she didn't like it. She wanted to find out more information about the place where she had taken John Paul.

Theresa Saint Clara told Gentillini that she found the place online and had researched the facility. But now the word *facility* began to bother Gentillini. When she had seen the actual Freedom Center for Boys, it looked nothing like a facility; it was an old house in the middle of nowhere that hadn't been cared for. She decided to call Theresa to find out exactly where she had learned about Joseph and the center.

She walked quickly and smoothly across Main Street in front of the church campus. She didn't want to take a chance that someone might hear the call. After she crossed the street, she walked through an alley and stood behind an abandoned store. She didn't see anyone around. She called the Saint Clara home.

"Theresa?" Gentillini said. "Yes, hello. This is Sister Gentillini. Do you have a minute?"

"Yes," Theresa replied. "I hope nothing is wrong with John Paul. I called school office today. That new secretary answered, and I told her that John Paul is being homeschooled for the next few months. She seemed confused. Is something wrong with the school?"

"Nothing is wrong with the school," Gentillini said. "I just wanted to check with you about how you discovered the Freedom Center for Boys, just for my information. So you found it by doing a search of Catholic reparative facilities?"

"Something like that," Theresa said. "I actually first talked to another mother whose son went there and did amazingly well. It had been quite successful for him. She gave me Joseph's number."

"You actually spoke to this woman?" Gentillini asked.

"Yes," Theresa said. "I mean, over the internet."

"So you never heard her voice?"

"Of course not. We were in a chat room for Catholic mothers. She knew exactly what I was going through."

"And then you called Joseph?" Gentillini asked.

"Yes," Theresa replied, "and then I called you and told you about it. And you told me that you then called and spoke to Joseph."

"I did. We had a wonderful talk."

"You sound like you are concerned," Theresa said. "Is there something I should know?"

"No, really," Gentillini said, "everything is fine."

"Joseph told us not to call or contact John Paul for a while because it could delay the therapy."

"Right, he told me the same thing. I think that's wise. Listen, Theresa, I really must get back to work."

"Well," Theresa said, "please call me if you think you need to. Otherwise, I'm putting my trust in the Lord that he is there with John Paul, Joseph, and the other boys that need help. We've been praying hard about it every night."

"Of course," Gentillini said. "That's the best thing to do. Well, you take care, and I'll talk to you later."

Gentillini ended the call. She immediately wondered how stupid a mother could be. Obviously, the other mother in the chat room didn't even exist. And she wondered how stupid she, herself, was for not investigating more at the time. What should she do now?

She walked slowly back across the street and toward the convent. It was in her nature to do nothing and let John Paul work it out himself. Didn't he deserve some pain for breaking God's law? But she couldn't get the image of the house out of her mind. It didn't look right. There weren't any other vehicles around. There was not another person in sight. There hadn't even been a sign stating the name of the center. Joseph was great when she spoke with him on the phone—a compassionate Catholic soul. But when she met him in person with John Paul, he was too quick to get rid of her.

Gentillini also couldn't forget the image of the book *Ancient Pride*, burning in the pot on the picnic table at the city park. She chastised herself for that. She never should have done that. Making him burn a book was just plain mean. She used to love books, and now she was burning them.

She went back inside the convent, using the back door. When she crossed the kitchen, she made a decision. After work, Gentillini decided to drive back up to the Freedom

Center for Boys. She'd insist on seeing the inside. If she didn't like what she saw, she'd bring John Paul right back to his parents. They'd start again somewhere else. At least, all of this was Theresa's fault for being so stupid—Gentillini could easily place all blame on her.

Then she saw something that changed her plan. As she walked up the first two steps, she noticed that Sister Gabriel Luke was sitting in the reception room, watching TV with two retired nuns. She heard the newscaster say something about a missing kid. She took a step back and looked at the TV. She saw Jayme Smith-Johnson's face and immediately recognized him as the boy in the photo with John Paul—the same boy he'd been kissing and the boy whose house she had visited early in the morning with a nasty note.

She walked into the reception room. She didn't look at the other nuns. She saw the Smith-Johnson parents on the television. The mom was crying profusely. The dad was talking about how much they just wanted their child back. Then she saw some of the news report.

"The Smith-Johnsons," said the newscaster, "believe that their transgender child was abducted by an ultra-right-wing fringe group. Mr. Smith-Johnson is running for Congress and is a well-known supporter of trans rights. In a recent campaign pamphlet, the family introduced photographs of their trans child, Jayme. Police are investigating and will hold a press conference this afternoon. In the meantime, police say that they have images from a doorbell camera on the Smith-Johnson's front door. They are looking for the person in the images and will release them at the press conference. If you have any information about the whereabouts of Jayme Smith-Johnson, please call the police immediately."

Gentillini wondered if she could wait until after work. Perhaps she might need to leave to retrieve John Paul sooner. She had no idea how things had gotten so out of control. But she was now wanted by the police, even though she had nothing to do with the disappearance of the boy—well, at least, *that* boy. She *did* have something to do with the departure of another boy whom she'd seen kissing the missing boy. What if she was taken by the police for questioning before she retrieved John Paul? What if John Paul saw this story on a television at the Freedom Center and had some sort of breakdown? What if Joseph hurt John Paul?

Then, a series of new thoughts took control of her. What if she was arrested or even questioned? Everyone would know what she had done. Even if she was found legally innocent, the convent might believe she was morally guilty. Gentillini was no longer as concerned about the boys as she was about her own future as a nun. She could never lose that. She was filled with panic. She needed to get John Paul immediately.

Gentillini ran through the kitchen. She grabbed the keys to the convent's car from a key rack by the back door. The door slammed shut. Quickly, she ran past the statue of the Blessed Mother without even looking at it and darted into the open garage. She got in the car and backed it out. She took off down the street, praying as she sped out of town.

CHAPTER 37

Jayme leaned against the side of the church, in the corner where one of the bell towers met the main structure. The courtyard was empty. He kept an eye on the back door of the convent. He didn't know anything about nuns and their schedules. He just wanted to talk to Sister Gabriel Luke— Gabs. He could have asked Bob to contact her, but he didn't want to get anyone else involved.

He was wearing black joggers, a black T-shirt, and a black hoodie that he had pulled up around his head. All of his clothes came from Hunter's closet. Now that he thought about it, he probably looked more conspicuous dressed like this than if he'd just worn something normal. But it was too late to go back and change.

He also wore his backpack, the one he'd taken with him from his bedroom, on his back. It was heavy. He'd packed it at Hunter's house with all the necessities he thought he'd need for a few days. He'd also put *Ancient Pride* in there. Jayme knew it would be lighter if he didn't take the book, but he really wanted it.

He'd seen a group of women walk from the convent to the school. He assumed they were nuns. None of them were Gabs. Then he saw no one for a long time. Eventually, a younger nun, the only one who wore a nun's veil, came out of the convent and walked across the street. He remembered Hunter talking about a bad nun named Genitals—that she was the only nun who wore a veil—and thought that this was probably her. But after a few minutes, she came back and went inside. Still no Gabs.

In the meantime, an older man, probably in his eighties, walked out of the church's side door. Jayme crouched down in the shadows to avoid being seen. The old man walked through the courtyard and toward the street. But he stopped in front of a large statue. Jayme knew that Catholics worshipped the mother of Jesus—at least, that's what he thought. Jayme studied the old man as he stood there in front of the stone woman in white. The man clasped his hands together and looked into the statue's face.

The old man looked so extremely peaceful. Peace seemed to radiate from him. The aura was so palpable that Jayme could almost touch it. He felt the peace himself.

Jayme hated Catholics for teaching gay children to hate themselves. Yet could a place that inspired so much peace be entirely bad? He knew nothing about this old man, but in this silent moment, the old man seemed both content and powerful.

After a few minutes, the old man simply walked away. Everything was still.

Then, suddenly, the back door to the convent burst open. The bad nun, the one with the veil, ran out and slammed the door behind herself. She moved stealthily and practically leaped into the garage. She tore out of the place like Cruella de Vil in the old Disney movie. If Jayme hadn't been so anxious, he would have found it humorous.

But then the back door opened again. Another nun ran out. This time it was Sister Gabriel Luke—Gabs. He recognized her from the bookstore. She chased the first nun. However, the car came out of the garage too fast for Gabs to catch her. He doubted that the bad nun even saw Gabs. But Jayme did, and he wanted to talk to her.

As Jayme ran across the courtyard, he watched as Gabs went into the open garage, put her hands on top of her head, and pressed herself into one of the walls. She turned suddenly as he ran in and said her name.

"Sister Gabriel Luke!" he said. "Do you remember..."

He stopped talking because she looked like she was going to faint. Her eyes grew wide, and she brought her hands to her mouth, like she was seeing a ghost.

"Jayme," she said, "is that you?"

"Yes," he said, "from the bookstore. We met the other night. Remember? I know John Paul and I—"

"You're missing!" she interrupted.

"No," he said. "That's the other boy, John Paul. He's missing. I'm trying to find him."

"No!" she said strongly. "I just saw it on the news. You're missing!"

"What?" he asked. Jayme had no idea what the nun was talking about. How could she know that he had run away from home?

"I just saw it on the news," Gabs said. "I saw your parents, the Smith-Johnsons. They said you'd been abducted, and they're trying to find you. Someone took you from your bedroom window—and they left a note! They think it's some transphobic people that took you. Oh my God, I have to call the police."

She started to move toward the courtyard. Jayme, starting to understand, put his arm out and stopped her.

"Gabs, no!" he said. "Wait! *You* don't understand. I wasn't kidnapped. I ran away. That's all."

"What? So you're okay?" she asked. "I still have to call the police. Everyone is looking for you. Your parents are beside themselves; I just saw them."

"My parents are doubling down," Jayme said. "They're calling my bluff, and I've seen enough movies to know that it will work. The story is out, and the media will love it. Nobody is going to believe the truth anymore—that they are horrible parents."

"I don't understand," she said. "What are you talking about?"

"My parents abuse me," Jayme said. "They have for a while. I ran away, and they are afraid that if I tell someone, it will hurt my dad's chances to be elected to Congress. So they're just saying all this stuff about kidnapping. I can't believe... well, yes, I can believe."

"If I don't call the police, then I'm committing a crime. I'm a guidance counselor! You're a missing kid, and I know where you are."

"Stop. Please, Gabs—Sister Gabriel Luke—please don't call. Nobody will believe me. I was locked in my room and abused since I was a kid. My friend had to rescue me with a ladder through the window. Nobody is going to believe that. The media will love that some conservative freaks took me because they hate my parents and their liberal ways. Trust me, that will be the story. If you call the cops, we'll be on the news tonight, all three of us, and my dad, the candidate for Congress, will be crying with joy that his trans kid is back from the evil clutches of the other side. The media will love it. They're not going to run with any other story—this is national-headline stuff, no matter what I say. And I'll be back right where I was in that house."

"But why are you here?" Gabs asked. "I mean, right here, at the church?"

"Because I want to find John Paul," Jayme said, "and I think you know where he is. Or at least, I think you can find out. Did that woman, or nun, who just left in that car have something to do with this? Does she know what happened to John Paul?"

"Yes," Gabs said, "I think so. But I'm not sure."

"They sent him away, didn't they? His parents sent him to one of those camps that I've seen in movies. One of those camps where they try to change gay people. That's what happened, right?"

"I think so. But, listen, there is nothing we can do about that until you are safe."

"I am safe!" he yelled. "It's when you call the police that I *won't* be safe. I'm not safe with my parents."

They both stood and looked at each other. It was a stand-off. Jayme wondered if he should just start running before she could call for help. But if he did that, he'd still have no lead on the location of John Paul.

"Listen, Sister Gabriel Luke," Jayme said, "you said you think they took him to a reparative therapy camp. That must mean you have a reason to believe that these parents would actually do something like that—and that scares me. Do you know what they do to guys in a place like that? They make them sleep in coffins and wash the floor with a toothbrush. I've seen it on TV. I thought it was fake—I guess I hoped it was fake. But now I know that it's not."

"What are you going to do if you do find him up there?" Gabs asked. "Rescue him and go off together in the sunset?

You're still going to have to come back to Kaiserburg and face all of this."

"What do you mean, if I find him *up there?*" Jayme asked. "That means you do know where he is. You know he's some-where north of here, probably in the country. People around here always use that phrase, *up there*, when they talk about the country. Just tell me where he is. John Paul and I didn't start any of this; we were just born."

"Jayme," Gabs said, "this is not a movie. This is real life. There are real people looking for you, and they deserve to know where you are. John Paul has real parents, and they have the right to raise him however they want. So don't try to manipulate me by pulling on my heartstrings and talking about all you did was to be born. This whole thing is now bigger than the two of you. This is a serious situation. You're old enough to understand that. Sometimes, this is just how life is."

"I'm sixteen! I'm not old enough to understand any of it! I'm supposed to be in school all day. At night I'm supposed to be gaming and cheating on my English essay. On week-ends, I'm supposed to be sleeping all day and making out with my boyfriend at night. That's what I'm supposed to be doing. But instead, I'm having drugs forced into me by my own parents, I'm crawling through windows, and I'm arguing with you in a damn convent garage. And to top it all off, the one guy that I can't stop thinking about, the one guy on this whole planet that makes my heart actually feel something for once—where is he? Well…he's in a prison, learning how not to love me. So that's life, right, Sister?"

CHAPTER 38

Jayme didn't have his driver's license, at least not technically. But he did have a learner's permit and had driven quite a bit with his mother. Even so, he'd never driven in a car all by himself. He certainly had not driven much outside of Kaiserburg. But none of this would matter if he couldn't get his hands on a car.

He'd just run through the church courtyard and circled around the convent. He pulled the black hoodie tighter around his face and crossed Main Street. If there was an army of people looking for him, they sure weren't looking downtown. He didn't see anyone else around.

He'd also left Sister Gabriel Luke behind. After she gave him a paper from her pocket—a paper with the location of John Paul written on it—she turned and walked into the convent. Jayme wanted to ask her about the other nun, the nun who had driven like nuts out of the garage, but when he followed Gabs, she just held up her hand, signaling to him that she was done with the whole situation.

After he crossed the street, he went through an alley and continued along the back side of a strip of shops and bars. He finally read the paper that Gabs had given him. John Paul was at the Freedom Center for Boys, Joseph. He didn't know if that was the name of the place, or if it was a place with a person's name written after it. Either way, he did not like the sound of Freedom Center for Boys. Not at all.

A list of directions was written on the paper. He'd lived in that area his whole life and knew, sort of, where he was headed. The problem was finding transportation. He couldn't go home for obvious reasons. Hunter didn't have access to a car, and he'd promised Hunter that he wouldn't involve Sophia. His one hope was the bookstore.

He knew that Fiona drove a twenty-year-old Toyota. He had seen it parked behind the bookstore. Jayme didn't want to involve Fiona. But he also didn't want to steal her car. His thought was to first check inside the car for the keys. If they were in there, he'd think about whether he'd just drive away. If the keys were not inside, he'd have to go talk to Fiona.

He walked up to the car, checking first that nobody was around. He looked through the driver's side window and didn't see any keys, but he did locate the push-button start. Maybe the key fob was somewhere inside. He pulled on the door handle. Suddenly, the car began to honk loudly.

He swore and ran to the side of the bookstore. He crouched down next to a dumpster. After just a few moments, Jayme saw the back door of the bookstore open. Bob looked out.

"Hey, Fiona, your car's going off again!" he heard Bob yell.

Bob went back inside. Soon Fiona came out of the door. She stood by the door, holding a key fob in her hand, and pressed a button. The car didn't stop. Fiona grimaced and walked all the way up to the car. This time when she used the fob, the car stopped. She began to walk back to the bookstore when Jayme decided to stand up.

Fiona was startled and jumped at the sight of him. She made a weird sort of high-pitched grunt in surprise.

"Jayme?" Fiona said. "Everyone is looking for you. Why are you here? Where have you been?"

"Hi, Fiona," Jayme said. "Yeah, I heard all about it. But, listen, it's not what they're saying on the news."

"You mean," Fiona said, "you weren't kidnapped by a bunch of right-wing wingnuts? Yeah, I figured that didn't happen."

"How did you know?" Jayme asked.

"Oh come on—I didn't believe your parents' act for a second. They made this whole thing up to get votes, right?"

"Well, you're closer than you think. I actually just ran away. They came up with the idea to use it for votes after I'd already gone."

"I knew it!" Fiona said with a laugh. "Politicians, right? I guess I'd run away too if my dad was running for Congress. Only the worst kind of person would ever think of doing such a thing."

"Fiona, I'm not trans," Jayme said. "I'm just gay."

"So?" she said.

"So," he answered, "it's a long story, but they want me to be trans, and that's basically why I ran away. But none of that matters now because I need to go and get John Paul. I know where he is."

"He's missing too? What the hell is going on around here?"

"I need to borrow your car."

"Oh, Jayme," Fiona said, "I don't know about that. People are looking for you. Do you know how much trouble I could get in? This could lead to jail. There has to be some kind of law against helping teenagers run away."

"But, Fiona," Jayme said, "John Paul's parents sent him to a reparative therapy camp. I have to get him."

"I'll drive," Fiona said decisively.

She walked toward the car. Jayme put his hand in front of her.

"No, you can't," Jayme said. "I would feel terrible if you got into trouble. Give me the car. This way, you can say that you didn't know anything about it."

"Who else knows about this?"

"Gabs. She found out where his parents sent him. I have the directions."

"Well, I don't like it," Fiona said. "But I really, really don't want to go to jail, and being with a minor that's missing is a pretty good way to end up there. I can't just let John Paul sit in a place like that."

"Give me the car," Jayme said. "Or let me steal it. You can deny it all, and I can get John Paul. We both win. Fiona…I have no other option. There's no other car I can take."

Fiona was silent. Jayme was in a hurry to get to John Paul. He had to leave in that car—even if he had to grab the keys and fight with her.

Fiona took a deep breath and said, "Okay, you can go. You can take the car. But what's your plan? Tell me you have something that sounds somewhat possible."

"I'm going to find him," Jayme said. "And then I'm going to call the media. Everyone is looking for me, right?"

"Yes, and they think you've been taken by dangerous conservative sycophants."

"So I'll call the media and tell them where to find me. When they arrive, they'll also find the dangerous conservative sycophants—the people that have John Paul."

Fiona just stood there and looked at him. Then she smiled. She threw the key fob to him.

"I'm impressed," Fiona said. "That might work. Just be careful. I want two guys back here for the book club, and I want them both in one piece."

Jayme moved toward the car. He reached for the door.

"Oh, Jayme," Fiona said, "you have to unlock the car with the fob before you touch it, or the alarm will sound. It's old and touchy."

Jayme used the fob to unlock the car. He opened the door.

"Fiona," Jayme said, "one more thing. I don't have a phone. GPS might be really handy."

Fiona rolled her eyes and shook her head. She gave him her phone.

"The passcode is 2-4-6-0-1," Fiona said. "It's Jean—

"Jean Valjean's convict number. Yeah, I know," Jayme said. "I've seen the movie."

CHAPTER 39

"People have cameras on their doorbells?" Gentillini said. "I can't believe it. How common is this?"

She was in the convent's car. She'd been talking to herself between sessions of listening to radio news reports. She was quite frustrated because she'd made a few wrong turns. She wished she would have taken the written directions to the Freedom Center for Boys with her. Her memory wasn't working like it usually did.

She had listened to the entire press conference about Jayme Smith-Johnson and their disappearance. She despised that the media and police kept referring to Jayme with "them" and "their" pronouns, mostly because it made it difficult to figure out how many kids had been allegedly abducted. She was especially angered over the sentence, "They have camera footage of whoever abducted them." It took her time to figure out that "they" were the multiple authorities and "them" was one person: Jayme.

The people watching the press conference were shown a still image from the doorbell video of the suspect. Of course, Gentillini wasn't able to see this image over the radio and had no ability to access the internet. She didn't know what a still image of a video meant and assumed it was probably one frame of film. She wondered what it looked like. Could they tell it was her? *Probably not*, she thought. If they had figured out exactly who was in the photo, they'd already have released more specifics about her.

She remembered that she had been wearing her veil when she delivered the letter to the Smith-Johnsons. She wondered what it looked like in the photo. Did it look like a veil? Or just black hair?

Three-quarters of the way to her destination, she needed to stop for gas. She worried that she might be recognized somehow. Gentillini really hated it, but she took off her veil. It had been the first time ever that she'd been in public without her veil since she had entered the convent at the age of eighteen. She had to go inside the gas station to pay with cash. She refused to carry a credit card issued by the convent's Mother House. All the other nuns had one, and she thought it was disgraceful and undignified to buy anything on credit. She didn't understand how a debit card functioned—or know that they even existed.

There were other people in the gas station. She remained aloof, even though she was full of paranoia on the inside. She paid quickly and left.

When not listening to the news, she focused on two things: the stupidity of Theresa Saint Clara and her complete innocence about Jayme Smith-Johnson's abduction. She did recognize that she had taken John Paul to the Freedom Center. And she did admit that she put an incriminating letter in the Smith-Johnsons' door. But it was too hard for her to deal with accepting any responsibility—she pushed those thoughts down.

At last, she was driving slowly down the long gravel driveway to Joseph's house. The sun was still up, and the entire place looked different. Now she really saw what a mistake the whole thing had been.

The house was actually an old farmhouse in the front. It was clearly in the middle of a renovation with missing siding and trim. There was no place to store any vehicles. There was no gate or guard house at the entrance. *Any reputable place,* she thought, *would be more polished.*

There weren't any other buildings on the former farm site. No barn and no sheds. However, the grass around the house had been meticulously maintained. She looked at the healthy lawn, which had been mown with perfectly straight lines. An old riding lawn mower, rusty and muddy, sat in the middle of the lawn.

Again, hers was the only vehicle on the property. She wondered how Joseph got around. The thought that something terrible was occurring inside that house took over her soul. No longer did she think about anything to do with herself or Jayme Smith-Johnson. Nothing about this place felt right. Her only focus was John Paul.

She stopped the car right in front of the house and stepped out. She checked that her veil was straight in the rearview mirror. She walked toward the three wooden steps that led to the front door. But before she reached them, the door opened, and Joseph walked out.

"Sister!" he said. "We weren't expecting you."

"Yes, well," Gentillini said, "I don't have a lot of time. John Paul's parents have decided to pursue other options with their son. I've come to take John Paul back to them."

Gentillini watched as Joseph's face went from a smile to completely flat. There was something horrifying about seeing each facial muscle change. It took him a few moments to respond.

"We are making excellent progress, Sister," Joseph said. "John Paul is doing great."

"Yes, well, that's good. But I still need to take him. They are his parents, you see, and there isn't much we can do about that."

"Well, Sister, that's not going to be possible. I have to rely on the Lord. Jesus tells me that John Paul needs to stay right here. They might be his parents, but Jesus is the Lord. You understand, of course, Sister. I have to listen to Christ."

She was alarmed at this kind of talk. Apparently, Joseph had crossed a line that she was uncomfortable with. She thought she'd try a different tactic.

"Yes, I can understand that," she said. "I'll just see John Paul and let him know we're thinking of him. Then I can go back and tell the parents that everything is fine."

"Oh, but that will set him back," Joseph said. "We're making progress, and he can't see anyone until it's all finished."

Ever since she was young, Gentillini had been a formidable woman. She'd always been as strong in her body as she had been in her faith. She took a look at Joseph, sized him up, and made a quick decision.

Joseph was standing on the bottom rickety step. Gentillini stepped up to him and pushed him to the side. He lost his balance and fell against the side of the house. He caught himself against the peeling paint of the siding. But that had given her the time she needed to get onto the small landing in front of the door.

Joseph was yelling something at her, but she wasn't listening. She opened the door and walked in. She took several steps inside, then stopped when a large dog appeared at the top of the staircase in front of her.

She looked around. She was standing in some sort of living room. She could see a kitchen in the back. There was a sofa in the living area and a stack of white PVC pipes of various lengths. The wood floor was unfinished. It did not look like a legitimate facility of any kind.

"John Paul!" she said loudly. "Are you in here?"

By this time, Joseph had sprung up the outdoor steps and was standing right behind her. She turned and looked at him, holding up her hand to keep him back. When she looked back at the stairs, she saw John Paul standing next to the dog.

She shuddered at his appearance. He was wearing an orange jumpsuit—like a common prisoner—and his face was smeared with grease. She wondered how he had gotten grease marks on his face. His hair was disheveled, and his school dress shoes were full of dust and dirt.

"Why is he dressed like that?" Gentillini asked.

"This is all part of the process, Sister," Joseph said.

"Come down here, John Paul," she said. "I'm taking you home right now. You don't need to get anything. Just come with me."

"Oh, no, Sister, you are not taking him," Joseph said harshly.

"John Paul, come here!" Gentillini yelled at the top of her voice.

The dog barked. John Paul nodded and started down the first few steps. Gentillini's senses were all heightened. She needed to keep an eye on both the dog and Joseph, while getting John Paul into the car.

"No!" Joseph yelled.

Joseph pushed Gentillini hard. She was taken aback by the extreme force of his strength and fell to the floor. She hit hard. But it didn't faze her for long. She quickly gathered her fortitude and stood from the floor. She backed up into the living room.

"Okay! Well, now we know what's going on here," she said.

As she spoke, Joseph walked toward her. Gentillini made a slow motion with her hand. She hoped that the motion would signal John Paul, letting him know that he should move slowly downstairs. But she didn't dare take her eyes off Joseph to check on John Paul.

"This whole thing is fake," she said. "This is a falling-apart house run by an obviously falling-apart man. Hitting me like that! How dare you! You could never run an actual facility like this—you can't even manage to finish one wall. This house isn't even fit for that dog, let alone a bunch of boys. John Paul is the only one here, isn't he? Well, that's a problem—a big problem. What is an old man like you doing up here all alone with a young boy?"

"Shut up, woman!" Joseph yelled.

"Christ would never want this," she said. "You think you're talking to Christ? Well, I've got something to say about that. You're not talking to Christ. You're being led by Satan!"

She kept her eyes focused on Joseph. He started walking quickly toward her. She held up her hand to keep him away. But Joseph reached and grabbed one of the pipes that was about three feet long. Gentillini screamed. He bashed it into the side of her head. She felt herself falling. She felt the hard floor as she landed on it. Through her terror and blood-filled eyes, she saw him over her. He hit her several more times with the pipe.

This was not the death she had ever imagined for herself. There was no bright light. Her life did not flash before her eyes. There was no beautiful Blessed Mother who came to escort her from her bedside. There was no triumphant chorus of angels leading her upward. Instead, Sister Gentillini just simply...died.

CHAPTER 40

John Paul had been working in one of the upper rooms, sealing an elbow joint with putty. He had not heard a car approach and didn't know why Joseph went unexpectedly downstairs. He was hot, and he wiped his forehead with a grease-covered hand. Then he thought he heard a voice. Max ran immediately from the room and down the upstairs hall. John Paul heard the familiar sound of Sister Gentillini's voice calling his name. He ran to the top of the stairs.

He never thought he'd be so happy to see Sister Gentillini. She stood at the bottom of the staircase. She said something about taking him home, and he was ecstatic. His only thought, as he started to go down the steps, was to ask Joseph if Max could come with him.

He stopped when he saw Sister fall. Joseph's push filled him with fear, but Gentillini got up off the floor. She started talking directly to Joseph, and John Paul saw her make a motion with her hand. He took it as a sign to walk slowly down the stairs. He heard her talking harshly to Joseph, but he didn't pay attention to the actual words.

But then he witnessed the terrible violence. He stopped moving and stood in shock. Max didn't move either, as if the dog knew there was nothing to be done to stop it.

John Paul heard the awful sounds of the pipe against the nun's head. She fell loudly onto the floor. A scream, followed by odd moans and gurgling, and then nothing. There was blood splattered everywhere around the room. Joseph's plaid flannel was full of it—so were both his arms. A pool of blood formed around Sister Gentillini's head on the floor. But Sister Gentillini's head did not look like Sister Gentillini's head. Instead, it was some sort of mass of skin, blood, and colors of fluids that John Paul didn't know existed. He wanted to look away, but he couldn't.

He didn't know how long he and Max stood like that—just staring. He didn't know how long Joseph stood, bent over with the pipe still in his hands. Eventually, Joseph stood straight and dropped the pipe to the unfinished wood floor.

"John Paul," Joseph said calmly, without turning to look at him, "put Max in your room and close the door. Then come down here and help me."

"No," John Paul said. "I don't want to."

Joseph stood there for a moment and then slowly turned to look at John Paul. He walked across the room, as normal as could be, and began to climb the stairs.

"Okay, John Paul," Joseph said. "Let's just get Max somewhere before the blood gets to him. He's a German shepherd, yes?"

John Paul didn't know what any of that meant. But he cared for Max a lot and didn't want to see him harmed. John Paul put his hand on Max's neck and guided him to his bedroom. He followed the dog inside. Joseph stood in the doorway.

"Sometimes," Joseph said, "it is difficult to do the Lord's work. But God called upon Joshua to kill—and many others. How many did David slay in the Lord's name?"

John Paul did not like hearing this. He knew, of course, from *Ancient Pride* that David, even though in a relationship with Jonathan, had killed. But to hear Joseph invoke that name at a time like this was repulsive.

"We have a mission," Joseph said. "You and me together. Jesus has shown everything to me. And he commanded that I stop anyone who stands in our way. This woman was not a holy woman. You didn't see what happened outside. She put her hands on me and shoved me so that she could get in here. And then she accuses me! Accuses me of poor quality! John Paul, she put her hands on me. Do you understand?"

John Paul thought he'd known fear before. He hadn't. Now he knew fear.

"I'm not a monster, John Paul. Nobody that acts in the name of the Lord is a monster. I am an agent of his will. And I can see that you're not well. Would a monster be able to see that? So I'll take care of everything. I'll do this for the two of us. You stay in here with Max. Then, when everything is done, we'll have a nice meal. We won't be able to install more plumbing today, and that will set us back. But if we work extrahard tomorrow, we should be able to get back on schedule."

Joseph turned and left. John Paul heard the lock and saw the door tremble as Joseph checked to make sure it was locked. He went to the bed and lay down. Max sat in the middle of the floor and whimpered. John Paul started to cry. He got up off the bed and laid himself on the wooden floor, next to Max.

CHAPTER 41

All the students at the public high school were talking about one thing: Jayme Smith-Johnson's abduction. The students fell into one of three groups.

One-third of the students were extremely upset and worried about their trans classmate. Many of these students cried and had to leave class to sit in the cafeteria, where three social workers were consoling those who sat on the plastic benches. These students were all—simultaneously—Jayme's best friend. They vowed to fight for justice and support Sammy Smith-Johnson's campaign for Congress.

Another one-third of the students thought that Jayme got what he deserved. Sure, kidnapping was wrong, but this group believed that if you played with fire, you got burned. And in their eyes, Jayme had played with fire.

The third group declared, vehemently, that they didn't care. However, inside, they were extremely dedicated to one of the first two groups.

Among all this were Sophia and Hunter—Hunter, who knew the truth, and Sophia, who thought she did. At the edge of the cafeteria, away from those with the social workers, Sophia was perplexed.

"You told me that you talked to him," Sophia said. "You said he was really sick. Was that before the kidnappers came? Did you see anything?"

"Listen, Sophia," Hunter said. "Let me explain. But you have to promise me that you're not going to be mad and freak out—at least not here. Jayme didn't think his parents would say anything, and that's why we didn't tell you."

"What are you talking about?"

"I did see Jayme on Sunday night. *I'm* the kidnapper."

"What?"

"I got a ladder, just like *you* told me to. But when I got up to his window, he wasn't sick. He was locked in there and his parents were...well, there was abuse going on. Bad abuse. He didn't give me much of a choice. He climbed out of the window, and we brought the ladder back to my dad's house. It was that easy."

"Where is he now?" Sophia asked. "How come you haven't told anyone? And why the hell didn't you tell me?"

"We didn't—*I* didn't—tell you because you're an adult or whatever. Even right now, in this minute, you are committing a crime. You know the location of a missing minor, and you're not reporting it. See? I was trying to protect you from that. I'm sixteen. I'm just a dumb teenager doing what dumb teenagers do to help their friends. They won't come down on me too hard for that."

She sat silent for a few moments and said, "Okay, I can understand that."

"Jayme is confused and upset," Hunter said, "and he's also in love. He's mad at his parents. He doesn't think anyone will believe the truth, and he just wants to find John Paul. So that's what he's doing."

"Where is he looking?" she asked. "Does anyone know anything?"

"I don't know," Hunter said. "The last time I saw him was when I left for school. He was going to talk to the good nun, Gabriel Luke. But I doubt she'll know anything. He said that he doesn't want to involve anyone else. But I think he won't have a choice. I think he'll probably hide out at the bookstore until he finds out something about John Paul."

"Bob," Fiona said, "what if I told you something that you might not want to hear?"

"I'm not stupid, Fiona," Bob said. "I know something's going on. You've been too quiet, and your car is missing, yet you're still here. And you always set your phone on the counter right here. Well, it's not right here."

It had been an hour since Jayme had left with her car. She should have realized that Bob would notice. She sat down next to Bob on her stool, and she told him everything that happened behind the store with Jayme. When she was finished, she got up from the stool.

"Fiona," Bob eventually said, "stop worrying about going to jail. I'm old—I can hardly walk since my fall. Jail might actually be nice for me."

"What are you saying?" Fiona asked, half laughing at him.

"You don't know anything about Jayme," Bob said. "This morning, *I* saw Jayme outside the store, and *I* stole your car fob and phone. I gave them to him. You don't know anything."

Fiona's heart melted. Bob was willing to take the fall for her. And she would let him.

"I feel terrible about worrying about me when those two guys have real problems. But thank you, Bob. You're a wonderful person."

"I know. Anyway, who knows how this will all play out? Maybe everything will be fine. But since you told me that Jayme talked to Gabs this morning, I think we'd…I mean, *I'd*…better give her a call."

Sister Gabriel Luke spent her time between watching the news in the convent's reception room and pacing the floor in her bedroom. She desperately wanted to talk to Gentillini. She wanted to know where Gentillini had gone. Gabriel Luke tried everything she could think of to get a number for Gentillini's cell phone. But nobody knew the number—not at the convent, not at the parish office, not at the convent's Mother House.

She was sitting in the reception room when her own cell phone rang. It was Bob. The retired nuns were still in the room. Gabriel Luke got up, went upstairs, and answered the phone in her bedroom.

"Hi," she said. "How are you?"

"Hi, Gabs," he said. "So we've got a bit of a situation going on." He laughed. It made her feel better.

"I just can't get my head around the whole thing," she said. "I can't figure out if I've done something wrong or not."

"It's going to take some time for any of us to figure that out," he said. "But I know you saw Jayme Smith-Johnson this morning and that you talked to him."

"How do you know that?"

"Because he came to the bookstore and told me."

"Oh," she said, "so you're in my same boat, huh? You know something, and you're not going to report it because you care more about those boys."

She instantly felt much better that someone else had seen Jayme and let it go unreported. She felt less alone and less wrong.

"Yep," Bob said. "I'm sailing right there with you. I couldn't call the police on the poor kid. He's been abused, and all he wants to do is stop someone else from getting abused."

"I think I found out where John Paul is," Gabs said. "I gave him the directions."

"I know," Bob said. "I gave him Fiona's car. And her phone. She's pissed at me."

"Well," Gabs said, "if I know Fiona, she won't be pissed long. You did the right thing."

"Fiona is one of the two most amazing people I've had the good fortune of knowing."

"Bob, I have to ask…and I'm sorry for bringing it up, but, is…I mean, does your devotion to Jayme and John Paul have anything to do with what happened to you about four decades ago?"

There was silence on the phone. Gabs regretted that she had brought it up.

"Of course it does," Bob said. "How could it not? It hits close to home. Why? Do you think I'm wrong or bad somehow?"

"No, not at all," she said quickly. "I'd be worried if you said it didn't have anything to do with John Paul and Jayme. And I know that I played a part in all that—what happened back then, I mean. Maybe that's why I'm willing to stick my neck out for these two."

"Gabs," Bob said, "I think we both want to think that we can smooth over the past by making things better in the present."

"I'm not sure it really works that way," she said.

"I don't care; I want it to work that way. But I think I don't need to talk to Gabs right now. It's too confusing. But I'd sure like to get Sister Gabriel Luke's opinion on something."

She couldn't remember the last time he'd called her Sister Gabriel Luke; maybe he never had. She didn't like it, but it was probably her fault for bringing up the past.

"What do you want to ask?" she said.

"If there is really evil in the world, it didn't come from me or you, or Fiona, or Jayme, or John Paul, or whoever got Jayme out of his bedroom. We've all acted according to what we deeply feel is right."

"So what's your question?"

"Well, if someone is evil, who is it? That other nun?"

She sat down on her bed. She sighed. Bob would never ask anything this spiritually extreme unless he was really bothered by it. She felt pressured to answer.

"I'd like to say that nobody is evil. That's what I'd love to say. But I can't. No, Sister Gentillini is not evil. She's a soul of the past acting in the wrong time. Like us, her intentions, however misguided, are to help John Paul get to heaven."

"Then who is the evil?"

"The parents. All of them. They all know better. Their sons have been nothing but wonderful gifts to them. I'd love to have either of those boys as my own. They know there is nothing wrong with their kids. But they needed something to be wrong so that they can remain devoted to their dogma. All four of them—evil."

Theresa Saint Clara sat at the kitchen table. Mary Clair was upstairs. She was waiting for Bernard to get home from work. It was quiet. She was praying her rosary. Her phone conversation that morning with Sister Gentillini still bothered her. Gentillini didn't sound like herself. Theresa worried that something was wrong with John Paul. She prayed, asking the Blessed Mother to come to their aid.

She heard the garage door open. Before long, Bernard came through the door that connected the kitchen to the garage. She stopped praying the rosary, but she kept the beads lying on the table. Bernard took off his jacket and hung it on a hook near the garage entrance.

"How was your day?" Theresa asked him.

"Just fine," he replied.

They spent the next five minutes discussing Bernard's day. He sat at the kitchen table, and Theresa made him a cup of coffee. She made excellent coffee, a skill she'd learned from her mother.

"Anything happen around here?" Bernard eventually asked.

"Mary Clair is upstairs," Theresa said. "She didn't have much to say about school today. Some kids were asking when John Paul was coming back."

"It's good he won't be totally forgotten by the Catholic schoolkids when he gets back," Bernard said. "He'll need to hang around a completely Catholic crowd I assume."

"I would think so," Theresa said.

She sat down with her own cup of coffee. She'd brought a small plate with three homemade cookies on it. She set it on the table in front of Bernard, and he took a cookie.

"Sister Gentillini called this morning," Theresa said.

"Is something wrong?" Bernard said quickly. "I knew it—he already messed up. They're not able to cure him."

He slammed his fist on the table. Then he sat back and pushed the plate of cookies away.

"No, Bernard," Theresa said calmly. "I know how you feel. My heart almost jumped out of my chest when she called. But it wasn't that at all. She just wanted more information about how I contacted the center and Joseph, the guy who runs it."

"So she hasn't heard anything?"

"No, and I believe that no news is good news. I'm sure John Paul is doing fine."

"Okay, well, I'm glad about that. I'm just so worried that he's going to mess up."

"We don't need to worry. We have the Lord on our side, and we made the right decision. God will reward us for that. Even though it was a difficult decision, we put our son's salvation ahead of our own needs."

"You're right," Bernard said. "Those parents that don't make their children fear the Lord will have to pay the price someday. Why, look at those parents of that missing kid on the news today. They let their son be a woman, or whatever, and now they have to pay for it."

"I've been thinking the same thing all day," Theresa said. "But I did say a prayer for those parents. Out of charity, of course."

Sammy Smith-Johnson left his home office and walked through the kitchen. There were two police officers waiting there. They sat on stools at the kitchen island with laptops in front of them. In his office, he'd left Brandon and two volunteers from his campaign.

He looked unkempt; he made sure of that. His tie was hanging down, his collar was open at the neck, and his shirt was half untucked. His hair was messy.

"How're you holding up?" one of the cops asked as he passed by.

"I'm not," Sammy replied. "I'm just trying to get through another minute without Jayme. Is my wife upstairs?"

"Yes," the cop said. "She said she needed to be alone for a while."

Sammy nodded at the officers and walked up the staircase. He took each step slowly as he attempted to portray a sluggish appearance. But once on the second floor, his demeanor seemed to improve dramatically. He went into their bedroom and closed the door behind him. He locked it.

Abygail was sitting on the bed. She was watching a newscast on the television. The newscast was about Jayme's disappearance. She had been dissecting her appearance on the program.

"Does it look like my crying is fake?" Abygail asked.

"No. Who said that?" Sammy asked as he sat on a chair next to the bed.

"Someone said it in a comment online. It was posted on the TV station's comment section."

"I told you never to read that crap," Sammy said. "I'll bet it was ten to one in our favor."

"I'd say probably twenty to one," she said. "One comment on my fake crying for every twenty saying how courageous we are."

"Exactly. That's what we need to focus on. And I have good news that will help you forget all about the fake crying."

"What's that?"

"Brandon is downstairs with some campaign people," Sammy said. "They've been going over the live donations coming in online."

"It's good, right?" Abygail asked. "I just feel all this momentum."

"It's real good," he replied. "We are raking in the money."

"See what happens when you listen to me?" Abygail said. "You get to be in Congress."

"Trust me," he said. "After this, I'll never doubt you again. I hope Jayme stays away for a few days. You still think he's at Hunter's?"

"I'm sure of it," Abygail said. "Hunter stopped texting Jayme's phone last night. So obviously, he knows where he is. If he didn't, he'd have texted Jayme's phone the minute he heard about all this on the news. Or at least, he'd have called us. But since we haven't heard a word from Hunter, I know that Jayme is over there."

"But how long is too long?" Sammy said. "I mean, we want the money to keep coming in, but at some point, we want to capitalize on the emotional reunion with Jayme."

"I don't think we should push it too long," she said. "We don't want to risk that Jayme figures his way out of this. I think tomorrow night we'll have to go over to Hunter's and get the ball rolling. We'll make a deal with Jayme and Hunter. If they play their cards right, they might be able to each get a car out of this."

"I was thinking the same thing," Sammy said. "We'll have plenty of money to buy a couple of used cars. That should keep Hunter's dad quiet too."

"But I don't want to go back downstairs," Abygail said. "It's too much work. But I guess the evening news cycle will be starting soon."

"Don't worry about it," Sammy said. "Maybe you're too grieved to be on TV. Let me do it. Besides, having you too messed up to be interviewed gives me more to be emotional about."

"Now that," she said, "is a great idea."

CHAPTER 42

The nice thing about the way that Joseph lived is that he had a lot of half-used construction supplies around. So it was easier for him to get rid of a body than it would be for someone else. It was also easier for him because he tended to not think things completely through.

He rolled Sister Gentillini in a blue construction tarp. He tightly secured the tarp with duct tape. He then dragged her body through the room and opened the outside door. He was strong, but it still took an immense amount of effort to drag her down the outside steps. He was surprised at how hard it was to drag her to the driveway. He made a number of comments about her dead weight as he moved her.

"These nuns have a nice car," he said to himself as he opened the rear driver's side door. It took quite some time to get Gentillini into the back seat. He almost gave up and went to get John Paul for help. But he was very glad that he didn't have to do that when she finally slid in. He closed the car door and went back inside.

He went upstairs to get a scrub bucket; he wondered what John Paul was doing. Hopefully he had calmed down. Joseph planned their menu for that evening as he filled the scrub bucket with warm, soapy water. He wouldn't be able to make anything that required too much preparation. He didn't know how long it would take to clean and dispose of the body. But he thought it would take long enough that he wouldn't be able to make a nice meatloaf. He thought he could handle hamburgers and Tater Tots baked in the oven. It wasn't the kind of food he liked to make, but it might have to do.

He went down to the now-infamous room. He worked on the walls first. The walls had been drywalled but not yet painted. Consequently, the water just soaked into the drywall, creating large wet circles that weren't going to disappear as they dried. Joseph was frustrated. Then he noticed that if he used a sponge and scrubbed really hard, he could remove the top layer of drywall along with some of the splattered blood. He'd have to let it dry before he could decide if he needed to scrub more tomorrow.

The floor was more difficult. It was unfinished pine. Here, the blood had penetrated the first few layers of the wood itself—like a good-quality wood stain. Scrubbing made no difference at all. Joseph didn't have a choice; he'd have to start sanding the floor.

He had an old standing sander that he stole from a construction site a few months back. He put a sanding disc on it and started to work on the floor. The machine was extremely loud. He worried that it might upset John Paul. He switched it off and went upstairs.

When he unlocked and opened the door, John Paul was lying on the floor. He was face down, with his head in a pillow. Max was lying next to him. They both turned and looked at him when he entered.

"I'm going to be using the sander for a bit," Joseph said. "It's loud. Then I'm going to have to take that car and hide it somewhere and walk back. I'll try to get back as soon as

I can. We'll have hamburgers, and I think I've got some ice cream in the freezer. But you should get up off the floor and lie on the bed."

John Paul showed no reaction. Joseph left the room and locked the door. He went back downstairs and started sanding. The machine was deafening, but he didn't have any type of ear protection.

This wasn't the first time he'd cleaned up blood in a house where he lived. It wasn't even the first time he'd cleaned up a woman's blood. But it was the first time that the woman had died.

Joseph had been married three times before. The first time was the longest. The marriage had lasted seven years. After many beatings, she finally had enough and ran away to her sister's house. She divorced him. Since Joseph wouldn't acknowledge the divorce or even show up in court, the judge gave her everything. Joseph spent a year in the county jail for contempt of court.

He met his second wife at church, on a Friday night during Lent. By Easter, they had been married. By the next Easter, after a series of charges for domestic assault, they were divorced. Again, Joseph spent time in the county jail.

He decided to move counties. He lived alone and actually had a fairly good life for a number of years. He got Max during this time from an animal shelter. His third wife volunteered at the shelter. They dated for a year and then were married. They were married for two years without an incident. Then one night, he snapped and started beating her. But she grabbed a baseball bat and beat the hell out of him. He was hospitalized for five days.

When he got out of the hospital, he was so demoralized that he picked up Max and moved to another state. He never heard from her again. He supposed he was still married to her, but he didn't know, and he didn't care. It was while he was in the hospital that he had his first vision from Jesus of the Freedom Center for Boys.

Yes, he'd cleaned up blood before. But never this much and never on unfinished surfaces. He did the best he could and decided to see what everything looked like in the morning.

He still had to deal with the car. And with Gentillini herself. He had several jugs of denatured alcohol for construction use. It was highly flammable. He grabbed four of the jugs and put them in the back seat of the car, next to the body. He also retrieved a grill lighter from the kitchen.

The kitchen cabinets had been assembled out of pieces of used cabinets that Joseph found somewhere. However, out of all the mismatched pieces, only one had a lock. The bottom drawer, next to the refrigerator, was locked. Joseph grabbed a ring of keys attached to his belt with a chain. He searched through them, then used one to open the drawer.

"She's already dead," he said, "but you never know who is out there."

The drawer contained a Smith & Wesson M&P Shield. This handgun was a semiautomatic pistol that Joseph had stolen from a truck he'd broken into two years earlier. The drawer also held a holster and several boxes of ammunition. He attached the holster to his belt. He loaded the gun and placed it in the holster.

When he walked through the house to go back outside, he saw that the crime scene looked worse than before he'd started cleaning. The wet walls were showing darker bloodstains as they dried. He could also see deep gouges in the floor from the sander. He grumbled to himself when he realized that he'd have to spend more time on that room before he and John Paul could get back to working on the rest of the house. He went outside, frustrated at having to delay his plumbing work.

He got behind the wheel of the sedan. It had leather seats. He'd never driven a car with leather seats before. Gentillini had left the keys in the car. He was glad for that because he hadn't checked her pockets before he wrapped her up. He would have hated to undo the tarp to look for keys.

Joseph turned the car around and drove down the long gravel driveway. The real trick was to decide how far to drive. He needed to go far enough that no one could connect the body to him. But he couldn't go too far because he had to walk all the way back to the house. He drove on a rural road for a mile or so, took a turn, and drove for another two miles. In the distance, he saw a grove of trees in the middle of a farmer's field.

He turned into the field and drove the car over ruts until he reached a tractor trail. Then he took the trail to the grove of trees. He didn't see a farmhouse or any structure nearby. He got out of the car.

Joseph poured the four jugs of denatured alcohol all over the inside of the car. He made sure that it covered Gentillini. Then he stopped and said a prayer.

"Lord, thank you for giving me the opportunity to prove my worth to you. Thank you for giving me the strength to follow your will. Please watch over John Paul and me. This woman is now in your hands."

He took the grill lighter and held it into the car. Immediately, the alcohol erupted into flame. He wasn't prepared for the outburst. His hair and eyebrows were singed. He backed away and fell to the ground. He felt a sharp pain.

When he looked at his right hand, the hand that held the lighter, he saw that it was badly burned. Some of the skin was even coming off. He looked around for water but didn't see any. So he did the only thing he could—he started running toward his house.

CHAPTER 43

It was dark as Jayme drove down a two-lane highway in the middle of nowhere. The journey had taken longer than it would have taken an experienced driver. He drove under the speed limit for much of it and stopped several times to check the directions against the GPS map on Fiona's phone. And although he knew it was taking longer, Jayme made a conscious decision to drive as carefully as possible. Being in an accident or getting pulled over by the police would ruin his quest to get to John Paul.

There were many concerns on his mind. The top concern was John Paul's safety. But a close second was the fact that he had put several people in bad positions. He worried for Hunter, Gabs, and Fiona; he suspected that Bob probably also knew by now. He worried that they might try to do something or even follow him. He thought that he should call Fiona and give her an update. Then they might not feel a need to involve themselves further.

He drove until he came upon a small town next to the highway. After passing several homes, he found a post office with a small parking lot. He pulled into it and retrieved Fiona's phone from the passenger seat. He used it to call the bookstore. He knew they were closed, but he hoped that either Bob or Fiona would still be there.

"Carlson's Used Books and Records," said a voice that he recognized as Fiona's.

"Fiona, it's Jayme," he said. "I'm really glad you're still at the bookstore."

"Bob and I both stayed here," she said. "We thought this is where you'd probably call. Just in case you need to know, Bob has his own cell phone that you can call—it's even a smartphone, if you can believe that. It's in my phone contacts under 'Fredricksen, Carl.' I should have told you that."

"After the old guy from *Up*," Jayme said. "I might have figured that out."

"Where are you?" she asked.

He took a deep breath. He tried hard to make sure his voice was confident and calm. He wanted them to know that he was capable of doing whatever he set his mind to. He would no longer be in the theater audience enjoying the movie; he was now director of the film.

"I'm calling to say that everything is fine," Jayme said. "I'm almost there, and I know that this will all be over soon. I want to thank all of you for caring and everything you've done, but now the ball is all in my court. I can do this, and I can accept whatever comes from my actions."

"Well, okay," she said. "I can respect that. I guess I have to respect that. What's done is done, and I...we...have to move forward."

Jayme took a breath. He didn't quite know how to respond.

"Thank you," he said. It was all he thought he needed to say.

"But just in case you need us," Fiona said, "Gabs is upset that she didn't make a copy of the directions that she gave you. Nobody knows where you are, and we can't find out anything about any gay reparative therapy places online, at least not anywhere close to Kaiserburg. Can you snap a photo of the directions with my phone and send it to Carl Fredricksen?"

"Sure," he said. "I'll do it right now."

"Okay," she replied, "but please drive safe, and let us know when you leave there. We're going to stay in the bookstore. None of us will be able to sleep anyway. And, Jayme, we're serious. If we don't hear from you within the next two hours, we're going to the police."

He felt bad when she said that. He didn't want to cause such a disturbance in their lives.

"I will call as soon as I'm heading back to Kaiserburg," he said. "But I should get back on the road."

They said goodbye, and he ended the call. He didn't want to give them a chance to follow him, so he ignored the request to send a photo of the directions. He set the phone on the passenger seat, next to his backpack.

He drove out of the parking lot and continued down the highway. There were just three more turns. After about twenty more minutes of driving, he turned onto a paved county road and then came to a long gravel driveway. He turned onto it and drove up the bumpy path.

Jayme noted that there wasn't any sort of sign advertising the place. When he got closer, a large exterior light lit the yard of an odd-looking house. This was not at all the place he'd imagined from piecing together what he knew about reparative therapy. There were no cabins around. No guards. In fact, there was nothing at all: no vehicles, no other build-ings...no people. Just a creepy old farmhouse and a single outdoor light on a high post.

He didn't think that there was any way this could be the right place. Maybe Gabs had gotten all of this completely wrong? Maybe he didn't follow the directions correctly?

There were scattered lights on inside the house. Someone could be inside, he guessed. He'd come all this way and had no other alternative to try. So he decided to knock on the door and just ask if anyone knew anything about the Freedom Center for Boys or anyone named Joseph. He kept the car running, with the keys in it, and left the driver's front door open—just in case he needed to make a quick escape.

Three wood steps creaked loudly as he stepped up to the door. There wasn't any sort of storm or screen door. He knocked. Almost immediately, he heard a dog barking. *There must be someone here,* he thought. But after several long moments, he heard no other movement, and nobody came to the door. He knocked again. Again, the dog barked, and nobody appeared at the door.

With a frustrated sigh, he decided to give up and leave. It was obviously not the right place, and there wasn't anyone there. In addition, he really didn't want to mess with a dog. Maybe he had made a wrong turn? He turned to walk down the steps.

Then he thought he heard a voice shouting. He turned back to face the door. It was muffled, and he didn't know for sure. But it sounded like a person and not a television or anything like that.

"Hello?" Jayme shouted.

The dog barked twice, and again, Jayme thought he heard someone shouting. He didn't know what to do. He tried the door. It wasn't locked. He opened the door just wide enough to stick his head inside. He didn't want to take a chance of being attacked by the dog.

Jayme looked around at what little he could see. He saw some sort of living room that was under renovation. Pipes and other construction supplies sat on the unfinished floor. A large standing sander sat on the edge of the room, next to a couch. The walls seemed as if they were in the middle of being painted—they had large wet spots all over them and were full of streaks and small blotches.

"Hello?" he said.

The dog barked once, then stopped. The bark came from the top of a staircase that was to the left of him.

"Hello?" he said, louder. "I'm looking for someone. Is anyone here?"

"Yes!" a voice shouted back from somewhere upstairs. "Yes—I need help."

This time, Jayme heard the words clearly. However, he was still apprehensive to enter the house.

"I don't think I should come in," he shouted. "But I can go and call for help. What do you need?"

"I'm here alone, and I need help," the voice said. "I don't want to be here."

His first instinct was to run to the car and grab Fiona's phone in order to call 911. He cursed at himself for not thinking to have the phone with him. Then the synapses in Jayme's brain fired fiercely. They made all the connections required for him to realize that the voice he was talking to was John Paul's.

"John Paul?" Jayme said. "Is that you?"

"Who is that?" John Paul said. "Yes, this is John Paul."

That's all that Jayme needed to hear. He opened the door completely and entered.

"Where are you?" Jayme said.

"Upstairs, first door," the voice said. "I'm in a locked room. Can you open it?"

Jayme ran up the steps, two at a time. He went immediately to the first door. It was locked.

"John Paul!" he said. "Are you in there?"

"Jayme?" John Paul said. "Jayme, is that you?"

"Yes. Are you here alone?"

"How are you here?"

"I came to find you," Jayme said. "How do I open the door?"

"You have to get me out of here," John Paul said. "He'll be back any minute. Just get me out of here. I'm scared."

The door wouldn't budge. Jayme was in a panic. John Paul did not sound okay.

"How do I open it?" Jayme said. "Do you know where the key is?"

"No," John Paul said. "Joseph will have it. He's coming back, and we can't be here when he does. I don't know…is there anything that can open the door? Please, please—"

"Okay, John Paul," Jayme said, "I'm working on it. Let me think."

John Paul's tone made the situation ten times worse. Jayme was frantic. He shook the doorknob as hard as he could. He kicked the door. The dog was barking again, but Jayme didn't care. He looked everywhere he could for anything he could use. He saw a light switch next to the top of the stairs and flicked it on. The hallway light, a single exposed bulb, turned on. He took a closer look at the lock.

"John Paul," Jayme said, "I see some screws on the doorknob. Is there a screwdriver around here?"

"Yes!" John Paul said. "Downstairs on the floor somewhere. One with a battery. It's in that first room. Probably on the floor in the corner where a bunch of other tools are. Hurry."

Jayme ran down the stairs. It didn't take long at all for him to locate a pile of tools in a corner next to the stairs. The screwdriver was on top. He grabbed it and quickly ascended the stairs.

Other than being locked in his bedroom for much of his childhood, Jayme had no experience with doorknobs or locks. He just hoped that by removing the exposed screws, he'd be able to do something to the door. The screwdriver had considerable power, and it slipped off the screws several times. He had to concentrate and try to keep his hands still. Finally, the last screw came out and fell to the floor. He tried the knob again. Again, it didn't move. He started shaking and pulling on it. A metal ring came off in his hand. He kept shaking, and other parts started coming loose. They dropped to the floor. Finally, the knob turned.

Now the door opened easily. John Paul stood in the middle of a small room. He was holding back a large dog that had, once again, started barking loudly.

John Paul looked awful. He was dirty and wore an ugly orange jumpsuit. The window in the room had been covered with wood. There was a dirty toilet and sink. Jayme was shocked.

"The dog won't hurt you," John Paul said, holding the dog tighter. "It's okay, Max. I know him."

Max stopped barking. Jayme walked up to John Paul. He wanted desperately to hug him. However, he wasn't sure of anything in the moment. So he just stood there.

"Jayme," John Paul said, "how did you get here? Are you alone?"

"Yeah," Jayme said, "I'm alone. It's a really long story, but you won't believe what I've been through since the last time I saw you."

"Well," John Paul said, "I've been through some things myself."

"I can see that," Jayme said. "What are you wearing?"

"Never mind that," John Paul said. "Listen, we have to get out of here. The guy, Joseph, is crazy. I don't know where he went. But Sister Gentillini…he killed her. I think he took her somewhere, and he'll be back."

Jayme didn't know how to respond to any of that information. Again, he just stood there. His brain needed a break, and it took one, whether he wanted it to or not.

"There is this monitor on my ankle," John Paul said. "But I'm not sure it really does anything. How did you get here? Drive?"

Jayme remembered where he was and what he was doing. Once again, his brain fired quickly. He moved toward the door.

"Yes, I drove," Jayme said. "I mean, I have a car here. Is there anyone else here?"

"No," John Paul said. "It's just me and Joseph—the crazy guy."

"And someone is dead?" Jayme said.

"Yes. Sister Gentillini from my parish," John Paul said. "She came here to get me, and Joseph went crazy. We really need to call 911. Can we just get going?"

"Oh. Right," Jayme said.

He moved quickly as he grabbed John Paul's hand and led him from the room. They started down the stairs.

"Can I take Max with us?" John Paul said.

"Who?" Jayme said, annoyed that he wasn't understanding everything.

"The dog!" John Paul yelled.

"Of course," Jayme replied. "Just get in the car."

Jayme opened the front door of the house, and the two of them ran outside with Max. Then Jayme stopped suddenly and held out his hand to stop John Paul. A man standing next to the car had just closed the driver's side door. The car was no longer running. Jayme heard John Paul gasp.

The man was extremely sweaty. There was dried blood all over his clothing and face. In his right hand, he held Fiona's key fob. The man used it to lock the car. Then Jayme watched as he put the fob in his pocket and grabbed a handgun from a holster at his waist. In his left hand, the man held Fiona's phone. The contents of Jayme's backpack were strewn around the ground. He saw his extra clothing and a toothbrush.

Then the man pointed the gun at the boys. He dropped the cell phone on the ground and smashed it by stomping on it with his work boot. Jayme saw the smashed phone lying in the mud, right next to his copy of *Ancient Pride*.

CHAPTER 44

After leaving the burning car in the grove, Joseph ran much of the way back to the house. Despite everything wrong with him, he was in great shape physically. But everyone had their limit, and Joseph met his about a half mile from the house. He slowed to a leisurely walk. His hand felt better; perhaps the burn hadn't been so bad. His mind was on one thing: making hamburgers for John Paul.

Joseph's route that night took him across farm fields, wild groves, and ditches. He avoided using the actual roads. He was elated when he finally came to a gravel trail that he knew was his driveway. He walked on the gravel.

Then he noticed a car parked right in front of his house. He made a growling sound. This was the last thing he needed, especially since he was in the middle of cleaning up after the nun. His immediate thought was about the front door. He wondered if he'd locked the door; he couldn't remember. But he did remember locking John Paul's room and was glad about that.

"Did that damn nun tell someone else?" he asked himself.

Suddenly, out of the quiet night, he heard Max barking. Now he knew that someone was inside his house. He started running as fast as he could.

When he got to the car, he saw that it was an older Toyota. Whoever was inside the house must be in a big hurry because they'd left the car's door open and the ignition on. Joseph ran over to the driver's side and peered inside. He switched off the car, then grabbed a cell phone, key fob, and backpack that were on the front passenger seat.

Holding the phone in one hand, he went through the backpack with the other. He threw the contents on the ground: men's underwear, socks, a toothbrush, toothpaste, deodorant, an empty water bottle, and a book. He was checking to see if there were any weapons.

He was about to take a closer look at the back seat when he heard the front door open. He saw a teenage boy whom he didn't know dressed all in black, leading John Paul from the house. Max followed close behind. They came down the steps. When they noticed him, they stopped.

Joseph didn't speak. He made sure they saw him lock the car. He got the gun from the holster and pointed it at the boy in black. In the process, he accidentally dropped the cell phone. He thought it was probably better if the phone was out of commission anyway. So he stomped on the phone hard. It cracked and shattered.

The boys didn't speak. Max didn't bark. The silence lasted for several uncomfortable moments.

"John Paul," Joseph eventually said, "go back to your room. Take Max. Close the door and wait for me. I'll be right in."

"No," John Paul said, "I'm not going back inside that house."

"Max!" Joseph yelled. "Go to your bed!"

The dog immediately obeyed and ran back inside the house. Joseph noticed that the two boys were holding hands as they stood frozen on the front lawn. He assumed they knew each other, and he wondered how the boy had located John Paul. He suspected that the nun was involved.

"You," Joseph said as he used the gun to point toward the stranger. "Walk to me."

"No," the boy in black said. "I'm not leaving without John Paul."

Joseph prepared the gun to fire. John Paul held up his hands.

"Jayme!" John Paul said. "Just go. He won't hurt me. Just go."

"He's right," Joseph said. "I won't hurt John Paul. But you need to listen, now. Just walk toward me, real slow. We're just going to go for a walk together. John Paul, I need you to go to your room."

"Jayme," John Paul said, "please, just go. Joseph, let him go. Just let him leave in the car, and you and I can go back to how things were yesterday."

Again, nobody moved. Joseph wondered how brave this Jayme really was. Then an idea came to Joseph. A brilliant idea. Surely, this kind of idea only came from God. If it worked, if this kid could be used in a new therapy, Joseph could surely create the best men's therapy center in the country. He said a quick prayer of gratitude to Jesus for leading this boy to him and for giving him the idea.

"Wait a minute," Joseph said. "I've had another idea. Remember, John Paul, I will shoot him. You know that I can't let Jayme leave because he'll bring others. So everyone just needs to listen, and we'll all get through this. Now turn around, both of you, and John Paul is going to lead us upstairs."

"I don't want to die," Jayme said.

"Then both of you need to listen to me," Joseph said.

Joseph watched as Jayme turned toward the house first. John Paul took the cue and walked up the steps. Jayme and Joseph, with the gun pointing right at Jayme's back, followed John Paul. They walked up the staircase to the second floor.

"Now go into your room, John Paul," Joseph said. "Get some sleep. Rest assured that Jayme will be just fine. Tomorrow morning, we are going to have a big day. There's also a lot of cleaning to do. We are really behind in our schedule to get the plumbing done."

John Paul didn't turn around. He walked into his room. Joseph bent around Jayme and slammed the door shut. He quickly grabbed the key ring from his belt, then noticed that the lock had been removed. He reopened John Paul's door.

"You're going to have to switch rooms, John Paul," Joseph said. "I'm sorry about that, but Jayme here ruined that for you. Go to the next room, and I'll come back to set up your bed."

"I can sleep on the floor," John Paul said.

"No, you can't," Joseph said. "You need a good night's sleep, and I'll move your bed. Come on."

John Paul left the first room and went into the second one. Joseph turned on the light, closed the door, and locked it, using his key.

"Okay, Jayme," Joseph said. "That open door, two doors down on your left. Go in there."

Jayme walked down the darkened hall and entered the open door. Joseph followed and switched on the room's light.

"You're in luck," Joseph said. "We just finished the plumbing in here. Sorry that there isn't a bed, but the floor will be fine for you I think."

Joseph turned to leave. Then he thought of something and turned back to face Jayme. Joseph needed to know if Jayme was a believer or not. It made a difference to the therapy.

"I have a question that I need to ask," Joseph said. "Have you accepted Jesus Christ as your personal Lord and Savior?"

"What?" Jayme asked, standing in the middle of the empty room.

"Have you accepted Jesus Christ as your personal Lord and Savior?" Joseph asked again.

"I don't even know what that means," Jayme said.

"You know who Jesus Christ is, right?" Joseph asked.

"Of course," Jayme said. "Born on Christmas, died on Easter."

"Died on Easter?" Joseph said. "Are you sure about that?"

"Yeah," Jayme said. "Died on Easter."

"And what happened to Jesus after he died?" Joseph asked.

"I don't know," Jayme said. "I think he cured Ben-Hur's sister and mom of their leprosy. Listen, man, I just watched the movie—that's all. I'm not religious. And you know, there are a lot of people looking for—"

That's all Joseph heard as he stepped into the hall and slammed the door with a loud bang. He didn't need to hear anything more. This boy was a perfect heathen. Joseph again said a prayer of gratitude to Jesus for sending Jayme. He was perfect for Joseph's purpose.

Joseph went downstairs and into the kitchen. He supposed that dinner was no longer an option because he needed to get back to cleaning. He despised having to change his routine, and he cursed at the dead nun for making this happen.

While he cleaned, he wondered how much time he'd have left in the house. He knew that they'd all have to leave for a while once law enforcement found the burned car. His hope was that they wouldn't be able to connect the car to him. As soon as the investigation went nowhere, he'd return with John Paul and the boy.

But he wasn't too concerned yet. He thought it would take them at least a week to find the car.

Back upstairs, John Paul stood in his new room. He knew this room because he had helped put in the sink. Joseph completed the piping and toilet earlier. He was alone for a few minutes when he heard the noise of Joseph moving his bed in the hall. The door opened.

Without speaking, Joseph brought in the cheap metal bed frame. He set it up and went back for the mattress and sheets. He put the mattress on the frame and threw the sheets on top. Without saying anything, he left. John Paul heard the lock.

He threw himself on the bed. Everything was ten times worse. Up until that afternoon, John Paul didn't know if Joseph was capable of physically hurting others. But that question had been answered when he witnessed Sister Gentillini's head get bashed with the pipe.

He wondered where she was. Where had Joseph taken the car? He felt bad for Sister Gentillini. She didn't deserve any of what happened to her. Yes, he knew she'd been misguided and was often mean, but she should not have died that way. He wondered how he'd be able to get over it. The images were clear in his mind as he replayed them over and over again.

Then he thought about Jayme. Joseph would never let Jayme leave. Finally, a terrible thought came to John Paul.

He assumed that all of this had started because he was gay. If he wasn't gay, they'd all be home, and Sister Gentillini would be alive. *Yes*, he thought, *it's all my fault.*

As soon as Joseph left and locked Jayme's room, Jayme went to check the window. It had been boarded up with a large sheet of paneling that was nailed—with many nails—all around its perimeter.

Jayme ran around the small space, checking all the walls and floor for weak spots. But everything was soundly built, and he found none. He tried the door. Considering how crappy the front door had been, this door was solid and unyielding. He checked the knob, and there weren't any exposed screws on this side.

He wished he could speak to John Paul. Together, they could work this out. He thought of yelling through the walls, but John Paul was at least one or two rooms away—Jayme couldn't remember.

He wanted to tell John Paul that he would be all right and that witnessing the nun's death did not have to haunt him. He wanted John Paul to know that none of this was his fault. The fault belonged solely to the adults around him.

Then he thought about himself. Had he overreacted when he climbed out of his bedroom window onto Hunter's ladder? Should he just have put up with his parents until the election was over? How much would two years of hormones really hurt him? When he turned eighteen, he could leave and never look back.

Jayme was not a scientist or mathematician. Logic did not direct his choices. Jayme was one of those people who loved the journey, no matter the destination. He loved movies, music, and stories about people who led with their hearts.

Then Jayme sat down on the wooden floor. He was about to pound his fists against the wood. But he stopped. He knew it would be bad to make noise. He yearned to scream at the top of his lungs; screaming was also not a luxury he could afford. He just wanted some peace.

He thought about that word, *peace*. He thought about the old man whom he'd seen praying to the church courtyard statue that very morning—the man who looked at the statue with a serene expression of peace. Jayme wanted that peace.

"I don't know which god is God," Jayme said. "But if Jesus is God, that's okay with me. So, Jesus, John Paul and I need help. Please help us. If you are God, then you are the God of gay people, straight people, and trans people. We need your help. Please help us."

He wanted to cry, but he hated Joseph too much to conjure tears. He thought about John Paul, stuck here with Joseph for these days. Then Jayme pictured his copy of *Ancient Pride* lying in the mud right outside the very house where he was now a prisoner. He looked up at the unfinished ceiling of his room. Out of nowhere, he felt a strength fill his soul. He stood.

"I don't know how…yet," Jayme said out loud, "but we will get out of this. I don't care what I have to do. As God as my witness, Joseph will pay for making that book dirty."

CHAPTER 45

Fiona loved the bookstore at night. There was something magical about being surrounded by so many words when the darkness made it seem more likely that the words would come to life. But that night, with so much stress hanging over all of them, she was restless.

Another problem was that she could not get comfortable. There were only two comfy chairs in the store. They were in one of the corners, under an old lamp, and created a sort of undignified reading nook. Bob was in one of the chairs, fast asleep and snoring. Gabs sat in the other, reading a book under the lamp. They looked like an old married couple.

Fiona decided that if she couldn't sleep, she might as well do something productive. She got up from her stool, stretched, and walked softly into the back room. The table where Jayme and John Paul once sat for their book club was now full of coffee and cookies that Gabs brought from the convent. Fiona didn't know much about religious life, but she knew that the nuns were excellent bakers. She grabbed a cookie on her way through.

Fiona opened the door into the storage room. She grimaced. At one time, she had this room completely organized. But Jayme used it a week ago to arrange his special first date with John Paul. Fiona helped to clear the room after Jayme promised to put everything back. He didn't. She shook her head and thought about what she was like twelve years earlier when she was in her teens—she probably wouldn't have put the room back either.

She began to pick up boxes and set them on the shelves. Many of the boxes contained old magazines that nobody was ever going to buy. She wanted to throw them away, but Bob would have had a heart attack and die. So she kept the boxes in order to spare his life. She understood that she couldn't love Bob's dedication to books and hate his aversion to throwing books away.

Since she had time—morning was hours away—she decided to check each box to make sure its label was correct. Most of them were. Every once in a while, she used a black marker to correct something on a label.

She had worked for over an hour when she came across a box of old business records from the bookstore. Fiona sighed with frustration. Bob was supposed to have gone through all the business stuff and given her the important items to be scanned. He must have missed this one.

Under a collection of property tax statements, she discovered several old Kaiserburg newspapers. The papers all contained articles about Bob purchasing the bookstore and renaming it. There was also a folder of cards that expressed congratulations and well-wishes for the new business. Some of the cards were from friends and relatives, and others were from people in the Kaiserburg business community, including the mayor. She enjoyed reading these, as they gave her a sense of Bob before she knew him.

Fiona got to the bottom of the box. Pressed between all the other stuff and the cardboard bottom, she found a large manila envelope—the kind secured with a small string that was wrapped around a riveted paper button. She undid the string and opened the envelope.

She pulled out a photograph. First, she admired the quality of the photograph's paper and the clarity of the print. She wished she would have lived in a time when she could have brought a camera roll to the grocery store to be professionally developed in less than an hour. Home printers just didn't do photography justice, and internet photo services took days to return.

The photo must have been about forty years old. A much younger Bob—probably in his mid-forties—sat with his arm around another man. Fiona smiled when she noticed how dashing Bob looked at the time. He was smiling and had the perfect amount of face stubble, and his hair was that salt-and-pepper color that Fiona loved. The other man was about twenty years younger than Bob.

Bob had never disclosed much to Fiona about his past. She suspected he was gay, but she never knew for sure. When she first started working for him, she quickly got the message that Bob was uncomfortable talking about things that were too personal.

Fiona looked at the picture; it made her happy. She loved thinking about the possibility that Bob may have been in love. The photo must have been taken in New York City. The two men were sitting at an outdoor table, and an NYC taxi was visible behind them. There were buildings and a street sign in the picture. She wondered if she could use the internet to find the exact restaurant where this photo had been taken.

The only other item in the envelope besides the photo was a handwritten letter. Fiona took a moment to consider whether it was appropriate for her to read Bob's stuff. But she really wanted to. So she did.

Dearest Bob,

This is the most difficult letter I've ever written in my life. (Yes, I can hear you now saying, "You're only twenty-six—how many letters have you written?") Okay, the point is taken, and it's the most difficult letter I've written so far.

Last night, you asked me if I loved God more than you. I'm ready to answer that question. I probably should have talked to you about it before, and I'm sorry about that.

Bob—I've loved all the time we have spent together these past two years. You are the best part of my day, and I can't imagine my time in New York without you. Our dinners, the road trips, the long talks about books—I would not be nearly as happy as I am without these things. Thank you so much for that.

I know you've been frustrated that we've never had sex. I want to apologize for that, but I can't apologize for who I am. I know you are under the impression that I've never had sex because I'm religious. That is very, very true. But there is another reason, and it hurts me to tell you. I should have been more honest. I do apologize for this. I'm not attracted to men. I'm so sorry that I led you to believe that I'm gay. Maybe in some way, I thought that I was.

After a lot of personal struggles, I have received a great calling that has given me a tremendous sense of peace. I've never felt this level of contentment before. I'm not gay, but I'm also not

a regular man either. I was born to be female. And
I was born to serve others. These two truths about
me are undeniable, and I must follow them.

Yes, Bob, I love God more than I love you—
more than I could ever love any human, man
or woman. I must follow what he has planned
for me. I must be a celibate woman who serves
the people of God. This is why I was born. I am
certain of this.

After I make my transition, I'm going to join
the Sisters of the Immaculate Heart of Mary. I've
become close to one of the sisters there, and she has
vowed to help me. One day, I hope that I can work
at their school in Kaiserburg—do you remember
Kaiserburg? It's that smaller town we drove
through last summer; it's the one with the bookstore
that you liked. I'm telling you this so that maybe
one day, you can write to me. I'd like to know that
you are okay. But I will understand if you never
want to think about me again.

I wish I could have it all. I want to serve
God, live in my truth, and maintain our close
relationship. But that would not be fair to you.
You deserve more from a relationship than what I
can give you.

You are a big part of my journey. Thank you.
I will pray for you for the rest of my life. May God
guide you, keep you safe, and hold you.

With love and prayers,
Lucas

Fiona sat on the floor and reread the letter. The letter answered a lot of questions that she'd wondered about over the past two years. She was a jumble of emotion.

"Wait a second," Fiona said aloud.

She looked at the top of the letter and noticed the date. Then she quickly set the letter aside, stood, and located another box that she'd already organized. She opened the box and pulled out a folder of real estate papers. She looked through them.

"Bob bought the bookstore one month before the letter was written," she said, still talking to herself. "But he moved here and opened the bookstore anyway."

She wanted to talk to Bob about the letter. She wondered if he'd be okay with that.

"But now is definitely not the time," she said.

She packed the real estate papers back where they belonged. Fiona carefully folded the letter and placed it back in the envelope. She took a closer look at the photo. She could see it now—Gabs, Sister Gabriel Luke, was inside the man who sat next to Bob.

CHAPTER 46

John Paul didn't sleep at all. He sat on his bed and leaned against a side wall of the new room. He cried some. His mind flipped between the horror of seeing Gentillini's death and the frustration of being so close to Jayme without being able to touch him.

Time passed—hours, probably. There was no way he could know. He wasn't sure if he wanted time to move quickly or slowly. He wasn't sure of anything.

At some point, he thought he heard sounds from the hall outside his door. But when he got up and listened closer, he heard nothing. Soon after that, Max started his daily wake-up call. At least John Paul now knew the time. Although, something was different about this morning because it took a while—much longer than usual—for Joseph to come upstairs and open his door.

Joseph had cleaned himself up. He wore fresh jeans and another flannel shirt. There wasn't any blood visible on his clothing or face. Around his waist, he carried the handgun in a holster attached to his belt.

"You're going to shower before we start the day," Joseph said. "We're going to mix things up a little."

"What about Jayme?" John Paul asked. "Is he okay? Did you check on him?"

"He's fine," Joseph said. "You won't see him until after breakfast. No more questions. Come on."

John Paul followed Joseph down the steps, across the kitchen, and into the first-floor bathroom. He'd become used to showering there during the past few days. Usually, there was a clean orange jumpsuit for him to put on. But this morning, next to the sink, there was a pair of jeans and a plaid-flannel shirt.

"I think you've graduated from the jail outfit," Joseph said. "I'm proud of you. So you can wear regular clothes. I'm not sure how they'll fit, but you can make do. I'll be standing right outside the door, like I always do."

Joseph closed the bathroom door. These past days, John Paul was surprised that he didn't mind showering. The bathtub was the only new fixture in the entire house. The shower had good pressure and was warm. Although, John Paul didn't want to linger in there long. He stripped off the jumpsuit and placed it on the counter. He took about a two-minute shower, then dried himself, and dressed in the clothing that had been laid out for him. The jeans and shirt were too big. He rolled up the cuffs on the bottom of the jeans, turned up the flannel sleeves, and tucked in the shirt.

Joseph was waiting for him when he opened the door. He nodded his approval and then went into the kitchen to start breakfast. John Paul sat at the table, in his usual space. Soon, Max came wandering in and put his head in John Paul's lap.

"Is Jayme going to eat?" John Paul asked.

"After us," Joseph said. "You'd better get this straight, John Paul, because it's important, and I'm only saying it once. Now I don't know what's going on between you two, but I assume it's not righteous. The only reason a boy that age is going to drive all the way up here is for sex. So I know what's going on between the two of you. It's disgusting. But this is a great opportunity for you. Jayme is going to help you get over your homosexual sinfulness. After that, you'll be glad to get rid of him, and the two of us will start things going with the center. If this works—like I know it will, because it was Christ's idea—we'll know how to cure many men of the same sin."

John Paul didn't like the sound of that at all. Last night, he had cried, thinking that he caused all of this by being gay. He thought that if he were straight, everything would be better. Now he realized that if the therapy worked and he were made straight, Jayme would probably die. He was damned if he did and damned if he didn't.

"Here's breakfast," Joseph said. "Eat up. Then we're going to have therapy and get to our work."

"I thought therapy was Monday and Friday," John Paul said. "It's Tuesday, I think."

"It is," Joseph said. "But today is different because we want to try out the new idea. Eat up."

Even though he wasn't hungry, John Paul ate well. He wanted to get as many calories into his system as possible. He was never sure when he was going to need a lot of energy.

When they finished breakfast, they did the dishes and cleaned up the kitchen. John Paul looked for an opportunity to grab the handgun. He didn't know anything about guns and had no idea what he'd do with it if he did grab it. But maybe guns were easier to use than he thought. Regardless, it was better for him to have the gun than for Joseph to have it. Perhaps he could just run with it and throw it in the woods.

The chance to obtain the gun never came. Joseph led John Paul to the basement stairs and walked down. To John

Paul's dismay, Joseph made sure that Max stayed in the kitchen.

When he got down to the basement, John Paul's eyes widened with shock. Just like the day before, the treadmill, chair, wires, and monitors were set in the middle of the room. However, the television had been pushed aside. In its place, Jayme stood, handcuffed by his ankle to the treadmill.

John Paul made eye contact with him. Jayme rolled his eyes and shrugged his shoulders. It was a strange move for Jayme to make, and John Paul thought it looked almost comical. At the same time, Jayme projected a sort of confidence with his movements.

Jayme was wearing the same black clothes as the night before. But he looked clean. Maybe Joseph had allowed him to shower that morning.

"Okay, John Paul," Joseph said, "take your seat."

John Paul sat down on the chair. Joseph grabbed the heart-monitor wires and unbuttoned John Paul's shirt. John Paul just looked straight at Jayme. Their eyes were locked. John Paul was afraid—his imagination ran wild thinking about what Joseph was going to do to Jayme.

Joseph placed the blood pressure cuff around John Paul's calf. Then he stood to the side and watched the monitors.

"Okay, John Paul," Joseph said, "go ahead and grab the metal plates. Let's get a baseline."

John Paul did as he was told. Jayme looked at him oddly, almost as if he were trying not to laugh.

"All right, got the baseline," Joseph said. "Now, John Paul, I want you to look at Jayme. Really look at him. But the whole time, you need to be repeating the name of Jesus. Oh, we forgot to pray."

Joseph set down his monitors and folded his hands together. John Paul stayed in the same position with his hands on the destroyed treadmill's metal plates. He noticed that Jayme just stood there, keeping his hands at his sides.

"Lord," Joseph said, "we ask you to bless this therapy session. Please help us as we purge John Paul of his sinfulness. Keep his mind on your holy word, your holy name. We ask this in the name of Jesus Christ. Amen."

John Paul didn't say anything. This time, he rolled his eyes at Jayme. Jayme smiled and shook his head. Joseph retrieved the monitors as John Paul held on to the treadmill. Joseph turned on the treadmill's motor, and it whirred loudly. Again, the gears rotated without having anything to turn.

"Okay, John Paul," Joseph said, "you can begin. Concentrate on the name of Jesus as you look at Jayme. If you start to imagine touching Jayme, or what he looks like naked, you need to focus hard on the name of Jesus. Focus, even if someone you dream about is standing right in front of you. The name of Jesus!"

John Paul didn't have to concentrate on the name of Jesus. The whole thing was about as unsexy as anything could possibly be. In fact, John Paul was so utterly turned off that he wondered if he had any pulse at all.

"John Paul, your signs are all going up!" Joseph said. "You need to concentrate on the name. The name!"

It was awkward for John Paul to just sit there, looking at Jayme. He assumed it was just as awkward for Jayme.

"What is this supposed to do?" Jayme asked.

John Paul gave Jayme a stern look. He didn't think that Jayme realized how crazy Joseph was and what he was capable of.

"You're not to talk!" Joseph shouted.

"Well," Jayme said, "the whole thing looks ridiculous. You ruined a good treadmill to make this crap?"

"The next time you open that hole in your face," Joseph said, "I'm going to shoot you."

"Did you get that line from *Titanic*?" Jayme said.

"The name of Jesus!" Joseph said.

"Jayme, please," John Paul said.

John Paul gave him a serious look. Jayme nodded and looked like he was ready to oblige Joseph.

"Oh, great," Joseph said harshly. "Now you've ruined it, Jayme. His signs are all down. This isn't going to work if you keep talking. Shut up. Take your shirt off. We need more stimulation."

John Paul's level of panic was beginning to rise. He wasn't sure at all what Joseph wanted and was convinced that none of the monitors worked. He wished he'd had a chance to tell Jayme that the blood pressure cuff didn't even inflate. He was worried that Jayme might feel real indignation at the request to take his shirt off. He hoped Jayme wouldn't do anything rash.

But Jayme didn't say anything. He unzipped his hoodie and took it off. Then he pulled the black T-shirt over his head.

This was the first time John Paul had seen him without a shirt. He wished it were under other circumstances. However, he was surprised at how fit Jayme was. He wondered how someone who spent so much time watching movies and gaming managed to have defined muscles. Still, even with Jayme standing there shirtless, John Paul was quite unaroused.

"John Paul!" Joseph shouted. "You must concentrate on the name of Jesus!"

John Paul looked at Jayme's face. It looked like Jayme, again, was trying hard not to laugh. John Paul hoped with all his might that Jayme would control himself.

Then John Paul thought how absurd this must all look to Jayme. Not just the weird equipment, but all the talk about the name of Jesus. To Jayme, there was no difference between this and believing that eating a rhino's horn could cure your cancer. John Paul hoped that Jayme wasn't going to judge his religion forever. But after this experience, he wouldn't blame him if he did.

"You're doing great!" Joseph yelled. "Really great! The name of Jesus is working!"

This went on for a long time. John Paul hoped that Jayme wasn't getting too cold.

Jayme put his shirt back on as Joseph led John Paul back to his room. Then Joseph came back down to the basement and unlocked Jayme's ankle cuff. He took Jayme back to his own room on the second floor. Jayme stood in the middle of the room while Joseph closed and locked the door.

"What the hell was that?" Jayme said.

He started laughing loudly. Then, he sat down on the floor and made himself be quiet.

ANCIENT PRIDE

THE GOD KING AND
THE SHEPHERD

This chapter deals with a myth that is extraordinary for two reasons. First, there is no ambiguity to this myth at all. All our sources tell us that the relationship in this myth was sexual and intimate in nature. Remember, myths were created by thousands of people around thousands of campfires over hundreds of years. Myths were told and retold as they spread across the countryside. The versions that we have now are the result of many minds. In order for a story to persist, it must have been important in some way.

The second reason this story is extraordinary is it involves a god—not just any god, but the king of gods himself, Zeus. Zeus reigned as the most powerful of all the entities that lived on Mount Olympus. He was responsible for uniting his siblings and defeating the Titans. The Romans called him Jupiter Optimus Maximus, which meant "Zeus, the biggest and the best."

Our story starts back in the fabled city of Troy, which we've read about before. Troy was founded and built by King

Tros; it was named after him. King Tros had three sons, and one of them was named Ganymede.

Back in this time, it was customary for young princes to be sent away from their palaces to learn how to live an ordinary life among ordinary people. Then when they came into adulthood, they returned to royal duties. Ganymede was sent away from the walled city of Troy and grew up on the slopes of Mount Ida. There, he lived with a peasant family and became a shepherd.

Ganymede spent long and blissful days watching the sheep graze in mountain grasses. He ran in the fields by day and slept by a campfire at night. He also grew in stature and beauty.

It became known around the countryside that Ganymede was the most perfect man alive. In fact, one historian discovered a version of the myth where Ganymede was described as the most beautiful human on Earth, man or woman. Surviving poetry says that he had a perfect body, a completely symmetrical face, and golden hair that fell in natural curls.

Zeus was not known for being devoted to his wife, the goddess Hera; that's probably the last thing anyone would ever say about him. He had multiple affairs with both immortals and mortals. Zeus fathered children with goddesses and human women.

One day, Zeus became aware of Ganymede. It didn't matter that Ganymede was male; Zeus was instantly infatuated. And since he was the ruler of the entire world, he made an instant decision. Zeus transformed himself into an eagle and flew to Mount Ida. There, he scooped Ganymede onto his back and flew him back up to Mount Olympus.

Zeus and Ganymede became lovers for a long period of time. We don't know how long because days don't mean the same thing for immortal beings. Suffice it to say, they were an item.

Zeus was so enamored with Ganymede that he gave him the greatest gift he could bestow on a human: immortality. In exchange for taking King Tros's son, Zeus gave him a pair of immortal horses. Two immortal horses were definitely worth more than one son. Tros could always make more sons.

Ganymede became the cupbearer to the gods. This was an extremely important role and one of great honor. (The constellation Aquarius, the cupbearer, is an image of Ganymede.)

Ganymede, as one of the younger beings on Mount Olympus, became friends with Aphrodite's young son Eros, also known as Cupid. In one myth, Ganymede was playing a dice game with Eros and caught Eros cheating. When Aphrodite found out, she yelled at her son, Eros, and told him not to cheat with a beginner like Ganymede. She command-ed Eros to be kinder to Zeus's favorite lover. She also said that it would be all right for Eros to cheat once Ganymede had more experience. (This is so typical of Aphrodite, god-dess of sexual passion.)

Ganymede was also indirectly the cause of Trojan suf-fering after the fall of Troy. Hera, Zeus's wife, was insanely jealous of Ganymede. Consequently, because Ganymede was a prince of Troy, she hated anything to do with Troy. She took the side of the Greeks during the Trojan War. After the Trojan horse brought defeat to Troy, Hera continued to tor-ment the Trojan survivors. For years, she threw every manner of obstacle at the Trojan prince Aeneas while he attempted to lead the surviving refugees to safety. While the wrath of Achilles is the main fuel of *The Iliad*, the wrath of Hera over Ganymede is the main fuel of *The Aeneid*.

As the gods lived forever, there was no end to this story. For all we know, Ganymede is still there on Mount Olympus, serving nectar to the gods and making out with Zeus when Zeus is not making out with someone else or arguing with his wife.

Certainly, his name lives on. Starting in the 1800s, the term *Ganymede* became an insult for gay men. Calling someone a *Ganymede* was the same as calling them a faggot. This term was used up until the 1970s. (Apparently, even homophobic people follow fads.)

But a much more fitting tribute occurred around four hundred years ago. On January 7, 1610, Galileo looked through his telescope and observed four objects floating around the planet Jupiter. ("Jupiter" is the Roman name for "Zeus"; the Romans named the planets.) He discovered that other planets could have moons, just like ours does.

He named the three smaller moons after three female lovers of Jupiter: Io, Europa, and Callisto. But Galileo named the largest and brightest moon after Jupiter's male lover. Today, anyone with a telescope can look to the sky and see Ganymede. He is there now, forever bound to Zeus in an everlasting dance.

CHAPTER 47

That entire Tuesday morning, the police station had become a zoo of confusion. Even before the sun rose, three anxious people arrived at the station and asked to speak with whoever was in charge of the Jayme Smith-Johnson case.

Bob sat on one side of a conference table. Fiona and Gabs sat to him. Two detectives sat across the table. It was cold in the room, and Bob was freezing. His cane sat next to him on the floor. He and Fiona had decided it would be smart to bring anything they had about John Paul and Jayme with them to the police station. Fiona's photograph of the boys, notes she'd taken during book club, and Bob's copy of *Ancient Pride* sat on the conference table.

Between sessions of questioning, the police left them for long periods of time. To calm their nerves, Bob read out loud from *Ancient Pride*. He'd just read the chapter about Zeus and Ganymede. None of the three had much to say about it. It was more an exercise in distraction than it had been about education.

Bob looked and saw the ever-present camera recording from above, in a corner of the room. Each detective also had their own recording device, and they took copious notes. The cameras implored him to be honest, even though he knew he hadn't been about Fiona's involvement.

They'd been in the conference room for over four hours. But Bob was shocked at how little they'd been seen by anyone official. Everything seemed to move in slow motion at the police station. One cop would come in and ask three questions, then they'd sit by themselves for an hour or more until another cop came in and asked the same questions. He was frustrated at how little information the group was able to get out. He wondered if the police cared at all about the vital information they had.

Finally, it looked like someone in charge was aware of their presence. A sergeant, who identified himself as the lead investigator for the city, arrived and questioned them. At last, it seemed that the law enforcement officers were beginning to listen and understand.

"Let's get this straight, one more time," a detective said. "We thought that we were looking for one teenaged boy. Now you are telling me that we're looking for two boys and a nun? I gotta say, it sounds like a joke."

"It's not," Fiona said. "You need to find out where this Freedom Center for Boys is located. John Paul Saint Clara's parents will know."

"We've got them coming in," the detective said. "But that's not my biggest problem right now. We need to get the conflicting stories from you three settled before we can trust anything you say. One untruth spoils the entire soup. Remember, there are young lives on the line. Now, Bob, you say that you saw Jayme Smith-Johnson in back of your store. He convinced you to help him, and you gave him Fiona's car keys and phone. But, Fiona, you say that you saw Jayme and you gave him your things yourself. So this means that one of you is covering for the other. Or neither of you is telling the correct story. I have to know."

Bob wanted to do the right thing. He was desperate to find the boys, even if it meant that his dear friend might get in trouble.

"Fiona is telling the truth," Bob said. "I never saw Jayme in back of my bookstore. I didn't want Fiona to get in trouble, but she gave him her car and her phone."

"It's good to clear that up," the detective said. "Now, Sister Gabriel Luke, you said that you saw Jayme Smith-Johnson before he went to the bookstore but after Sister Gentillini left quickly in the convent's car. Do you have anything—*anything*—to prove that you gave him the directions? Did anyone else see you? Do you remember anything at all about what was written on that paper? Give us something to prove that you're telling the truth."

"I've tried," Gabs said, "but I just didn't look at the paper long enough to remember much about it. I took the paper directly from Sister Gentillini's room. We wanted Jayme to text us a photo of it—we asked him when he called last night, but he never did. I feel terrible. How stupid could I have been?"

"Pretty stupid," the detective said. "You let a missing kid go on his own to find other missing people. I'm not beating around the bush here, not when there are people missing."

"I understand," Gabs said sadly.

"What about my phone?" Fiona said. "You must be able to track it. I promise you: Jayme Smith-Johnson has my phone right now."

"It's not like in the movies," the detective said. "It takes time. If you'd have had the phone-finder feature turned on, well, we'd already know. But as it is, we'll have to wait for the cell phone company to review the case. It's going to take time."

Bob looked at Fiona. He saw how troubled she looked. Now she was also being blamed for not using technology correctly. Gabs also looked horrific. He didn't even want to know what he looked like at this moment.

"Sister Gentillini," the detective said. "She has a phone. She has the convent's car. But nobody knows anything about the phone—either her number or the name of the carrier. And the car, who is it registered to?"

"Our Mother House," Gabs said. "The religious order owns the car, the Sisters of the Immaculate Heart of Mary. I told that other cop that the people at the Mother House—the secretary, for sure—will know all about the car."

"But you've never talked to either of…what was the Catholic boy's name?" said the detective.

"John Paul Saint Clara," Gabs answered. "His parents? No, I know them, but I never spoke to them about anything having to do with John Paul, at least nothing about his sexuality. That must have been all Sister Gentillini."

"So here's my other problem," the detective said. "All I have to go on is a feeling that this boy's parents worked with some nun to send their kid to some sort of same-sex-attraction therapy—a feeling that *you* have. But there's no proof. How do I know that Sister Gentillini is involved at all? Maybe you're covering for yourself, or someone—"

"Wait!" Gabs interrupted. "The directions…I remember. I didn't give Jayme the page from Gentillini's notebook. I wrote them down in my own handwriting. It all happened at once, and I didn't want Gentillini to know. I didn't remember until now because there is so much going on. But the page is still in her notebook, in the convent. She didn't go up to her room before she took off in the car—I don't think she did—so I don't think she has the page. The page is in the convent."

Bob stayed with Fiona in the freezing room. A cop came to take Gabs to the convent to look for the paper. The main detective left.

Theresa Saint Clara was nervous as she sat with Bernard in the police station. Not because she was afraid of getting in trouble but because she was terrified that the news of this situation would get out. If John Paul really was involved with the missing Smith-Johnson boy, it would be all over the news. Everyone would know that they had a homosexual son. Everyone.

The door opened, and a detective who had talked to them earlier walked in. Theresa was growing impatient with the long breaks between questions.

"All right," the detective said, "I'm starting to make a picture here. You don't know anything about Jayme Smith-Johnson?"

"No," Bernard said sternly.

"And you have no reason to believe that your son knew him?"

"No," Bernard said again.

Theresa let him answer all the questions, unless she was specifically asked one. She was proud of Bernard for retaining his composure and strength.

"You sent your son to stay with a cousin north of here?" the detective asked.

"Yes," Bernard said.

"And the nun, Sister Gentillini, brought John Paul to his cousin's house?"

"Yes."

"And we can't contact the cousin because he took John Paul on a trip to Rome?"

"Yes."

"And you have no reason to believe that your son is gay?"

"Absolutely not!" Bernard said loudly.

"Okay," the detective said. "Then I want to show you this."

The detective opened a folder that he'd brought with him. He took out a photograph and slapped it harshly on the table in front of them. Theresa looked at it and stared with panicked eyes. It was the photo that Sister Gentillini told her about—the photo that Gentillini had seen in the bookstore, the photo of John Paul and Jayme Smith-Johnson. For the first time, Theresa saw with her own eyes that her son was a homosexual.

"Where did you get that?" Bernard asked.

"From the employees at the bookstore," the detective said. "They say that your son and Jayme were in a book club together. They were in a relationship. Mrs. Saint Clara, you knew about this photo; I can see it in your eyes. Did you send your son away with the nun without telling your husband?"

"No," Theresa said. "Absolutely not. John Paul is with his cousin at the Vatican. In Rome."

"That does not sound right," the detective said. "I mean, you gotta do better than that. If my own mother said that, I'd tell her, 'Momma, you have to do a lot better because that sounds ridiculous.' You know, they have phones in Rome. Who travels with someone else's kid to Italy and doesn't take a cell phone? And you don't even know what flight they were on. So you've got a choice to make. You can either produce your son right now, or you can give me the name of the person that has your son in Rome. That's it—you need to do one of those two things. If not, then I'm arresting you both for endangering a child."

"Oh here now," Bernard said. "I want an attorney. You can't talk to us like that."

"You can have an attorney," the detective said. "But I won't be able to talk to you anymore if you get one. Do you want an attorney, or do you want me to keep looking for these missing boys?"

"Attorney," Bernard said.

"Well," the detective said, "I'm going to leave this picture here so that you can think about it. But don't touch it. It's evidence."

The detective got up and left the room. Theresa sat next to Bernard in silence.

Abygail Smith-Johnson sat in another room at the police station. Sammy was next to her. As were Brandon and an attorney from their political party's state office. In the long breaks between questioning, they talked about the campaign. Abygail thought it was quite warm in the room. She took off her sweater and hung it on the back of her chair. She hoped that she wasn't sweating through her blouse; she didn't want to go on television looking that way.

The detective, the one in charge, entered the room once again and sat down at the small table with them. It was crowded.

"So," the detective said, "some things are lining up here, and we need to get to the bottom of it. Remember when I told you before that I'm real good at making a picture? Well, the picture is starting to come together."

"Don't play those games," the attorney said to the detective. "Just ask your questions, and they will answer. It's not your job to insinuate anything."

"Okay," the detective said. "Now that we have that out there, let me ask you a question. I just talked with our detective that's over at the high school, talking with your son's friend Hunter. So we didn't prompt him or anything—we have the body cam video to prove that. We just asked him what happened, and he told us the same story that we heard from the other witnesses at the bookstore. He just said it, as plain as fact. How would he, and the other witnesses, know about Jayme escaping from the bedroom window because he was being abused? How would they all know the same story if there is no evidence that they ever spoke to each other? The only way they'd all know that information is if it was true and they heard about it from Jayme himself. Correct?"

"Don't answer that," the attorney said. "We don't know that there even is a detective at the school."

"How do you explain the note that was left on our door?" Abygail interjected. "And the doorbell footage? Someone that looked questionable was at our door."

"Abygail," the attorney said, "please don't speak unless the detective asks you a direct question."

"Sorry," she said and sat back in her chair.

"Maybe the woman with the note and the disappearance of your son aren't related," the detective said.

"That's not a question," the attorney said.

"Fine," the detective said. "Sammy, how would a kid at the high school know the exact same story as the witnesses from the bookstore if it wasn't true?"

"Because this whole thing is coming from those conservative bastards," Sammy said. "It doesn't surprise me that Hunter is involved—his dad told me that he voted for that horrible governor that we have. They're doing this because they know I can beat their asses in the election, and they're scared. Hunter—and all those other so-called witnesses—are conservatives."

Brandon held up his hand as a signal that Sammy needed to shut up. Abygail agreed and hoped that Sammy got the message. She worried that he'd crossed that ever-important line between controlling the narrative and being just plain crazy.

"But the bookstore people are hardly conservatives," the detective said. "They are pretty much the opposite. I'd call them flaming liberals, actually."

"Then it's my opponent in the primary doing all this," Sammy said. "She's afraid of me too."

"Everyone needs to stop," the attorney said, leaning forward toward Sammy. "Let the detective ask a question, and then give a simple answer."

"Let me ask: Did you drug your son against his will?" the detective asked.

"No," Sammy answered.

"Abygail, when we searched your house," the detective said, "we found a heavy latch on Jayme's bedroom door. What's that all about?"

"We are well-known political people," Abygail said. "We have a trans child. We are terrified of what the right-wing extremists will do. And apparently, we were right to be terrified. We installed that latch so that we could keep anyone that got inside the house out of Jayme's room. We did it to protect him."

"Protect *him?*" the detective said. "Hmm. Odd choice of pronoun. But how is putting a lock on that side of the door going to protect Jayme if the bad guys can just unlatch it? If you don't want anyone getting into the bedroom, you put the lock on the inside. Where it is now—well, that's where you put it if you don't want anyone getting out."

"This is over," the attorney said. "We are leaving. Do your job, and find Jayme Smith-Johnson."

"I intend to," the detective said.

Abygail, so confident all morning, started to get the smallest butterfly in her stomach.

The detective had completed the third round of questioning and was about to regroup with the other cops before beginning round four. Perhaps the nun was back from the convent with the directions to the therapy center.

"Detective," a young police officer said, walking quickly. "I have a message. They found a car up in Gitchegumee County. The woman we're looking for—the nun—was inside. She's dead."

CHAPTER 48

Joseph had a smartphone. He used it to keep an eye on John Paul's ankle monitor. He believed it worked. Whether it really did or not, he didn't know. He sat in his bedroom on the first floor, another room that was half finished and half not. Max was lying on his dog bed, a large pillow, at the foot of the bed. Joseph needed to get to work cleaning the living room, but he was taking a break to relish the success of the morning.

He was elated that the therapy had worked. He was tremendously proud of himself and thankful that Jesus had provided the new boy, the key to the therapy's success. The boy was a nonbeliever, a heathen. Satan was in him. This was no longer just therapy—this was the actual battle of good versus evil, occurring in his own home and under his guidance. The boy was key to the whole project. Joseph would never again refer to him by his name, Jayme. He was now something else. He was the boy.

The real trick was going to be keeping the boy in line and making him cooperate. Satan was always difficult to control. Joseph would need to think about that. He also planned to make the boy exercise and eat only protein. In order for this to work, the boy needed to stay attractive. He would, at some point, get older. But Jesus would provide a new boy when this boy was no longer effective.

Perhaps, when the center became the best therapy center for men in the country, Jesus would send multiple boys to be "the boy." They would need their own dormitory with special security. Joseph would think about that. He thanked Jesus for another great idea.

While he wasn't the best with technology, he knew how to do a few things on his smartphone. One of them was to check the running log of Gitchegumee County's sheriff's department. All calls that came on a county law enforcement radio were converted into text and placed on the log. By scrolling through the text, Joseph could get a picture of what deputy sheriffs were doing around the county. He often looked through it to see if anything was going on close to his house. He decided to check the phone for any updates.

"Darn it!" he yelled to Max as he stared at the phone.

When he read the newest posts, he learned that all the county's police activities were focused on one spot, just a few miles from his house. To his dismay, a car had been discovered in a grove of trees near a private farm field. The car had been burned. There was a burned body inside the car. The posts started coming in about forty-five minutes ago.

"How did anyone report this so fast?" he said. "No doubt Satan is behind this. Probably, he's leading the police."

Joseph had been caught and sent to jail before. He had no intention of allowing that to happen again. He'd need to take John Paul and the boy somewhere else, and he'd need to do it quickly—there wouldn't even be time for cleaning the living room. They wouldn't need to stay away too long, just long enough for all this to cool down. Then they'd return and build the center. Once he became the most prominent and respected Catholic men's expert in the country, no one would dare disrupt his duties to the Lord.

"Oh, Max," Joseph said. "What should we do with you? I'm not sure you can come with us. Your morning barking might be a problem. You better just stay here."

Joseph got up from his bed and walked to a well-organized closet. He grabbed a duffel bag from a shelf and began stuffing clothes into it. Then he left the room, making sure to close the door with Max inside. He carried the duffel bag and set it down in the middle of the living room. He remembered that he'd forgotten the gun. He went back to the bedroom to retrieve it. Max stayed on his dog bed while Joseph quickly went in and out of the bedroom.

Keeping the gun in his hand, Joseph climbed the stairs and went to the boy's room first. The boy was in there, stretched out on the floor.

"Get up," Joseph said. "We're leaving. Come on."

To Jayme's surprise, he'd actually fallen asleep on the hard floor of the room. He didn't know how long he'd been sleeping when the door unlocking woke him. Joseph came into the room and told him to get up.

Jayme didn't know what he should do. He wondered if it was better to just be shot here or to take the chance of going somewhere else. His experience that morning during the therapy session led him to know that Joseph wasn't competent at really anything. Maybe he and John Paul should just ambush Joseph?

Jayme looked up and saw Joseph with the gun. He didn't want anything bad to happen to John Paul—well, anything worse than what John Paul had already seen. *And,* he thought, *the only thing worse than seeing a violent death is experiencing one.*

Joseph pointed out into the hall. Jayme got up off the floor with a loud sigh.

"Don't take an attitude with me," Joseph said. "You get off the floor without a sound and listen to what I tell you. Now walk ahead of me, and go to the stairs. Stand there at the top."

Jayme did as he was told. He stopped at the top of the staircase and waited. Joseph opened John Paul's door. Jayme turned, but he couldn't see inside the room.

"All right, John Paul," Joseph said. "We're going away but just for a little bit. Then we'll come back here and finish our empire. I've got some clothes for you, so you don't need to bring anything. Just follow the boy down the stairs and go right outside."

Jayme finally saw John Paul walk out of the room. He looked so much better not wearing the orange jumpsuit. The plaid-flannel shirt looked nice on him. Jayme took a moment to admire how handsome John Paul was, just in case it was the last time he could do so.

"Go on," Joseph said. "Let's get to the car."

Jayme began to walk down the stairs. At the bottom, he kept walking until he was at the door. He opened it and went outside. He turned to see that the other two were behind him. He walked up to the car.

"Hey, boy," Joseph said, "pick up all that crap, and put it back in that backpack. We don't want to leave a trace that you were here."

Jayme went to the car, bent down, and started picking up his things. He stuffed them into his backpack. The last thing he put in was the muddy copy of *Ancient Pride.* As he held the book, he remembered the vow he'd made the night before: to make Joseph pay for getting his book dirty.

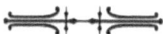

John Paul followed Jayme as he walked outside the house. He could feel Joseph behind him. He watched Jayme pick up his stuff.

"John Paul," Joseph said, "you're going to drive. Get behind the wheel. I'll have the gun on this boy here."

"I don't know how to drive," John Paul said. "I've never driven."

Joseph sighed loudly and said, "Then get in the back seat. Boy, you'll have to drive."

John Paul started to move. Joseph was right behind him. Jayme quickly grabbed the handle of the driver's door. Suddenly, the car began to honk loudly. John Paul jumped.

Jayme, acting quickly, took his backpack and swung it at Joseph. It smashed into his head. Joseph yelled and dropped the gun. John Paul saw Jayme throw himself on the ground to grab the gun. Joseph threw himself on top of Jayme. John Paul ran toward them.

Then Joseph was able to get ahold of the gun. He shouted something that John Paul could not understand and stood. Jayme was lying on his back. Joseph pointed the gun straight at him. Jayme's face was frozen in terror. Jayme sat on the ground, moved back, and leaned against the car. He held his hands up, as if to stop the bullet.

Nisus sacrificed for Euryalus. Antinous sacrificed for Hadrian. Patroclus sacrificed for Achilles. The Sacred Band of Thebes sacrificed for each other. Now it was John Paul's turn.

John Paul ran to the car and leaped toward Jayme. He heard a loud bang. He landed on top of Jayme. The last thing he felt was Jayme's arm around him.

For Jayme, smashed up against the side of the car, everything was moving in slow motion. But it was not like a movie; it wasn't anything like a movie. The sound was different—much, much louder. There was a smell. John Paul's body had weight to it when Jayme caught it in his arms. There was yelling from the shooter and odd, muffled sounds from the victim's throat. And there was an emotional impact that no movie could ever, ever replicate.

Jayme, in shock, looked up at Joseph as the man screamed, "No!"

The car was still honking, but that scream was deafening. The scream stopped time for a brief moment, and then it turned into a fuel that fed the rage within Jayme.

He pushed John Paul off himself and rolled on the ground, swinging his backpack over his head. He found himself shouting loudly, but he had no idea what words he was saying. He heard the gun fire again. As a bullet hit the backpack, he felt the backpack get ripped from his hand. He let it go and watched it fly through the air. But he did not stop advancing. He was a physical mass of emotion.

Jayme grabbed Joseph's legs and pulled him to the ground. In the process, Joseph kicked him hard in the side. Jayme took both his hands and wrapped them around Joseph's forearm, the one that held the gun. He smashed Joseph's arm into the ground, over and over again, still shouting the unintelligible words.

The gun came free and bounced on the grass. Joseph was on his back. Jayme took his right fist and smashed it into Joseph's face. Instantly, Jayme winced with the great pain in his hand and side. But that did not stop him. He rolled over and got his hand on the gun. He sprang up quickly, pointing the gun directly at Joseph on the ground.

"You don't know how to shoot," Joseph said.

Joseph's voice was garbled; his face was full of blood. But it was true: Jayme didn't know how to shoot a gun. He hoped that it was somehow automatic. He pointed the gun at the ground and fired. It went off. Again, there was the unexpectedly loud sound and a smell of fire. The bullet hit the ground and caused dirt to fly up around it. Joseph looked absolutely stunned, but he just lay there, staring at Jayme.

Jayme stood, strong, and held the gun directly at Joseph. Besides the honking car, his brain heard another sound that it couldn't process yet. Jayme wanted help, and he didn't know how to get it. John Paul still lay next to the car. He wasn't moving. Jayme was about to start yelling for someone, anyone, to help him, when he realized that the sound he was hearing was a siren. He looked up. A police car was speeding down the gravel driveway, throwing dirt and rocks everywhere. Still, Jayme stood, strong and brave.

ANCIENT PRIDE

TRUE GOD OF TRUE LOVE

Piccadilly Circus is London's version of Times Square. It's a place where several main thoroughfares meet among expensive shops, gourmet restaurants, and luxury hotels. The term *circus* comes from the Latin word for *circle*.

A large, ornate fountain stands in the circus. On the top of the fountain, there is a statue, eight feet tall, of a man. The man has giant wings and seems to be in flight. He carries a bow in one hand. He is extraordinarily beautiful, with a perfect body and face.

The statue is often misidentified. Londoners, including tour guides, regularly identify the statue as a depiction of the Greek god Eros, more commonly known by his Roman name, Cupid. However, educated people know that this statue is not Eros. Eros is the God of unrequited love, the love when one person loves another, but that person doesn't love back. Eros—Cupid—is a trickster.

The statue in Piccadilly Circus, the centerpiece of one of the largest cities in the world, actually depicts the Greek god Anteros. Anteros is the god of selfless love, of requited love. This is the love between two people who cannot bear to be separated.

Then why is the name of Cupid so famous, while nobody has ever heard of Anteros? The reason lies in the origin myth of Anteros. Classical historians generally do not like Anteros's origin because it does not fit into their narrative. I will tell the story, and you can decide.

Long, long ago, deep under the ocean, two minor sea deities were married. Nereus, often called the "Old Man of the Sea," and his wife, Doris, a sea nymph, had fifty-one children. The first fifty of them were girls. Among these girls was the immortal sea nymph Thetis, who would one day become the mother of Achilles. The last of their children was a boy named Nerites.

Nerites was mainly raised by his sister Thetis. As he grew, he became handsome and was envied for his athletic abilities. In fact, he became so handsome that he garnered the attention of many who met him.

Thetis became concerned, for there was one god on Mount Olympus that was notorious for ruining the lives of beautiful people: Aphrodite, goddess of sexual passion. Thetis attempted to hide her brother from Aphrodite. But it was futile. Aphrodite had seen the beautiful young man and had to have him.

Aphrodite made several attempts to seduce Nerites. But each time, to Thetis's delight, the immortal boy chose to stay with his family under the sea rather than go to Mount Olympus with the goddess. Aphrodite made a last attempt to win him. She gave him a pair of magnificent wings. Still, he scorned her, rejected the wings, and told Aphrodite to go back to Mount Olympus alone.

Nerites eventually revealed to his sister Thetis that the reason he rejected Aphrodite was not because he disliked her; it was because he was already in love with another Olympian god. Thetis was shocked, as she thought she knew everything about her brother, and she wanted to know who Nerites was in love with. The truth was eventually revealed: Nerites was in love with, and having a sexual relationship with, mighty Poseidon, god of all oceans, one of the two brothers of Zeus.

At this point, Thetis seems to disappear from the myth. Perhaps she, being a sea nymph, was intimidated by Poseidon's power. Perhaps she was amazed and delighted for Nerites. We don't know.

However, according to Nerites, he and Poseidon were passionately and eternally connected by an undying love. Poseidon felt equally strong emotions for Nerites, so much so that the two of them had a child together.

What? Two men had a baby? How could this be? Well, we need to take a step back and look at how the ancient Greeks viewed reproduction in general. The ancient Greeks did not have microscopes or any other tools to scientifically figure things out. All they had was the power of observation.

They knew that animals, humans, and gods reproduced through the sexual act. But since they couldn't see exactly how this was accomplished, they turned to botany. Consider a seed. A seed will do absolutely nothing except sit there—until you put it into the exact right conditions. Then it becomes a baby plant and eventually a full-grown plant. They thought the same thing happened with humans and animals.

The ancient Greeks believed that somewhere inside the male semen, there was a tiny seed that they couldn't see. But the seed did absolutely nothing unless it was put into the perfect condition: the womb of a woman. When male semen, or the seed, was put into a woman, it became a baby human and eventually a full-grown human.

Now let's return to Nerites and Poseidon. We must recognize that we are not dealing with ordinary humans here. These were powerful entities that controlled waves and earthquakes. So it is not that unbelievable that a god as powerful as Poseidon had the ability to nurture a seed, just as a human woman could.

While we don't know exactly how it was accomplished, or even which of them birthed the child, Nerites and Poseidon's love was so great that they had a son named Anteros. This boy, the son of two gods, was born with beautiful wings. He was the embodiment of mutual love.

Meanwhile, Aphrodite was so upset about being scorned, she turned Nerites into a shellfish. (There was nothing Poseidon could do—the Greek gods were not omnipotent or all-powerful over other divine beings.) And she was so jealous of Anteros that she took the wings she'd made for his father Nerites and gave them to her own son Eros (or Cupid).

Eros was the son of Aphrodite and Ares, the god of war. Although Eros was also the son of two gods, they were two very different gods. Aphrodite and Ares had a tumultuous relationship at the best of times, mostly because Aphrodite was already married to Hephaestus, the blacksmith god. Thus, Eros was formed from unrequited love. He tricked humans into love by shooting them with arrows.

Anteros, the son of immortal love, grew into the god of requited love. He was present when two people, without intervention, loved each other fully and without hesitation. Anteros caused them to feel pain when they were separated from each other. And he caused them to feel great joy—not sexual passion, but actual joy—when they were together.

Over time, the myth of Anteros became confused with the myth of Eros, so much so that those in the Middle Ages believed Anteros to be the son of Aphrodite and Ares—and a true brother to Eros. Most of this confusion was probably because it was difficult for us regular humans to believe that two men could have a baby. Even today, many internet sites devoted to Greek gods will list Anteros's parents as being Aphrodite and Ares. Some more enlightened sources might mention Nerites and Poseidon. However, it's wise to know that there are centuries of homophobia behind the myths that tell of Anteros belonging to Aphrodite and Ares—homophobia that the ancient Greeks themselves did not possess.

If you find yourself in London, go to Piccadilly Circus. Stare at the beautiful image of Anteros, and think about the wonder of true love. Look at the thousands of people around, and consider how many of them have ever met Anteros. Probably not that many. True love is indeed a rare thing to find.

Look not for Anteros in grand weddings and the sweeping off of feet. Look not for him among beautiful gowns and shining horses. Look not in a new home or new baby. Look not in Christmas letters, celebration cakes, or delivered flowers. Instead, look for Anteros inside the grieving heart of one whose love has died. There, you will find Anteros, in the silent stillness of a million memories.

CHAPTER 49

" *There*," said Jayme, "*you will find Anteros in the silent still-ness of a million memories.*"

"Read that one again," John Paul said.

"No," Jayme replied, "the nurses have already been on my case once tonight. That cop in the hall has been giving me the evil eye, but I think he might understand. Anyway, I have to get back to my room, or they won't let me come over here anymore."

But instead of getting up, Jayme sat back in a large up-holstered chair next to John Paul's hospital bed. Jayme was wearing pajamas and looked quite comfortable—except for the cast on his entire right arm, various bandages in several places on his body, and an IV that was still running into his left arm. It turned out that he had an internal bleed from his fight with Joseph. He had become quite ill. Three days ago, he'd had surgery to remove an infection and was feeling much better now.

John Paul was in bed wearing a hospital gown. He was hooked up to an IV and several other monitors. When they had arrived five days ago, John Paul had been rushed into emergency surgery. The bullet had entered his lower back on the left side, penetrated his colon, and exited out the front. He had been lucky that the bullet spared his kidneys and liver.

"How's your drainage tonight?" Jayme asked. He thought this was a fairly odd question to ask any other human being. But he asked out of his need to play nurse.

"It's less, I think," John Paul said.

Jayme got up, walked around to the other side of the bed, and checked a plastic cylinder that had a clear hose running into it. The cylinder was about 20 percent full of a murky liquid.

"It's a lot less than last night," Jayme said. "I think that's good. How is your bandage? Any seepage or anything?"

John Paul threw back a blanket. He unsnapped the top part of his gown to expose a large white bandage wrapped around his entire abdomen. Jayme looked at the front, then told John Paul to roll on his side.

"It's clean," Jayme said. "I think you'll be going home soon."

"I don't even know where that is though," John Paul said. "Are you still leaving tomorrow?"

"Yeah," Jayme said. "If I don't run a temperature tonight, they're going to let me leave."

Jayme snapped up John Paul's gown and placed the blanket neatly over him. He tucked it in around him. Then he went back to the chair and sat down.

"You figure out where you're going?" John Paul asked.

"To Hunter's dad's house," Jayme said. "At least for a few days. Maybe longer. I'm not sure."

"Did your parents come here to see you?" John Paul asked.

"Yeah, twice," Jayme answered, "but each time was with a lawyer. It's weird. The media is all over the place, and they're both loving and hating it. I think they are doing everything they can to stop all the rumors of child abuse. But at the same time, they love all the attention. Remember, to them, the only bad publicity is no publicity."

"Is it working for or against them?"

"Who knows? Have your parents been here?"

"No, they would never come to see me. I doubt I'll have much contact. I'm sure they're afraid of everything coming out. But I can't stop any of that now. Joseph will have to go on trial at some point, and everyone will know why I was up there. They can't escape it anymore. This morning a nurse told me that Joseph and Sister Gentillini are all over the true-crime internet."

"You're done calling her 'Genitals'?" Jayme said. "Do you forgive her?"

"No," John Paul said. "Maybe. She tried really hard to save me, and it got her killed. I feel bad. But I really need to focus on getting better and figuring out where I'm going to go."

"You can think about Joseph and all that another day," Jayme said.

"Exactly," said John Paul. "Wouldn't it be great if I could just stay in the hospital until I'm eighteen?"

"Shut up! Don't say that."

"I know. I can't stay here forever though. Like you said, my gunshot wound is healing."

"Can your parents make you go back to them?" Jayme asked.

"I don't know," John Paul said. "Fiona was here this morning, and we had a long talk about it. She's got a friend who is a family lawyer, and he's coming to see me tomorrow. Obviously, it's not safe to go back to my parents' house—especially since they can't even look at me. Fiona said it's probably good that they never visited me here. I might get put in a foster home. The hospital social worker thinks I've suffered way too much trauma to go to a home without adults that are trained to work with me. I'm not sure what that means. I think I'd prefer a foster home over a mental health place."

"Don't worry," Jayme said. "I'll be here, and we'll work it out together. I might not be trained—but look at how fast I learned to check your bandages!"

"Jayme," John Paul said, "do you think I'll ever stop seeing those images? Especially Sister Gentillini, I mean."

"I don't know," Jayme said. "I wish I could say that I did, but I'm not sure I'll get the image of Joseph shooting you out of my mind. But I guess we don't have much control over that right now. That whole 'It gets better' thing might be a lie. Maybe it'll get better? Probably. I've learned a lot these past few days."

"Like what?" John Paul asked.

"That I can handle life," Jayme said. "Also, that there is value to things I've been taught are worthless. Like religion. All I've heard my whole life is how stupid religious people are. But now I know that there is a peaceful and confident side that I like. I don't know what I think, really. But I'm proud of myself for learning."

"I can't even think about religion now," John Paul said. "It's just too close and too much. Maybe that's the worst part of all of this. Joseph made me witness these horrible things, then he took away my biggest tool to get through. He did those things in the name of Jesus. How can I pray to that name? I guess I don't know any more than you do."

John Paul reached his hand out from under the blanket. Jayme took it with both of his hands and held it.

"Are you proud to be gay?" John Paul said. "Like the guys in that book?"

"Yeah," Jayme said. "I've never been anything else. I might not be Sacred Band of Thebes material, but yeah, I'm proud."

"You seemed a lot like the Sacred Band to me," John Paul said. "When you were saving my life."

"Ha! Please!" Jayme said with a laugh. "You took an actual bullet for me. You threw your body in front of an actual freaking bullet. I think you're going to win this round."

They smiled at each other. Jayme stood up, still holding John Paul's hand.

"What about you?" Jayme asked. "Are you proud to be gay?"

"I was so ashamed of it," John Paul said. "I hated being gay—I would have given anything to change. But not now."

"What made the change?" Jayme asked. "The book? Your survival instinct?"

"No, it wasn't the book," John Paul said. "And it's not that I appreciate life more after almost dying. Don't laugh, but the more I think about it—as ironic as it is—it was Joseph's therapy machine."

"What?" Jayme said. "I don't understand. Are you joking?"

"Nope," John Paul said. "It was just so damn crappy! What a joke. When I think about it, I am bothered that he didn't care about having quality in the things that he said he cared so much about. Does that make sense? Joseph actually thought it was an amazing invention. That is a joke. I don't want to ever live like that. I'm not a joke. I want quality and to care about the things that I care about. If I make a therapy machine, it's going to be nice, look nice, and actually work. If I make a cabinet, it's going to be finished and complete. My house is going to have worth and strength. Michelangelo was gay, and he didn't just paint half the ceiling with cheap paint—no! He painted the entire damn thing with unbelievable art. So if I want quality for the things around me, then I have to want that for me. I have to be complete, strong, and worthy. Yeah, I'm proud to be gay."

"Can I stay in here?" Jayme said. "Let them come and make me go back to my room."

John Paul scooted over to one side of the bed. Jayme got in and lay next to him. They held hands and turned to look at each other.

"Anteros is here," Jayme said.

"Anteros is here," John Paul said.

ANCIENT PRIDE

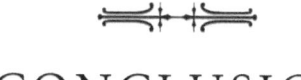

CONCLUSION

I n the introduction to this book, I told you that writing it had been a labor of love for me. A labor of love—working on something you love—is still work. Many people love woodworking. They relish the hours they can spend in their workshops, crafting furniture and art. But woodworking involves lifting heaving things, sweating, cleaning sawdust from every surface, and bending in odd positions to reach a far corner with a paintbrush. Even though they love it, woodworking is still a lot of work.

The men in this book, either mythical or real, all had one thing in common: They were not idle. At a time when there were no machine guns or hospitals, they marched for months to fight with swords. They did this because they believed it was the best way to protect their homes and bring honor to themselves.

But you don't have to be a mighty emperor or powerful god. Remember, this book told of only the smallest fraction of gay men who lived in the ancient world. There were thousands of gay couples living over thousands of years. We don't know their names, but we can be assured that they also protected their homes and brought honor to themselves.

Did honor die with the ancient people? Of course not. Do you know how many people died so that we can enjoy the benefits of same-sex marriage today? They didn't die in glorious battles doing heroic deeds. Instead, they died of homelessness after being kicked out onto the street. They died as bullies beat the crap out of them. They died after decades of stress from fighting in courtrooms and legislative chambers. They died of an autoimmune disease that nobody else cared about. We don't know all their names, but they were as strong as Achilles and as dedicated as Patroclus.

So now we come to you and your labor of love. It's your turn to protect your home and bring honor to yourselves. In the introduction to this book, I stated that the ancient people knew that sharing stories was the best way to impart knowledge from one generation to the next. That's the work you need to accomplish. Telling your story can be as scary, difficult, and dangerous as going into battle. It will take work—lots of it. But if you channel the pride of the ancients, our future will be better.

May the spirit of Anteros fill your work with love,
Dr. Madison W. Freeman
Professor of Egyptian, Greek, and Roman studies

CHAPTER 50

Sophia didn't date Hunter. She also did not go to Ohio Valley Catholic University. She wrote about the events of that week in her college admissions essay to Yale. She will start school there in the fall.

Sister Gabriel Luke was charged with endangering a minor and obstruction of justice. She pleaded guilty and took a plea deal for two hundred hours of community service. She has not disclosed whether she was disciplined by the Mother House for her involvement. There is an empty spot in her soul when she thinks about Sister Gentillini. She doesn't know if it will ever be filled. However, this whole ordeal brought her closer to Bob than they'd been for the past forty years. She is grateful for that.

Fiona was also charged with endangering a minor and obstruction of justice. She pleaded guilty and spent thirty days in the county jail. She could have done community service, but she wanted to try jail and thought it was good for her. She still works at the bookstore and has not talked to Bob about the letter she found. She just enrolled at a local university and is looking forward to studying archaeology there.

Hunter was never charged with anything. The authorities chalked it up to a kid trying to help his friend. He is happy to have a new roommate at his dad's house. He's been running a lot more and gaming a lot less lately.

Joseph was charged with the first-degree murder of Sister Gentillini, the attempted murder of John Paul Saint Clara, the attempted murder of Jayme Smith-Johnson, two counts of holding a person against their will, one count of practicing medicine without a license, one count of abandoning an animal, and several counts of building without the proper permits. His high-profile trial will begin sometime next year. The media has turned the trial, and everything involved with it, into an internet sensation.

Bob fully recovered from his fall and doesn't use a cane anymore. He is healthier than he's been in years. There was a big change inside his house that helped him to feel young again. He still goes to the bookstore every day. He is proud of himself and happy.

Sister Gentillini was laid to rest in the cemetery of the Sisters of the Immaculate Heart of Mary. Her grave site is near a large statue of Our Lady of the Seven Dolors. It is peaceful there. Sister Gabriel Luke visits often.

Sammy Smith-Johson lost the primary, mostly due to all the conflicting reports over the events surrounding Jayme's abduction. He and Abygail were apoplectic. However, the winner of the primary was killed in a car accident two weeks before the general election. Sammy took her place on the ballot. Despite all the allegations of child abuse and obstruction of justice, Sammy easily won the election because they lived in a district that tended to vote liberal. Abygail loves living in Washington and hopes to visit Kaiserburg as little as possible.

Theresa and Bernard Saint Clara moved away from Kaiserburg. But that didn't stop authorities from charging them with neglect of a minor for sending their son to a facility that had not been properly vetted. For lying about John Paul being with a cousin in Rome, they were also charged with obstruction of justice and the abandonment of a minor child. Their judicial cases are still moving through the court system. They no longer attend Our Lady of Seven Dolors and are dedicated to the Catholic church in their new town.

Jayme Smith-Johnson threatened his parents with filing for emancipation. Abygail and Sammy knew that a series of family court hearings would ruin any chance they had for a future in politics. They made a deal with Jayme that allowed him to live with Hunter. They paid him a large stipend. Jayme has become obsessed with the ancient cultures of Egypt, Greece, and Rome. He is saving to take a graduation trip to the Mediterranean in two years. Because he has sworn to dress as Achilles next Halloween, he's been lifting weights.

John Paul Saint Clara successfully petitioned to become a ward of the state. It helped that Theresa and Bernard eagerly waived all their parental rights. He doesn't see them and attends the public high school. He found the perfect foster home when he moved in with Bob. Every Wednesday night, Jayme, Fiona, and Gabs come over for dinner. John Paul always places the bronze statue of a Greek warrior on the table when they eat. He intends to become a physician someday so that he can heal wounds like Patroclus.

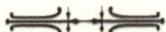

After being discovered alone in Joseph's house, Max was taken to a rescue shelter. He was soon adopted by Jayme and John Paul. He lives in a comfortable corner of Carlson's Used Books and Records.

EPILOGUE

Professor Madison W. Freeman left the lecture hall after turning off the lights. She walked through hallways crowded with college students hurriedly attempting to leave campus for the weekend. She wished that the lecture hall was closer to the humanities building, where her office was located.

Dr. Freeman entered her building. There weren't any students around, and it was quiet. She laughed when she thought about how slow the students moved in the mornings and how fast they could vacate entire buildings on Friday afternoons. She took an elevator up to the tenth floor. The building was old, and the elevator was slow. She was alone.

As she rode up, she reflected on the lecture about Anteros that she'd just given. She didn't think it went well. She felt uninspiring. Was it her, or was it the students? Was she too old to inspire, or were they too young to care? She wondered if it was time to retire. Perhaps that lecture would be one of her last.

The elevator door opened on the tenth floor, and she walked out. Her office was at the end of the hall, but as she walked past the Department of Human History, a secretary called her name.

"Dr. Freeman," the secretary said, "there are two students here to see you. They are waiting in your office. I didn't think you'd mind, and I let them in."

"Thank you," Madison said.

She was a bit annoyed that the secretary would just let people into her office. But the secretary had only been there one month, and he didn't know how things worked yet. She was also annoyed that students would just blatantly show up when it was not time for her posted office hours. However, she considered that she couldn't blame the students for not caring and then chastise them for wanting to visit a professor.

The door to her office was open. When she walked in, two young men were sitting in the two chairs in front of her desk. They stood when they heard her enter.

"Hello," Dr. Freeman said. "Please sit. I'm not used to people being so polite! Do you have a question about a class? Which class are you taking from me?"

She sat on her big desk chair. It was good to sit in her comfortable surroundings. But when she looked at the two young men, they stared back with a look of amazement. She was taken aback. She was glad that she left the office door open.

"No," one of them said, "we're not your students. At least, not yet."

"We're in high school," the other one said.

"What can I help you with?" she asked.

"I'm Jayme, and this is John Paul," Jayme said. "We drove sixteen hours during our spring break to meet you."

She certainly was not expecting to hear that. She took off her glasses and leaned forward across her desk.

"What?" she said. "Why?"

"We hope it's okay," John Paul said. "We just really wanted to meet you."

"And we found out where you teach," Jayme said.

"Yes, but why?" she asked.

Jayme reached into a backpack leaning against his chair. He pulled out a very dirty, and very crumpled, copy of her book *Ancient Pride.*

"We really wanted to ask you to sign this," Jayme said.

Dr. Madison Freeman was actually speechless. Of all the days that something like this could happen, this was the most perfect day for it to occur.

"I'm so touched," she said. "I'm not sure what to say. Sixteen hours?"

"Your book means a lot to us," John Paul said. "It got us through a really difficult time."

Tears started to form in her eyes. She took the book and put it on her desk.

"You know," she said, "I can give you a brand-spanking-new copy, right now."

"No!" they both said at the same time.

She jumped back a bit. Then the young men laughed loudly.

"Sorry," John Paul said. "We sort of have an attachment to this copy."

"Yeah, it's been through a lot," Jayme said.

"I can see that," Madison said. "Well, I'll be very happy to sign this. And maybe then, if you want, you can tell me the story of how this book got to look like this. I have a feeling it might be something like a Greek epic."

When she looked closer at the book, she noticed a round hole that had torn through the pages of the entire thing. If she didn't know better, it looked like this book had been shot with a bullet. She just ignored it and opened the cover. Luckily, there was a space that was clean enough for her to write. She grabbed a pen.

Madison had always been good with words. She wrote:

> *You are just starting out in life. Always know that you have the spirit of all these great gay men in your souls. Do not let anyone—ever—take that away. Live a life that brings honor to yourselves and to the people that came before you.*

> *Dr. Madison Freeman*

They sat in her office and spoke for the next four hours. They ordered pizza. Madison pointed out that pizza was not Italian; it was Trojan. They thanked Nisus and Euryalus for the pizza. Madison was proud of them—and proud of herself.

THE END

ABOUT THE AUTHOR

M ichael Fridgen has written both adult and young adult
fiction and is a previous winner of the Minnesota Book
Award. His book about gay people during the Holocaust,
The Iron Words, spent several weeks as Amazon's bestselling
World War II title. *Jacob Marley's Ghost*, a prequel to Dickens's
A Christmas Carol, has been featured in school library pub-
lications and is included in collections across the country.

Fridgen recently completed new versions of Homer's *Iliad*
and Virgil's *Aeneid*. When not traveling to theme parks, he
lives in the Smoky Mountains with his husband, who shares
his love of Christmas and theme parks. *Ancient Pride* is his
sixteenth book.

Michael loves pianos, snow, theme parks, Christmas, and
Dolly Parton.